"Then I'll have to go,"

Susannah said, feeling the sudden sting of tears.

"I don't want you to," Edward murmured.

Susannah dropped her gaze to the glass she clutched in her hand. "I have no choice," she answered. "I'm afraid there'll be trouble if I stay here."

"Trouble from what people think? From outside?"

"Or from inside," she replied. Though her cheeks were burning, she made herself meet Edward's eyes.

She couldn't measure the silence, but it seemed to stretch on and on. Then Edward said very softly, "Do you *want* trouble, Susannah?"

Dear Reader,

As the green of summer fades into the warmer colors of fall, it's time to put away your beach chairs and think about curling up on the couch with a good book. With this month's four titles from Harlequin Historicals, we hope that every reader will find a story to pique her interest.

In *To Touch the Sun*, newcomer Barbara Leigh gives historical romance a new twist with a tale of a man and a woman who meet as enemies and equals on the field of battle. We hope you will enjoy this unique and enchanting love story set in the British Isles during the early 1300s.

Passionate Alliance, Lucy Elliot's sixth book for Harlequin Historicals, takes place in New York City during the closing days of the Revolutionary War.

Maureen Bronson's *Ragtime Dawn*, the lighthearted tale of a minister's daughter with her eyes on Broadway and a handsome music-hall owner, and *Tender Feud*, a fiery romance set in Scotland from Nicole Jordan, round out the month.

Coming up next month, look for Bronwyn Williams, Kate Kingsley, Nina Beaumont and Laurie Paige.

Tracy Farrell
Senior Editor

Passionate Alliance
Lucy Elliot

Harlequin Books

TORONTO • NEW YORK • LONDON
AMSTERDAM • PARIS • SYDNEY • HAMBURG
STOCKHOLM • ATHENS • TOKYO • MILAN

Harlequin Historicals first edition October 1991

ISBN 0-373-28695-3

PASSIONATE ALLIANCE

Books by Lucy Elliot

Harlequin Historicals

Shared Passions #8
Frontiers of the Heart #24
Summer's Promise #44
Contraband Desire #64
Private Paradise #79
Passionate Alliance #95

Harlequin Books

Historical Christmas Stories 1989
"A Cinderella Christmas"

LUCY ELLIOT

is a happily transplanted Easterner living in northern California with her husband, son, dog and any neighborhood cat who wants an extra meal. She has been making up stories for her own entertainment since earliest memory—full of romance, adventure and, of course, happy endings.

To my father, Sidney Greenman,
who came along that hot, muggy day when the car
broke and the bank card didn't work—and the guide
at Fraunces' Tavern told us about Washington's
triumphant entry into New York.
For your patience, interest and good humor on that
day and all the rest.

Part I

Chapter One

Kingsbridge Checkpoint
New York
April, 1783

"Name?"

"Susannah Beckwith."

"Age?"

"Twenty-four."

"Married or unmarried?" With the slightest twist of his lip, the redcoat sergeant managed to give the question the sting of a subtle insult.

Susannah felt her whole body stiffen in response. "Now who do you think I'd have married with all the good men off fighting the war?" she snapped before she caught herself.

Damn! She was too late. A gleam of malice was sparking in the sergeant's pale eyes. If you're not suitably humble, his look said, I can keep you out of New York.

"Many did marry," he noted. "What is your residence?"

"One hundred and forty-seven William Street." Susannah's cheeks were beginning to burn, but she forced herself to ignore them and to keep her mind on the desperately needed British pass, which lay at his hand on the table.

"William Street in New York City? How long since you've lived there?"

"Seven years," said Susannah. *Ever since you British swine forced me to flee,* she added silently.

"Seven years?" The sergeant clucked impatiently. "If you haven't lived there in seven years then it's not your residence."

"It's my home," Susannah said softly.

"Your home!" the sergeant jeered. "And what makes you so certain that it hasn't burned down? A good half of the city was burned, you know—by rebel arsonists."

"That's a—" blurted Susannah before she could stop herself. She bit her lip. If she called the man a liar, she would never get her pass. And she had to get it. Her heart yearned for home!

"And even if the house is still standing," the sergeant went on, "it will be occupied by His Majesty's forces or by loyal citizens. You won't be allowed to live in it. You lost that right when you ran away."

Susannah's cheeks were flaming at the terms he used—calling traitors "loyal citizens" and accusing her of cowardice. But this was no time for anger. This was the time to be calm. "Then I'll find other lodgings," she said, meeting his eye. "Besides, I've got a brother who'll be coming off a British prison ship. I want to be there to meet him."

"I see." The sergeant smirked, as though Alex were a common criminal and not a prisoner of war. Then his smirk faded and his pale eyes hardened. "Is that all, Miss Beckwith?"

Oh God, thought Susannah. *He means to turn me down!* This was no time for false pride—or any pride at all. "Please," she entreated softly, "I don't mean any harm. I don't want any trouble. I just want to go home."

The sergeant's scornful glance informed her that her plea had come too late. Her shoulders sagged. Then, to her amazement, he dipped his pen in the inkwell, pulled the form to him and began to fill it in. "You can have your

pass, Miss Beckwith. But you'll have to sign this parole."
He pointed to a blank space where he'd made a little *X*.

Susannah stared at him, shocked beyond self-control.
"Why, I'll bet you never really intended to turn me down!
I'll bet you were only—"

"Only what?" he asked, the expression in his pale eyes
warning her that he could still change his mind.

You worm! raged Susannah, but for once she held her
tongue. "Nothing," she muttered as she bent to sign an
oath not to aid the rebellion against England so long as she
was in New York—quite an ironic statement, considering
the fact that the war was over and the patriots had won.

Five minutes later she stood outside the guardhouse,
giddy with relief. She'd been traveling for six days, but this
was the first time she'd noticed that the sky was blue, and
that the Post Road was abustle with other travelers. Some
of them were riding, but most were on foot. She looked at
the riders with envy as she remembered the fifteen weary
miles that still lay between her and New York.

Suddenly she realized that her legs were trembling. She'd
been through enough in these last years to know what it
came from: a combination of an empty stomach and a case
of delayed nerves. She couldn't recall when she'd last eaten,
she'd been so worried about getting a pass. Now, catching
a whiff of the meat pies a woman was selling across the
road, all at once she was overwhelmingly hungry. She
turned to dart across the road, barely noticing the large
farm wagon bearing down on her.

"Hey-up!" the farmer shouted, yanking hard on his
reins to avoid her. "Looking to get yourself killed?" he
yelled, but Susannah could see that he was really more
frightened than irate.

"I'm sorry. I wasn't thinking," she apologized shakily,
her hunger frightened straight out of her mind. As she
squinted up at the farmer, another thought took its place.
"Are you going to the city?" she asked. Seeing him draw
back, she added quickly, "If you are, could you take me
with you? For a fee, of course."

"You've got money?" he asked skeptically, assessing her well-worn shawl and bodice and her linsey-woolsey skirt.

"I wouldn't have offered if I hadn't," she retorted, neglecting to add that her money was Continental paper, not coin. She'd tell him that once he'd let her up on the high wagon seat. Once he'd let her up there, he'd be less likely to put her down. "Five shillings," she said firmly, holding her shabby bag as though it contained something valuable enough to protect.

The farmer hesitated for a moment longer, then agreed. "Can't say you'll add to the horses' burden," he observed, helping her up. "I took you for a child when you darted out like that."

"I'm old enough to know better," she allowed good-humoredly. My, but the world looked lovely from up on a wagon seat!

"Come a long ways?" asked the farmer, clucking to his horses to move forward.

"From Albany." She sighed. "Before that from the Mohawk Valley, and from Kingston before that." Always one step ahead of the redcoats, she might have added, but there was no need. The farmer understood as much. She could see it in his face. "What about you?" she asked him.

"We were lucky. We stayed put. The Brits came through three times but the worst they did was to set fire to our barn. Put out they were that time, because we'd had an hour's warning and managed to hide the stock."

"That sounds like the redcoats," Susannah agreed, casting a scathing look back toward the guard at the bridge. Now that the ordeal was behind her, resentment was replacing fear.

"Gave you a hard time at the guardhouse, did they?" the farmer asked.

"As hard as they could!" she said with a disdainful toss of her head. "From the way they're acting, you'd think they'd won the war! You'd think that they were holding more than just New York. And they're only holding New York until the final treaty's signed!"

It was eighteen months since Cornwallis's surrender at Yorktown, but it had taken all this time for King George to acknowledge that he'd lost the war. For eighteen months he'd kept his soldiers on American soil—and kept Susannah a refugee from her rightful home.

But after all the rumors and hopes and frustrations, two weeks ago news had come that preliminary terms had finally been reached. The British would give up all they held except for the city of New York. That they would surrender when the final treaty was signed.

The farmer glanced at Susannah. "You're a quick one, mistress, to be out on the road so soon after word of the treaty's come through."

"Quick!" Susannah's anger flared at the very word. "It's not quick when you consider the seven years I've been gone! Besides, you're going, aren't you?" she added, glancing back to the barrels that filled the wagon bed.

"Flour," he acknowledged almost apologetically. "After the years of embargo they're so starved for goods they'll pay any price."

"I wish they *had* starved!" she vowed. "Every last one of them! I wish the Continentals could have kept every mouthful of food from New York. I wouldn't have cried a single tear if every last redcoat had died, clutching his belly and wishing he'd never left home!"

The farmer stifled a grin at her feistiness. Then sobering, he added, "You'll find New York greatly changed. After all the fires, there's not much place left to live, and what's left is full of Tories. You'd best prepare yourself."

"I don't care," she assured him. "Whatever damage the redcoats and the Tories have done, we'll repair it when they're gone. We'll rebuild the city better than it was before!"

"That's the spirit, mistress!" He bobbed his head, then pulled the reins as a carriage swept past them, almost forcing them from the road.

"Tories!" Susannah glared at the lacquered door panels and the footman clinging on behind.

"Aye." The farmer nodded, wiping his face with his sleeve. "You'll find them thick in the city, staying near to their British friends. Well, they won't have their friends long. Then we'll see what's what. Have you got family to meet, mistress?"

"Not much," Susannah admitted, quieting at the question. "My mother...my mother died. And the last I heard from my father, he was sailing for the Orient. But I do have my brother. He's on a prison ship. He was captured in the fighting, but now they'll be letting him go."

Her eyes softened at the thought of Alex, and she hugged herself as though to master the sudden rush of joy. Alex wasn't just her brother, he was her twin. Her other half. Now they'd be together, both of them whole again. They'd be a real family. A real family with a home. And surely soon her father would come back and he'd be with them, too. She turned her head from the farmer so that he wouldn't see the tears that blurred the bright spring colors and threatened to overflow.

"Who knows," she added, sniffing. "He may already be free. His fiancée's family may already be back. If they are, I'm sure they would have moved heaven and earth to get him out." She smiled to think how glad Alex would be to be reunited with pretty Marguerite Dawes. Marguerite's family had fled south, and the last that Susannah heard, they'd been living in Maryland. But that had been well before Yorktown, so who knew what had happened since.

Thoughts of Marguerite and Alex led to other memories, not grim ones of wartime but scenes from the good old days when they'd all been children growing up in New York, sons and daughters of the prosperous middle class. The day was warm and pleasant, and she hadn't slept much the night before. The swaying of the wagon must have rocked her to sleep, because the next thing she knew, the farmer was shaking her by the arm, saying, "Wake up, mistress. We're here. We've reached New York!"

"New York," Susannah mumbled, rubbing her eyes. Then she sat bolt upright and stared about her. They were lumbering past the Commons and onto the upper Broad Way.

"There's the Hopwell house! And the Browers' and the Dawes'!" She pointed excitedly. "Oh, please, can you put me down here?"

She would have clambered down in the next moment, had the farmer not grabbed her arm. "Seems you're bound and determined to get yourself killed today!" he said with a chuckle, drawing up on the team. "And then there's the matter of my five shilling fee."

His fee. It had slipped her mind in the thrill of being home. Feeling suddenly guilty, she opened her bag, counted out the paper and handed it to him. "I'm sorry. It's only paper."

"That's all right," he said kindly. "You were good company. Good luck to you, mistress."

"Good luck to you," she replied, turning away even as she spoke to feast her eyes on New York.

There was no sign of fire this far up on the Broad Way, though the appearance of every building spoke of years of sorry neglect. The Hopwells' lovely garden had completely disappeared, as had every one of the Browers' shutters and the front fence. New York had been under Continental siege for seven years and Susannah had heard rumors of shortages of fuel. The British must have burned shutters and fences in order to keep themselves warm.

"I hope they froze all the same!" she muttered, shifting her valise from hand to hand. Looking at the Dawes house, she saw with pleasure that it had fared better than the others. She took a few steps toward it and almost stepped into a puddle in the road. Catching herself in time, she was just stepping around it when a carriage clattered past, spraying filthy water clear up to the fringe of her woolen shawl.

"Why, you—" she sputtered, then realized that the carriage was stopping outside the Dawes' house. Were these the creatures who had usurped Marguerite's rightful home?

Mud spattered and disgusted, she watched as the footman leapt to the street, pulled down the carriage step and opened the door. He reached forward with a flourish and carefully handed out a British colonel whose scarlet uniform was so gold-encrusted, befringed and emblazoned that the weight of the decoration alone would have crushed a smaller man. But the colonel was enormous, with an ugly, arrogant face. Susannah guessed his hair would be white beneath his powdered wig. He stood with haughty impatience, tapping the scabbard of his sword against his polished boots as he waited for the footman to hand his lady down.

This was no easy process, for her skirt was very wide, and her hair had been powdered and padded and piled so high that she had to angle her head with precision to get it through the carriage door.

Susannah felt her stomach tighten in disdain. The couple's pomp and finery only made her proud to be wearing her own well-mended dress. Poor Marguerite, she thought, hoping with all her heart that these vile creatures would be long gone before Marguerite returned.

The lady was out now, headdress and all. As she gave her hand to her husband, she turned in profile. Susannah's jaw dropped open as she recognized Marguerite.

"Marguerite?" she murmured disbelievingly. *"Marguerite?"* she repeated, more loudly.

Marguerite turned. When she saw Susannah, her mouth opened in surprise. "Susannah?" she faltered, her cheeks flushing a deep shade of red. "I didn't know you were back, Susannah," she said in a strange, stifled voice. Then, gathering her wits, she gestured to the colonel. "May I present Lord Bridgeham, of Stanleigh and Ware, and colonel of the Queen's Fortieth Royal Surrey Regiment. This is Mistress Susannah Beckwith, a former acquaintance from New York."

"Mistress Beckwith." The colonel's eyes flicked over Susannah, taking in her shabby valise and her mudspattered skirts. His nostrils narrowed as though he'd smelled something foul, and the corner of his heavy lip curled with distaste.

Susannah hardly noticed. "Former acquaintance?" she said. "Marguerite, what is this? You're my brother's fiancée!"

Lord Bridgeham sputtered. "What impertinence!" he snapped.

Susannah whirled on him. "To the contrary, your lordship, I'm only telling the truth. Marguerite is engaged to my brother. Isn't that right, Marguerite?"

Marguerite turned pale. "N-not exactly," she stammered. "I'm Lady Bridgeham now. Lord Bridgeham and I were married—"

"Married!" Susannah gasped. "What are you talking about! What about Alex! You were supposed to marry him!"

"Young lady—" began Lord Bridgeham. A crowd was beginning to form.

"Have you told him?" demanded Susannah, ignoring both the crowd and the purple-faced lord. "Or were you waiting to meet him like this on the street? Was this how you meant to tell him?" She swept one arm out angrily.

"Susannah, really! This is not something to discuss in the middle of the road," Marguerite reasoned, attempting to calm her down.

But Susannah was beyond calming—or caring what people thought. "Of course you haven't told him!" she raged at Marguerite. "Right now he's sitting in his prison cell, believing you've been true. Marguerite, how could you, after what he's been through!"

"Lady Bridgeham, you must come away!" Lord Bridgeham took Marguerite's arm.

Stung by Susannah's last comment, Marguerite broke from her husband's grasp and spun to confront Susannah. "What he's been through!" she snapped. "How typical of you Beckwiths, always thinking about yourselves! But what about me? What about wearing shabby dresses and never having enough to eat? Being hounded night and day and always being afraid? And for what? For the promise of some rebel rotting in a cell? How could I know if he'd survive, and even if he did, what would he have to offer—nothing but more promises!

"I've had enough of promises to last me all my life! I wanted the real things that Lord Bridgeham could give." Marguerite glanced at her husband, who looked on the verge of a fit. "Lord Bridgeham's got fine houses, wealth and family. As soon as the war is over we're going to England to live!"

Susannah's head swam as she searched for a fitting response. For an awful moment she thought she was going to faint. Then the faintness vanished as the words arrived.

"Why, you, you—Tory traitor!" she cried. Without thinking, she brought her hand back and swung it at Marguerite's cheek, welcoming the stinging that exploded in her palm.

Marguerite gasped in pain and horror. Her hand flew to her cheek. "You'll see, Susannah Beckwith! I can have you arrested! Lord Bridgeham has powerful friends!"

"Enough, Lady Bridgeham!" Lord Bridgeham grasped Marguerite's arm and, with the help of the footman, practically dragged her up the front walk.

"Go ahead!" Susannah shouted after them. "Have me arrested! I'd rather spend a year in prison than one night in a traitor's house!"

She was shaking with anger when the front door slammed shut, leaving her to her audience, who numbered some two dozen by now.

One of them, an old woman, advanced to touch her on the arm. "You look peaked, mistress. Would you like to sit a spell?"

"What? No, thank you, I'm fine," murmured Susannah, though she didn't feel fine at all. Her hand was burning from hitting Marguerite, and she felt empty and light-headed and leaden all at once. A crisp loaf in the woman's market basket reminded her that she still hadn't eaten anything today. But at the moment all she wanted was to get away from the sight of the Dawes mansion and Marguerite's treachery.

"I'm fine," she assured the woman as she backed away. She crossed the street quickly, walking blindly for several blocks—or perhaps not so blindly, because when at last she stopped she found that she was on William Street, only a short walk from her home.

Home! Dear Lord, how sweet a word! How could she resist at least looking at it when she'd come so far? She didn't care if other people were living there—so long as the house was standing, she'd be satisfied.

She could tell from the corner that the house was still there. She caught a glimpse of the dormer windows angling from the roof and her heart lurched so sharply that she had to lean against a hitching post until she could breathe. But a minute later she was standing at her own iron gate, feasting her hungry eyes on each beloved inch.

The outside was shabby but it was intact, thank Providence. The cherry trees were gone, but they could be replaced. She scanned the windows, trying to see some sign of the condition of the interior. But the windows stared back blankly without yielding a clue. Were the things she had left behind still there, or had they been stolen or sold? The lovely rosewood sofa and the china plates that hung above the sideboard on either side of the clock.

For seven years she'd forced herself to forget these things. But now they rose up in her memory, filling her with longing. Without really thinking, without sparing time for thought, she pushed the gate open and started up the walk. The light-headedness she had felt before was with her again, but she ignored it as she climbed the five steps to the door.

The paint on the door was peeling, but the knocker was intact. She raised it with an effort and let it fall back. When nothing happened, she raised it once again. She was reaching to raise it a third time when she heard footsteps in the hall.

Chapter Two

Edward Steel, captain in the Prince of Wales's own Yorkshire Royal Twentieth, fastened the knee buckles of his dress breeches, then sat on the bed to pull on his polished boots. Beside him was arranged the rest of his dress uniform: white waistcoat, scarlet jacket, crossed belts and tricorn hat. His valet, William, had laid them out before disappearing—as was William's habit—to who knew where. New York was not London, that much was for sure. Edward wasn't sure how he felt about being back again. He would make up his mind once Carleton let him in on the secret of what his mission was to be. All Carleton had told him so far was that the job would be challenging.

Challenging. Edward grinned as he reached for the second boot. Carleton had scarcely seen him in years, but he'd read him well. The more work, and the more difficult, the happier Edward was. Work kept him from dwelling on personal concerns. Or it had, during the bad time, and it was habit by now. And a man could have worse habits, Edward thought to himself.

His long legs snugly booted, he shrugged into his waistcoat, then coat. This wasn't his first encounter with New York. He'd been here five years ago, for long enough to form a grudging respect for the rebels, who always fought harder with their backs against the walls. If you stripped them of provisions, they seemed to exist on fresh air. When their shoes gave out, they'd march barefoot in the snow.

They were full of vigor, perhaps too full for their own good—a veritable nation of gamecocks, always spoiling for a fight.

They'd had their fight and they'd won it, and now Edward was back again, though in what capacity he had yet to learn. His official appointment was as personal physician to Sir Guy Carleton, commander in chief of His Majesty's forces in America. Edward was a doctor, so in that way the post made sense. But to his knowledge, Carleton was in perfect health—besides which, Edward's wartime training had not been in medicine.

He was fastening his belts when he heard a sound below. Someone was knocking. Perhaps the cook had gone out in search of something—he couldn't remember what, though he was sure she'd told him when she'd met him in the hall. It was the cook who'd told him how the house had been before. When the war was raging, the house had been fully staffed and all of its rooms taken by His Majesty's officers. Five days ago, when he'd arrived, he'd made the fourth in the house, but yesterday the other three had sailed—bound for distant India, where the King had another war. So now he had the run of the house to himself—and no servants but an absent cook and an equally absent valet.

The knock sounded again as he came down the stairs.

"All right, all right!" he muttered. "I'll answer it myself!" Perhaps it was a message from headquarters. Perhaps his meeting with General Carleton had been postponed. That would be a pity after he'd gone to the pains of trussing himself up in his dress uniform like a Christmas goose. And then, too, he was anxious to hear what he'd been assigned. He'd had five days to roam the city and now he was ready for work.

Ready and willing, Edward was thinking as he yanked open the door. But it wasn't a messenger from headquarters on the stoop. It was a woman, dressed in dusty clothes—and whose dark bonnet contrasted sharply with her pale skin, skin that grew even paler as her eyes fixed on his uniform, on the gold buttons of his jacket, which her pupils reflected as they grew and grew. He thought he saw her swaying.

"Are you all right?" he asked, but she didn't answer. Slowly her knees gave way, and she started to crumple toward the floor. Dropping his hat and moving quickly, he managed to catch her before she hit the ground.

The first thing Susannah was aware of was a wonderful smell, composed of soap and clean wool and warmth and something else that would have made her smile if she wasn't so lethargic. Cool fingers rested lightly on her brow and a deep soothing voice murmured softly from overhead. At that she did smile. She felt so comfortable—more comfortable than she could remember feeling in a very long time. The voice was so restful and the pillows were so soft. She could lie here forever and be perfectly satisfied.

Pillows? A little alarm sounded in her mind. Deep voice? Cool fingers? What was this about? Her eyes sprang open despite her lethargy and she found herself staring up into the face of a very handsome man. Blue eyes. No, blue-gray with black around the rims. Strong mouth, fair eyebrows beneath a powdered wig. Bronzed skin with laugh lines. Aristocratic nose. She was lying on a sofa and he was sitting on its edge, one hand braced against the back as he leaned over her. They were so close that she could feel the heat of his leg stealing through the thin wool of her petticoat. Her gaze slid lower and she saw that his broad shoulders were encased in the brightest red.

Her heart froze. The man was a British soldier!

"Stay back! Don't touch me!" she gasped, her heart racing now.

All action, she cringed backward, trying to move beyond his reach, but the arm of the sofa prevented her escape. She braced herself against it with her knees drawn up, ready to spring into action at his slightest move.

"Who are you? Where am I?" She wanted to look around, but she was afraid to take her eyes off him.

"Edward Steel," he answered. "Captain Edward Steel." He touched his hand to his forehead as his expression changed from a look of startlement at her sudden commotion to one of mild amusement. She noticed he made no effort to give her more room, but neither was he being openly aggressive.

She relaxed slightly, but frowned in confusion. "What's happened? How did I get here?" Her eyes still fixed on the red coat, Susannah racked her brain for an explanation, but nothing came except for a disturbing buzzing in her ears, as though there were a hive of bees loose in the room.

"You walked here," he told her. "At least I didn't see any form of conveyance when I opened the door. When I opened it, you fainted. Then I carried you in here. That's all I know. Don't you remember?" he asked her hopefully.

To her great relief, he moved away at last, shifting back toward the opposite end of the couch. This allowed her enough room to swing her feet onto the floor, which she did with caution and with her eyes glued to him. When he remained in his corner, she risked a glance around—and the shock of what she discovered almost caused her to faint again. She was in the drawing room at William Street! She was home! She must be dreaming. Then it all came back: the checkpoint, Marguerite, standing at the gate.

She'd been remembering the rosewood sofa, and here she was sitting on it! And there, over the mantel, was the portrait of her grandfather. The statues of the four seasons were missing from the mantelpiece, but then she remembered that she had hidden them in the frantic hours before the British came. The windows still had their curtains, and the floor still had its rug, though both looked rather the worse for these last seven years' wear. There was her mother's worktable, with its French design. Susannah's eyes moved quickly, hungrily, around the room. Then they swung back to the sofa as she remembered Captain Steel.

He was watching her with interest, his blue-gray eyes steady on her face, though behind their calmness she sensed the activity of his mind. She could imagine what he was thinking, and it made her blush. What sort of a woman faints at a stranger's door? His arm was resting along the back of the sofa, the tips of his fingers absently rubbing the seasoned wood. According to his explanation he had answered the door. Then he had carried her in here, carried her in his arms. This day had begun as a trial and ended as a catastrophe.

"Do you remember?" he repeated gently.

"Of course I remember!" she snapped. She brushed both hands severely down the front of her skirts, seeking to bring what order she could to them—seeking to bring order to the entire day. Straightening her back, she turned to face him. "I came here for the purpose of inspecting my home."

That startled him, Susannah noted with satisfaction. His hand came down off the back of the couch and his eyes widened with surprise.

"Mistress—Beckwith?"

Susannah nodded.

For a moment he studied her. His next words were unexpected. "You must be relieved."

"Relieved?"

"To find your house still standing after all the fires."

"I'd have been relieved to find it empty!" she retorted, forgetting the joy she'd felt when she'd spotted the dear, familiar roof.

She saw his eyes absorb the force of her reproof. But in the next moment, his mouth tilted in a smile that scooped a small dimple into the corner of his lips. "I declare, Mistress Beckwith, if this were my introduction to the colonies, I might find reason for believing that American women were rude."

She brushed her skirt a second time, offended by his wit. "Your findings, Captain Steel, are of no interest at all to me. If you'll excuse me—"

He caught her before she could rise, moving swiftly from his corner of the sofa to lay one hand on her shoulder while the other one reached for the bell.

"What are you doing?"

"Calling for some tea. We can't have you fainting on the street again."

"I never faint!" she said cuttingly.

"But you did just now. You might have hurt yourself if I hadn't been there."

"If you hadn't been there, I wouldn't have fainted at all! I don't want to stay here." She shifted beneath his hand.

His hand shifted with her. "And I insist you do. Anyway, you haven't finished your business yet."

"What business?"

"Have you forgotten? Your inspection of the house. What, is that cook still missing?" He released her shoulder to ring again. This time there was a brief bustle at the door, heralding two women, one older than the other, but both of them equally stout.

The older one was talking as soon as she came through the door. "Captain Steel, my goodness! I thought you'd be alone. I'll only take a moment. I thought you'd like to know. This is my daughter, Milly. She's come to help. I thought that we could use her. I didn't think you'd mind. Shall I send you tea up? I thought you were going out. If I'd known—"

"Thank you." Captain Steel firmly stemmed her flood of words. "Tea would be just fine. And if there's any cold meat, you might give us a plate."

"There's mutton from dinner. Milly can slice it up. Can't you, Milly?"

"Yes, Mother." The younger one bobbed her head. They bustled out together just as they'd bustled in.

"You see then!" Captain Steel declared when they had gone. "It's not worth protesting. Tea is on the way, and the cook will be insulted if you try to sneak away. Not to mention the eager Milly," he added, raising one fair brow and holding both hands up, palms outward, as though he meant to push Susannah back down if she tried to rise.

She knew that she ought to do exactly that, if only from pride, but the truth was she doubted her legs would carry her to the door. Just the mention of meat and tea had made her feel faint. She'd take only enough to make her feel better, then she'd be on her way. Anyway, it wasn't as though this were charity. This was her own parlor, for heaven's sake!

She couldn't resist stealing another glance around. The screen at the fire was the one from Alex's room. She wondered if the one that should be here had been stolen or damaged or moved upstairs. And where was the mirror that had hung on the wall? And the brass candle holders had turned almost black. She wondered if Milly polished. Then she caught herself.

She looked back at Captain Steel and found him watching her again, with an expected eagerness in his eyes. "Susannah—that's your name, isn't it?" he asked. When she didn't answer, he explained, "I saw it in a book. Shakespeare's sonnets. I borrowed it to read."

Susannah nodded. She remembered that book. Her father had brought it back from one of his voyages, and to please them both she'd learned all the sonnets by heart. Once, sitting in an unfamiliar kitchen while soldiers were searching the house, she'd warded off panic by repeating sonnets silently. Over and over, for hours—or so it had seemed at the time. They had been British soldiers.

"The book is mine," she said, laying her emphasis on the possessive, as though his borrowing it were a theft. But her tone lacked spirit. She felt empty and cold inside to be sitting in her own drawing room as no more than a guest. Part of her wanted to ask him how long he'd been here. But the other part of her didn't want to know. She felt him watching and sensed his sympathy. She didn't want it. All she wanted was what was hers.

She met his eyes coolly to show him how she felt. "So what is your role in this occupation?" she challenged.

"I'm attached to Sir Guy Carleton's staff. As his personal physician. I imagine you've heard of him."

"I imagine I have," she said coldly, though Carleton wasn't so bad. Then again, he was British.

At that moment Milly returned, as energetic as ever and with a loaded tray.

Susannah recognized the service from halfway across the room. It had been her mother's, a part of her dowry. Before she could stop them, tears of pain stung her eyes. She turned her head away, praying they would not fall.

"Where shall I put it? On the table here? I've brought cheese and meat both. Mother thought you'd approve." Milly's chatter filled the silence in the room, and through the mist of pain Susannah heard her setting down the tray. "Well then, I'll leave you. Unless there's something else."

"No, thank you, Milly," she heard Captain Steel say. "Mistress Beckwith?" he added after the door had closed.

"Yes?" Susannah slowly turned her head back to him. She couldn't see him clearly, but she sensed his sympathy, as though he'd understood her feelings about seeing her mother's things. But how could he understand her—a redcoat officer?

"Will you do the honors?"

He meant, would she pour? She nodded, took a deep breath and reached for the pot, whose handle fitted her fingers like the grasp of an old dear friend. She managed to fill a cup without spilling and handed it to him, but he was already busy filling a plate from the various dishes crowded on the tray.

He set the plate before her. "I want you to eat every bite. There's always illness in a city. It's best to keep up your strength."

"I've lived well enough so far without British advice," she retorted, but she couldn't help being touched. It had been many, many months since someone had looked after her. Some of the people she'd stayed with had been friendly, but the war had given everyone their own concerns. For a time there had been her mother. But then she'd been all alone.

Meanwhile, Captain Steel had risen, glancing at the clock, whose pendulum was swinging as it always had. "You'll have to excuse me, but I'm already late to head-

quarters. Please stay as long as you wish. I meant what I
said about keeping up your strength." He hesitated, then
added, "And feel free to inspect the house to your heart's
content. Just let yourself out when you've finished. I'll tell
Milly before I go."

"B-but..." Susannah stammered.

"But what?" He paused.

"You'd trust me to do that?" she blurted out, then
cringed when she saw the glimmer of his dimple again.

"What should I be afraid of—that you'd steal your own
things?" His smile broadened into a full-fledged grin.
"Besides, in case you haven't heard, our countries have
signed a truce. Good day, Mistress Beckwith." His eyes
held hers for a moment and then he was gone. She heard
him speaking to someone—Milly, she assumed. Then she
heard the muffled thump of the front door.

"Well, of all the nerve!" she muttered. "Giving me leave
to look at my own house!" But the truth was that she
wasn't really angry at all. In the first place she was too tired,
and even beyond that, it was hard to feel angry curled up
on the rosewood sofa with a cup of wonderfully hot tea
vying for her attention with a plate heaped high with food.

Suddenly she was famished, so hungry she was glad that
Captain Steel was not present to witness her gobbling
practically with her hands. He needn't have worried about
her keeping up her strength. The way she was feeling, she
could finish every bit. The cheese was soft and tangy and
the meat was cold roast lamb. They were perfect together,
melting in her mouth. She chewed and swallowed, then
took a deep sip of tea, closing her eyes as she felt the
warmth stealing down through her.

"Home," she murmured, feeling her body relax bit by
bit to the familiar ticking of the clock. This morning at the
guardhouse she'd hardly dared let herself dream of such a
moment and yet now the moment was real. Her lips curved
in a smile and her head rested back. She could stay here
forever, she felt so safe and good.

Home. The ticking of the clock grew fainter and Susannah's head lolled back as she slipped gently and deeply into exhausted sleep. She didn't stir when the clock struck the hour, or even when Milly eased the teacup from her hand.

"Poor thing," murmured Milly, setting the cup on the tray. "We've all been through enough in these last years that we can use a little rest!" Leaving the tray to prevent it from rattling, Milly tiptoed from the room to resume her chat with her mother in the kitchen below.

Chapter Three

Riding north through the city in full uniform, Edward drew bitter looks from rebels and loyalists both. So this was New York moving toward peacetime, he thought ironically. Carleton would have his work cut out for him, keeping the two sides from each other's throats until the final terms were reached.

Giving up America had been a bitter pill for Britain, as Edward ought to know, since he'd spent the past five years coaxing King George to swallow it. Edward had initially shared the King's belief that America should be forced to remain a colony, but his first trip to America had changed his mind. He'd spent the past five years working for the peace that he believed might very well achieve what the war had not.

Everyone knew that the colonies were only slightly less suspicious of one another than they were of the King. So why not take away their common enemy and let them spar among themselves? Given the present chaos of their economy, it wouldn't be very long until they'd come crawling back in need of English aid. Of course they wouldn't submit to being colonies. But some sort of union would surely be possible. The King had resisted, but at last he had given in, and now Edward had been summoned to play a role in the final act.

After the hostile stares of the city it was a relief to reach the countryside of sunlit fields and wooded hills and pretty

country mansions that showed hardly a sign of the war.
There was a scattering of ramparts near the water and on
the heights, but otherwise this section of the island had
come through the last years unscathed. Of course the rebels had been exiled from their homes, but those who had
occupied the rural mansions had done them no visible
harm.

The thought of rebel exiles brought Susannah Beckwith
to mind, and Edward grinned as he recalled his initial impression of her. First she'd fainted on his doorstep, then
she'd refused to respond to the wrist chafing he'd offered
on the stoop, so he'd had no choice but to carry her into the
drawing room. She'd looked so young and fragile lying on
the couch that he'd been absolutely certain of what sort of
a woman she'd be when she opened her eyes.

She'd be one of those women who lay back languidly and
expected the rest of the world to step and fetch for her.
When she'd decided that she'd been asleep long enough, her
lids would flutter open over eyes full of limpid appeal,
which she'd employ without scruple to wrangle whatever
she wanted from him. What might she want? he'd wondered. Want something, she would. Women always wanted
something in his experience, and most often what they
wanted had nothing to do with love. That was the truth as
he'd learned it, and he'd also learned that a man could save
himself a great deal of heartache by keeping that truth in
mind.

Smoothing the thick tangle of her hair back from her
pale face, he'd tried to imagine just what this woman might
want. Why had she turned up on *his* doorstep? He'd studied her features, searching for a clue: black hair and black
lashes curled thickly against white skin, with just a sprinkling of freckles scattered across the nose. The nose was
slightly upturned, the lips saucily bowed. Then her long
lashes had fluttered and she'd opened her eyes.

The big bay mare shied sideways as Edward laughed
aloud. He'd been wrong about Susannah Beckwith, about
as wrong as a man could be! He'd hardly had time to no-

tice the color of her eyes before she'd doused his foregone conclusions with a strong dose of vinegar. But he had seen the color. Charcoal gray. He'd never seen any others quite that shade. And as for distracting feminine wiles . . . !

Edward was still chuckling when he turned down the lane of the Beekman mansion, which housed Carleton and his staff.

Two orderlies were waiting to receive him at the house. One accepted his reins while the other led him into the drawing room, where he found Carleton being lectured by a man finely clad in plum-colored velvet and looking extremely perturbed.

"Without guarantees," the man was saying, "we shall be thrown to the wolves! After our loyalty to His Majesty, surely it's not too much to ask!" He broke off at Edward's appearance long enough to be introduced as Myles Porter, a New York gentleman.

Hearing that Edward had worked with the peace party, Porter turned his attack on him. "It's fellows like you, Steel, who have landed us where we are! Therefore, let me ask you. What do you plan to do?"

"Do?" Edward glanced at Carleton, who made no move to interfere, seeming content, if anything, to be delivered from Porter's wrath.

"Yes, do!" exclaimed Porter. "Do for the very people who have put all their trust in you. I'm speaking of the loyalists, we who have stood by the King! Oh, it's very well for you to wash your hands of the whole affair. You can give up our city and go back to your own home. But what will happen to your former friends after the troops have gone and left the rebel riffraff to run the game? We'll be thrown to the wolves, Captain, without that guarantee!"

"A guarantee of safety for all loyalists." Carleton straightened, drawing in his long legs. In person the general was tall and dignified and was said to resemble George Washington almost uncannily. The two men were similar in other ways, as well, for Carleton's long service to Britain had been distinguished by courage and common sense.

Edward could not imagine anyone better suited than Carleton for his present job, which would—heaven only knew—demand a great deal of both qualities.

Edward nodded. "Yes. I understood. But it's been brought up with the American negotiators in Paris and they've said that guaranteeing loyalists' safety is up to each individual colony."

"Then bring it up again!" blustered Porter. "Bring it up again with more force. And please don't tell me about the land in Nova Scotia that Parliament has set aside for loyalists. I'm a New Yorker! I have a right to remain! I have property, interests—I won't see that all thrown away!"

"It won't be thrown away, Mr. Porter," Carleton said patiently. "I've already established a commission to guarantee that fair value is given for everything."

"Fair value—ha!" Porter snorted. "The rebels are cutthroats and thieves! They'll never pay fair value for loyalist property!"

"In my experience people rise to the trust one puts in them," Carleton observed mildly. "In any event, Mr. Porter, your petition will be passed on. Thank you for your trouble in coming here today."

In response to the general's summons, an orderly appeared to show Mr. Porter out. Porter left looking as though he would have preferred to say more.

"Welcome to New York," Carleton said with a sigh after the door had closed. Then his expression softened as he came to his feet. "How are you, Edward?" He extended a warm and welcoming hand.

"Forewarned," Edward answered, returning Carleton's grip. He hadn't been surprised by the general's summons, for Carleton and his father had been childhood friends.

Carleton chuckled appreciatively. "And well you should be! I wish I could tell you that Myles Porter is unique, but he isn't, not a bit. There are plenty more like him in New York—and plenty of Americans who hate them bitterly. I believe I can safely say that trust is not the prevailing mood in New York."

"I sensed as much," concurred Edward, "just walking in the street."

"I know. I've felt the same thing." Carleton sighed again. Then rousing himself, he gestured Edward to a chair. "Sit down and tell me, how are things at home?"

"In a state of confusion," Edward said honestly. "Although the King allowed the preliminary treaty, he still disapproves of it. And the people, who were so eager for the war to end, are now just as eagerly searching for someone to blame. Everybody in the government is fighting with everyone else—and they won't make final peace with America until they've made it among themselves."

"All of which leaves us stranded here in New York, while the Americans accuse us of intentionally dragging our feet." Carleton shook his head. "Well, what can we do but the best we can? Which means protecting both sides from each other's wrath."

"Both loyalists and rebels."

Carleton paused to smile. "Patriots," he corrected. "Or Americans. The term 'rebel' is a fighting word these days, and the last thing we want here is another fight. Which brings me to your job, Edward."

"Yes, sir." Edward leaned forward with an eagerness he could not hide.

"Officially," said Carleton, "you'll be in charge of making sure that the Tory emigration goes along without a hitch. At last count there were twenty thousand Tories in New York and more arriving every day, since this is the one place in America they feel safe. But they won't be safe for long, so they've got to leave. And as much as Porter hates it, Nova Scotia is their best hope. A quick and smooth emigration is the best way I can see to avoid the sort of confrontations we've been talking about."

Edward nodded. "And unofficially?" He knew without being told that the job Carleton had just described was to serve as a cover for something more closely tailored to his particular skills.

His skills were in espionage, or they had been these last five years. Using his cover as a physician to various British diplomats, he'd traveled on the Continent, collecting information from the French and the Americans—information that had been used to coax King George toward peace.

Carleton smiled at Edward's eagerness. Pointing across the room, he said, "Knock twice on that door, if you will."

The door quickly opened to Edward's repeated knock. It led to a small chamber, whose sole occupant was a man in civilian dress. The man was in his mid-twenties and wore an unpowdered wig. His clothes and appearance suggested he was some sort of craftsman, recently out of work.

But, as Edward immediately suspected, this appearance was a disguise. Carleton introduced the man as Lieutenant Aaron Franks—lieutenant in the King's American Regiment. "Lieutenant Franks is from North Carolina," Carleton explained. "He's unknown in this city, where he has been posing as a Carolina regular recently released from jail. A Continental regular.

"It's not Porter's bluster we've got to worry about," Carleton went on. "It's the hidden bitterness of men who want revenge. Most men will be happy to get on with their lives, but there will be a number who can't let the fighting go."

"Loyalists or Americans?"

"Particularly Americans. Men who want their last shot before the enemy disappears. There were vigilante groups before the war began and we fear that now there may be again. Lieutenant Franks has been watching out for the first sign of such a group. He's been frequenting the taverns and the markets, keeping his eyes and ears open for the signs of discontent. When asked, he professes opinions that extremists are likely to share."

"Anything so far?" Edward addressed his question to Franks.

"Nothing specific," Franks replied in a voice that was softened by just the hint of his Carolina slur. "I've met a few who'd be willing to follow. But no leader as of yet."

"With luck, there will be none," Carleton put in. "But given British luck in America, I fear that there will be. If he does find something, Lieutenant Franks will report to you, Edward. And you will take what action you feel is appropriate."

"On my own?" asked Edward, feeling more and more alive. This *was* his sort of assignment. Carleton had been right.

"Consult me, if you feel you should. I leave that to you."

"How will we make contact?" Edward turned back to Franks.

"There's a tobacconist, James Waller, just off Water Street," Franks explained. "He's got no objection to our meeting in the room behind his shop. I'll send a message through Waller when I've got anything." He turned to Carleton. "If there's nothing else, sir, I think I'd better go."

"So is this assignment to your liking?" Carleton inquired after Franks had gone. Without waiting for a reply, he continued, "I have every hope it is. You remind me of your father. He was a regular hound for work, even when he was a boy. I think you'll be busy enough in these next months."

"I think so." Edward grinned. He was feeling very happy, very glad he'd come. But then—suddenly—Susannah Beckwith emerged in his thoughts. Only Susannah wasn't smiling. She was looking at him with reproach, as if to say, How could you? Spying on me and mine?

It's for your own good, Edward thought. It's for the good of everybody.

But Susannah didn't change. She was still watching him reproachfully when he took his leave a few minutes later and struck out for home.

Susannah woke with a start. For the first moment she couldn't recall where she was. When she did realize, she thought she was still asleep. Then, as her mind cleared, everything came back: coming to the city, Marguerite, Captain Steel.

Captain Steel! Her eyes flew to the clock. Half past four, and it had been just before three when he had left. He could be back at any moment! Susannah leapt to her feet, retrieved her shawl from where it had fallen and hurried to the door.

In the hall she was greeted by an unfamiliar silence. The house as she had known it had always been bursting with life; full of friends, family, servants and the acquaintances that her father had met in his travels and brought home for a meal. Once, before the war had started, Benjamin Franklin had come to tea, which had turned into Madeira and a lively good time indeed!

She heard the sound of voices coming faintly from below: Milly and her mother, both of them talking at once. She hadn't seen the hall yet, since she'd been unconscious when Captain Steel had carried her in, so now she spared a moment for a look that showed her the walls in need of paint and plaster and the wood a good polishing.

The dining room door was open. She couldn't resist a peep, and then the other rooms in their turn each beckoned. Like the drawing room, they were worn but mainly intact. As she came back toward the front door, she paused to glance up the stairs, and that glance filled her with longing to see the familiar rooms.

No, she really couldn't. What if Captain Steel returned and found her there? Then her shoulders stiffened. What was she thinking of—tiptoeing around like a little mouse? This was her own house, after all! She had a right to see it for as long as she pleased, and if Captain Steel came in and found her, she'd just—well, she'd deal with him. Squaring her shoulders, she marched up the front stairs, though not quite so loudly that Milly and her mother could hear.

Alex's room was the first she came to on the right. Alex's style had always been spartan, so there was nothing much to have changed. She peeked inside the blanket chest, which held only a few odds and ends, before she tiptoed across the hall, to her own room, with a rapidly beating heart.

The sun had passed the horizon long since and begun to fall. It lay across the floorboards and the flowered rug, which she remembered down to the very last thread. It lay across the carved headboard of the bed, across the green bolsters, across the green cover, which had been ripped and mended since she'd last been here. She touched the tear with one finger, wondering who had slept in this bed. The presence of strangers made her shiver and she turned away.

Strangers had shifted the big things and removed some of the little ones. The knickknacks on the dressing table weren't there anymore. She pulled open the drawer, but it was empty, save for a small pile of letters that were dry and brittle with age. Letters from a school friend who'd moved away. They'd lost touch with each other over the course of the war. Her heart throbbed with a pang of longing for all that had been lost. Then she reminded herself brusquely that she was lucky still to have a house.

Captain Steel had chosen her parents' room for himself. Thanks to his presence, it had an inhabited look: clothing in the wardrobe, towels on the rack, an ivory comb-and-brush set on the dresser top. A wig, unpowdered, stood on its stand, and a suit of clothing was scattered on the bed: a shirt, a pair of light gray breeches, a coat and waistcoat of deep blue. It was nosy and foolish to stay here. But she didn't leave. Curiosity sent her toward the bed.

The coat was made of broadcloth, the waistcoat of tabinet, of newer and finer materials than she'd seen in years. She touched the coat's tapered sleeve, savoring the spring of the woven cloth, that took her back to better days she'd known in this very room. She could close her eyes and see her father dressed in the same handsome cloth and her mother in the satin or taffeta she wore when they were going out.

The shirt was white lawn. Its softness beneath her fingers brought other, newer, memories: a handsome face, blue-gray eyes, the heat of a hard-muscled thigh. Her hand closed around the fabric and she lifted it to her face, rubbing it against her cheek the way that a blind person might.

The smell of it was familiar. She turned her face and inhaled the same scent that had greeted her when she'd awakened from her faint. She found it as deeply satisfying now as she had done then, the only difference being that now she knew what it was: the scent of a redcoat captain.

She dropped the shirt on the rest of the clothes and had already turned to leave the room, when she caught sight of the books stacked on the table beside the bed. One in particular caught her eye: the second in the pile. She recognized the leather spine. Her book of Shakespeare's sonnets. She opened the cover and read her name in the girlish script of ten years before. One page was marked with a ribbon. She turned to it and glanced at the final couplet:

For sweetest things turn sourest by their deeds;
Lilies that fester smell far worse than weeds.

She stared at the printed page, her heartbeat curiously slowed. She knew from the selection that she hadn't left the ribbon where it was. In a volume of love poems, Edward Steel picked the least forgiving one. Why? she wondered, recalling his handsome face. What had happened in his life to have made him choose this poem? Or had he slipped in the ribbon at random? Strangely, she found herself hoping that he had. A kind thought about a redcoat: likely the first in her life.

A sound caught her attention, as if a floorboard had creaked. Swiftly she looked up. Captain Steel himself was standing in the door, looking amused. All thoughts of kindness fled her mind.

"What do you mean by sneaking up to catch me?" she snapped.

"Sneaking?" he repeated without a trace of guilt. "I didn't sneak, Mistress Beckwith. I walked like a normal man, but you were obviously too engrossed to hear me coming up. And in case you've forgotten, this happens to be my room." As if to claim it, he stepped inside the door.

"Temporarily," Susannah retorted, standing her ground. "You may have it now, but you'll be gone soon enough!"

"But not soon enough, eh, Mistress Beckwith?" He cocked one brow teasingly as he glanced around the room.

At that, Susannah bristled. "I didn't take anything, if that's what you're wondering! Though I might have. They're my things, after all!"

"So they are," he acknowledged, his eyes sweeping her up and down. They settled on the book of sonnets still open in her hands. "I see you've found your Shakespeare."

She had forgotten the book. As she glanced down, her first instinct was to snap it shut and return it to the pile beside the bed. But before she could do that, her eye fell on the poem she'd been looking at when he'd appeared.

She glanced from the page to Captain Steel, sensing her chance for revenge. "'For sweetest things turn sourest by their deeds,'" she quoted calmly. "'Lilies that fester smell far worse than weeds.'"

She'd intended to pay him back for surprising her, but she was astonished by the response her words evoked. His face blanched beneath his deep tan and his jaw went taut. Crossing the room in three long strides, he seized the book from her grip and shut it as though he were crushing something to death in his hands. His eyes closed for a moment, and when they reopened they were flat gray with an anger that sent a shudder down her spine.

"I'm sorry," she whispered, afraid to speak aloud—afraid that he might turn his anger against her. He might without even realizing who she was, since his eyes seemed to bore straight through her with the force of his hate. The bed was behind her and Captain Steel blocked her way to the door or she might have responded to her urge to flee.

Time stopped for a frozen moment. Then he seemed to recover himself. She watched as his eyes focused in surprise on her, as though he'd expected to find himself looking at somebody else.

At the lily who had festered, Susannah thought to herself as he stared down at her in a silence that wiped her fear away, only to replace it with a new kind of uneasiness.

They were standing close together. She could feel it when he breathed, feel the heat and the movement of his chest beneath his uniform. He was taller than she'd remembered, broader-shouldered and longer-limbed. He filled all the space around her, seizing her consciousness in a way she'd never experienced before. She tried to concentrate on his scarlet jacket—a color she despised—but the whiteness of his breeches was tugging at her eyes and making her remember the pressure of his thigh.

She felt her cheeks flushing as they would from the heat of a fire as she stared fascinated at his hands clasped on the book. She remembered his hand on the back of the sofa stroking the polished wood. For one crazy moment she imagined his hands on her arms. She took a step backward, feeling for the bed and meaning to edge along it until she was past his reach. At her movement, however, he suddenly became aware of how close he'd been standing and how he'd been staring at her.

He blinked, stepping backward to open the path to the door. "Excuse me. I didn't mean..." He let his voice trail off. Catching sight of the book he was holding, he held it out to her. "It's yours. Go ahead. Take it."

"No, thank you." She shook her head, shrinking away as though he'd offered her something poisonous. Her hand, groping behind her, grazed the lawn of his discarded shirt, the one on which she'd inhaled his scent when she'd pressed it to her cheek. At the memory her heart gave an awful lurch. "I—I really should be going," she mumbled, edging around him and toward the door.

He turned to watch her. "Mistress Beckwith, I didn't mean—" But he had no more luck in completing the sentence than he had before. Spreading his arms, he added, "You're right. These things are yours. If there's anything you wish to—"

"No! No, thank you!" Susannah exclaimed, wanting only to be gone—from the room and the house, but mainly from the presence of Edward Steel. "No, thank you!" she repeated as she reached the door. Turning without a backward glance, she fled toward the stairs.

Edward stood where she had left him, listening to the sound of her footsteps descending then crossing the hall. He heard her pause for a moment to snatch up her valise, which he had brought in from the doorstep when she'd fainted in his arms. He'd seen it there five minutes ago when he'd come in from headquarters, which was how he'd known that she was still in the house.

He'd smiled when he'd seen it and crossed to the drawing room. He'd expected to find her asleep in a chair, and when he hadn't, he'd thought she might be upstairs.

She was right. He had tiptoed up so as not to startle her. And yes, he'd also tiptoed so as to catch her unawares. If what he'd done was dishonest, she'd more than paid him back by quoting that sonnet. It had reminded him of Catherine and, by reminding him, brought back the old pain.

He was still holding the book. He recalled how Susannah had shrunk back when he'd offered it to her. He'd frightened her with his anger. He regretted that, but it was probably all for the best. He was sorry that she'd run away, but all the same he didn't need another lesson in women's fickleness.

Chapter Four

"Just one more cruller, Susannah!" coaxed Mrs. Van Rijn as they sat in the cosy kitchen of their rented rooms. Mrs. Van Rijn had been Susannah's mother's friend and at the present moment she was trying to make up for three years' worth of a mother's care.

"Honestly, I couldn't." Susannah held up her hand.

"Give her one for her pocket," suggested nineteen-year-old Amy with a toss of her red curls. It was Amy who had found Susannah yesterday afternoon, almost running down the street in her headlong flight from Edward Steel. Discovering that Susannah had nowhere to stay yet, Amy had insisted that she come home to the Van Rijn's. And, overjoyed to find old friends, Susannah had accepted willingly.

But it hadn't been the roomy Van Rijn mansion to which they'd gone; it had been three cramped rooms on the back of Golden Hill. The Van Rijn house had been burned down, as had their store, which had been one of the finest in New York before the war. Instead of sleeping in the guest room at the end of the upstairs hall, Susannah had shared a bed in the parlor with the two Van Rijn girls.

"Why should I wrap a cruller?" clucked Mrs. Van Rijn. "You'll be coming home for dinner, and hopefully bringing Alex, too."

Susannah smiled at her generosity. Then her eyes filled with tears at the thought of what the family had lost. "Your house and your store both. It seems so unfair."

"War is unfair," Mr. Van Rijn said, sucking on his long Dutch pipe. "But the war is over now, and there's no point in wasting more time grumbling over what's been lost."

"Father says now's the time for rebuilding," fourteen-year-old Maria chimed in.

"That's right!" Mr. Van Rijn exclaimed in a cloud of smoke. Brushing it away, he added, "We'll put this city back together even better than it was before!"

"With what?" asked Susannah. "There isn't any wood."

"But there will be," Mr. Van Rijn declared. "And in the meantime there is brick that's survived the fires and only needs to be rearranged. We'll start with the foundation and go on from there!"

"When Papa says 'we' he means 'we'!" Amy gave a comic roll of her eyes. "He intends to put us all to work. He says it's a patriotic effort and we're all patriots! For that matter, so are you and Alex—maybe you'd like to help us too! Here's a chance to learn brick-laying, a very useful trade!"

The mention of Alex brought Susannah to her feet. It had been too late yesterday to make inquiries about securing his release, but this morning she meant to get an early start.

"You're sure you're not still hungry." Mrs. Van Rijn rose with her.

"I'm sure!" Susannah said, laughing. "After two crullers and two cups of coffee and milk I'd be lucky if I can waddle down to the Commandant's office."

"It's at the Kennedy mansion," Mr. Van Rijn advised. "You know where that is, just before the Bowling Green."

"Yes, I know. And thank you."

Mrs. Van Rijn walked her to the door. "I mean it about you and Alex staying here. Rooms are scarcer than gold in the city and we'd love to have you here." She paused, then she added, "I don't want to touch a sore spot, but I want you to know that I miss her. She was a very good friend."

Susannah knew Mrs. Van Rijn was talking about her mother. "I miss her too," she murmured, gratefully returning the pressure of the older woman's hands. "Thank you for all your kindness."

"I wish we could do more. Would you like Amy to go with you? There's likely to be a crowd."

"No, I'll be fine," said Susannah. "If these last years have taught me anything, it's how to take care of myself. The crullers were delicious. Goodbye, Mrs. Van Rijn."

Five minutes later she was hurrying up Maiden Lane toward the Broad Way—hurrying as best she could, given the condition of the streets, which didn't appear to have been repaired since the Continentals had ripped them up to defend against the British seven years before. The ditches and mud holes were littered with all manner of filth, through which vagrant pigs were rooting hungrily, dodging the wheels of wagons and the prancing horses' hooves.

On another morning, the sight might have made Susannah sigh, but on this particular morning it only made her smile. Even before the war, visitors had complained about the condition of the New York streets. New Yorkers had complained, too, but with an affectionate note. Dirty, disorganized and stubborn, New York was still New York. Home. Susannah mouthed the word silently. Then she turned onto the Broad Way and her happiness disappeared.

From here she could see the damage that she had missed before, the devastation of the fires creeping up to her. The skyline was vacant where roofs should have been, and the roofs that existed seemed lonely and forlorn. And with her every step southward, the scene grew worse. To the right loomed the blackened remains of Trinity Church, to the left a stretch of wasteland where houses once had been, with nothing now to mark them but a crumbling wall or a skeleton chimney. In lieu of the houses, tents and huts had been thrown up, crowded and dirty, disheartening to see; and the few houses that rose among them only increased the desolation of the scene.

Susannah felt a hard lump rising in her throat. It was gone, disappeared. Her city. The place she had always called home. The heart of New York had vanished. How could the rest survive?

But it seemed to be surviving, she realized foggily as she found herself in the midst of the bustle that filled the wide Broad Way. New York's lots might be empty but its streets were far fuller than they ever had been. Teamsters shouted warnings as they urged their horses on past muffin men and fishmongers, broom sellers and dumpling girls, honeycomb women and mousetrap boys whose voices clashed in competition to draw attention to their wares. Housewives hurried toward the markets with their stout baskets on their arms, Negro slaves dawdled and British soldiers paraded by, scuffing up the city's dust beneath their tramping feet.

Susannah turned her head to follow the marching troop, just long enough to confirm that the captain had dark hair. Realizing what she was doing, she jerked her head back, shocked. Ogling after redcoats! She ought to be ashamed. Drawing her shawl closer, she set off again, toward the Kennedy mansion, whose walls she could already see by virtue of their being almost the only walls on the remaining length of the street.

The crowd grew denser as she neared the mansion, until it blocked her completely a good dozen feet from the door. My goodness, but what were all these people doing here? They couldn't all have relatives in prison, could they?

"Excuse me." She attempted to elbow her way in, but other elbows blocked her progress.

"Well, I never!" a woman clucked. "I suppose she thinks she's too fine to wait her turn!"

"Is everyone waiting?" Susannah asked, looking around. None of the faces was familiar and none expressed the least interest or sympathy. Meanwhile, more people had arrived after her and were pressing forward, trying to push toward the front. Susannah did her best to resist their pressure, but it was no use. She was thrust into the woman in front of her, who responded in kind with a none-too-subtle shove.

She felt her chest contracting—she'd never been good in small places ever since the time she'd accidentally locked herself in the root cellar as a child. She tried to draw a long breath, but it was cut off when she took another sharp push from behind. She knew she couldn't stand it. She'd be crushed to death. Panic rose within her. Turning, she began to battle her way blindly toward fresh air—or where she imagined fresh air to be, though in her confusion she was no longer sure.

"Excuse me," she mumbled. "Please let me pass!" The less yielding the bodies, the harder she pushed. Then all at once the crowd ended and she felt herself launched through clear air.

"Oof!" she heard a man grunt as she barreled into him. Strong hands grabbed her shoulders and held her back. "Why, if it isn't Mistress Beckwith!" she heard a familiar voice say as her eyes traveled up a dark blue waistcoat to the face of Edward Steel.

He seemed to have recovered from yesterday's pain. Once again she saw amusement in his eyes, whose gray seemed to have been sucked away by the blueness of his coat. When she didn't answer, he pretended to frown. "You're not going to faint again, are you?"

"Of course not!" she snapped. Glaring at him, she realized what was different about the way he looked. "You're not in uniform."

She realized she'd said it almost accusingly, which brought a new spark of humor to his eyes. "No, I'm not," he admitted, glancing down.

Susannah glanced down, also, and saw he was wearing the same clothes she'd seen lying on his bed: the same blue coat and waistcoat, the same white lawn shirt she'd rubbed against her cheek. Even the same gray cashmere breeches molded the muscles of his long legs. She caught herself staring and snapped her head up.

Too late. He'd seen her looking and his eyes met hers with a glint. "Are you sorry I'm not in uniform?"

"Of course not!" she gasped, furious at having been caught at her weakest, yet again. "I couldn't care less what you're wearing!" she declared with a toss of her head. Taking a step sideways, she attempted to pass by him.

He took a step in the same direction and succeeded in blocking her way. "I apologize, Mistress Beckwith. I didn't mean to tease," he assured her, pulling off his hat. "The truth is, I detest wearing a uniform. You left so quickly yesterday I didn't have a chance to ask whether you'd found everything in its place."

She knew he was referring to her tour of inspection of the house, and her first reaction was to assume that he was teasing her again. But when her eyes met his, her sharp retort died on her lips, for she saw only interest and concern.

"In the main things were in order," she admitted warily. "Though some things were missing. I suppose it's to be expected."

"Expected but not admired," he answered, his tone no longer light. He paused a moment, then added, "I meant what I said yesterday. No doubt there will be things that you'll want from the house. If you send me a list of them, I'll see that they're delivered to you."

She wanted to refuse him. She wanted to say no. That look in his eyes brought the same uneasiness she'd felt yesterday afternoon when they had stood so close in his bedroom.

"Thank you," she muttered, knowing she had to leave. But the growing crowd behind her had made that impossible. During the few minutes since Edward had arrived, the new arrivals had been steadily nibbling away at the space she'd put between the crowd and herself until it had finally reached her back. Undaunted, the next arrivals attempted to wedge themselves in, with the result that Susannah felt herself suddenly shoved. For the second time in minutes, she was thrust into Edward's arms.

But this time was very different from the last. This time she was all too conscious of the hardness of his chest and the corded muscles that tensed along his thighs. He didn't grunt this time, though she heard him suck in his breath with a suddenness that erased every other sound, so that for a moment she forgot about the crowd.

She felt the grasp of his fingers fanned along her arms, the heat and strength of them biting into her flesh. For the briefest moment he held her so close that she imagined she could hear his beating heart and feel the warmth of his breath stirring against her hair. She knew she ought to struggle, but for a moment she did not. Instead, she rested against him, absorbing his hardness and heat. She forgot that he was British and knew only that he was a man; a man whose heady, vital scent did strange, subtle things to her. She felt his fingers tighten, then release her arms. In the same breathless instant, the two of them broke apart.

"Goodness!" exclaimed Susannah, looking everywhere but at Edward, as her fingers performed small, useless fluttering acts: smoothing her shawl's fringe, tugging at her sleeves, touching the brim of her bonnet as if to be sure that it was still intact. "These people are so heedless!"

"Aren't they?" he agreed. The way he was breathing made her afraid to look up, but at the same time tempted her to do just that. She surrendered to temptation and saw that his face was deeply flushed beneath his tan and that the black around his irises had turned the centers a brilliant blue. "If you haven't any reason to be here, I'd urge you to come away," he suggested, though the look in his eyes made her wonder whether he was paying the least heed to what he said.

His eyes, she suddenly realized, were fixed upon her lips with an intensity of purpose that brought her heart to a sudden stop, then sent it racing madly ahead. Her own lips began to tingle and the tingling quickly spread into goose-flesh all up and down her legs. She felt herself sway toward him—Toward a redcoat, for heaven's sake!

"I can't!" she muttered.

"Can't what?" he asked.

The soft insinuation of his voice only made things worse. With a supreme effort, she dragged her eyes from his to whatever would save her—to the Kennedy mansion and the jostling clamorous crowd. That returned her to her senses.

"I can't leave," she said. "I've got business with the commandant. I've got to get inside."

"What business?" Edward asked, pulling his eyes away from her lips with no less effort than it had taken Susannah the moment before. He felt that he already knew her, from living in her house. Last night he'd read her sonnets until sleep had finally come. For once he hadn't read only the angry ones. He'd also read the others, the ones that spoke of love—with a pleasure he hadn't felt in years. "Maybe I could help you."

"I doubt it," Susannah said. "I can't think what a doctor would have to do with releasing prisoners."

"Who's a prisoner?" he asked her, and saw her hesitate.

"My brother, Alex," she said finally. "The last that I heard they'd moved him up from Charleston to a prison ship here."

"He might be out already. A lot of the prisoners are. It would be in the commandant's records."

"If I could get inside." Susannah sighed at the prospect, which seemed increasingly dim. At the rate that the crowd was moving, she'd be here for several days. "Who are all these people?" she wondered. "What do they want?"

"They're loyalists mostly," Edward replied. "Trying to settle their affairs. They've fled all the other colonies and now most of them are trying to leave America."

"Tories!" sniffed Susannah. "No wonder they push and shove. Tories haven't the least concern for anyone but themselves!"

Edward stifled a smile at her sudden change of mood. "I'm not so sure a crowd of reb—that is, of patriots, would be much gentler. Come on," he added before she could take issue with his last remark. "Most places have a back door. Let's see what we can find."

She knew she ought to protest when he took her arm, but she suspected that her protestations would only make him laugh. Besides, he was moving so purposefully that she doubted he'd even hear her if she did protest. She wondered if she could be thought a traitor for accepting his help, but then she thought of Alex and the crowd out front. And what could be treacherous about passing Tories in line? If Captain Steel wanted to trump his own allies, then who was she to protest?

There *was* a back door, though it was well guarded.

"Wait here," Edward commanded, leaving Susannah a few yards away while he approached the sentry for a murmured conversation that she could not hear. She saw him reach into his pocket and draw a paper out. Whatever the paper contained must have been important, for as soon as the sentry read it, his whole attitude abruptly changed.

"Come along, Mistress Beckwith." Edward beckoned unceremoniously as the guard opened the door.

She scooted through the open door before the guard could change his mind. "What was that paper?" she demanded when the door had closed and she and Edward were alone in the hall.

"What paper?"

"You know. The one you showed the guard."

"It's just a note from Carleton, describing my job."

"I thought you were his doctor?"

"I am," Edward agreed. "But since he's in such good health, he's given me something else to do. Shall we—?"

"Do? Such as what?" demanded Susannah, her eyes narrowing suspiciously. The subdued hum of voices reached them where they stood, along with the sound of footsteps trooping up and down the stairs. But Susannah ignored them, waiting for his reply.

Edward hesitated only briefly before he said, "Such as helping the loyalists who want to emigrate. Now, as to your brother..." he prompted, laying his hand on her back in an attempt to end the conversation and guide her down the hall.

She ignored his prompting and stood her ground, though his hand was distracting, resting on her back with the tips of his fingers just tickling her ribs. The spread of his fingers made her feel small and feminine. It also made her disturbingly aware of her breasts, either of which he could have touched by the least little shift of his hand. "You mean those people outside. You're here to help them leave?"

"That's right. Do you have an objection?" he asked, inclined to be annoyed at the stubborn suspicion printed in her eyes. Here he was trying to help her and she was interrogating him as though she were the King's Attorney and he a common criminal.

Susannah frowned. "No. Why should I? Good riddance to them all, I say! Where are we going?" She turned in the direction in which Edward had been guiding her and took a small but firm step away from his distracting hand. Her freedom from him offered her relief and disappointment both.

"Second door on the right," he directed, following her down the hall. His annoyance had vanished—replaced, to his surprise, by the amusement she seemed to rouse in him. Perhaps because she was so little, he thought of her as a precocious child. But looks were deceptive, he reminded himself. And women even more so.

Susannah reached the door first but waited for Edward to open it. He knocked once and they entered to find two sergeants at ease—one with his white-breeched legs crossed up on his desk. Both of them eyed Susannah with impudence, but their manner changed quickly when they saw General Carleton's note.

"Yes, sir!" exclaimed the first sergeant as his feet crashed to the floor. He listened closely as Edward explained why they had come. After Edward had finished, he flipped through a log. Finding no record of Alex, he went to look in another room. He was back in several minutes, with a strange look on his face. "Captain, may I see you—alone?" He gestured to the door.

"I'll be back," Edward told Susannah as he and the sergeant left.

Susannah stood where they had left her, trying not to wring her hands, for the second sergeant was still eyeing her as he worked. What had that strange look meant? What had the first sergeant learned? Was something wrong with Alex? Was he ill—or worse? But she had gotten no further in her thoughts when the two men returned, the sergeant looking puzzled while Edward—was it possible?—seemed to be amused.

"What is it?" Susannah demanded before she could catch herself.

"Your brother is still in prison," Edward replied. "He was offered the chance to go free but turned it down. It seems there is some problem about his giving his parole." He kept his expression solemn as he imparted this news, but Susannah could very clearly see the laughter in his eyes.

"Can't let him out without it," the sergeant explained. "Most everyone else gave his. War's over, after all. At this point it's nothing more than a formality. There is a way around it, like I was telling the captain here, if someone else was willing to give their parole instead. 'Course, that person would be responsible. If anything was to happen—"

"What could happen?" Susannah snapped, annoyed with the sergeant and with Alex both. And annoyed most of all with Edward Steel for taking the whole situation as a joke. "I fail to see the humor," she said in an undertone.

He shrugged. "I was only thinking that it runs in the family."

"What runs?" she demanded.

He opened his mouth to reply, caught himself, then answered, "Conviction," in a tone that told her just exactly what he had meant to say.

As her brows dropped low in reaction, he had the nerve to grin. Ignoring him completely, she turned to the sergeant, instead. "I'll sign for my brother," she declared, hoping that Alex wouldn't be angry with her. Too bad for him if he was! she retorted to the thought. She hated the British as much as anyone, but the war was over, and surely it would be better to be out and active than brooding in some filthy hold.

Susannah glanced at Edward and saw that at least his grin was gone. "When will they release him?"

"As soon as it can be arranged," the sergeant replied. "I'd say tomorrow morning. If you're going to meet him, you can go down to Coenties Slip. It's the brig *Hesperian*. You can see it from there."

"Mistress Beckwith, if you're ready?" Edward stood at the door. Susannah swept past him, down the hall and out the back.

Outside, the sunlight was briefly blinding. Susannah blinked as her eyes adjusted, then turned to squint up at Edward. "You think he's foolish, don't you, for refusing to give his word."

"Not foolish, no." Edward chose his words. "Just typically American."

"Meaning what?" she demanded.

"Meaning that he's got too much fight for his own good. We British may have too little, but you Americans have too much. It keeps you from knowing when it's time to stop. And it will probably keep you from stopping before it's too late."

"Too late for what?" she asked him, curious despite herself.

"Too late to take advantage of the freedom you've just won. Self-government is achieved by men who can compromise—not men who stay in prison to prove an empty point."

"And I suppose that you English are experts in self-government—with generals who can't win battles and a king who's lost a war but who doesn't want peace!" She faced him, triumphant, hands planted on her hips, pleased to note that the twinkle had vanished from his eyes.

But he seemed more thoughtful than daunted when at length he replied. "Yes, we have lacked strong generals, and yes, we have lost the war. But it's not those things that matter in the longer view. It's not how often we stumble, it's how we recover from our falls. And we've always recovered, for almost one hundred years. We've got a certain maturity that America seems to lack."

"Maturity, ha!" she flung back. "What you've got is arrogance! We'll manage in the peacetime as well as we have in war—and no thanks to you English!" she ended angrily. She spun around to leave him, then remembered and turned back. "Thank you very much for helping me today."

His eyes blazed with repressed laughter at her unyielding tone. "You are too gracious," he answered, executing a courtly flourish with his hand. "I shall look forward to hearing from you."

"From me?" That stopped her. She stared at him, confused.

"With the list of possessions you want from the house. Remember, I said I'd send them if you'd send me a list?"

Now she remembered. "I've changed my mind!" she snapped. "I believe I'll get on well enough with exactly what I've got until the last redcoat soldier is long gone from New York!"

"Whatever you say," he replied, doffing his hat as she spun away for the second time. Then, because he could not resist, he called after her, "Good luck with your brother!"

She didn't deign to reply. But as she strode away, he saw her shoulders rise in the same way that boiling water raises the kettle's lid.

Chapter Five

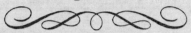

Barnett Silver sat with his mug of beer, watching the British regular fondle the serving girl. Goddamn redcoat, Barney thought to himself. And goddamn the Tories, who were even worse. The soldier hooked his arm around the girl's waist and pulled her down onto his knee. She protested with a laugh, but Barney could see she didn't mind. This wasn't at all the way it had been for Barney's wife when the redcoat soldiers had found her all alone at the farm that day.

Barney had been gone that day, to have his wheat ground over at the mill, and by the time he'd gotten back there hadn't been much to do except listen to her raving until she'd finally died, from grief and brain fever, but mainly from British abuse. After he'd buried her, Barney had sold the stock. Then he'd joined the Continental Army to kill all the British he could.

Now the soldier was trying to get his hand in the serving girl's stays. She struggled with him until he drew out his knife and cut the lacings so that her breasts sprang free. There was a whoop of approval from the other men that drowned out the girl's screeching as she fled the room, clutching stays and bouncing bosom as she ran. Chairs thudded to the floor as a couple of still-whooping regulars leapt up in clumsy pursuit.

But not the one who had wielded his knife. For one thing, he was laughing too hard to find his feet. For another, he was too drunk. Patient as a spider, Barney bided his time until, sometimes afterward, the soldier lurched to his feet and made his rambling, shambling way toward the tavern's back door, his hand on his breeches' fall leaving no doubt that his intention was to relieve himself. Then Barney rose and followed him out through the door, knowing that no one would notice him leaving. No one ever did.

The alley was deserted, malodorous and dark. Barney joined the soldier, both of them facing the wall.

"You've got a way with women," he remarked conversationally.

The soldier guffawed. "Bloody flirt," he muttered. "I should have bedded her myself."

"I could introduce you to much better," Barney offered, rebuttoning his fall. "Unless your friends are waiting."

"No friends," the soldier slurred, fumbling with his buttons. "Take me to the wenches!" he commanded with a belch.

He hardly noticed as Barney led him toward the slip—not until they'd reached the bottom step, with the water lapping at their feet like greasy ink. Then he tried to protest, but to no avail. Barney grabbed him and forced him under and held him until he went limp, after which he gave the inert body a good push toward the harbor. When they found the soldier in the morning, they'd assume he'd fallen in. No one would think of Barney. No one ever did. In the war they'd all been astonished that such a meek-looking man could be so good at killing, even with his bare hands.

Goddamn redcoats, Barney thought as he walked away.

The meat pasty woman was insistent on crying out her wares. "I've got good pasties, nice mutton and beef! Fresh made this morning, the best in all New York!"

Susannah bought one, though she had little appetite. She was too excited and, at the same time, too depressed. She nibbled on a corner as she crossed to the slip, straining her eyes across the water toward the brig *Hesperian*. Almost at once she saw the blackish smudge that must be Alex's barge pulling away from the brig.

At the sight her heart began to race with all the emotions she'd mastered for so long. Again she remembered the day seven years ago when Alex had marched off to Long Island with the rest of Washington's troops.

"I wish I could go with you," she'd murmured as she'd watched him pack.

He'd paused in his packing. "So do I," he'd confessed, and she'd understood then that he was scared, for all the bravado he showed to the rest of the world. He'd reached across the knapsack to squeeze her hand. "No matter what happens, Susie, I'll see you afterward."

"No matter what," she'd whispered, smiling through her tears.

She'd probably seen him three weeks altogether in the next four years. Then he'd gone south and been captured and she had not seen him since, though hardly a day had gone by without him in her mind.

She watched the black smudge growing as the barge cut through the harbor waves. What if he wasn't on it? What if he'd refused to leave the prison even on her parole?

"No, Alex!" she murmured. "Enough is enough!" But the thought of him not coming spread like a stain on her mind, reaching out to merge with the other source of her unhappiness.

She'd stormed away from Edward Steel in a high dudgeon yesterday, but six hours of searching for lodgings had more than humbled her. All of the best housing had been assigned to officers or to the most important of the Tory refugees. The less important Tories had snatched up most of the rest, leaving little open to returning patriots. She'd begun in the better neighborhoods and quickly worked her way down toward the worst, though she'd promised herself that she'd never stoop to a tent or a shack. In her search she'd heard of families who'd already given up and gone back out to the countryside to wait until the British had left—families who had houses still standing but occupied.

In view of that, she supposed she should feel lucky for having found anything at all.

But it was hard to feel lucky after having spent the night in two squalid chambers over a butcher's shop, and those just a few blocks short of Beekman's Swamp. She'd spent most of yesterday evening doing her best to transform the dingy rooms into a home, but the light of morning had showed her how miserably she'd failed. It pained her to think of bringing Alex to such a home. The next time she saw Edward Steel she wouldn't swoon or faint. The next time she'd see him as what he was: the redcoat who'd forced her to bring Alex home to a slum.

The barge was coming close now. Gloom and anger slipped away and Susannah stood on tiptoe, searching for her first glimpse. Suddenly she saw him. Her hand went to her throat and the words failed her completely to utter what she felt. At last, the war was over! Tears filled her eyes and ran unheeded down her cheeks.

"Alex!" she called, waving, but no words came out. She saw she was waving the meat pasty. Hastily she tucked it away. When she looked up she found Alex's eyes on her.

Dear God, he was so thin! The jacket he was wearing hung loose as a tent and his face, always so handsome, was haggard and so pale that his eyebrows and lashes stood out like sharp exclamations of darkness slashed across his brow. The clothes that he was wearing all looked freshly washed, but they also had the look of belonging to someone else. Imagining what he must have worn on the ship, Susannah felt an awful constriction in her throat.

But Alex was grinning as he leapt the last three feet of water to the wharf. "Susie!" he was calling, then he had her in his arms and she was laughing and crying both at once as he spun her around. Then he was seized by a fit of coughing and had to put her down.

"Alex! Are you all right?" She leaned over him, breathless from laughter and now breathless with fear.

"Just a ship's fever. From the damp." He shrugged it off. Putting his hands on her shoulders, he turned her to the light. "Look at you," he murmured, his voice rough from his cough. "My God, you're all grown up!"

"Grown up! I'm an old lady!" she scoffed with a smile. "Have you got any baggage?"

"Nothing but the clothes on my back. And even they weren't mine until a couple of hours ago."

"Never mind," she told him. "We'll get you whatever you need. Are you hungry?"

"Famished, and dying of thirst! Here, let me see you! Let me see everything!" He turned from her to the city and whistled beneath his breath.

"The fires," she murmured, following his gaze as it passed over the denuded skyline and the tent-filled fields. "Our house is still standing. But it's occupied," she said, and saw the sudden bitter twisting of his mouth. "Never mind," she repeated, linking her arm through his. "Soon the city will be ours again—just like the rest of the country. The United States!"

That made him smile, to her great relief. Arm in arm they walked up Great Dock Street, Susannah trying to ignore the sharpness of Alex's ribs against her arm and the way he wheezed after he exhaled. They found a tavern above Hanover Square that suited their taste. The parlor was empty so they chose a table and sat.

"Tell me," he commanded after they'd ordered food and drink from the tavern keeper's wife.

"Tell you what?" asked Susannah.

"Tell me everything!"

Looking at his thin face, she thought of Marguerite. But that tale was too painful, as was the one of their mother's death. For a long minute she sat in silence, racking her mind for something she could tell him that wasn't fraught with hurt. Finally she told him about her night with the Van Rijns, dwelling upon their high spirits and Mr. Van Rijn's determination to rebuild what had been lost.

While she was speaking, the food and ale arrived, and though Alex drank deeply, he hardly touched his meal. "Alex, you aren't eating," she murmured in concern. His skin, which had been so pallid, had turned feverishly bright.

"I'm too wound up," he apologized. "Have you heard from Marguerite? I haven't had a letter in over a year. I believe she must have written but they kept my mail. Damned bloody redcoats!" he muttered.

Susannah bit her lip. "It wasn't the redcoats. Well, in a way it was," she said. As kindly as she could manage, she told him the truth.

All of the feverish color drained from his face and Susannah could not help flinching before the raw pain in his eyes. "How could she?" he whispered, staring at his hands as though they held the answer. "How could she have done such a thing?"

"She was weak." Susannah reached out to grip his arm. "She was weak, Alex. You've got to let her go!"

He returned her hand's pressure as he struggled for control. In the end he found it. "Yes, you're right," he said. "Have you had enough here? I'm ready to go home."

She paid for their ale and for the food they hadn't touched, then led him with a heavy heart to their rented rooms. "It's only for the time being," she explained as they felt their way up the unlighted stairs. "As soon as they sign the final treaty, the British will be gone, and we'll be free to go home to William Street. In the meantime I'll sew curtains—" She opened the door and stood back so that he could have his first view of their interim home.

Alex sucked his breath in then let it out again. "Compared to where I've been, it's a palace!" he declared stoutly, which only succeeded in making her feel worse.

But she forgot her feelings when he started coughing again. She led him to the second room and helped him down onto the bed, loosened his collar and pulled off his well-worn shoes. When he was settled, she sat at his side, stroking his forehead and humming a lullaby that their mother used to sing to them when they were small.

He lay with his eyes closed and silent for so long that she was certain he'd drifted off to sleep. But when she gath-

ered her skirts to leave him, he reached out to keep her
there.

"Tell me about Father."

"The last I heard he'd left France for the East Indies on
the *Melissa.*" The *Melissa* was the best, and also the last,
of their father's ships, all the others having been lost in the
blockade. "He sent me a letter through his factor, Monsieur Binchot, who we're to write to until Father returns."

"How's the money?"

"There isn't much," she said. "That's why he went to the
Indies instead of coming home. But I have a little left, and
there should be something Monsieur Binchot can send.
We'll write to him as soon as we can find a ship to take a
letter to France."

Alex assented with a slight movement of his head. She
knew what was coming from how quiet he was. "Tell me,
now," he murmured.

"No, Alex. I can't." But even as she said it, she realized
that she could. More than that, she realized that she wanted
to—that she'd been holding the pain inside her until she
could share it with him. They had shared a mother, as
they'd shared everything.

"It was terrible," she whispered, "the very worst of all.
We were in the Mohawk Valley, staying at a farm. Mother
had been feeling poorly ever since we'd come. The travel,
the constant worry—her strength had slipped away. I tried
to find a safe place but it seemed that wherever we went, no
sooner did we get there than the redcoats arrived. And if it
wasn't the redcoats, it was the Tories in their stead.

"That day she was running a fever and unable to get out
of bed, when a boy rode up in a great hurry shouting from
below that the redcoats were coming, headed straight for
us. Mother had heard the boy's alarm and begged me to go,
but I told her I would stay there with her. I told her I wasn't
afraid of the redcoats, which was the truth. I wasn't so
much afraid of them as I was furious—furious at what
they'd done to Mother—done to all of us."

She drew a deep breath and continued. "Within the hour they came. I heard them approaching and went down to speak to them. They had Indians with them, but the Indians stayed outside. I explained about Mother being so ill. I asked them if they wouldn't please leave us alone. It was a poor farmhouse, there was hardly a bite to eat. I had a bit of money. I offered what I had.

"They laughed in my face," she said, swiping a distracted hand at the tears that had begun. "They called me a rebel wench and—something even worse. They made me sit in the kitchen while they ransacked the house. They took everything they could carry, right down to the quilt from Mother's bed. I suppose we were lucky they didn't set fire to the house. I suppose I was lucky that they left me alone, though at the time I was so angry I didn't really care.

"I found some sacks in the barn and put them on Mother's bed. But they couldn't keep her warm, and then there was the shock. She lingered for three days, but in the end she died. I did my best, Alex. Honestly I did. Just before the very end, she blessed both of us. Then she whispered Father's name. And then she died." She twisted her hands together, the tears pouring down her cheeks.

"Hush, now, Susannah. I'm here now. It's all right," Alex comforted her. He sat propped against the wall behind him and held her in his scarecrow arms, rocking her against him until the tears had spent themselves.

She rested her head on his shoulder, feeling drained but also at peace. A tight knot inside her had finally been untied and she felt as though she could breathe deeply for the first time in years. She was beginning to drowse off when Alex's voice shook her awake.

"I'll pay them back." He spoke the words as a solemn vow.

She roused herself to face him. "No, Alex. There's no point. The best you can do is forget them and get on with your own life. We wanted our independence and we've got that, finally. We've beaten them, Alex. That's got to be enough."

"It's not enough," he answered in a voice she knew—the same voice she imagined he'd used when he'd refused the parole. She knew better than to argue when he spoke in that voice. Right now he was ill and tired. When he was feeling better he'd see things differently.

"Rest now," she coaxed him, and though she was relieved, she was also depressed by how little persuasion he needed to lie back down in the bed. His head had hardly touched the pillow when he was deeply asleep.

She sat beside him, frowning into space. From below she could hear the voices of the butcher and his wife. The voices were angry, raised in a fight. Something crashed and shattered, then a door was slammed, rattling what was left of the windows and shaking the walls. How could she heal Alex in a place like this? How could she heal his body and his bitter heart? He needed nice things around him, good familiar things.

With a pang she thought of Edward Steel's offer yesterday. She'd turned him down in anger, but now she regretted it. Pride wouldn't help her make Alex whole again. She needed bed linen and warm covers and something to cheer his mind as he went through the recuperation that so clearly lay ahead. She'd swallow her pride and write to Edward tonight. Let him think what he would of her change of heart; she had her own concerns. She tossed her head in defiance as she rose to begin the task.

She sent the note that evening, with the butcher's boy, then spent the night lying awake on her thin bed in the front room, listening to Alex mutter and cough through the wall. In the morning he said he was tired, so she urged him to stay in bed and went out in search of breakfast and some material with which to fashion curtains in order to cheer up their rooms. She spent an unconscionable amount on two lengths of calico and a loaf of white bread, which she toasted at the fire. She told herself the expense was worth it when Alex ate the toast. He also ate part of her pasty from the day before and washed both down with a quantity of tea. By the time she'd cleared up, he was asleep again.

She was measuring the calico in the front room when she heard footsteps on the stairs. Who could it be? she wondered. The drayman with her things? Her heart rose at the possibility and she hurried to the door, carrying the fabric with her. The footsteps were coming slowly—because of the absence of light and also because of the ricketiness of the stairs.

"Up here, straight on!" she called out, throwing open the door. To her surprise she found herself looking down at Edward Steel. "You!" she gasped without thinking.

He seemed as nonplussed as she by her sudden appearance and accusatory tone. He put one hand out to steady himself on the wall, then glanced down behind him. "I've brought your things. The draymen are waiting down below. I—I wanted to be sure that you were in before I sent them up." Slowly he came up the last few steps.

She fell back before his approach. "I—didn't expect you!" she stammered, feeling like a fool. He more than filled the doorway, seeming to occupy all the room and making her conscious of his presence in strange, disturbing ways. Today he wore a dark coat and dark breeches; she thought they were chocolate brown, though she couldn't be certain in the dim light of the hallway. But that only intensified his effect on her. She couldn't look at him without recalling how he had felt when she touched him. She took another step backward. "Won't—won't you please come in?"

With a silent nod he accepted, sweeping off his tricorn and ducking as he came through the door. "It was thoughtful of you to be so prompt," she said belatedly, keeping her hands clasped before her to prevent them from fluttering, as they'd done in his presence yesterday and seemed prepared to do again. Her heart was also fluttering as though beset by butterflies. One would never have guessed from her reaction that this was her enemy, she thought crossly. But she couldn't stop herself when he stood so near. It crossed her mind to step back again, but this time she did not. "I didn't imagine you'd bring the things yourself," she murmured, looking up at him.

"I was coming in this direction," he explained, but the look in his eyes informed Susannah of the real reason that he had come. He had wanted to see her! She was suddenly filled with a gladness that was quick and warm, and she smiled with pleasure before she could catch herself.

Edward returned her smile. "I couldn't find some of the things on your list. I don't know if they're missing. They might have been put somewhere else. I didn't want to rummage around any more than necessary."

"Whatever you found will be fine," she replied, touched by his delicacy. He might be a redcoat, but he was an unusual one. She saw his eyes drop briefly to her lips, then pull away with an effort she could almost feel.

His eyes settled on the calico she was still holding in her hands. "I see you're sewing."

"What? Oh, yes. Just curtains." Idiotically, she held the material up to him.

He examined it as closely as though it were the finest silk. "The color suits you," he said presently. "You ought to use it for a gown." His eyes left the calico and rose to her face just as she felt his fingertips brush lightly against hers. She jumped at the contact and her fingers began to burn.

"It's just calico," she murmured, her heart hammering. She knew she should move her fingers but she kept them where they were. She knew she should hope that he'd move his, but she prayed that he would not.

Her prayer was answered as his hands slid under hers, cupping them lightly before his fingers began to stroke. "Sometimes," he murmured, "the simplest things have the most appeal."

The pads of his fingers caressed hers, while his thumbs stroked her palms in a way that made her remember his hand resting on her back. Her breasts also seemed to remember the nearness of his touch, for she felt them tingle as his thumbs moved back and forth. The tingling spread through her until it met the butterflies and turned into a trembling down along her thighs. His eyes told her that he'd felt it, too. They seemed to swirl and smolder, neither blue nor gray. She knew it would be wiser if she looked away, but found she had no more power over her eyes than she had her hands. Instead, her gaze seemed to be fused with his, and she felt him drawing her deeper with every beat of her heart.

His fingers were moving with slow authority, stroking and tickling along her sensitive skin. She realized that she and Edward were both breathing shallowly, as though they were waiting for something. Then she knew what it was. He was going to kiss her. She could feel it on her lips as though his lips had sent them a message and they could hardly wait. I can't kiss a redcoat, she thought dazedly, but it seemed unimportant, a concern that had mattered to someone else. His eyes were the color of a mountain lake. A secret lake tucked away where only they could go.

"Ahhhh!" She felt the warmth of his sigh as he bent to her. Slowly she rose on tiptoe until she felt the first unimaginably soft brushing of skin against skin. His fingers tightened. She shuddered.

And then, through the partition, came the sound of Alex coughing.

Susannah jerked. Edward froze. She knew that he meant to release her, but just before he did his hands gripped hard and his lips opened over hers. For a blinding, red-swirled minute he claimed her hungrily and she knew the texture and feel of his teeth, his tongue, his open mouth on her stunned and willing lips. Life stopped for that minute while sensation raged.

Then the minute was over and they were standing apart, the calico abandoned between them on the floor.

"My brother," Susannah said lamely, referring to the noise. She was shocked, disappointed and frightened all at once. Every part of her body hated to let Edward go. But her mind knew what would happen if Alex opened his door. She shuddered to think of the reception he would give an

Englishman in his home and shuddered again to contemplate what he would say to her. "He—he's resting," she faltered. "He shouldn't be disturbed." She raised her eyes to Edward's, full of mute appeal.

"No, of course not," he answered, glancing toward Alex's door. Then, perhaps for the first time, he became aware of the room. His eyes made a slow circuit, and as Susannah watched she saw first shock, then pity, steal into his face.

She saw him try to mask it as soon as he realized, but far from helping, that only made it worse. A dreadful mortification burned hotly through her chest and her back went rigid with blind, instinctive pride. How dare Edward Steel, or anyone, look that way! How dare he pity her—as though she were some object for his charity! Did he think her weak and pathetic because she'd melted in his arms? Well, let him take note that she wasn't melting now!

"Have you some objection to this chamber?" she demanded as her limp hands clenched into fists and settled on her hips. She gave him no time to answer but plunged ahead down the turbulent path blazed by wounded pride. "Personally I prefer this room to a vermin-infested house." What she meant by the word *vermin* was unmistakable. She saw Edward color and defiantly tossed her head. "I'm sure your draymen must be wondering where you are," she concluded, looking behind him and down the stairs.

Edward's glance followed hers, then swung back again. "Susannah, please," he reasoned.

"Please, nothing!" she snapped. "And I'll thank you to call me Mistress Beckwith—Captain Steel!"

"Mistress Beckwith—"

"Really, you've got to go! There's no telling what my brother will do if he finds you here. He's got a terrible aversion to vermin after his time in that British brig!"

The first time he could forgive her, but the second time it stung. That's what you got when you trusted a woman, Edward told himself. Tall and regal or small and pert: they kissed you, then kicked you while they had you down. Of course. He should have known. Rebel or British, they were all the same.

"Have it your way," he said shortly. "I'll have your things sent up. It seems you've dropped your curtains," he added, glancing down at the calico on the floor before he turned and strode from the chamber and down the unlighted stairs.

"The devil take you, Captain Edward Steel!" Susannah cursed after him through clenched teeth. "And the devil take the curtains!" she added, giving the calico a kick that sent it skidding across the floor and into the spindly chair, which, besides a bed and table, was the room's only furnishing.

There was a noise behind her as Alex opened his door, blinking and still drowsy as he looked around. "Are you all right, Susannah? Is somebody here?"

She brushed her skirt quickly. "Only a drayman," she said. "He's got some things to bring up—some things from William Street."

"From William Street?" Alex stared in disbelief. "But I thought the redcoats—"

"They are," she cut him off. "But that doesn't mean they have a right to our things. I had a list delivered to the present occupant and now he's sent what I requested."

A slow grin of admiration spread across Alex's face. "Trust you, Susie, to have the British army eating from your hand!"

"From my hand!" she muttered, half-tempted to laugh bitterly at how far wrong Alex was. But the temptation to laugh left her when Alex had gone back to bed and the draymen had delivered the things and gone. Alone, she opened the first case, and there, on the very top, she found one item that hadn't been on her list.

It was her book of sonnets, the one she'd last seen in his hand. His hand. Susannah closed her eyes and tried hard not to think of what had just happened. In her efforts she recalled something her mother had told her shortly before she had died. Susannah had been saying that she was too worried to respond to the advances of the American soldiers who'd been camped nearby. Her mother had smiled sadly and replied, "The right man can make a woman forget even a war."

Until this moment, she hadn't understood what her mother had meant. For one crazy minute Edward Steel had made her forget—about war and pride and loyalty, and even Alex next door! A redcoat, of all people, she thought bitterly. And one who patronized her with his pity after he'd stolen her home. If she couldn't forget about Edward, then she'd remember today as a lesson in behavior to avoid.

She put aside the sonnets and, kneeling beside the crate, set about the business of creating a home.

The guards had the dead soldier's body under a dirty tarp, which they unfolded for Edward when he arrived at the wharf. The coat was unbuttoned and the shirt filthy from the mud. The crossed belts had come unfastened and were lying at his side.

"The belt's what caught on the moorings," one of the guards explained. "Wrapped around one of the piles and pulled him under but left his boot sticking out. One of the men from the ferry happened to catch sight of it." The guard looked down at the body with evident distaste. "Must have got drunk and fell in. Can't see why General Carleton's concerned."

Ignoring the soldier's comment, Edward knelt to examine the corpse as best he could with a crowd looking on. The rest could be accomplished when they'd moved it to the morgue. Rising, he noticed a familiar figure loitering nearby. He gave the guard his instructions, then briskly walked away.

A little bell rang tinnily as the tobacconist's door swung shut, plunging Edward into a dim, pungent-smelling world.

"Sir, what's your fancy?" The tobacconist looked up from the counter on which he was weighing out ounces of snuff.

"My name is Edward Steel."

"Steel?" The man peered at him for a moment before he abandoned his scales. Opening a door behind him, he ushered Edward across a hallway and into a little room in which Franks was already awaiting him.

Franks's teeth flashed in the dimness. "I took a shortcut from the wharf. What did you make of the body?"

"Not much. That he drowned. I found nothing to indicate that he hadn't tripped and fallen in. He didn't strike me as a man who took great care of himself. He could have slipped and hit his head, or he could have been pushed. What do you know about him?"

"Not much," said Franks. "He was in one of the taverns, fooling with the serving wench. The next anyone can remember, he had disappeared."

"Did the girl have a jealous lover?"

Franks shook his head. "I mean to go back to the tavern and spend the evening there. Perhaps there's something to discover. At least it's worth a try."

"Be careful."

"Yes, sir. I will."

Edward sat in the pungent dimness after Franks had gone, thinking less about the dead soldier than about the way Susannah had felt in his arms—soft and supple and firm all at once. She'd felt better than a woman had felt in a long time. But she wasn't just any woman. She was an American and he happened to be the redcoat who was living in her house, which made the chances of something between them almost impossible. But even so Edward couldn't get her out of his mind.

Chapter Six

Susannah sewed her curtains and arranged the things from William Street in the two rented rooms. Alex said that their own things made all the difference, but privately she found they emphasized the very shabbiness they were intended to hide. But when she thought of the pity she'd seen in Edward's eyes, she tossed her head in defiance and told herself that she didn't care. She wasn't a weak-willed Tory who needed silk-papered walls. She was an American and she could do without.

But if her pride could make her forget the rooms, it couldn't cure her worry over the state of Alex's health, which continued to deteriorate despite her best efforts to nurse him back to health.

One problem was money, since good food was dear. She'd written a letter to Monsieur Binchot urgently requesting funds, and though Mr. Van Rijn had promised to find an American ship bound for France, she knew that it would be at least two months before she could hope to receive a response.

Meanwhile she nursed Alex as best she could and tried not to worry, which grew harder by the day. She would have gladly paid for a doctor, but Alex refused to be seen by any physician who'd treated Tories, which included virtually every one. It certainly included Captain Edward Steel, the personal physician to Carleton himself. Not that she would have called Edward, she assured herself—but without the spirit she'd felt too weeks before.

In her years in the country, she'd learned something of healing with herbs. As did most refugees', her possessions included a small stash of remedies, most of which she tried on Alex to no avail. The fever she'd noticed the first day continued to come and go, until one day when it caught hold and began to mount steadily. Then she did call a doctor, who bled him and gave him a purge, but by the next morning the fever was worse than before.

She sat with him throughout the day, laying cool rags on his forehead and feeding him spoonfuls of a tea made from her dried herbs, watching for improvement that didn't come until her eyes began to ache.

Alex became restless as evening gathered and darkness crept through the rooms. He began to mutter and finally to rave, imagining himself alternately back in prison and in the war. Once, she had to hold him to keep him from getting up.

"Let me go!" He fought her with feverish strength. "I've got to go with the men!"

"Alex, no!" she pleaded. "You're not in the war anymore. You're with me, Susannah. The war's over. You're at home!"

She saw that he hadn't heard her, but then he began to cough and doubled with the spasm as she bent over him. When it was over he fell back, exhausted and burning hot.

"Alex, please," she begged him, cooling his face with a cloth. "Please, please get better! Please don't leave me alone!"

The memory of her mother's death gripped her throat like a clammy hand. She swallowed hard on her panic. She had to remain calm. With shaking hands she wrung out the cloth and smoothed it on his skin, but as she did the heat of his fever burned through it to her palms.

There was an apothecary on the far side of Golden Hill, a cold-eyed Tory who remembered her from before the war. She'd been to see him a couple of days before, and though she'd seen his full jars with her own eyes, he'd coolly informed her that the rebel embargo had exhausted his stock. Perhaps if she begged him. Perhaps if she offered a bribe. Her eye fell upon the silk paisley scarf that Edward had sent with the things from William Street.

Edward, she thought.

"Don't," she said aloud, firmly. But the firmness didn't help. She was too frightened and Alex was too ill to stem the flood of images evoked by Edward's name. Strong hands on her shoulders, a deep voice in her ear murmuring, "I can help."

He could. He was a doctor. But even more than that, he had helped her almost every time they met. He was a redcoat and her enemy but she trusted him, and right now she was too worried to regret that trust.

Then she remembered the last time that they'd met, how she'd called him a vermin and practically thrown him out. He'd left angry. Maybe he was angry still. If she sent him a message, maybe he'd tear it up.

"Forward!" Alex muttered, thrashing his head from side to side. "Down . . . down! Take cover . . ."

"Hush, darling." She stroked his cheek. He was so hot. Burning. She knew what she had to do. With one final look at Alex, she went to fetch her shawl and a shilling, which she hoped would persuade the butcher's fat, argumentative wife to sit with Alex for the half hour she'd be gone.

"Oh, Captain Steel, do tell us what you think of our New York." Marguerite Bridgeham raised her voice to make herself heard above the chatter of her supper guests. They were twelve that evening, including the commandant and the irascible Myles Porter, who took predictable issue with Lady Bridgeham's words.

"Ours!" Porter grumbled. "It doesn't seem so to me—unless you mean the city is ours to throw away!"

"Now, now, Mr. Porter!" Marguerite silenced him laughingly. "You know Nova Scotia's a very lovely place. Please do tell us what you think of our fair city, Captain," she implored, turning her back on Porter before he could interrupt again.

"I think it's borne up very well, given the circumstances," Edward answered politely, vowing to himself that the next time the Bridgehams asked him, he'd find an excuse not to dine.

"Diplomatically said!" Marguerite applauded, tinkling her jewels.

"Where are you staying, Captain?" From the far end of the table, Lord Bridgeham craned his neck over the line of platters all piled as high as if there had never been such a thing as shortages.

"On William Street," Edward answered. "In a house that belongs—"

"To some rebel family that doesn't deserve as much!" Marguerite interrupted with a smile. "You mustn't mention the Beckwith name to him," she added confidentially when Lord Bridgeham had gone back to his food. "They're a difficult family—rebel through and through. The father was a rogue even before the war. He traded in the Netherlands, regardless of the law. When the war began, he took to privateering and managed to lose most of his ships. It seems he's sailed the last one off to the Orient. Who knows if he'll ever come back.

"The children are cut of the same cloth," she went on, leaning so close to Edward that her bodice warmed his arm. "The last I heard of the son, he was in jail. And as for the daughter—she's hardly civilized. Do you know she actually yelled at me in the street! So of course any mention of her throws Lord Bridgeham into a rage!" Marguerite glanced at her husband, then her eyes swung to Edward again. "To tell the truth," she confided, "I wouldn't put it past Susannah Beckwith to approach the house. My advice to you if that happens is not to answer the door!"

Edward freed his arm from her clutches by reaching for his glass. "Thank you, Lady Bridgeham. I'll keep that in mind."

He left as soon after supper as he possibly could, though Lady Bridgeham put up quite a fuss. Then, when he'd gotten past her, Porter trailed him to the door. He thought Porter meant to ask about his petition, but he had other things on his mind.

"You're staying at the Beckwith house, aren't you?"

Edward nodded reluctantly, preparing himself for a repetition of Lady Bridgeham's tale—but not for Porter's next comment, which came as a total surprise.

"I heard Lady Bridgeham describing the family to you. But I wonder if she added that she'd been engaged to the son?"

"The one who was in prison?" Edward stared at him in shock, unable to imagine a brother of Susannah's in love with the beribboned Marguerite. Or the reverse, for that matter.

Porter nodded, pleased by Edward's shock. He was still smarting from Marguerite's remark about Nova Scotia being a pretty place—as though she hadn't sold her soul for an English estate!

"She was Marguerite Dawes back then, and a rebel to boot. But when she had the chance to hook his lordship, she changed her feathers fast enough. Naturally her marriage offended the Beckwith girl, who said so in no uncertain terms the first chance she got—which happened to be in the Broad Way, on her ladyship's front stoop!" Porter chuckled, imagining the scene. "From what I hear, his lordship almost had a fit."

Forgetting Porter, Edward smiled at the thought of the outraged Susannah berating the sputtering pair. But after he'd said good-night to Porter and was walking home alone, he found that the entire evening had left a bitter taste in his mouth. The story of Lady Bridgeham's betrayal cut far too close to home. It brought back his own betrayal at the hands of Catherine. And the memory of Catherine left more than a bitter taste. It left the dull aching of deep and unhealed wounds.

Catherine Hargreave had been blond, like Marguerite, and beautiful and accomplished. And Edward had been young—young enough to believe that she loved him for his soul instead of for the title that had tumbled into his lap with the death of his beloved older brother, St. John. Because both of their parents had died many years before, St. John had been more than a brother to him. He'd been a friend, teacher, confessor and advocate. St. John had been the one who'd encouraged Edward to pursue his interest in medicine when others had frowned on it as below his station in life. He'd just finished his medical training when the news had come that St. John had died in a storm at sea. The news had hit him very hard.

And then he'd met Catherine.

She'd comforted and soothed and dazzled him with her beauty and soft words. He'd believed himself the luckiest man on earth when she'd promised to marry him as soon as the official mourning was through. But before that time came, the wonderful news arrived that although St. John's ship had gone down, St. John had survived. Edward had been ecstatic, but Catherine sent him a letter saying that she'd changed her mind. She realized she didn't love him and so the marriage was off. He'd been too stunned to guess her reason until two months later, when she'd become engaged to the oldest son and heir of the Duke of Darbyshire. She'd only wanted his title and never cared for his heart.

"Ten o'clock!" the watch was calling as Edward turned into William Street. "A clear and warm night. All is well!"

All is well! The words echoed with bitter irony in his mind. He'd come to New York five years ago to flee the memory of Catherine. He couldn't stay in England to bear witness to the spectacle of her brilliant marriage and her equally brilliant hypocrisy. New York had served its purpose, giving him time to form a tough layer of experience over the tender wounds. Thanks to Catherine, he'd learned a lesson that he'd never forget. He'd learned that if you trust a woman, you do so at your risk.

On that note, he arrived at the gate of William Street, which brought to mind a woman as different from Catherine Hargreave as a woman could be: Susannah Beckwith, she of the forthright tongue. And of the sweet lips, he added, recalling that one stunning kiss. As always, when he recalled it, his body began to react, skin and blood and muscle responding by memory.

He paused with one hand on the gatepost as a sound came to him. The sound of running footsteps. He turned toward their approach.

His first thought was that desire had conjured the image of her. But as he watched her come nearer, he knew that she was real.

"Susannah?" What was she doing, rushing about in the night with her shawl all loose and flying and her hair all coming down? She was headed in his direction, though as usual she was too preoccupied with her errand to see him standing at the gate. He reached out and caught her just as she turned in.

"Ooof!" She jerked to a sudden halt, too breathless to scream. Then she looked up and saw him and her expression changed. "Oh!" she gasped. "Oh, Edward!" Then she caught herself. She pulled back.

But he held her. "What is it? Is something wrong?"

She looked up. Her chest was heaving. Her dark hair framed her face. He could see that she was frightened and reluctant, both at once. Her parted lips, her urgency made him forget about wisdom and risk, and his mind still echoed with the sound of her gasping his name.

"Tell me," he urged her, tightening his grip.

Fright overcame reluctance. "It's my brother," she confessed. "He—I'm afraid he's not very well."

"Not well? Do you mean he's ill?" The doctor in him took charge while the man was still responding to the feel of her in his hands. "How ill? Describe it."

"He's got a fever," she said. "He's had it since the beginning, but only off and on. He must have been sick in prison, and he coughs and coughs. Then, yesterday morning, the fever took hold. I sent for the doctor. He bled him, but that didn't help." Once she released them, the words tumbled out in a rush and her eyes clung to Edward's, petrified with fright.

"Does he spit blood?" he asked her.

"No. Not yet, in any case. Does that make a difference?"

"It could," he replied. Tendrils of her dark hair had broken loose in her flight and now formed a halo around her face. Without thinking, he released her shoulder to smooth those tendrils back. "Would you like me to come and see him?"

"Oh, would you?" Susannah breathed. Then, before he could answer, her expression changed. She broke away, turning toward the gatepost to avert her face from him. "I know I've got no right to ask you, after what happened," she said in such a low voice that he had to lean forward to hear her words. "That is, after what I called you when you brought me my things. But if you could find it in your heart to forgive me, or at least to call a truce—"

"I forgive you," he said softly. He watched as she heard him and turned.

"You do?" She looked up, tears trembling in her eyes.

He nodded. For a moment he was overcome by a wave of such aching tenderness that he couldn't speak. When it ebbed enough to permit him, he murmured, "Yes, of course. I'm only sorry that you waited so long."

"I'm sorry, too," she whispered as the first of the tears splashed down. "Oh, Edward, I've been so worried! I didn't know what to do. I'm so afraid of losing Alex—" But she couldn't go on. She clutched her throat as though she were strangling and her face contorted with pain.

Before she drew her next choked breath, he had her in his arms. "You won't lose him, Susannah. Hush, don't think about it." He felt her body tremble and gathered her closer yet.

"I can't help it! I can't help it!" she sobbed heartbrokenly against his chest. "Hour after hour, it's all I've been thinking of. After what happened to Mother, I can't get it out of my mind. I'm so afraid, Edward! Oh, God, I've been so afraid!''

He held her tightly to him, his lips pressed to the silk of her hair, feeling cruel and selfish to be reveling in her grief. She felt as weightlessly fragile as she had that first day. When her fiery spirit wasn't burning she was as delicate as a child. "Hush! Don't cry, my darling," he murmured into her hair.

"I'm sorry!" she wept. "It's just I've been so worried. I promise that I'll stop."

She did stop, almost too soon for Edward's wish, but for a time she seemed contented to nestle in his arms. When she sighed against him, the heat of it scalded his chest. Then he felt her hand stir, fumbling in her skirts. "Oh dear. I've lost my handkerchief."

"Take mine." He shifted her against him in order to fish it out. When she bent to blow her nose, her hair fell across her face. He tucked it back behind her ear, feeling the same tenderness aching in him again.

"Keep it," he told her when she held it out. "Come inside and wait now, while I get my bag."

Obediently she let him lead her up the steps. He was fitting his own key into the lock when Milly opened the door.

"Captain Steel! And Mistress Beckwith! This is a surprise! Shall I—"

"No, thank you, Milly," Edward cut her off. "Mistress Beckwith's brother is ailing. I'm just going to fetch my bag then we'll be going out. Don't wait up for me. I can let myself in. I'll be down in a minute," he told Susannah, starting for the stairs.

"Ailing? I hope not badly. There's so much going around. But don't you fret, mistress, Captain Steel will see to him!" The sound of Milly's chatter followed him up to the second floor, where he lost no time in collecting what he'd need.

Milly was still fussing when he came down again, but in the short space Susannah had lost her helpless-child look and had changed back into the familiar straight-backed American, who beckoned to him impatiently as soon as he appeared. "I've already been gone longer than I told the butcher's wife, and I don't trust her to stay beyond her time!"

They hurried in silence through the lamp-lit streets, Susannah's face once more drawn and preoccupied. Glancing across at her, Edward wondered if she'd already forgotten crying in his arms. Would she regret such a weakness when she did remember? He suspected that she would.

The butcher's wife was still with Alex when they arrived. She shook her head darkly. "He don't look too good to me. If you ask me, he'll be lucky to last the night. He's skinny as a bean pole. He ain't got any strength."

"Thank you for your opinion," Edward said, moving her past Susannah and out through the front room. "Do you have another candle?" he asked when she had gone, less because he required it than to give Susannah something to do—other than sit and worry while he examined the sick man. When she'd fetched the candle, he'd think of another task. He crossed the room to the mattress and set down his bag.

He got his first jolt of surprise when he saw her brother's face. The same sweep of dark lashes, the same dark arching brows—even the same sprinkling of freckles scattered across the nose. Take away the two weeks' growth of sickroom beard and you'd have Susannah, albeit haggard and flushed.

"Your brother—is he older?" he asked when she returned bearing the candle, which she held over the bed, adding to the light of the lantern that was burning on the table at his side.

"By five minutes," she said with the ghost of a smile. "He always called me his little sister—as a joke, that is." She looked down at her brother and Edward saw her lips compress and knew that she was holding back another rush of tears. This time she was successful. "How is he?" she asked, her eyes seeking Edward's, torn between hope and despair.

"I'll tell you in a minute. Have you got a kettle on? I'd like a basin of hot water, if you can manage it."

"What about the candle?"

"The lantern will do while you're gone."

The water wasn't quite hot, but by the time she returned, he'd finished his examination and composed his thoughts. "I wish I could say that he wasn't, but your brother is very ill."

"Will he die?" she whispered, her color draining so fast that he half rose in the expectation that she was about to faint. She understood his motion and held a restraining hand. "I'm all right. Please. Tell me."

"I don't know," he said. "That will depend upon how strong he is."

"He's so weak from prison," she murmured, her face still very pale.

"I know that," Edward acknowledged. "But I meant something else. If he's anything like his little sister, I'd say he's got a fair chance."

At his words a flash of gratitude sparked in her dark eyes. But the flash was short-lived. "Can you help him?" she asked.

"I'll do my best," he promised. He looked around the room. She'd made every improvement that was humanly possible, but she couldn't change the underlying wretchedness of the place. The room was close and airless and smelled strongly of decay. Most doctors favored closed sickrooms, but such squalor could not be healthy, in his book. "I'd like to move him," he said slowly, watching her face. "I think he'd have a far better chance at William Street."

He wasn't sure what he'd expected: anger or pride or hurt. To his puzzlement he saw only reluctance before she turned away.

In any event, she nodded. "Yes. I think so, too. You'll need a stretcher."

He'd already thought of that. "I can get one easily. If you've got ink and paper, I'll send for one right now."

She brought him both and he wrote on the table beside the bed, addressing the note to the nearest hospital, at what had been King's College before the war. He blotted it and sealed it, then had Susannah take it down to the butcher's boy with a half-penny fee.

To Susannah it seemed forever before the stretcher arrived. She would have filled the time with packing, but there was no point, since, except for the few things that Edward had sent, most of Alex's possessions were still at William Street. She sat in silence, her eyes fixed on Alex's face, memorizing his features—as though they weren't hers, too—and trying not to cry.

"Are these yours?" asked Edward. He was examining the bottles of herbs that she'd lined up on the table beside Alex's bed.

"I brought them from the country when I came back." She watched as he opened each bottle and shook the herbs into his hand, sniffed them, then held them up to the lantern light. One by one, he quizzed her about them: their names, where they grew, what their flowers looked like, what she knew of their use. She answered his questions as best she could, convinced that he was cringing before her ignorance. It was only later that she realized he'd only been helping to pass the anxious time.

His questions did help. He still had two bottles to go when they were roused by the commotion of heavy boots on the stairs. She stayed with Alex while Edward went to direct the men in.

"You'll have to tie him to it to get him down the stairs," he was saying as he led the two redcoat regulars into the room. When they had Alex tied securely, he stood at the top of the stairs, holding the lantern with which to light their way.

At first Susannah stood at the bottom, but she was too afraid that they'd come crashing down, so she ended up standing in the street with her hands pressed against her ears. The descent also seemed endless, but at last they got him down, after which they would have rested, but Edward hurried them on their way.

He would have followed hard on their heels, had Susannah not caught his arm. "Forgive me, but if it's not too much trouble, could you send me word? You could send it with Milly. Or I could send the butcher's boy."

"Word?" He'd been watching the stretcher being borne away. Now he turned back with impatience. "What are you talking about?"

"Of how Alex is doing," she said quickly, blushing at her selfishness.

His brows swooped down disbelievingly. "But of course you're coming. I thought that was understood!"

"I didn't—" she stammered.

But Edward was already gone, running after the stretcher, his steps echoing in the night.

"I'll just put out the candles!" she called after him, and when he didn't answer, she ran quickly upstairs.

One of the two stretcher bearers opened the door to her knock at William Street. "They've got him upstairs," he directed, stepping out of her way as she hurried past him with a hastily murmured thanks.

Lights were blazing in the sconces all along the stairs, and she could hear Milly's voice from above. She met Milly herself in the hallway.

"Where is he?" Susannah asked. But before Milly could answer she saw the light coming from Alex's room. She heard Edward speaking as she came through the door, but she didn't see him. Rather she saw a servant she'd never seen before. He was in the process of stripping off Alex's shirt—and having a hard time of it because Alex was thrashing again.

"...down to the kitchen," Edward was saying as Susannah came in. "And, while you're about it, you can hurry them up with that tub."

"Tub?" Susannah repeated as Edward emerged from the gloom beyond the bed. He'd taken off his coat and stock and rolled up his sleeves. "Surely you don't mean to give Alex a bath?"

"Indeed I do," he said crisply, advancing toward the bed. The servant finished with Alex's shirt, covered him hastily with a sheet and beat a retreat toward the hall. "He's burning up with fever," Edward explained in the same brisk tone. "There's nothing like tepid water to cool him down."

"But a bath, when he's sick!" She'd never heard of such a thing. She came to stand by Alex. Shirtless, he looked so thin—even in the candlelight she could count his every rib. Edward was right about the fever: she could feel it from where she stood. He was radiant with it, like a Franklin stove. "Won't a bath chill him?"

"Not if we're careful," Edward replied. The brusque tone he was using bruised her, though she knew that she shouldn't mind. He was helping Alex. That was the important thing. And she had to trust him. Really, she had no choice.

A few minutes later the two soldiers appeared, one lugging the bathtub, the other two buckets of water, one hot and one cold. Milly and the servant followed with two buckets more apiece. As soon as the tub had been set down, they emptied the buckets in.

Edward felt the water. "All right." He glanced toward the bed. "Let's get him in."

The men moved to obey him as Milly fled the room. Susannah stayed where she was. She'd seen Alex before. What alarmed her was not his nakedness but the sharpness of his hips. The two soldiers carried him between them, but he looked so wasted that one might have done it alone.

Alex groaned and thrashed his arms when they put him in the tub, but gradually he quieted until even his head was

still. Edward knelt beside him, dipping in a cloth and letting the tepid water flow over Alex's body in slow rivulets.

The three men and Susannah stood watching in a row.
The soldiers' heads were nodding, then one of them began
to snore. The other one nudged him sharply, but not before Edward glanced up.

"You can go," he said. "Thank your sergeant on my
behalf."

"Yes, sir." They saluted, relieved to be released.

The servant looked hopeful, but Edward shook his head.
"Sorry, William, but I'll be needing your help to get him
out."

"I can help," offered Susannah, taking a step toward the
tub. "He's not very heavy. I've been nursing him myself."

Edward's eyes shifted from the servant to her with little
more interest than he had shown in the men. "Very well."
He nodded. "William, you're dismissed. But don't go off
tomcatting in case I need you later on."

"Oh, no, sir!" William looked shocked by the very idea.
A moment later he, too, had disappeared.

The room seemed very quiet after they had gone. The
only sound was the gentle splash and trickle of Edward's
cloth. Susannah stood for a moment, watching, then joined
him at the tub. "I could help with that," she offered.

"I'm fine. Thank you," he said without looking up. But
just at that moment, Alex struck out. His dream of battle
must have come back, because suddenly he was thrashing
as he struggled to get up.

"The men!" he cried hoarsely, flailing with scarecrow
limbs as Edward and Susannah both lunged to hold him
down. Edward grabbed his shoulders.

Susannah seized his arms. "It's all right, Alex. You're at
William Street. You're home!"

For a few minutes more he struggled, but then his frenzy
passed. He gave up and fell back, limp and exhausted in the
tub. By that time Edward and Susannah were both more
wet than dry. Susannah felt great curls of hair plastered to
her neck, and her bodice was soaked clear through her

stays. Edward's waistcoat was dripping. He unbuttoned it and peeled it off, tossing it over the back of the nearest chair.

His white shirt clung damply to his shoulders and his chest. It molded to his muscles, transparent to his skin, which was glowing softly in the flickering light. Susannah knelt at the tub, watching despite herself. He had a magnificent body, like statues she had seen. For a moment she forgot Alex and her worries—everything. She heard a measured thumping that was the beating of her heart.

Edward glanced down and saw her looking up at him, her lips slightly parted, her eyes wide and dark. He knew what she was thinking. A thrill shot through his loins. How had it happened, this attraction between them? He'd never felt so much with any other woman, not even with Catherine.

Susannah swallowed and dragged her eyes away, to Alex's wasted form. She felt a stab of guilt. She dipped the cloth and washed him. "How long will you leave him here?"

Edward bent to touch first Alex's forehead, then the back of his neck. "We can take him out now. Can you manage without William's help?"

"I can," she assured him, waiting while he spread clean towels on the bed. Then he took Alex's arms while she took his legs. The move cost her little effort, since Edward bore the brunt. They laid Alex on the towels, and she dried him carefully, after which she covered him with a clean linen sheet. She laid her hand on his forehead. "He doesn't feel so hot."

"That's good," Edward murmured. He was mixing something in a glass. When he'd finished he directed her to support Alex's head. "I want to try to get this into him," he said, holding up the glass. "Wrap a towel around his neck to catch whatever spills."

What spilled was two-thirds of the contents of the glass, but Edward seemed satisfied that Alex drank at all. Next he mixed a poultice to spread on Alex's chest.

"Now what?" asked Susannah when he'd finished and Alex was covered again.

"Now we wait," said Edward, looking up at her—and as he looked, he realized that she was as wet as he. The scarf crossed at her bodice was soaked through, molding with the wet fabric beneath it to the contours of her breasts. Just then she took a sharp breath and he watched her breasts rise and fall. Unconsciously his tongue came out to wet his lips. Her lips parted as they had before and he knew she had shared his thought.

"Susannah," he said softly.

"No." She shook her head, taking a step backward into the gloom, which only threw her wet body into higher relief. He thought he could see two sharp points pressing against her stays—imagined or really saw them, it was all the same.

"I ought to change," she murmured quickly. "There'll be something in my room. Or something in my mother's..." She edged sideways toward the door.

"You don't have to run. I won't jump you," Edward said, but he wasn't completely sure. He felt as though his body were connected to hers by strings. When she tugged, he reacted—and she was tugging now.

She flashed him a nervous smile and murmured something about "being safe." Her words had hardly reached him before she was gone from the room.

The watch was calling midnight—and still clear—when she returned.

"Any change?" she murmured, pulling up a chair across the bed from him.

"Neither for the worse nor for the better. Which isn't bad," he said. She was wearing something frilly and low cut in front.

"I've grown," she said self-consciously, seeing his eyes on her gown. "I couldn't wear my own things, they were all too small. And my mother took everything except her very best. I suppose she thought she wouldn't need them where we were bound." She stopped abruptly and bit her lip, looking down.

"What happened to your mother?" he asked before he thought.

"She died," she answered shortly. "After a British raid." He cringed at that. "I'm sorry."

Her shoulders rose and fell. "It was wartime. And in wartime, people die."

"That doesn't mean it hurts less," he murmured in the same gentle tone.

She looked up, her eyes hard in contrast to her frills. "What do you know about it? You come and go at your pleasure. You weren't touched by the war."

"That's true," he admitted. "I was just trying to help."

She glared at him across the shadows. Between them, Alex groaned. At the sound, her eyes faltered. Then she nodded and her shoulders slumped. "I know you were. I'm sorry. I was very rude. After what you've done for Alex..."

Her gaze dropped to the bed. For some minutes she sat in silence. Then her shoulders heaved with a sigh. "What you said before, about inner strength... Alex has always had a lot. But then I wonder how much a person can take. He's been through so much—and not just the war...." Her voice trailed off.

He watched her, recalling what he'd learned from Porter earlier tonight. Had it only been tonight? It seemed like years ago since he had started home. "You mean about Lady Bridgeham?"

Her head jerked up. "How do you know about that?"

"I had supper there tonight."

Her lips curled in derision. "I'm sure the food was excellent. No doubt you enjoyed yourself."

"It was, and I didn't," he answered, meeting her eyes. "Your name came up at the table. Her ladyship warned me in confidence that you might approach my door."

"Did she!" Her eyes narrowed.

He nodded. "Yes, indeed. And if you did, she advised me not to let you in. She also warned me that the mere mention of your name was enough to send his lordship into fits."

"Did she tell you why?"

"She did not. But later one of the guests filled me in." In spite of himself, he smiled. "It must have been quite a scene."

Susannah's jaw went tight at his smile. But after a moment it relaxed and she grinned. "I slapped her," she admitted. "Right across the face. But she deserved even worse. Both of them deserve much worse."

"After this evening, I'd have to agree."

Susannah's amusement faded as she studied him. "I don't understand you," she said finally. "In some ways you're so British, but in other ways you're not."

"What's British?" he asked her.

She thought, then replied, "Arrogance, shortsightedness, self-love, conceit. Cruelty. Avarice." She paused in further thought.

"Please! I'm sorry I asked." He held up his hand to restrain her. "And which of those am I?"

"Arrogant," she said promptly. "You believe that we Americans are too immature to govern our own lives. Just because we don't act like Englishmen. That's British through and through."

"And in what way am I not British?"

Again she sat in silence, which deepened as their eyes met and held. "You're kind," she murmured softly. "And you're generous. Thank you for coming with me and for bringing Alex back here. I believe that being home can cure him as much as anything."

Edward felt a stab of ridiculous jealousy at her expression as she looked down at her brother's face. "He does look more peaceful," she said after a spell. When she looked up a moment later, her eyes were twinkling. "Just don't ever tell him how he was moved. Carried by a couple of redcoats!" She grimaced in mock despair.

Jealousy forgotten, Edward smiled back. "I'm surprised he didn't argue, even in his unconsciousness."

Downstairs, in the parlor, the clock struck the quarter hour. "I don't mind sitting with him, if you want to get some rest. I doubt you got much last night."

"I didn't. But that's all right. You go ahead if you want to. I don't mind sitting up."

But wild horses couldn't have dragged him away from her. In any event she dozed off a few minutes after that. When he tried to move her, she protested in her sleep, so he covered her with a blanket and propped her legs up on the bed.

He looked from her face to her brother's, so different and yet so alike. Arrogant, conceited . . . he heard her thoughtful voice say. You're kind and you're generous. He wanted to be with her. He'd held back from women ever since Catherine. Holding back from women had felt natural up till now. But when he was with Susannah he wanted to let himself go. With an American woman? He had to be out of his head. Or maybe he wasn't. Maybe he was attracted to Susannah because, in a way, she was safe. No matter what happened between them, in the end they'd go their separate ways. She'd never come to England any more than he'd stay here in this dirty burned-out village with its brash bumptious ways.

"The men!" Alex muttered. "Got to help the men!"

Edward laid a hand upon his shoulder and he quieted again. The fever had lessened, but Edward knew well enough that it could return at any moment and worse than before. And so it did, toward morning. Edward must have been asleep, because when Alex started shouting, he jumped out of his skin. So did Susannah. They both leapt at once, swooping down upon Alex to hold him in the bed.

"'S'all right," muttered Susannah. "War's over. We're all safe. It's all right, Alex darling." Groggily she shook her head.

She was leaning over as she had last night, but now she was wearing her mother's dress, which dipped deeply across her chest. She'd also taken off her sodden stays and chemise, so that Edward found himself staring at the plunging valley between her rounded breasts.

Stupid with sleep, he could not will his eyes away. When they had been woken, he had been dreaming that he was kissing her. Now, at the sight of her soft, full breasts, he remembered the dream, and found himself fired by the way they trembled as Alex struggled against her grip.

Alex. His patient. Edward came awake. Blinking, he focused on the tortured, feverish face. "It's come back," he said tersely, feeling his spirits drop. "I can restrain him here by myself while you call for another bath."

Chapter Seven

The day that followed passed much the same as the preceding night had done. Working in shifts or together, Edward and Susannah kept vigil at Alex's side, assisted in small ways by Milly and by William, the valet. They bathed Alex again at midday, after which his fever dropped. But it was back up again by supper, so they gave him another bath, this time wrapped in huge aprons that Milly's mother, the cook, had sent up. She also sent up supper, which they were almost too weary to eat.

"You've got to eat," coaxed Edward. "You'll make yourself ill if you don't."

"I know." Susannah stared listlessly at her plate. She picked at a piece of chicken. "Life is ironic," she said. "There've been times when I was so hungry I would have blessed Satan himself for this meal. There've been times in these last years when I've kept myself awake at night recounting every time I've turned up my nose at good food and swearing before heaven that I'd never do it again." She carved off a mouthful of chicken and began to chew dutifully. Then her eyes met Edward's, and she swallowed, pointing with her fork to his plate. "What's good for the goose," she advised him.

He speared a piece of meat at random and brought it to his mouth. But he chewed without tasting. He was thinking of something else. He was thinking of the challenge Susannah had flung at him last night. What do you know of it? she'd demanded, referring to the war. Not as much as he'd thought, he conceded. Not about the fear or the hunger she'd just described.

For him, war had been a diversion and a chance to hone new skills. For her, it had been a nightmare and a series of tragic thefts. It had snatched the end of her girlhood and her mother from her very arms. It had subjected her to trials that no young woman ought to have endured. No wonder she hated the British.

He watched as she chewed and swallowed another bite, her eyes resting on Alex, who was quiet once again, his chest wrapped in a fresh poultice, his hair still damp from his last bath. Her face changed as she watched him. To Edward, it seemed to dissolve into a pool of such profound longing that he wondered how she could not drown. What would he do if he lost her? he thought—as though she were his. The aching he'd felt last night rose in him again, but this time instead of tenderness, he felt a wave of guilt: guilt for all she had suffered at his country's hands.

"I'm sorry," he heard himself murmur before he could still his tongue.

"For what?" Her gaze left Alex, and she looked up in surprise. He could almost see the curtains drawing across her face. Those curtains were a warning, reminding him of her pride.

"For nothing." He shook his head briefly. "Eat your supper," he urged, and bent to address the food remaining on his own plate.

Later, when they'd lighted the candles, he made no attempt to persuade her to leave. As before, they sat up together until she began to nod. This time when he tucked her in a blanket, she sighed wearily. Nor did he struggle against encroaching sleep. He'd sat vigil over patients enough times to have faith in that sixth sense that would pull him back into consciousness if there was a need.

But it wasn't intuition that pulled him from his dreams. Instead, it was a light hand touching his arm.

"Edward!"

It was Susannah. The candles had burned down, but even without them the room was vaguely light. Dawn must be breaking. Alex! he thought with a start. Had his senses betrayed him? He jerked upright in his chair.

Susannah's hand restrained him from coming to his feet. He blinked and saw she was smiling. "He's still cool," she said. "The fever's broken. He slept right through the night. I'm sorry, I know you haven't slept much. I shouldn't have woken you...."

Groggily, stiffly, Edward unfolded himself from his chair to lean over Alex. Susannah was right. He was as cool at this moment as if he'd just been in the bath. He listened to his breathing and counted his pulse.

She watched, standing beside him. Edward could feel her holding her breath. Finally she released it. "I know you can't be certain... I know it's too soon to be sure, but do you think that maybe...?" She caught the last words and held them back as the air between them pulsed with her unspoken hope.

The doctor in him counseled caution, based on experience. "You're right," he answered slowly. "It is too soon to know. He's very weak, Susannah. He could slip back at any time." Then he relented. "But the fever breaking is a hopeful sign. If he does stay cool, and if we're lucky—"

A sound from her made him turn. She was crying, the tears pouring down her cheeks. But she was also grinning so broadly that the tears ran in crazy rings. As it had done last night, her soul lay open to him. But this time, instead of sorrow, she was showing him her joy.

Darkness ended abruptly. He felt her soul touch his, coaxing it from its shell. He was filled with a light and a sweetness that made him want to laugh. If possible, her smile broadened, brilliant as the sun. "Oh, Edward, I'm so happy!" she whispered in a voice that sprang his arms open and swept her into them.

He hugged her in pleasure, in comradeship and in peace. As he held her, he had the feeling that he was the one who'd been cured. A vitality flowed through him such as he'd never felt before. It struck aside walls and defenses, secrets and regrets, flowing from him to Susannah in a magical, unbroken ring.

It continued to flow even after he'd released her and she'd leaned away, her hands on his shoulders, his ringing her waist. She was still smiling, though her tears had stopped. One clung to her cheek. He raised a thumb to brush it away. She wrinkled her nose to sniffle, and when he kissed the tip of it, she laughed unselfconsciously. Then she dropped her hand from his shoulder to search for her handkerchief.

She didn't find it. "Do you eat them?" he teased, and found her the one he'd put into his pocket yesterday morning, when he'd changed his linen last.

"I must," she admitted, giving her nose a good blow. "I'm hungry enough—Lord knows! The way I feel right now, I could eat a whole bolt of cloth!"

Her vehemence made him smile. His hands still circled her waist. With the slightest effort, he could claim her lips, and from the way that she was smiling he knew that she wouldn't object. But he also knew how quickly this lightness could disappear. Torn between two pleasures, he picked the simpler one.

Releasing her, he stepped back. "I can think of tastier things than raw cloth."

"So can I." Her eyes grew dreamy. "Such as soft cheese and bread."

"Bacon and meat pie," he responded.

"A perfectly fried fish."

"Two fish."

"Fresh jam. Strawberry!" She licked her lips.

He laughed. He hadn't felt so hungry in years. "Let's send down for breakfast."

"Let's send for enough for four!" She grinned.

Susannah's lightheadedness lasted through the day. After an enormous breakfast, Edward changed and went out, leaving her the address of where he could be reached in case she should need him. She'd expected him for dinner, but he sent a note, saying he was dining with General Carleton. Even the mention of his connection to the general didn't change her mood. Instead, after dinner, she treated herself to a quarter hour in her father's library, then returned to Alex's room armed with enough volumes to keep her busy for a month. She spent the afternoon happily reading in her chair beside Alex's bed.

Alex spent the day lost in profound sleep, from which he emerged only vaguely when she dosed him with the medicine Edward had prepared. He had one bad fit of coughing, but even that didn't wake him up, and he was still sleeping when she heard Edward come home. Her heart beat faster as his footsteps came down the hall, and she felt herself smiling broadly when he opened the door.

"All well?" He turned his head toward Alex, but his eyes lingered on her. She knew what he was feeling because she felt the same herself: little prickles of pleasure because she hadn't changed and because she was exactly where he'd expected her.

"All well," she answered. Then self-consciousness struck them and they both turned to Alex. "I gave him his medicine," Susannah murmured, watching as Edward checked his vital signs. "He's spent the whole day sleeping."

"That's good, very good," he approved, drawing the covers back up over Alex. "I spoke to the cook when I came in," he said without turning around. "Supper will be at six-thirty in the dining room. William will sit with Alex." He shot her a glance. "Those are doctor's orders."

"Well, in that case," she said.

On her way down to supper, Susannah stopped in her own room to brush her hair and wash her face. Her mother's dress was still lying on the bed, where she'd left it yesterday morning when she'd changed back into her own clothes. The sight of its low-cut bodice brought back the look in Edward's eyes when she'd caught him staring at her. Her breasts began to tingle at the memory of how his tongue had emerged to flick around his lips. She hugged herself with pleasure and smiled a secret smile, feeling feminine and powerful in a new, exciting way. She leaned closer to the looking glass, studying her face. Then, swiftly and impulsively, she began to unfasten her skirts.

Changing into her mother's dress made her a few minutes late coming down, but she noted Edward's approval as she entered the dining room. His eyes swept over her with the same expression she'd recalled, and the same sensation tingled through her in response.

But this time they weren't alone in a shadowed room, enveloped in the intimacy that a shared crisis creates. This time they were seated formally in bright light, with Milly as their witness and four courses to endure. The shyness that had struck her before upstairs returned to cling all during the endless meal. And though Edward did his best to pretend he was relaxed, his every word and gesture told her he felt the same.

She winced through the strained silence they maintained during the soup, gritting her teeth at the unnatural loudness of her spoon's chink against her dish. She racked her brain for conversation as Milly brought the fish, but despite her desperate efforts, nothing came to mind. Looking up during the meat course, she caught Edward's eye. She jerked her gaze away but felt her cheeks burn.

She sat up straight to keep her bodice as high as she could and deeply regretted her frivolous choice of dress. What had she been thinking in tempting Edward's eye when, if anything, the circumstances had called for modesty? She was exhausted by the time the trifle arrived and could tell from how quickly Edward cleared his plate that he felt the same. She swallowed her last mouthful with a sense of profound relief and hardly paused to excuse herself before she fled the room.

But a few minutes later, in the safety of her own room, she was forced to admit that she had a good deal more than a silent supper to worry about. Two nights ago, with Alex so desperately ill, it had seemed perfectly natural to come to William Street. But now the crisis was over, she saw her situation in a very different light. Then she had been a frantic sister willing to go to any lengths to save her brother's life. Now she was a single woman voluntarily sharing a house with a redcoat captain—and without a chaperon. Either situation was sufficient to sink her reputation, even in war-torn New York. And she dared not even think what would happen when Alex was well enough to understand where they were living, and how, and with whom.

But as troubling as those things were, there were deeper worries yet. There was Edward's way of looking at her, and her feelings when he did. There was also the fact he'd kissed her, and the virtual certainty that if they remained in close contact, it was only a matter of time until he would kiss her again. And when that moment did arrive, she knew she'd welcome it. She, welcome the kiss of a redcoat? It seemed impossible.

There wasn't a time in her memory when she hadn't hated all Englishmen. Long before the war had started there'd been the Townshend Acts: taxation without representation—the bane of the colonies. She and Alex had been raised on protest and patriotic zeal. Then the war had come and confirmed each of her beliefs. The British had killed her mother as surely as if they'd shot her with their guns. And if Alex didn't survive, they'd have killed him, too.

But Edward would have saved him if he did survive. And Edward had helped her every time she'd asked. He'd treated her with kindness and generosity. The most patriotic patriot couldn't have done more for her. She couldn't hate Edward, it would be pointless to try. But that only furnished all the more reason for them to move apart. Either she or Edward would have to leave William Street.

Two weeks ago she wouldn't have wasted five minutes on the thought. She'd have said, "Well, of course it should be Edward. It's my house, after all!"

The house was still hers, but everything else had changed. Now, even as she posed the problem, she knew how Edward would respond. He'd say she should stay with Alex and offer to move out himself. Then she, who already owed him so much, would owe him even more. The debt made her uneasy, but there was nothing else she could do. Honor and reason both required that she and Edward part.

She opened her door and listened. There was no sound from below. Milly must be in the kitchen helping her mother clean up from the meal. She wondered if Edward had gone out. She thought she'd have heard if he had. Chances were he'd been thinking along the same lines as she.

She crossed the hall to Alex's room. Alex was still asleep. William was also sleeping in his chair beside the bed. Not the best of nurses, but he'd do for a few minutes more. And a few minutes was all she needed.

She started toward the stairs. Then, on second consideration, she stopped at her room to fetch a scarf to tie over her bodice.

The drawing room was empty, but the library door was closed. She knocked and heard Edward call out. "Come in!" The sound of his voice made her heart jump—and strengthened her resolve. She opened the door and saw him sitting in a chair.

He had a book open on his lap and was drinking a glass of wine. He rose to his feet when he saw her, setting both aside. "Is something wrong with Alex?"

"No, no. Alex is fine. That is, he's still sleeping. William is sleeping, too."

"At least he hasn't vanished," Edward remarked. "Can I give you a glass of claret? I was just having one myself."

"No, thank you. Don't bother." She came in and shut the door behind her so they wouldn't be overheard, though there was no one but Milly, and she'd feel no compunction about bursting into the room.

Despite her refusal, Edward poured her a glass. "You see, it's no bother." He smiled and brought it to her.

She almost let the glass fall, trying to keep their fingers from touching as she took it from him. Despite her efforts, their fingers touched anyway. She jumped and their eyes swung together.

Her heart started pounding again. "We have to—that is," she stammered, "there's something we should discuss."

"Sit down," he invited, gesturing to a chair. He'd gotten over the tension of dinner and seemed to be relaxed.

She accepted his offer, if only to increase the space between them, picking the hardest chair and perching on the edge to show that this was anything but a social call. She waited until he had reseated himself in his chair and retrieved his glass. Then she cleared her throat and began.

"First of all, I want to thank you for everything you've done. No, please don't stop me. I want to," she said when he tried to protest. "As you know, I've never had a very high view of Englishmen. I guess you've showed me that there are exceptions to the rule."

"You flatter me," he murmured, his eyes gray and twinkling. He took a sip of claret.

"Please," she repeated. "You're not helping when you tease. I'm trying to be serious."

"I'm sorry. Please go on."

"Thank you." She swallowed and retrieved her thread. "I know it's still too soon to say for sure that Alex will get well. But, on the other hand, there's certainly strong hope that he will." She paused, her eyes on Edward, waiting for his accord. When he nodded, she continued, "And that being the case, there's something else to consider. Propriety."

Edward raised one brow. "Who sounds British now?"

"Americans are just as proper!" she retorted, taking offense.

He accepted her retort with a shrug and another sip of wine. "What about propriety?"

She sipped her wine to gather her thoughts. "The point is this. No matter how much I might trust you, there's still the rest of the world. How do you think it will look to people if we all stay here? You, a redcoat captain, and me, an American. And without a chaperon.''

''So I've reverted to being a redcoat, have I?'' Edward observed. ''And what is your solution?'' he asked before she could reply. ''Are you suggesting we bring in a chaperon? I suppose Alex doesn't count?''

''Under the circumstances, no. And I don't believe it would help things to bring in someone else.''

''Then what?'' Edward asked. ''Is this your way of saying that you're planning on moving out?''

She stared at him, bewildered by his response. This wasn't at all the way she'd imagined he would react. Upstairs, in her room, she'd imagined a solemn interview in which Edward very gallantly offered to leave the house. But instead he was acting, well, almost amused. And he seemed to be suggesting that she ought to leave!

She took another sip of wine and a second thought came to her. Perhaps his mind was elsewhere and he needed a gentle hint. She set her wine down. ''I will, if I have to,'' she said. ''But I thought it might make more sense if you were to go. Temporarily,'' she added quickly.

''Temporarily?''

''Just until Alex is well.'' She held his gaze trustfully. Now, surely he'd understand.

But to her astonishment, Edward shook his head. ''I'm sorry, Susannah, but I'm afraid that wouldn't work. For better or for worse, this house is assigned to me. If I were to move out, then it would be reassigned—to the next likely candidate.'' And though he didn't add it, they both knew that he meant a Tory family or a British officer.

''I thought if it were informal—''

''What? In New York? With every bed accounted for and every corner full?'' He paused and his eyes narrowed. ''Or did you mean for me to spend the interim in your vacant rooms?''

She flushed hotly. She hadn't thought of that. She wouldn't voluntarily consign a dog to those rooms. But on the other hand, if he was a true gentleman . . .

Edward's eyes lost their teasing glint and became serious. "It's not a bad idea, Susannah. But you know how people are. As soon as the word got out that you and Alex were here alone, someone could cause you a lot of trouble—trouble you wouldn't want."

"Then I'll have to go," she told him, feeling the sudden sting of tears.

"I don't want you to," he murmured.

She dropped her eyes to the glass she clutched in her hand. "I have no choice," she answered. "I'm afraid that there'll be as much trouble if I stay here."

"Trouble from outsiders?"

"Or from inside," she replied. Though her cheeks were burning, she made herself meet his eyes.

She couldn't measure the silence, but it seemed to stretch on and on. Then Edward said very softly, "Do you want trouble, Susannah?"

His words, their softness, seemed to flick across her skin. She shivered and her fingers tightened on her glass. She knew the answer to his question, but she didn't want to know. "It doesn't matter what I want. It's wrong, Edward. It's all got to stop. I'll leave before I let anything happen. I'll take Alex, too."

"No." He shook his head, as serious as she had ever seen him before. "Alex can't be moved now, and he needs your care. We'll adjust. We'll be careful. It is possible. We won't repeat this evening's fiasco. We'll take our meals separately. I'll move all my things down here. You and Alex will keep the second floor and I'll have the first. I can have a bed made up right here in the library."

Tempted, she felt herself waver. "I still don't think—"

"But I do. Trust me, Susannah," he said in his doctor's voice—the voice that had brought her safely through these critical days. In a softer tone, he added, "And it's not only me. The servants will bear witness to our propriety."

In spite of herself, she smiled at his use of the word.

Edward relaxed when she smiled. "That's better," he approved. "Now drink your wine like a good girl, then we'll say good-night." He raised his glass in a toast. "I give you propriety!"

"To propriety!" she repeated, touching her lips to the glass.

As she drank she realized how much better she did feel. Edward had that ability to make things come out right. They'd divide the house between them, just as he'd said. She could almost hear Milly reporting to her friends: "I declare, they even take their meals apart. It's like they're living in two different worlds!" Then Alex would get better and—well, she'd think of that then. For the present, things were settled.

When she'd finished, Edward stood. "We might as well go up together. You can take William's place, then I can use him to help me move my things."

And witness our arrangement, he meant. Susannah came to her feet, smiling in gratitude. But her smile faded when she passed him at the door. Her arm brushed his lightly and both of them jumped. They'd have to be very careful. Very careful, indeed.

Chapter Eight

They were. Susannah kept to the second floor and Edward kept to the first, except for the two times a day when he checked on his patient's progress. At those times they were careful to stand on opposite sides of the bed, or Susannah left the room completely until he was gone. Edward was very busy so he wasn't around very much, and Susannah suspected that he dined out whenever possible. Still, she was always conscious of when he was in the house, and despite what she'd said about trouble, just knowing that he was nearby made her feel secure. As for the other feelings, either distance kept them at bay or what she and Edward had felt for each other was dying a natural death. A part of her was sad to let it go, but the rest of her was relieved. They had no future as lovers, and this way they'd part as friends.

Alex's progress was slow. Prison had left him badly weakened and the illness had sapped him of everything but the barest will to survive. But at least his cough was fading, to Susannah's profound relief, and slowly but surely he was recovering his health. Two days after the fever broke, he opened his eyes, and at the end of the two weeks he was able to sit up.

As Alex grew stronger, he grew more curious. He wanted to know how Susannah had managed to reclaim the house. He also had questions about who his doctor was. Susannah gave him answers that trod the far reaches of truth. She also instructed Milly and William as to what they must not say. Finally, as Alex's curiosity grew, she told Edward that it would be better if he didn't come. But even those measures soon wouldn't be enough. It wouldn't be much longer before Alex would take his first faltering steps—his first steps toward discovering that he and Susannah were only guests at William Street.

And it wasn't only Alex. Susannah was restless, too. Since Alex had come out of prison, she'd been tied to his side and only vaguely aware of what was happening in the world outside. She hadn't seen the Van Rijns since she'd come to William Street, and by now other patriot families must have returned. As her worries for Alex diminished, curiosity took its place and she began to look forward to seeing old friends again. But she felt that she couldn't do that so long as she was at William Street. She couldn't entertain patriotic acquaintances in a redcoat's house. Brutal as that sounded, it was the way she felt. She would have felt like Marguerite, asking people here.

The brutality of the comparison informed her that it was time to prepare herself for leaving Edward and William Street. The thought filled her with sadness, and not just for the house. Moving away from William Street would be only temporary. But her separation from Edward would be permanent. Which was all for the best, she told herself, but still it took her two days to gather her courage to take the first step. That evening, after she'd settled Alex for the night, she sent a note downstairs with Milly, asking Edward if she could speak with him.

Milly returned at a trot. "He's in the drawing room, mistress. He says he'd be delighted if you'd join him there."

Delighted. Susannah wondered whose word that had been. She straightened her skirts, then went down, silently rehearsing the speech that she'd prepared.

The drawing room door was open and he was on his feet, one elbow hooked on the mantel, which was bare except for the clock. His eyes lighted up when he saw her in a way that made her heart give a quick little leap of pleasure before it sank back with dread. So much for the natural death of her feelings. But their coming separation would serve the same end.

"Alex is much better," she said without preamble. "Soon he'll be walking. It's time for us to leave."

He must have been expecting it, but even so she saw him flinch as though she'd said something intentionally cruel. But he hid his reaction quickly. "Do you think he's well enough?"

She nodded. "If not right now, then in several days."

His fingers stroked the mantel and he turned his head to study the carved decoration as though he'd never seen it before. "I suppose you'll go back to your rooms," he said without looking at her.

His tone was conversational, but she heard his concern. "We'll be all right there," she answered. "Now that Alex is better. And—well, we'll be all right." She'd wanted to add that the move there wouldn't be for very long, but she couldn't bring herself to say that to him.

"If there's anything you'd like to take with you..." He looked around the room.

Only you, thought Susannah before she could catch herself. Then his fingers tapping the mantel gave her another thought. "Actually, there is something. But I'd need your help."

"Anything," he promised. "Just tell me what I can do." He looked so very eager she couldn't resist a smile.

"You can find a shovel."

"A shovel?" He looked taken aback.

Grinning now, she nodded. "And maybe a pick."

Edward leaned on the shovel and wiped his forehead with his sleeve. He'd been digging for an hour and hadn't struck a thing except for a broken stave from a barrel that had rotted long ago. "Are you sure this is the place where you buried those statuettes?"

"As sure as I can be." From her perch, Susannah scanned the sand-strewn dirt floor, trying to recall. "After all, it was seven years ago and a lot has happened since then. Maybe you ought to try a bit more to the left."

"You said to the right last time," he grumbled, but he complied. The root cellar in which he was digging was dark and damp and so cool that Susannah was wrapped in a woolen shawl. She was perched on an apple barrel, holding the lantern to guide Edward in his work. She sat on his coat and waistcoat, which he'd taken off to dig.

The light of the lantern threw shadows on the wall. At the sight of them, Susannah shuddered. "I was locked in here once by accident, when I was too little to reach the latch." She shuddered again. "It was awful. I've hated this place ever since."

"Who buried the things then?"

"I did," she said. "The British were coming. There was no one but me and Mother, and she was busy with other things. She said to leave the statues, but they'd always been special to me. I guess I was already too panicked to feel any worse."

"Or to remember just where you were digging," Edward added with a grunt as he tossed another shovelful of dirt onto the pile.

"Or to remember where I was digging," she agreed peaceably, watching the play of his muscles through the cotton of his shirt and admiring the snug fit of his breeches across his hips. Her eyes drifted lower, then she jerked them away before her own body could begin to react.

"If you don't find the box I hid, you'll probably find some of Alex's things," she said, looking around. "This cellar was always his favorite hiding place. I remember after he'd enlisted he hid his uniform down here until he got up the nerve to tell Mother and Father what he'd done."

"When was that?" asked Edward, pausing to wipe his forehead with the back of his sleeve.

"Right after the battle at Concord. When Alex heard about that, nothing could hold him back. He was too young, just sixteen, but he lied about his age. I wanted to enlist, too," she added with a laugh. "We were all so proud

of those farmers for turning the British back with nothing
but their muskets and their bravery!''

Her eyes shining, she gazed up at him. "Oh, you call
Americans immature and undisciplined, but we started with
almost nothing and look at what we've done!''

"I didn't say you lacked courage," Edward pointed out.

"Of course not. You wouldn't dare," she replied with a
toss of her head.

"Now who's being 'British'?''

"I'm not being arrogant. I'm being honest," she retorted, and he laughed. The shadows shimmered as she
laughed with him, shaking the lantern she held.

Edward leaned against his shovel, studying her face,
trying to memorize it to carry in future years. She was so
bright and vital, maybe her spirit would keep her alive inside him after he was gone. "What will you do when we're
gone?" he asked, following his thoughts.

"We?''

"The British.''

"Oh . . ." She rested the lantern on her knees. "Fix up
what needs fixing up and wait for Father's return. He's
gone to the East Indies. I'm not sure when he'll be back.
Even before the war came, his voyages were long." She
stared at the shadows, remembering.

Edward watched her stare. "Who takes care of you in the
meantime? Who watches his affairs?''

"A man named Binchot. My father's factor in France.
He's the one who sends us money—what money there is to
send." She turned away from the shadows with a rueful
smile. "And once Alex is better, he'll look after me.''

"Of course," Edward said briefly, wondering just how
much a man who refused to leave prison could be counted
upon for care. A zealot and a sailor: it didn't inspire much
hope. "Is Binchot an honest man?''

"I don't know," she said. "I suppose so. I've never met
him." Her smile rekindled about the edges of her lips.
"He's probably as trustworthy as Father when it comes to
funds. Father's very courageous, but he's not very practi-

cal. He lost six ships challenging the British rule. Now there's only the *Melissa*. But she's a very good ship." She kicked her heels on the barrel. "Who knows—maybe this voyage will restore Father's wealth. Maybe he'll sail into New York harbor with a hold full of gold!"

"Would that make you happy?"

She laughed. "I wouldn't mind. It would be nice not to have to worry for a change. Why? Do you hate money?"

"I don't hate it," he said. "Not half as much as titles." He began to dig again.

Susannah watched him, puzzling on the anger she'd heard in his voice. In some ways she felt she knew him better than any other man, but in other ways she hardly knew him at all. And why should she know him when, after tonight, she and Edward would never be together this way again? Never, she thought with a tremor. Then she put the thought from her mind. "If you don't like titles, you ought to like America, because we don't have any."

"You're lucky." He thrust his shovel hard into the earth. The thrust ended in a sharp noise. Suddenly he was alert. "It's probably just another busted stave. But can you give me more light?"

She scrambled down from the barrel and held the lantern up as he probed with the shovel's blade. It wasn't another old stave but the corner of a box. A few minutes later he had the whole thing free. He knocked the dirt off the latches, and Susannah opened the lid. Reaching in, she unwrapped the first of the statuettes.

"Fall," she said softly. "My favorite." She ran a re-membering finger along the graceful china draperies and over the tiny grapevines twined through the porcelain hair. The one below was Summer, with flowers in her hair. She laid one beside the other and leaned back on her knees. "They stood on the drawing room mantel, the four seasons, in a row. I remember, when I was little, I used to pretend that they were alive, and I'd make up stories about how each one would be—which would be the nicest, which would make the truest friend... I couldn't bear to leave them to be stolen or hurt." She stared at the statues, recalling the panic of that day.

"It seems like another lifetime," she said at last. "The day I hid these down here I had no idea what would happen. No idea at all." She looked up at Edward and found him watching her with understanding. And tenderness. And also with desire. Nothing had died between them. It was all right there, smoldering in his eyes. As hers locked with his, she felt a fire kindle in a place so deep within her she'd never known it was there.

"No, Edward," she whispered. "We mustn't!"

He didn't move except to hold his hand out and murmur, "Come here!"

She laid her hand in his and he pulled her to her feet. They were very close together; her skirt brushed his thighs. His finger traced the cool, trembling line of her jaw. Then, very gently, he raised her chin. "I want you," he murmured, and bent to kiss her lips.

Closing her eyes, she remembered the softness of his lips, but not the sweet, hot, faintly claret taste, or the cool firmness of his hands spanning her back, first bunching the shawl between them, then sliding under it. The shawl slipped backward onto the freshly dug earth, fanning the lantern so the flames leapt and fell. Susannah's lips opened and she pressed against Edward, conscious of a hardness she'd never felt before.

He flattened her against himself, his hand lower on her back, moving her in circles as his tongue reached out to taste the corners of her lips. Her lips opened wider and his tongue slipped in between, touching hers, then stroking, then pulling out again. In and out his tongue slipped as his hips moved slowly around, making things happen inside her, in that secret place. Then his tongue left her mouth and his lips abandoned hers to trail a line of kisses across her cheek to her ear.

"Want you!" he murmured thickly. She felt the fire searing in her chest and abdomen. Her head fell backward as his lips moved down her neck toward the gathered bodice of her dress. She clung to his shoulders so that she couldn't fall. Her legs were shaking but she wasn't afraid, only caught up in a whirlwind that she feared would end before she discovered what it was all about.

His lips stroked and tickled the bare skin below her throat. She felt her breasts thrusting toward him, stiff with eagerness. His tongue snaked between them and she squirmed, gasping in his arms. He lifted his head to smile. "You like that," he purred.

"Yes—oh, yes!" she whispered. She was afraid that he might stop, but she need not have feared. His lips touched her shoulder and in tandem with his tongue made their slow, exploratory way along the bodice hem, sensuous and teasing until she was standing on tiptoe to coax him on—to coax him in, down deeper where the fire was.

His hands left her back then and moved around beneath her breasts, pushing them up above her lacings as his mouth came down to bury itself in the soft flesh, moving from side to side. Then his thumbs grazed her rigid nipples over the tops of her stays and she cried out in amazement, a startled, wordless cry. She heard something ripping: his shirt, she realized. She was twisting it so tightly the seams had begun to give. Letting go, she grasped his broad shoulders instead, feeling the heat of his skin stretched over the muscles beneath.

Something had happened. His mouth was on hers again, open and demanding. Her arms were around his neck. This time when he held her, her feet left the floor. Then they were touching and he was bending down, his hands cupping her buttocks, then slipping down her thighs. She felt a draft of cold air against her legs. It rose higher and higher, then the fingers of his right hand grazed the bare back of her left thigh.

His fingers froze when she went rigid, then they began to move again, bunching up the petticoat she wore beneath her dress. She was melting beneath it, burning between her legs. She was afraid of his moving fingers but she wanted them. She wanted him in so many places her body was coming apart.

His fingers moved higher as his lips rediscovered her breasts. She was arched over backward but pressed against him in the front. The higher his hand reached, the closer their bodies pressed. She could feel the individual buttons of his breeches' fall. Beneath the buttons she could feel everything.

Her skirt had vanished. His hands cupped naked flesh. They opened wide on her buttocks, then shut, fitting her against him, circling her around and around. "No, no!" she whispered, but he knew what she meant.

He was burning for her. He'd never felt this way. She was fire, delicious, soft and fierce and sweet. Right or wrong didn't matter. She was his destiny. His right knee edged forward, working its way between hers, while his mouth drew her hot tongue deep into its depths, pulling and releasing in the rhythm of his need.

Then something scuttled past his ankles, and the shovel he'd leaned on the barrel came crashing to the earth, striking the side of the open crate and bouncing away.

Susannah jerked and screamed. Edward released her and her skirts tumbled free. They stood facing each other, too shaken to see anything: not each other, not the cellar, not the dancing light. Susannah's entire body was trembling violently. She was trembling with fear and wanting and couldn't control either one.

Edward's eyes were depthless, neither blue nor gray. "I'm sorry," he whispered. It wasn't a total lie. Truly he was sorry he'd broken his word, but he wasn't sorry he'd held or tasted her. How could he be sorry for that? His vision restored, he looked at the chest, the shovel, searching for something to do. But he was still too shaken to be practical.

Susannah's lips were swollen, her hair wild, her bodice askew. Her breasts were heaving. Oh, God, her luscious breasts. And that baffled yearning still smoldered in her eyes! She stared at him unspeaking, then her hand pressed to her mouth. He thought she might start crying, but instead she turned and fled, the cellar door banging behind her and her feet flying up the steps.

Edward stood alone in the dimness, which thrummed to the beat of his heart, letting the damp air of the cellar cool his burning skin. From the street up above him he heard the watchman's cry. "Eleven o'clock. High clouds and full moon. All is well!"

All is well. His breathing was almost normal, though his skin was still on fire wherever she had touched him, which was almost everywhere. He squeezed his eyes tightly shut, but that couldn't bring her back. So he opened them and reached for the shovel to knock the rest of the dirt off the box. He brought the box up with him when he came so that she could find it tomorrow and take it when she went.

He climbed the stairs silently and listened outside her door, but he heard nothing, not even her breathing, so he set the box on the floor. For a moment he stood in the hallway, but there was nothing he could do either to make things better or to make them go away. So in the end he went back down as quietly as he'd come up, to spend another sleepless night in the library.

Milly skidded to a stop outside Susannah's door. She raised one hand to knock, then didn't, not just yet. "Oh dear, oh dear!" she muttered. "How could I be such a fool? And especially this morning, when she's already got more than enough to worry her!"

Milly's face screwed up with the same reluctance that was staying her hand, and she cast a quick nervous glance back toward Master Beckwith's room. From its direction she heard a muffled rustling and a thud. "Oh dear, oh dear!" she muttered. And then, because she had to, she rapped on Susannah's door.

Susannah heard Milly's knock halfway across her room, where she was pacing the familiar track she'd worn through since last night. She'd spent the whole night trying to put a name to the tumult of feelings that threatened to shatter her. Was this love, this crazy fever that made her whole body shake at no more than the thought of what she and Edward had done? She'd always imagined that love was a sweet thing, not wild and fierce and frightening—scaring her half to death. She felt as if a giant hand had laid a grip on her life and her only hope for salvation was to wrest free of its grasp.

One thing she knew for certain: she had to get away. That's what she'd concluded in her pacing last night. She had to get away from Edward, at least until she understood what was happening between them and what she ought to do. A few more days at William Street might benefit Alex's health, but he'd have to do without them, because she couldn't stay. Not so close to Edward. Not after last night. Not knowing so clearly what could happen if she did. That's what she'd concluded last night, at any rate. But then, this morning, all her plans had changed.

It had started with Milly bringing the early tea—and the box of statuettes Edward had left in the hall. She'd heard him leave them when he'd come up last night. She'd held her breath and listened, terrified that he'd come in—and terrified that he'd leave her trembling here for his touch. Even after she'd heard him going back down, she'd left the box in the hallway, afraid to open her door—as if she'd be sucked into the hallway and down the stairs into his arms by the sheer force of the desire roiling in her.

So the box had still been waiting for Milly to lug in with the tea, chattering with a curiosity Susannah refused to satisfy. She'd left the box unopened while she'd drunk her tea. Then she'd gone across to wake Alex and to break the news that they'd be leaving William Street as soon as they were packed.

But then disaster had struck. She'd found Alex awake and feverish again. He wasn't hot enough to be delirious, just enough to make her afraid that if she did try to move him, he'd go into a decline. How could she let her weakness jeopardize his health? Regardless of what she was feeling, she knew she'd have to stay, at least until his latest bout of fever was gone.

Grimly she'd dosed Alex with Edward's medicine, then she'd retreated to her room—back to her worried pacing and her chaotic thoughts.

"Mistress Susannah!" Milly knocked a second time, and more insistently.

Susannah stopped and sighed. "Come in, Milly." She glanced at the unopened box, wondering if Milly's curiosity had gotten the best of her. But she forgot all about that when Milly burst through the door, red-faced and apologetic.

"I'm sorry to bother you. But Master Beckwith—"

"Is he worse?" Susannah blanched.

Milly shook her head so vigorously her mobcap slid over her eyes. She shoved it back and answered, "No, no. He's still the same. But I'm afraid I told him, well, about Captain Steel. I swear I never meant to. It just slipped out. And then, once it had slipped—"

But she never finished, for her words were interrupted by a crash from Alex's room. Susannah sprang toward the hallway with Milly at her heels, still in the midst of her muddled apology.

The little table next to the bed had toppled to its side, scattering glass from broken bottles and the lamp flue at Alex's feet. Alex's feet! Susannah froze in shock at the sight of Alex standing on the floor beside the bed, clutching the bedpost with one thin hand.

"Alex! What are you doing!" she gasped as she jumped to his aid.

"I!" He uttered the single word with enough venom to stop her in her tracks. "What am I doing? Ha!" he barked, the force of his anger swaying his body precariously. "I'd ask you the same question if I didn't know by now! It's too late, Susannah. You can't lie to me anymore!"

"I haven't—"

"Yes, you have!" His cheeks were feverish, two bright spots of color in his otherwise ghostly face. "You lied to me about this house. You never did reclaim it. There's a red-coat living here still. Captain Steel is still here—in fact, he's keeping us! Kept by a redcoat! How could you do such a thing!" He trembled with indignation, his hand clutching hard to the post.

The unfairness of his accusations made Susannah forget his health. "How could I? I'll tell you!" she hurled back, rigid-jawed. "You were dying, Alex! Captain Steel saved your life!"

"I'd have rather died!" he exploded.

"Oh, yes! That's just like you! Selfish to the end, aren't you? Marguerite was right! It wasn't enough to lose Mother, I was supposed to lose you, too—and all because of your damned pigheadedness!" To her dismay, she burst out crying as her already strained nerves gave way.

"Susannah—" Alex faltered, almost as dismayed as she. "Susannah, I didn't—"

"Oh, never mind!" She fumbled in her pocket and, finding no handkerchief, used her apron to blot her cheeks.

Meanwhile, Milly, who'd been watching saucer-eyed, seized the moment to bustle forward and catch Alex before he fell. "Shame on you," she scolded as if he'd been a child, easing him down so he was sitting on the bed. "Causing more worry when your poor sister has so many cares! Why, she's watched over you like an angel! Like an angel, I declare!"

"Let him be, Milly." Susannah sighed, smoothing her apron down. The sight of Alex's weakness had cooled her ire as the sight of her tears had cooled his. "Anyway, he's right. I would have left this morning if your fever hadn't come back. As soon as it's broken, we'll go back to our rented rooms."

"No!" Brushing away Milly, Alex struggled to rise again. "Not when I'm better. Now! This very hour!"

"Oh, Alex, be reasonable! You're still so weak! You're sick and all this fussing will only make you worse." Susannah came forward to take Milly's place. She put her hands on his shoulders.

He gripped them with all his strength. "I mean it, Susannah! I refuse to stay. And I won't let you stay, either. Susannah, can't you see? Staying under these conditions makes you no better than Marguerite!"

"Alex, what are you saying!" She jerked away, averting her face from him as it flushed scarlet with guilt. She wished that she could say more, but she didn't trust herself.

"Susannah?" Alex's voice shook with a note of fear. "He—Captain Steel... Tell me that he hasn't... taken liberties."

"Alex! What a question!" She forced herself to turn back, but she still couldn't manage to meet his eyes.

"If he has—" he whispered. "If he has, he'll pay! I'll kill him—"

"Please, Alex!" In terror, she seized his hand. "There was nothing. Nothing! I give you my word!" She raised her eyes to his, feeling worse than she ever had, but knowing that she had to lie, for everybody's sake. Whatever had happened had happened, and it wouldn't help for Alex to hate Edward any more than he already did.

His eyes met hers and held them, and she felt even worse to see what the effort of the fight had taken out of him. He fell back against the pillows. "Then promise me, Susannah. Promise me we'll leave." His eyes weren't so much angry as pleading now—pleading with her not to forsake him for their enemies.

Pleading with her! The thought of it twisted Susannah's heart. She stared into his dark eyes, so identical to hers, and suddenly the turmoil inside her subsided and everything fell into place. In Alex's plea she saw clearly what she'd been denying up till now. Edward hadn't made things better when he'd arranged for them both to live here: he'd only disguised the truth. Now she saw that truth all too plainly in Alex's pleading eyes.

"Promise me?" he repeated. His hands were trembling.

Slowly she nodded. "Yes, Alex. You're right. We can't stay another hour. If you promise to stay quiet, I'll ar-

range for the move.'' She covered his shaking hands with
hers and laid them on the sheet. He looked ill and wasted,
but she had no choice.

His eyes closed, then they opened. "I'm sorry," he said.
"Sorry about implying that you and Captain Steel . . ."

"Hush. Forget it.'' She laid a finger on his lips and gave
him as much of a smile as she could muster for his sake.

To her shock, she found Edward standing in the hall
outside Alex's room. From his expression, she knew he'd
heard everything. Their eyes met and he opened his mouth,
but she shook her head. "Don't. It doesn't matter," she
murmured, and turned away. But she didn't try to stop him
when he followed her into her room.

He shut the door behind him. She was about to protest
when she realized that it would be better if they weren't
overheard. She stood looking out the window, holding the
picture in her mind of thin, wasted Alex pleading with her
to leave. As long as she didn't look at Edward, she thought
that she'd be all right. She jumped when he spoke from
behind her.

"Your brother's wrong. Whatever has happened between us, you aren't like Marguerite. You haven't jilted a
fiancé and you haven't betrayed your cause.''

"Not yet," she answered. "But that's where it always
ends once you start fooling yourself about the truth. I lied
to my brother, Edward. I'd never lied to Alex before I
brought him here.''

"You did it for his sake," said Edward. "To avoid his
prejudice. Some lies are justified, Susannah.''

"So you say," she replied. "But I've seen the damage
this kind of lie can do. I've seen this same thing happen often enough to people during the war. You get so tired of
doing without that when a little pleasure comes your way,
you can't resist. You rationalize. You tell yourself it's
harmless. You take the first little step. And before you
know it, you've gone too far to turn back. Marguerite

wasn't evil. She was just a little weak—and she didn't have a clear-eyed brother looking out for her.''

"And what about your brother?" he asked, trying another tack. "If his fever's come back, he's not well enough to be moved.''

"He'll be all right," she said slowly. "He'll be worse if we stay. We have to leave, Edward. You can't change my mind.''

There was a long silence. Then he said, "I'll leave.''

"You!" In her amazement, she forgot her resolve and turned. He was standing in the sunlight, wearing the same brown coat that he'd worn to the rented rooms that morning when she'd kissed him first. He didn't have his wig on and the sun turned his fair hair to butter, all glittery and bright. Just seeing him in the sunlight hurt sharply in her chest. She slid her hands beneath her apron as though she meant to hide them from him. "But what about rules and regulations? What about reassigning the house?''

He shrugged. "I'll arrange it. Don't worry. You won't be put out. I'll get my things together and leave right away. I suppose that will satisfy Alex.''

She nodded in a daze. "You? Leave?" she repeated as if she hadn't heard him right. After that evening when he'd explained why he couldn't go, in all her ponderings and preparations, she'd been the one to leave. She'd never considered Edward leaving her, and though she knew it should please her, it did the opposite. It made her feel bad and lonely, and angry and afraid. Afraid—Susannah Beckwith, the feisty, fearless one!

"Yes, leave," he repeated. "This morning, within the hour. Whatever I can't take with me, I'll send for later on.''

"Just like that?" she murmured, feeling worse and worse. He made it sound so simple, as though it were nothing at all. As though she'd been nothing more than a passing whim, fun for the moment but easily let go. In the heat of the moment, her mind swept back to that night in the library when she'd been sure that he'd offer to leave but instead he'd convinced her that they both could stay. That night he'd surprised her with the lightness of his tone. Now that lightness came back to mock her.

"What else?" His fair brows angled down. "My leaving solves all your problems. I should think that you'd be glad."

He was right. She should be. But she wasn't glad at all. She felt hurt and angry and betrayed, and worst of all, she couldn't shake loose from the memory of how he had acted that night. If Edward had left then, when she'd asked him, there wouldn't have been last night or fighting with Alex or this sharp pain in her heart at the way his hair shone in the morning sun. And now that those things had happened, Edward was walking away. Just walking away. Just like that. How could he leave so easily if he really cared?

Tears of hurt stung her eyelids, but she blinked them away. "You know what I think, Edward?" she said in a strange, strangled voice. "I think that you knew all along that you didn't have to stay. All that business about the house being reassigned if you left—If you could arrange all this right now, you could have arranged it back then. Couldn't you have?" she demanded, wanting him to answer "No!" She wanted to see that this parting was also hurting him. She wanted to see it and hear it in his voice.

He seemed about to deny her accusation, but then he shook his head. "Maybe I could have," he admitted. "But it didn't seem necessary with us dividing the house."

Maybe. Maybe! He made it seem almost offhand. The hurt in her heart grew sharper, the grip on her throat more intense. "A convenient arrangement! Was that all I was to you?"

"Convenient—what are you saying?" He stared at her as if she'd gone mad.

She felt as if she had, or were at least on her way. "I'm saying that you stayed as long as it pleased you to. You were glad to have me as long as Alex was too sick to know. But now, at the first threat of trouble, you can hardly wait to go—probably onto your next fling with some other poor innocent girl!'' She raised one hand and snapped her fingers. " 'Just like that'—to use your own words.''

"Those were your words,'' he ground out. His face had gone ashen. "I can't believe you really mean this!''

"Yes, I do! I do! I mean every word!'' The only reason she wasn't shouting was for fear that Alex would hear, but the strain of keeping her voice down only fed her rage. She knew she was pushing him further away from her, but she didn't care. If she didn't push him, he'd still go on his own. "You had me, and now you're leaving, and if you have any regrets I bet it's that we were interrupted before you'd bedded me! 'Trust me,' you murmured. And so I trusted you!''

"Susannah!''

"Oh, don't 'Susannah!' me! I know that I've been stupid, but even dumb Americans can wake up! Why, I bet you only cared for Alex to get your hands on me! Bringing him to William Street in hopes that I'd follow along! Don't bother to deny it. You know that it's the truth!''

He didn't bother. He was too shocked to try. He was also too angry at the way she was twisting things, turning his innocent intentions into motives so base that he'd call another man out for doing things half as bad. And what made him angriest of all was that she was partly right. Maybe he could have arranged to move out of the house before now. And if they hadn't been interrupted, he might well have bedded her. But what she said about using her brother as bait to get her here! And to think that he'd spent the whole night agonizing over her—over this bad-tempered fury with her way of twisting the truth!

She took a step toward him, her eyes narrowing. "I was wrong about you, Edward. You're no different from the rest. You're nothing but a redcoat!''

His head snapped up at that. "And proud to be!'' he retorted, meeting her steel for steel. "The more I see of you Americans, the prouder I feel! Just wait, Susannah, until we 'redcoats' have all gone away and there's nobody left for you to blame and berate but yourselves! Then watch how quickly your 'United' States will disunite! Think of me,

Susannah, when it's all come apart and you're secretly wishing that you'd never cut yourselves off."

"Never!" she gasped. "No, never! I vow that I'd rather die than ever be tied to England—or to an Englishman!"

"No Englishman would have you!" he fired back. "Goodbye, Susannah. I'm sorry that we ever met!" He didn't wait for her answer before he yanked open the door. He snatched the last word from Susannah by slamming it hard in his wake.

She glared at it, her fists clenched. "Good riddance!" she shouted, not caring if Alex did hear. The wooden box he'd disinterred was lying a few feet away. She took two steps and kicked it—so hard that she bruised her foot.

"Ow! Damn!" she gasped, hopping in pain as the tears stung her eyes.

"Mistress Susannah? Are you all right?"

Double damn! It was Milly again. "Right as rain, Milly!" she gritted out, hopping to the door. She yanked it open and limped past Milly and across the hall.

"What was all that shouting?" Alex asked when she came in. "And why are you limping?"

"I had an accident. We don't have to leave, Alex. Captain Steel is moving out."

"Is he? When?"

"This very hour—to quote his words. He's probably gone already."

"Good riddance!" Alex sniffed.

"He saved your life!" snapped Susannah and shocked them both. As if she hadn't just shouted exactly the same words as Alex herself—and loud enough for him to have heard across the hall.

Alex's eyes opened wider. Then he caught her hand. "I know that whatever happened, you did it for my sake. But you don't have to worry about that anymore. I promise I'll get better, then I'll take care of you. I promise," he repeated.

Susannah didn't respond, but she squeezed Alex's fingers so tightly he winced in pain.

Part II

Chapter Nine

July, 1783

Barney Silver drained his tankard in a single draft and raised it to show the serving girl that he required a second one. A man worked up a stiff thirst toiling his days away at a hot forge—though a day's wages of four shillings hardly left him enough to quench his thirst after paying his room and board. And at New York prices, Barney added silently as the girl saw his gesture and acknowledged him with a nod.

Barney supposed he should feel lucky to be able to earn his keep. There were plenty of able-bodied men knocking about the city for want of something to do. Then again, he reflected, idle men had their purposes. It was easy to stir up resentment among idle men. Barney sat down his empty mug and returned to his scrutiny of General Washington's circular as printed in *Rivington's Gazette.*

Speaking of resentful men, Barney thought, scanning the page, on which the general pleaded for all good patriots to dig deep into their pockets to pay the new nation's debts—especially those owed to soldiers who had fought to make the country free. It was no secret what had prompted the general's plea. Three weeks ago two companies of Pennsylvania recruits had scandalized the government by marching on Congress to demand their pay. There'd been a pitched battle with hastily called regulars while the besieged legislators had cowered in the hall. Now Washington was pleading for "a sacred regard for public justice," and also for the suppression of all "local prejudice." Too bad, thought Barney. The general was a fine man and he wished he could support his plea. But he couldn't—at least, not until a private justice had forced the redcoats and Tories to pay. After that had happened, Barney could endorse Washington's peace.

Blacksmithing from dawn to dark was no holiday. Barney's mouth felt like old cotton wadded up with tar. Where had that girl gotten to? Looking up, he located her across the room. She'd stopped at the elbow of a fellow who was hunched over another copy of the *Gazette*. The fellow also had a tankard, and as Barney watched, the girl was evidently asking if he needed it refilled. The fellow didn't hear her or even sense her at his side. He was reading the paper with so much concentration that Barney half expected the pages to burst into flame.

The girl repeated her question, thrusting out one hip and planting her hand upon it to show that she meant to stay. This time the fellow heard her. He looked up and shook his head. He didn't need a refill. He wanted to read in peace.

But she didn't want to let him read. She wanted to flirt with him, and as he turned in profile, Barney could see the reason why. The fellow was handsome in a dark, hawkish way. He was also a patriot, with a tricolored cockade clipped to the rim of the tricorn he'd laid on the tabletop.

The girl leaned forward, pretending to read with him but really only wanting to thrust her bosom in his face. He tolerated her presence until at last she gave up and straightened with a good-natured shrug. Then the fellow went back to his reading.

For the second time, Barney raised his tankard aloft.

"I'm coming! I'm coming!" the girl grumbled, threading her way through to him. "What's your pleasure?" she asked, arriving.

"Another."

"The same?"

"If you please."

She swept up his tankard and left with hardly a glance. If asked later to describe him, she'd most likely say, "I don't know. I didn't notice. He looked like anyone else."

Barney returned to the paper after she was gone, but there wasn't much of interest other than Washington's speech. Advertisements for cloth and tonics, and notices of sales. Warnings from the commandant about keeping the gutters clean.

He looked up as the sounds of a commotion reached his ears. Whatever it was, it was coming from the hallway outside the taproom door. Then it spilled into the taproom in the form of two men and a woman. Both of the men were very young despite their silk breeches and fancy powdered wigs. Tories, thought Barney, his lip curling at the word, and the woman must be a prostitute they'd picked up in the street. They kept her between them as they wove their way to the nearest table with three vacant chairs.

"Landlord! A good Madeira!" called one of the men. His wig was slightly awry and his face was flushed. The other one leaned forward, lost his balance and practically sprawled on top of the girl. She pushed him back with a burst of laughter. Barney's hands curled into fists. Then he noticed the dark-haired fellow whom the serving girl had liked. The fellow was watching the Tories with as much hate as Barney had ever seen printed on a human face.

The dark-haired fellow wasn't the only one to react, for this was a tavern frequented by patriots. The room was deadly silent except for the trio of drunks, who continued to call for Madeira and laugh as the landlord approached.

He spoke to them in an undertone.

"What! No wine!" they cried. "Then bring us a rum punch!"

The landlord shook his head. With the serving girl to assist him, he managed to get them up from their seats and out the door of the taproom before anyone started a fight. The men were too drunk to understand what was happen-

ing, but the whore realized and did what she could to hurry
her companions out of the room. From the hallway Barney heard them complaining bitterly that there ought to be
a law against taverns that didn't have punch!

"A Brit law, I suppose!" someone growled, and everybody laughed, except for Barney and the dark-haired fellow with the cockade. He kept on staring at the table where
the Tories had been, as though he hadn't had quite enough
of hating them.

Barney watched the fellow from across the room. Even
from this distance, he could tell certain things about him;
it was obvious he'd seen fighting in the war. He had that
curved-in wariness that came from watching for the enemy
on too many dark nights. He also had the tension of a
coiled spring.

Barney's eyes narrowed and his mind became alert. He'd
spent many an hour watching men in taverns since he'd
come to New York. Finding men who hated the redcoats
wasn't hard to do. But finding men you could depend on
was a different thing. Men were lazy and men forgot.
They'd tell you their stories and listen to yours, but when
it came to action, too many would shrug and say, "Why
bother? All that's over. Besides, I'm sick of it."

They were wrong, it wasn't over. It was happening every
day, right here, in this taproom, wearing powdered wigs. It
was strutting through the markets twirling walking sticks.
It was moldering in forgotten graves and burning in Barney's heart. Barney Silver wasn't lazy. He had a job to do,
and he meant to do it just as soon as he'd gathered his
troops. And finding a first lieutenant was the cornerstone
of his plans.

"That's twopence for the ale, sir!" The girl slapped his
tankard down. Noting the object of Barney's attention, she
shook her head and sighed. "He'd be a fair sight more
handsome if he ever smiled!"

"Maybe he does," said Barney, "when he's got something to smile about."

"I don't think so," the girl said candidly. "I already offered him that." She held out her hand for the twopence, pocketed it and left. Barney drank enough of the ale to wet his throat. Then he carried the rest with him as he crossed the room.

The dark-haired fellow started when Barney sat down across from him. He'd still been staring at the table the Tories had left. Now he rubbed his eyes as though he'd just waked up and, with a nod to Barney, returned to his *Gazette*. As he read, Barney observed him from the corner of his eye, adding to his store of impressions that he could see at closer range. Such as the fellow's clothing, which, although not silk, was definitely of a better grade than most of the rest in the room. And the fellow's fingers, which were smooth and clean. He didn't work for his living, and he washed regularly.

He looked younger across the table, small and light-boned as a girl. But there was nothing feminine about the set of his jaw. He didn't look healthy. He was thin, as if he'd been sick. He was reading the paper as if he'd been to school: not struggling and stumbling, but moving right along, his forefinger whizzing down the page. That feeling of a wound-up spring was stronger, closer up.

He read without consciousness of Barney, as though he were alone in the room. Barney waited patiently until he'd finished the circular. After all, he had nothing better to do than to watch and wait until he'd recruited his troops. Then the waiting would be over and he'd be ready to act.

"What do you think about it?" Barney asked when the fellow looked up.

The dark eyes sharpened as they surveyed the questioner. "It makes some sense." The fellow glanced down at the open *Gazette*. "What he says about the states all uniting under a strong federal head. I believe that we've got to do that if we're to succeed."

Barney nodded slowly. "But that's a ways down the road. New York won't be uniting with anyone until after the redcoats have gone. And from the way they've been dragging their feet, it doesn't seem that will be very soon."

"It can't be forever," the dark-haired man replied.

"Maybe not for the British," acknowledged Barney. "But the Tories are a different case." He glanced over at the empty table and felt his companion tense. "I've heard that some Tories aren't so anxious to move to Canada. They don't want to give up their fine mansions and fancy carriages—and whatever they've managed to steal from the patriots during the war!"

At that, the thin hands curled into fists as Barney's had done before. "They've got no choice, have they?" the fellow gritted out.

"Haven't they?" Barney asked. He nodded to the paper, half-hidden by the man's angry fists. "Didn't you read what Washington said about forgetting prejudice? I suppose he'd have us make the Tories our newest friends."

The dark eyes fixed on Barney's with that same smoldering intensity with which he'd been reading before. Barney thought he meant to answer, but instead he grabbed his tankard for a long, thirsty gulp.

"You fought, didn't you?" asked Barney.

The man slapped the tankard down. "What if I did?" he challenged. "You're very curious."

"I believe we've got things in common."

"What sort of things would those be?"

Barney didn't answer until he'd glanced all around the room to be sure that no one was listening. Then he said, "We both hate the redcoats and Tories. We both believe they should pay."

"How do you know I believe that?"

"Don't you?" Barney asked, wondering for a moment whether he might have been wrong. Maybe the fellow had been angry about something else. Maybe he'd had a fight with his girl and come to drink and forget. But he wasn't drinking, he was reading. And Barney had seen his hate.

Barney tried another tactic. "I fought, too," he said. "Ever since the day the redcoats attacked my farm. They burned the buildings and killed my wife."

"They killed my mother," his companion replied in a low voice. "They take our women. They treat them like—" He shook his head. "I'll never forgive them, no matter what Washington says!"

"They don't deserve forgiveness," Barney said, leaning close. "They deserve revenge!"

The dark eyes flew to his and there was no mistaking the flame that flared up as they did. "Revenge?" he murmured. "What do you have in mind?"

Barney laid his palm flat on the table, each of the fingers outstretched. "A man alone is no stronger than one finger of a hand. But a group of men, pulled together..." He drew his fingers in and slowly curled them into a fist.

"Is there a group of men?"

"What if there was?" Barney said.

Slowly the other man grinned. The girl had been right, Barney realized. He was handsome when he smiled. Barney released his fingers and held out his hand. "The name is Silver. Barnett Silver. Barney to my friends."

The fellow's hand was slender, but the grip was cool and firm. "Alexander Beckwith. What have you got in mind?"

Susannah chose a melon from the pile and tested it between her hands. Holding it up to her nose, she sniffed deeply, closing her eyes to concentrate.

"Firm and sweet," promised the melon woman, who'd been watching with an eagle eye. "And fresh just this morning. I picked the lot myself from the best Brook Land fields."

"I'll take it." Susannah handed the melon over for the woman to weigh, though she knew very well that it hadn't been picked that day. There wouldn't have been time, since the melon woman would have had to leave before dawn in order to catch the market ferry that would bring her across from Brook Land.

On the other hand, she didn't need the woman to tell her if the melon was sweet. That she'd learned from her mother, long before the war. Every self-respecting New York housewife marketed for herself. The rich ones brought their servants to carry their bundles home. The rest brought their daughters or carried their things themselves.

From the time she could remember, and when she hadn't been in school, Susannah had come along for the marketing. Her mother had been a careful shopper and had passed the skill along. She'd had her special vendors whom she'd patronized and others whom she'd avoided. "Bad eggs," she'd murmur to Susannah, steering her past a stall. Or, "She always slips the spoiled tomatoes beneath the perfect ones."

Susannah used to catch some of the vendors exchanging looks when her mother passed. "She's never satisfied, that one," their looks implied, and Susannah had stood up straighter so they'd be sure to know that her standards were just as high as her mother's were.

Most of the city's markets had been closed during the war, either because of damage or from the lack of goods. The Continental Army had blockaded the city from all sides so that whatever New York received had had to come in from the open sea. Americans had taken a fierce pride in New York's shortages. The British might hold the city, but they would not get fat in it. They wouldn't be throwing the sort of fancy balls they'd had in Philadelphia.

Now that the war was over, the markets were starting to be rebuilt. A number of the old stalls had reopened in the last few weeks, and every day more vendors arrived to set up shop. Little by little, the city was regaining its old shape. The stage had resumed service to Philadelphia, and the various ferries had begun to run. Of course there was still a daunting amount to be done—and still thousands of Tories to dispatch upon their way.

Susannah paid for the melon and added it to the other purchases in the basket over her arm. She was moving on to the next stall when she saw a commotion up ahead.

Chickens were shrieking and furious wings beat the air. In the midst she recognized a flash of brightness that was Amy Van Rijn's red hair. She hesitated a moment, then pushed her way forward toward the scene.

By the time Susannah reached it, the hubbub had ended, though both Amy and the chicken seller were out of breath. On the ground between them was a crate containing two hens, one of whom looked half-dead, while the other pecked at the crate's slats and muttered mutinously.

"I've never seen such a thing!" the seller was exclaiming when Susannah arrived.

"I guess chickens know when you don't really like them." Amy shook her head ruefully. The shake dislodged a feather from the lace of her cap; it hung in the air for a moment then floated down to earth.

"Nonsense!" sniffed the seller. "Chickens are too stupid to know anything! But, as I told you, these ones lay good eggs. May the Lord curse me if they don't give you a half dozen each a week."

"Mmm, no doubt," agreed Amy, eyeing the crate with mistrust. Looking up, she saw Susannah and her skepticism disappeared. "Susannah! What a nice surprise! Which way are you going? Wait, I'll walk with you as soon as I've arranged to get these home."

Susannah waited while Amy found a carter who was willing to deliver the chickens to the Van Rijns'.

"Where will you keep them?" she asked Amy, thinking of their three rooms.

"Oh, out in the yard. The landlady lets us have a coop in exchange for fresh eggs. I'm not so sure it's our bargain," she added with another rueful laugh. Then her expression brightened and she squeezed Susannah's arm. "I'm so glad to see you! It's been so long! How are things going for you and Alex over at William Street? I've been meaning to come calling, but we've all been so occupied! Do tell how you arranged it. I'm so envious of you!" Amy concluded with a smile to show that she wasn't at all.

Susannah laughed, as always, at Amy's effusiveness and wished she'd paid a visit on the Van Rijns long before. Even with Edward long gone from William Street, she'd found other reasons for keeping to herself—such as her worry over Alex and the guilt she felt about having her own house when other good patriots were living in rented rooms. But one smile from Amy shouldered those worries away. "Things are going well enough. How about with you?"

"Oh, fine. Just fine." Amy beamed, then glanced away, momentarily distracted by a pile of squash.

"Fresh today!" the seller informed her. "I picked this lot myself."

"That's what they all say!" said Amy with a giggle as she and Susannah moved on. "But tell me now, how did you manage to reclaim your house?"

"It's a long story."

"Is it? Let's walk slowly then. I've been going so fast these last weeks, I don't mind the rest! Rebuilding things better than ever may be an inspiring idea, but it's also a lot of work!" Amy grimaced and rolled her eyes. She held out her hand for Susannah's inspection. "Look at those bruises and scrapes! You'll never guess what they're from. I've been helping Father to rebuild the store. Me, with a saw and hammer—can you just picture it! I believe I hit my fingers more often than the nails!"

Susannah shifted her basket and held out her hand to compare. "I've been working in the garden. I've put in vegetables. What with things being so expensive, I thought that it made sense. I've already got lettuce and beans. And I ought to have tomatoes and squash very soon."

"But not melons." Amy grinned and tapped the melon Susannah had bought.

"I did plant them," Susannah admitted. "But they never came up. The cook is of the opinion that I put them in too late. But the cabbages are coming—by the hundreds, or so it seems!"

"Shall I tell you a secret?" Amy looked around with exaggerated suspicion, as though they were in the midst of spies. "I'm glad we're in rented rooms without our own yard, because if we had one, I'd probably be weeding a garden in addition to everything else! To tell the truth, Susannah, chickens are quite bad enough!" She rolled her eyes again with feeling.

Susannah laughed. "You don't need a garden, Amy. You can share what I grow in mine! Honestly—if you saw it, you'd know that it was true. Hundreds and hundreds of cabbages and legions of lettuce plants! And when the tomatoes and squash come...!" Susannah shook her head.

"Why not can them?" Amy suggested.

"That's what I said to the cook. And she said that there'll be so many that if we started now, we'd still be canning when it was time to plant next spring! So you see what you'd save us by taking a share of the crop. I tell you what," she added when she saw Amy still holding back, "if it will make you feel better, you can pick for yourselves. Just send over one of your sisters for whatever you need."

"All right. I'll send Maria," Amy said with another grin. "She swears that touching chickens makes her come out in hives, so she doesn't have to help with them. Picking beans and cabbages will pay her back! And do make her help with the weeding," she urged wickedly.

The two of them laughed together. Then Amy said, "But, Susannah, you still haven't told me the story about the house!"

"There's not much to tell."

"You just said the story was long! You're not trying to evade me, are you?" Amy teased.

"Of course not." Susannah blushed and made a great show of examining braided onions in the stall they were passing just then. She even bought one, despite having plenty of onions at home. She added it to her basket as they began to walk. "You remember that day when you met me coming out my front gate. I'd just gotten back to the city."

"Of course. And you spent the night. I remember you'd been inside your house and met the man who lived there— I was so impressed! You said he was a redcoat captain."

"Yes. And a doctor, too. And later when Alex got to be so ill and I didn't know how to cure him, I went to him for help. And he, well, he insisted that we move Alex to the house."

"Did he!" Amy's hand squeezed Susannah's arm. "How very gallant! And how fortunate for you!"

"It was," Susannah admitted. "Very fortunate. Of course I'd have never accepted if Alex hadn't been so sick. He was so sick," she repeated, "that he couldn't be safely moved. So for several weeks we had to divide the house. The redcoat doctor lived downstairs, and Alex and I had our own rooms on the second floor."

"Then when Alex was better the captain left?"

"That's right." Susannah nodded. "He—um, arranged for us to stay."

"He does sound very gallant! Why, Susannah, I've made you blush!"

"Of course you haven't!" Susannah protested. "It's all this talk of gallantry—as though it weren't all based on strict necessity! Everything that happened was because Alex was sick. And as soon as he was better, the redcoat doctor moved out."

"Of course he did," agreed Amy. "I only meant that helping you and Alex was a very thoughtful thing. I don't suppose most redcoats would have done the same!"

"Not likely," agreed Susannah, letting down her guard enough to remember those nights that she and Edward had nursed Alex together and Edward had been so kind. Then she caught her guard down and snapped it back again. "But," she added quickly, "he was a redcoat, nonetheless!"

Her strictest rule these past weeks had been to bar Edward from her thoughts. The feelings he'd left were open wounds that needed care to heal, and she had nothing but time and distance with which to cure herself. That was another reason for keeping close to home—and for only frequenting places, such as the markets, where she was sure he would not be.

But sometimes even these rules and precautions were not enough. Sometimes the littlest things would flood her thoughts with him. The quality of light would remind her of the dawn after the nights they'd sat up. Or she'd come into the drawing room and imagine him standing there with one arm on the mantel, smiling his smile. Or she'd catch sight of a tall man in the street and her heart would lurch painfully before she saw it wasn't him.

In the house nobody mentioned his name, though every so often Milly would slip, then catch herself.

"That was when Cap—" Milly would say, then stop. Or, "Mother's roast turnips were—well, some people favored them!"

When she was lucky, Susannah could imagine that it had all been a dream. She hadn't really lived with Edward so intimately, and she certainly hadn't done with him what she had. But for the most part she wasn't lucky, and she knew it had all been true. She had shared more than a house with him all those weeks. She'd shared her body and all her most intimate gifts. But for one scuttling creature interrupting them, she knew she would have allowed him the ultimate intimacy.

And he would have taken it. After her first explosion of anger at him had passed, she realized that Edward had not been solely to blame. She'd accepted her portion of the guilt for having welcomed his caress. But she continued to fault him for having stayed at William Street when he could have left after Alex's crisis had passed. She faulted him for having encouraged her to care, for having lighted her fires and for then having walked away.

The fact that she still cared for him was a deep wound to her pride, especially since she suspected that he'd forgotten her. In any event she'd put a name to the feelings that they'd shared. Those feelings hadn't been love at all, they'd been pure animal desire. She didn't love Edward Steel, and he surely didn't love her. You didn't love someone one day, then walk away the next, the way Edward had left William Street without a second glance.

Amy brushed a stray chicken feather off her sleeve. "And what about Alex? I take it that he's well? What has he been doing?"

"Oh, this and that." Susannah gave a vague wave of her free hand. "He's completely better, but he's still weak. He can't do too much. If he does, I'm afraid that the fever will come back."

"Of course," agreed Amy. "You don't want to take any risks. It's almost a miracle that he survived the prison ship, when you think of how many died! Thousands!" She shuddered. "He must feel very grateful to be alive!"

"I'm sure he does," agreed Susannah in a tone that made Amy turn.

"You don't sound so certain." Amy's brown eyes were serious as they studied Susannah's. "You sound worried, Susannah. You look worried, too."

"Of course not." Susannah gave a quick laugh and looked away. "Why should I be worried when Alex is well and we've got our own house! Everything is fine!"

"Is it?" pursued Amy in the same serious tone. "As Mother says, worries are always lighter when they're shared."

Susannah's mother had always said the same. She sucked in her lower lip, then let it out with a sigh. "Well, maybe things aren't completely fine. I guess I have been a little worried by the way that Alex has been. I don't mean his physical condition. I mean the way he acts. What you said just now about prison—I know you're right. He's been through some awful things, and they must have left scars. But I'm beginning to wonder when they'll start to heal.

"He's so bitter, Amy," she confessed. "It's as though whatever sickness got his body also got into his heart, and I don't know what medicine will make it go away. At first I tried cheering him up, but that only seemed to make him worse. If I say something hopeful, he answers something bleak. Most days he mopes around the house, but then he goes out at night. He goes out to taverns and drinks alone. He's quiet when he comes in, but I hear him anyway.

"I thought when he got better he'd take over things. You know, find out about Father's business. Help me decide what to do. I've mentioned those things to him, and he nods and says that he'll get to them later, he's got other things on his mind. I don't know what's on his mind, Amy. But it's making me afraid. I have this awful feeling that unless he changes, he's headed toward something bad. I feel it, but I don't know how to stop him. That's the worst part of all!"

She stopped to catch her breath and realized that she'd just poured her heart out to Amy without ever intending to. "Just listen to me!" she apologized. "Babbling on like a fool. As if you haven't got enough worries of your own."

"Oh, hush!" Amy chided gently. "What else are friends for? You don't sound like a fool, Susannah. You sound like any sister who's concerned for her brother's health. Poor Alex, he sounds so unhappy."

"He is." Susannah sighed. "We've all had our hard times to get over, but he can't seem to get over his. I wish I could think of something to take his mind off whatever it is. I try coaxing him out to the garden—"

"But he didn't want to weed?" Amy finished with a lopsided grin. "Frankly I don't blame him. Wait! I've got an idea. Maybe he'd want to help Father with the store. I hate to say it, Susannah, but building is a far sight more entertaining than scrabbling around in the dirt. And you know Father. He's got enough optimism for all of New York. Maybe if Alex were around other people he'd stop brooding over whatever is on his mind."

Amy finished as breathless as Susannah had been. She waited, looking hopeful, while Susannah considered the thought.

"It might work," she conceded. "If he'd agree to try— and if it was presented to him in the right light. Not as if we're trying to help him cheer up. But if it seemed like a favor he'd be doing your family..."

"Maybe Father could ask him," Amy suggested. "He could write him a note or stop by the house."

"Too formal," objected Susannah. "Alex might suspect. I know, I could have you to dinner, and then it could just come—" But she never finished her sentence. Glancing casually ahead of her, she saw Edward no more than a few yards away.

He was wearing light breeches and a black coat. The starkness of the colors set him off from the rest of the crowd—though perhaps that was only to Susannah's eyes. Her heart froze with a painful suddenness, and her hand tightened its grip on her market basket so hard that the handle creaked.

He looked wonderful. Terrible. What was she thinking of? She hated and despised him for what he'd done. What was he doing here at the produce market, where she'd thought she would be safe? It wasn't fair that he'd come here. She had to get away! She glanced quickly behind her, seeking a route of escape. But when she glanced around again, she saw that it was too late. Edward had caught sight of her.

She watched in frozen comprehension as his eyes swept over her, recording random details just as hers had done. She watched him register what she was wearing and how she looked. In the first shock he must have, like her, forgotten that they'd parted as enemies. She saw the moment at which he remembered and watched his expression change. His jaw tightened and his eyes moved quickly away. Humiliated, she watched them search from side to side. He'd just as soon avoid her if he could manage it. But Edward was no coward, whatever else he might be. He caught himself, squared his shoulders and began walking to where she stood.

"Could just come—what?" Amy was saying, still pondering Alex's state of mind. "In any event, I think dinner would be very nice. Of course I'd coach Father on what to say—and coach the others on keeping still!" Amy chuckled, then realized Susannah had stopped, though she clearly hadn't stopped to peruse any of the stalls. She wasn't looking to either side, where the vendors were. She was staring straight ahead—at a tall, well-dressed man who had stopped for a moment but was now approaching them. Well-dressed and very handsome, Amy added belatedly.

"Do you know him?" she murmured to Susannah. But Susannah made no reply. She didn't seem to know Amy had spoken, she was watching the man so hard. She didn't look happy to see him—and when she addressed him a moment later, she sounded distinctly displeased.

"What are you doing here?" Susannah blurted before Edward could greet her—before he could say anything. She cringed at her own stupidity, but at least he looked taken aback.

"What does anyone do at the market?" he asked, recovering.

"They shop," she said bluntly. "If you're shopping here, then where's your basket? Where are your purchases?" This time Edward was not the only one to recoil. At her side she felt Amy stiffen with shock at her impoliteness. In that moment she regretted that she had not fled. Cowardice would be preferable to standing here with Edward's cool and baffled eyes staring down at her.

The censure she saw in his eyes only nudged the demons prickling beneath her skin. "Or maybe you're not shopping because the goods are beneath your tastes? Maybe you think British markets have superior goods? Maybe you prefer the markets of London, which haven't gone through a war?" She met his cool gaze with her hot and angry one.

"And what if I do?" he asked evenly.

"If you do, then nothing!" she snapped back. "Then keep your British silver—we don't want it here!"

"Is that so?" His brows rose as he glanced around. His eyes settled on the nearest vendor, an old woman selling peas. "Do you think she shares your opinion? Shall I offer her my British silver and see if she turns it down?" He took a step in her direction.

Susannah tossed her head. "Offer what you like!" she retorted. "In any case, she wouldn't be the first honest woman to be tempted by British charm!"

She'd expected her barb to sting him, but to her chagrin, instead of anger she saw the familiar gleam spark in his eyes, brightening their grayness with a flash of blue.

"And what makes you think she's honest?" He cocked his head. "In London the canny housewife takes every vendor's boasts with a grain of salt. Are American vendors more honest? Or could it be that American housewives might be more naive?"

Damn him for turning her insult back on her! Susannah shifted her market basket more firmly on her hip. "I'm surprised that you even have time for marketing! Your General Carleton protests so strongly when he's accused of procrastinating. I guess he doesn't know his officers are using working hours to shop. No wonder there are still so many Tories fouling the streets of New York!"

He clucked his tongue chidingly. "What would *your* General Washington say to such a speech? I thought he was urging the end to local prejudice and the propagation of universal goodwill."

"That's goodwill among the states," Susannah replied.

"Is that so?" Edward pretended to be surprised. "And here I was thinking that the states already got along! At least that's what I heard from certain Americans. I guess my American sources must have been misinformed."

"Misinformed!" she sputtered, but Edward had turned away. He'd turned his attention to Amy, who'd been gaping from side to side, trying to follow the barrage of their repartee.

He doffed his tricorn. "I apologize. I know Mistress Beckwith wouldn't have forgotten her manners, so she must have forgotten my name. Please allow me to introduce myself. Captain Edward Steel."

"Amy Van Rijn," Amy stammered, shooting Susannah a sideways glance of apology. Her eyes were bulging with curiosity. Why on earth was Susannah being so rude to this man?

"Captain Steel is a redcoat," Susannah put in, as though she'd read Amy's mind. "He's on General Carleton's staff. His job is to clear all the Tories out of New York."

"I see," murmured Amy, who didn't see at all but knew that Susannah would not like her trying to find out. "It—it sounds like a big job," she faltered, searching for neutral ground.

"It is," Edward agreed. "It isn't very often that I have time for marketing." He smiled at Amy, a smile that Susannah knew, and Susannah wasn't a bit surprised when Amy smiled back. The smile was purely friendly, but it hurt her anyway—hurt her in the deepest places, as his teasing hadn't done. It stripped away the hard shell she'd formed over her wounds. She hadn't recovered when he turned back to her.

"How is your brother?"

"He—he's fine." She met his eyes, driving every bit of weakness out of hers. Or trying to drive the weakness out—meaning to drive it out.

"Is he really?" Edward's brows came down as both his smile and the twinkle in his eyes disappeared. His eyes no longer jabbed at her or teased. He waited for her answer with that look she recalled—a look that made her want to tell him the truth. A look that made her want to go back to depending upon him as she had before. And then what had happened? she reminded herself.

"Yes, really." She drew back—past the pull of Edward's smile and past the temptation of his strength. But she couldn't push herself past the memory of his embrace. She'd been right. She needed time and distance to forget, and evidently more of each than she'd had so far. Even bearing the wounds he'd inflicted, she could be moved by him yet.

She tightened her hold on her basket with one hand and with the other gripped Amy's arm. "Since you are so busy, we won't keep you here. Good day, Captain Steel." She tugged on Amy's arm.

"Good day." Amy nodded, following Susannah's lead.

"Goodbye," Edward murmured, stepping back to let them pass, but Susannah felt him watching as they walked away. For that reason, she forced herself not to rush—at least until she was certain that they were out of his view.

Chapter Ten

"**Y**ou! Watch where you're going!" an indignant voice cried out as Susannah dragged Amy down the crowded market aisle.

"That's the third person we've bumped!" panted Amy. "And I've got a stitch in my side! Whoever he is, I promise, we've left him far behind!"

Susannah slowed with reluctance. Given her own way, she would have kept on running all the way home to William Street. She was breathing as hard as Amy, and her neck was damp with sweat, for the day was hot and muggy with the promise of afternoon storms.

"That's better!" gasped Amy, fanning her flushed face with her hand. Then she stopped fanning and looked at Susannah hard. "Well? Are you going to tell me now?"

Susannah looked away. Frankly, she didn't want to. She preferred to forget the whole thing. But refusing to speak about Edward would give Amy ideas that she vastly preferred not to give. So she pushed back her damp curls and shrugged with nonchalance. "Of course, if you want me to. But there's nothing much to tell. Captain Steel was the redcoat who took care of Alex when he was sick."

"The—him!" Amy ground to such a sudden stop that Susannah almost tripped. "You mean the one who was living at William Street? The doctor, do you mean?"

"What of it?" Susannah retorted, wishing that Amy wouldn't gape at her that way.

"Well, nothing—but he's so handsome! You never said he was. When you said doctor, I thought of an older man. You know..." Amy trailed off vaguely, her expression still amazed.

Frustration washed over Susannah. "He's a *redcoat!*" she declared. "Like the redcoats who seized the city and burned down your house and your father's store. Like the redcoats who killed my mother and your brother, Gilbert. Just because he's handsome doesn't excuse him from what he's done!"

"But he's a doctor," protested Amy, though with less conviction than before. "I don't think that a doctor would have done any of those things. Even if he was in a battle, he'd only be saving lives. And look what he did for Alex, and giving you your house..." Amy pursued exactly the line of reasoning Susannah didn't want to hear—the reasoning that had already caused her so much pain.

"I'm surprised at you, Amy," she said soberly. "Being so ready to excuse the enemy while they're still holding New York. Captain Steel might not wield a gun, but he heals the men who do so that they can go back out and kill good patriots. If it wasn't for the British, you'd be living in your house instead of taking care of chickens and hammering your hands!"

"You're right," admitted Amy, with a smile at Susannah's last words. But her smile quickly faded and she sighed. "I know he's a redcoat. It's just that I get so tired of everybody having to be so angry all the time."

"War makes people angry." Susannah tugged on Amy's arm and they began to walk again, toward the market entrance and Water Street.

"But the war is over," Amy pointed out. "It's what you were saying about Alex and the hate getting into his mind. I don't like the British or the Tories for what they've done. But I'm tired of being angry. I want to get on with my life. I want to get back to peacetime."

"And look who's stopping you," Susannah retorted as they came down the market stairs. "The King, who won't sign the final treaty, and General Carleton, who'll stay in New York till he does. And Captain Steel, who's shopping instead of clearing the Tories out! Which way are you going?'' she asked as they reached the street.

''That way.'' Amy nodded toward the left. ''I've got an errand at Hanover Square. What about you?''

She'd had enough of the markets. ''I'm going back home.''

''Then this is where I leave you,'' Amy said, but she didn't leave. ''You know what, Susannah?'' she said thoughtfully. ''As much as I hate all the damage and the death, I can't help but thinking that if it had never been, right now I'd be at home doing women's work instead of— as you put it—hammering my hands.'' She raised her free hand and regarded it with a rueful smile. Then she looked at Susannah. ''I know this sounds very strange, but the truth is that I'm really enjoying the work. I'm getting better with the hammer, and I'm learning new things every day—things I'd never have had a chance to learn if there had been no war.''

''Amy!'' Susannah stared at her with dismay.

But Amy met her reaction with a gentle smile. ''And another thing, Susannah. About Captain Steel. You say his being handsome doesn't excuse what the British have done. But what about the good things, like saving Alex's life? Should his being British take that away?''

''Alex would never have been ill, but for his treatment on a British brig,'' Susannah replied stubbornly.

Amy shook her head slowly. ''You do sound like Alex now. Will we never forgive them?''

''I don't know,'' Susannah said. ''I suppose we will one day. But now it's still too soon.'' But even as she said so, she knew in her heart that the blame she had laid upon Edward had little to do with the war.

Amy sighed and squeezed her arm before she let it go. ''I hope it won't take much longer. I hope so with all my heart. In the meantime I'll speak to Father about Alex helping with the store.''

"And send Maria to pick from the garden," Susannah reminded her. She hesitated and added, "I'm sorry I scolded before."

"That's all right." Amy grinned. "If we didn't think with our mouths open, we wouldn't be American!"

Susannah walked slowly toward William Street. She didn't share Amy's enthusiasm for her present life, but apart from that she couldn't fault much of what Amy had said. Amy was right about anger, it did feed upon itself; and the only way to stop it was to let it go.

She remembered those weeks when Alex had been too ill to object to all of them living together at William Street. Reflecting on Amy's words, she realized now that one of the things that had made those weeks so comfortable had been laying aside the anger she'd been lugging around all these years. She hadn't realized how heavy that anger was until she'd set it aside. Then Alex had recovered enough to make her see that laying aside her anger too soon had been dangerous. So she'd picked it up and carried it with her ever since. But now, reflecting on Amy's words, she wondered if Alex had been wrong. Maybe Alex needed to hear what Amy had said.

And what did that mean about Edward? she was wondering, engrossed by her thoughts, when she heard her name called from across the street.

"Why, it's Susannah Beckwith!"

Looking up, she saw Marguerite, Lady Bridgeham, dressed in a gown that took up every bit as much space as a carriage would have done. Marguerite was going to market, with a maidservant at her side dutifully lugging the basket while Marguerite sailed along. Now, to Susannah's amazement, Marguerite crossed the street to her. Her amazement was quickly doubled by the teasing smile on Marguerite's face.

"Why, Susannah, you sly thing!" Marguerite began. "Carrying on like a daughter of liberty, when all the while you were also carrying on with Captain Steel!"

"Carrying on!" Susannah sputtered. She couldn't believe her ears.

But Marguerite smiled coyly. "Do you think it's a secret? Why, the whole city knows how the two of you were living together—until you threw him out." She paused, eyeing Susannah, then added, "He told me himself! Of course, I'm sure you had plenty of reason for gratitude, what with him caring for Alex." She gave the fan in her gloved hand a little wave.

When her fan descended, it rested on Susannah's arm, and Marguerite leaned forward as far as her skirts would allow. "Personally I'm astounded that you'd throw him out. Everyone's in agreement that he's the handsomest man in New York. And his older brother is an influential man. Of course Edward will never get the title, but even without it, he'll do very well—better, I assure you, than any American."

She tapped her fan lightly on Susannah's arm. "Perhaps you should reconsider. It might not be too late. He's got his choice of women, but we all know how very energetic you can be!" Before Susannah found the breath to respond to this latest outrage, Marguerite disengaged, leaning back again. "In any event, it's been quite a treat running into you. Good day, Susannah," she concluded, snapping open her fan and waving it once at Susannah before she sailed away.

Susannah stared at her departure, dumbfounded with shock and rage. The whole city was talking! Edward had told Marguerite! No, it was impossible—Edward scorned Marguerite. Or so he had told her. But he'd also assured her that he couldn't leave William Street.

A wave of awful nausea swept over her. Had Edward betrayed her? The very thought of it made her ill! And to have done so with Marguerite, when he knew her history. As hurt as she was feeling, somehow she couldn't believe that he had. Or maybe she just wouldn't let herself believe. On the other hand, she had no trouble believing what

Marguerite had said about him having his choice of women—and that hurt her, too.

Even from a distance she could still see Marguerite's powdered hair bobbing along toward the market. The sight of it made her ill. So much for forgiveness. Amy had been wrong. The time to forgive and forget hadn't come at all.

Edward made his way slowly to the market's Queen Street door. He hadn't been shopping, as Susannah had guessed. There'd been trouble in one of the markets a few days before and he'd come here to listen to gossip and gauge the prevailing mood. The trouble had been mild, as such trouble could go: just a spontaneous shoving match between an American vendor and a loyalist customer that had spilled over into the crowd before it had been stopped by a passing troop. Given the numbers of both sides crowding the city these days, the British were lucky that the trouble wasn't worse. And Edward couldn't help but wonder how, with his days already so filled by his official job, he'd be able to discharge his secret one, should the need arise.

In any event, the prevailing mood in the market seemed calm—calmer than Susannah's, he thought with a fleeting smile. He recalled how she'd crackled with indignation at him. Nobody else got angry the way Susannah did. Beside her, other women seemed insipid and pale. Then his smile faded as he thought of something else.

Susannah was worried about her brother. He'd seen it in her eyes when he'd asked about Alex. Now, as he left the market, he wondered what was wrong. Had Alex's illness come back? Was he not getting well as he should? Or was there another problem that didn't concern his health? He knew that Susannah wouldn't confess to him, but perhaps if he spoke to Milly—

Edward caught himself. He had no business poking into Susannah's life. In the first place, she didn't want him—she'd made that plain enough. And in the second, he'd promised himself to let whatever he'd felt for her wither from lack of care. They sparked something in each other that he'd never felt before. Just thinking about that night in the root cellar could take his breath away. But passion alone was a shifting sand that couldn't support the trust or love it took to build a life. And an Englishman couldn't build anything these days in America.

He remembered the shock in Alex's voice when he'd questioned her, and he remembered the rage in Susannah's when she'd sent him away. He'd gone away in anger, but the anger hadn't endured. Later, in calmness he'd admitted to himself that they'd been playing with a fire as powerful as the one that had destroyed New York. And they'd both had enough of destruction in their private lives.

Besides, he added silently, Susannah had friends—American friends—upon whom she could rely. Like her red-haired companion, Amy Van Rijn, who'd witnessed their conversation with eyes that had seemed ready to pop. He wondered what Susannah had told her friends about him. Nothing, he suspected from Mistress Van Rijn's look. She was probably trying to forget him as quickly as possible. Despite his resolution, he couldn't help but feel more than a twinge of satisfaction at the realization that she hadn't succeeded yet.

As Queen Street crossed Cooper, he glanced around and saw Lady Bridgeham advancing toward him. He saw that she hadn't seen him and dodged quickly out of sight, hurrying on up Queen Street before she could arrive. The last time he'd run into Lady Bridgeham on the street, she'd pestered him for details on his move from William Street and he'd exhausted his manners in refusing her request. He regretted that the Bridgehams were taking their time leaving New York. Marguerite had become the toast of loyalist society, such as it remained, and he supposed she wanted to milk that pleasure dry before she went on to the next.

There were so many loyalists yet to leave. Sometimes, when he felt tired, the sheer number daunted him. By his best estimate twenty thousand had already gone, and an equal number remained in the city still. Add to that the returning Americans arriving every day and you had to wonder how they could all fit in. He considered himself lucky to have found a decent room, and only Carleton's personal exemption had kept Susannah at William Street. Carleton had asked no questions when Edward had gone to him, but Edward could guess what the general had been thinking when he'd signed the pass, which he'd sent to Susannah through a neutral messenger. She hadn't thanked him for it, but he hadn't expected her to.

Franks was already waiting at the tobacconist's when he arrived.

"What news?" Edward asked, as his eyes adjusted to the dimness of the tiny back room.

Franks shrugged briefly. "Mostly the same as before. A good deal of harmless grumbling but nothing rising to a threat. But there is something . . ."

"Go ahead," Edward urged.

"It's a man I met," Franks confided. "In a tavern the night before last. I was having a game of checkers. A few men were watching us. By and by the talk turned, as it does, to the war. Somebody expressed the opinion that it would be a relief when the last of the British were gone. Somebody added, 'Aye, and the Tories.' The things that everyone says. But then someone else put in that that time might never come. He said he'd heard that the Tories were changing their minds and deciding to stay."

Franks paused, recalling how the exchange had gone. "I didn't call his statement. I was just listening. But one of the others asked him where he'd heard such a thing. He said he worked for a smithy and he'd heard it in the shop. He said that if anyone listened, they could hear it in the street. He said that some men in Congress were saying that if the Tories left, they'd take out all the brains and money and the country would fall apart."

Franks sucked his breath in slowly. "As you can imagine, that didn't sit well with some of the men. They thought that American brains could run things well enough, and if they'd won the war without money, they could build a country, too. This fellow let them go on until they'd gotten their tempers up, then he said that maybe those men in Congress don't know how the people feel. Maybe they needed to see that true patriots wanted the Tories out.''

Edward leaned forward. "Did he suggest how?"

"That he didn't." Franks shook his head. "But he seemed pleased when somebody said that maybe they ought to pluck some chickens and heat up a pail of tar. He seemed very pleased, indeed."

"Did you get his name?"

"Silver. Barnett Silver. And there was something else. Were you ever in battle?"

Edward shook his head.

"Well, there's a look some men get sometimes, in the heat of the worst fight. It's not uncommon for a man to lose his fear and start caring more about killing than about being killed. But some men stop caring about being killed at all. I've seen it happen sometimes. There's a look that comes into their eyes."

"And this Silver had it?"

"Yes, sir. That he did." Franks's own eyes flickered. "It's a funny thing. Except for that one expression, you'd never pay Silver any heed. He's the type of fellow you'd overlook in a crowd."

"The type who could come and go without being seen."

"Exactly." Franks nodded. "I was thinking just the same thing."

"I think you should stay with Silver."

"I intend to," said Franks. "Of course, he could turn out to be nothing."

"Let's hope so," Edward said.

Chapter Eleven

"Down!" whispered Barney.

Alex dropped to the ground, still holding the bundle of firewood he'd been carrying in his arms. He clamped his jaw to stifle his exclamation of pain as half a dozen barbed edges jabbed into his chest. He forced his heartbeat to steady. Through it and Barney's breathing he heard the muffled clang of a cowbell and a voice coaxing, "Come on, Bessie girl, come on!"

The bell stopped clanging. "Damned stubborn cow!" cursed the voice. "All the others come back when they're meant to. But you, you've got to drag me out to search for you in the middle of the night! You could give pure West Indies rum instead of milk, for all I care. I swear, I mean to sell you! I'll slaughter you for feed! I'll trade you to a farmer who'll work you with a plow!"

There was a brief scuffle, then the clanging recommenced. Instantly the voice changed. "That's a good girl, now," it crooned. "Come on now, Bessie. You know I didn't mean what I said about selling you. It's not so very late, either. Hardly eleven, I declare! You come on home to the barn now..." The voice faded away.

Despite himself, Alex was grinning when Barney whispered, "Coast is clear." He rose, still gripping his bundle, and followed Barney's bulky silhouette around the skeleton walls of the ruined church.

Inside it seemed quieter than it had in the yard. Their steps echoed in the roofless nave as they came to a halt beneath a pier that had somehow survived the fire. Here they dropped their bundles and stood gazing up at the ghostly crossbar backed by the moonless sky.

"Was this your church?" murmured Barney.

"Trinity?" Alex shook his head. "Trinity was for Tories. We were Congregationalist. Our church burned. But I guess it could have been worse. Look at St. Esprit and the North Dutch—they made those into jails."

"Bloody redcoats! Bloody redcoats and Tories both," muttered Barney, drawing his knife to cut the cord that bound the sticks.

The watch was approaching by the time they'd finished arranging the wood. They let him pass, both of them lying flat against the wall, next to another wood stack Barney had stowed there earlier.

"All is well," chuckled Barney after the watch had gone on. "It ain't all well for someone—I wonder who!"

They had no particular victim, which Alex had seen as a mistake when Barney had first explained the plan. But Barney had brushed off his objection. "Town's crawling with them," he had said. "Besides, if you're counting on someone in particular, you're more likely to get caught. Always take what you're offered, that's the surest way. The less connection between you and your victim, the less chance of being tracked." Barney had explained his theories with a calm that had made Alex wonder if he'd done all this before.

"Personally, I'd rather have a redcoat," Barney confided as they left the church, carrying a stout sack and a length of rope. "Then again, a Tory would be easier to take. Less experience fighting, since most of them were too scared to enlist. Besides, His Majesty's forces might feel obligated to avenge one of their own. They'll never avenge a Tory. It's not worth the fuss." He paused to consider. "A drunken one would be best—and small, since we've got to haul him back to Trinity. A small, drunken Tory," he said reflectively.

"Why not a child?" Alex suggested sarcastically.

To his surprise, Barney shook his head somberly. "That would turn sentiment against us, sure as you're standing there. It would push away the very people we mean to attract."

The people they meant to attract were other patriots who shared their hatred of the British and their belief that even a lifetime of exile wouldn't pay the Tories back for what they'd done. Tonight they meant to serve notice that a new order had begun, and that any American enemy remaining in New York would be subjected to its justice when and as its enforcers chose.

When Barney had first announced to Alex their plans to strike, Alex had assumed that there would be more than the two of them. He knew the taverns and wharves of New York were filled with bitter, disgruntled men. He assumed that Barney meant to organize them in a group—much as the Sons of Liberty had been organized before the war.

But Barney was less of a one for organization than for secrecy. He believed that the taverns were crawling with British spies. Indeed, Alex was surprised that Barney trusted even him. As it was, Barney hadn't divulged the specifics of the plan until this evening, when they'd met up toward Greenwich Street to fetch the rest of the wood.

Barney's theory was that if you held meetings before you took action, you were likely to pull in the talkers, who'd balk when it came to real work. But if you *began* with an action—and especially a striking one—you'd weed out the fainthearted and save yourself a good deal of time. As for spies and traitors, you dealt with them as you went along. And you didn't trust anyone who hadn't proved himself. Privately, Alex thought Barney was too suspicious for his own good, but he was also flattered at having been chosen to come tonight.

They walked along the Broad Way north, toward the City Arms Tavern, probably the best known of all the Tory inns.

As if they shared the same thought, their steps slowed as they passed. Light shone through the windows. Although the hour was late there were still a few stalwart souls tipping a cup inside.

"Drinking away their troubles," Barney murmured, sounding pleased. "So I guess they'll need some new ones." He chuckled to himself.

Alex squinted at the windows, trying to see inside. Barney might be right about random victims, but picking someone who deserved what they meant to give him had a greater appeal. He thought of Marguerite's gross husband almost wistfully. His own connection to the Bridgehams would be all too easy to draw, but that didn't stop Alex from wishing it was Lord Bridgeham they were watching for in the darkness right now. Maybe they'd get him later, when they were more numerous. The idea sent a surge of power flooding through his gut. After all those months in prison, that power felt very good.

"Let's wait here for a few minutes," he suggested, nodding toward the tavern's door. "Maybe someone will come out soon and we can follow him."

"Can't hurt." Barney shrugged. "It's a long time yet till dawn."

They sheltered in the shade of an elm tree that had survived the fires. They settled themselves among its roots, but their wait wasn't long. They'd hardly been there five minutes when the door swung wide, pouring a wedge of bright light into the moonless night and silhouetting briefly the form of a man. The sound of voices swelled for a moment, then the door shut again.

"We're in luck," whispered Barney. "He's not big, and he's alone."

He was heading up the Broad Way, toward the streets behind St. Paul's.

"Whoring," muttered Barney, unnecessarily, for the streets between the church and King's College had been notorious even before the war. "Best grab him before he gets started. Here. Give me the sack."

Alex handed the sack to Barney, who fished inside for a length of cloth. "We'll gag him and bind him. Then we'll carry him."

Alex nodded in agreement, though, to his surprise, he felt a twinge of doubt. It was different than he'd imagined, different from the war. But this was a war, too, he reminded himself. This was more like what had happened before the war. Like the Stamp Act protests or the tea parties. Silent-footed, he padded along in Barney's wake.

They caught the Tory half a block up Courtland Street. They stopped at the corner to tie handkerchiefs over their faces so he wouldn't see who they were. Then, moving together, they took him all at once. He turned at the last moment and his eyes bulged with fear. No doubt he took them for the robbers that the town was crawling with. Perhaps he thought they were murderers, for he fought with surprising strength. Before Barney had the gag tied, he shook it off and screamed, so Barney slugged him hard across the face. Alex heard the soft crunch as the Tory's nose broke. He knew that Barney had to do it, but still it made him sick, just the way that battle had made him sick at first.

With a good deal of clumsy grappling, they got him bound and in the sack, headfirst, as far as he'd go. Barney picked up his hands and Alex took his feet.

"Get his hat," whispered Barney. So Alex got the hat and, for want of a better place to put it, stuck it on top of his own.

They couldn't carry him down the Broad Way without risking being seen, so they took him the back way, through blackened, empty yards. Alex was sweating profusely by the time they reached the church. There they unwrapped him and unbound his arms in order to retie them along the crossbar of the pier. Except for muffled groaning, he'd been quiet while they carried him. But once his hands were free, he began to fight again. He made a grab for Barney's mask but Barney jerked away. He looked ready to haul back and slug him again, but Alex intervened.

"Let's hoist him up," Alex muttered as he propped the Tory up beneath the arms. Using a rope as a lever, they pulled him up on the makeshift cross and bound him securely to it, both hand and foot. Then Barney reached into his coat pocket and took a paper out, which he unfolded and pinned to the Tory's chest. It read: "This is for burning our city—all Tories out of New York in two weeks!" It was sighed "Sons of Justice," Barney's choice of a name.

Meanwhile, Alex was busy with flint and steel. He had a bit of cotton, which flamed as it caught the spark, then burned with enough strength to light Barney's torch. Barney held the torch up to the Tory's face, and for the first time Alex got a good look at him.

He was older than Alex had thought, closer to forty than thirty, though it was hard to tell exactly since his face was distorted with fear, his eyes goggling practically out of their sockets and running with terrified tears. The gag was stained and dirty with blood from his broken nose, while his wig had fallen off and his real hair stood on end. Sweat poured down his forehead and mingled with his tears.

"Look at him," sneered Barney. "He believes he's going to die!"

Alex looked at the Tory. He didn't feel the way he used to feel before a battle. Before a battle, he'd felt completely there. At this moment, by contrast, he felt slightly removed, as though he were watching someone else doing this. He didn't feel the anger he'd imagined that he would, that bright and purifying rage that seemed to light the way. He felt slightly hollow and also slightly sick. But there was nothing to do but to go forward tonight and hope that the next time he'd feel that rage. Maybe if he knew the victim.

Barney was muttering something that Alex couldn't hear; he had his eyes closed as if he were speaking a prayer. Opening his eyes, he touched the torch to the wood on the ground. It was as dry as tinder and caught right away. "Good luck, Tory!" Barney snickered, holding the torch up high so that he could see the desperation contorting the Tory's sweat-soaked face.

The wood was burning more quickly than Alex had thought it would, and though they'd tied the Tory up high, the flames nipped at his feet. "Come on," he urged Barney. "We'd best be on our way."

Barney appeared not to have heard him. He was still looking up. "My Sarah looked that way when I found her," he said in a low flat voice. "Couldn't talk—just stared at me till she died."

"I'm sorry," muttered Alex. "Come on. We've got to go!" He gave a tug on Barney's arm.

Barney glanced around. His eyes flicked over Alex with just a hint of disdain. "Worried about our friend, are you? I wouldn't waste my time. He's not worth it," he said flatly, and made as if to throw down the torch. But at the last moment he changed his mind. Raising the torch, he touched it to the Tory's limp coattails. One of the tails began to smolder. "Let's go, then," Barney said, tossing the torch onto the fire and starting toward the hole where a window used to be.

"God!" muttered Alex, sweeping off his hat to beat out the smoldering coattail before it could catch. Realizing then that he still had the Tory's hat stuck on top of his, he took it off and tossed it behind him on the ground. Then he ran after Barney, who was already out of the church.

They cut down Wall Street, where they pulled off their masks and began to shout. "Fire!" Barney hollered. "Fire in Trinity Church!"

In less than a minute, voices rang out in the street and buckets banged against one another as the people appeared in their doors, paused and then set off in the direction of Trinity. Barney would have followed along, but Alex held him back. "He might recognize us, for God's sake! He could point us out!"

"He won't," responded Barney, disturbingly cool. "He was scared out of his wits. Besides, I'll bet that Tory will be gone within the week. Within a day, if he can manage. Did you see his face? Did you see his expression?" Barney chuckled to himself. Then he began to whistle softly beneath his breath. Glancing across at Alex, he slapped him on the back. "What's the matter, Beckwith?"

"You shouldn't have lit his coat. That could have killed him."

"Aw, I knew you would put it out. I only wanted to scare him. Forget it, I'm telling you. Well, Alex, my boy, we did it! You ought to be proud of yourself! Just wait until tomorrow. Then you'll see a thing or two! Come on! Fire makes me thirsty. I'll stand you to a drink!"

Half an hour later, after two cupfuls of strong punch, the chill had worn off Alex and he felt differently. He remembered his first battle and how appalled he'd been at its gore and sloppiness. Compared to that, he and Barney had done admirably. And at least they'd done something, instead of sitting around on their tails and grumbling about injustice into their tankards of ale!

Edward stood in silence, gazing down at the smoldering remains of the fire still sparking embers at the foot of the ghostly pier.

The church was empty. They'd carried the terrified victim away and the fire fighters had gone back home to sleep. Identifying himself as a doctor, Edward had had an excuse for interviewing the victim, as much as was possible, given the man's state of mind. Now he was contemplating what the man had said.

"I'd say it is beginning," Franks said quietly at his side.

Edward glanced over without surprise. He'd seen Franks among the onlookers when the fire had been put out and had assumed that he would come forward once they were alone. In response, he nodded briefly. "I suppose we should consider ourselves lucky that it's held off this long."

"Lucky." Franks gave a toneless laugh. "Did the victim say anything useful?"

"Maybe," Edward replied. "There were two men, both wearing masks. They must have picked him by random, coming out of the City Arms. They followed him up Courtland and jumped him from behind."

"Don't tell me where he was going."

"Actually, he was on his way to his lodgings on Greenwich Street. He's from Charleston. He came here a few months ago. After tonight, I imagine he won't be staying long."

"Did he see them?"

Edward shook his head. "I'm not sure he'd have noticed even if he had. He was sane enough to remember that there were two of them. One was big and one was little. Of the two, the big one was by far the rougher. He's the one who broke his nose."

Franks glanced around the silent church as though the walls might have developed ears. "What did the note say?"

"Just the usual about revenge. It gave a two-week grace period and was signed the Sons of Justice. Have you heard of that before?"

Franks shook his head slowly. "It's all new to me. I had no idea—nothing—that it would be tonight."

"What about that man, Silver?"

"I wish I could say for sure. He wasn't at his favorite taverns tonight, but that doesn't necessarily tie him to this. Anything else that might be helpful?"

Edward nodded. "Two things. They didn't mean to burn him. They hoisted him up too high for that and built the fire too low—and from what he said I'm fairly certain that they were the ones who gave the alarm. But at the last moment before they left him, the big one changed his mind and touched the torch to the victim's coattails. The small one snuffed the fire out."

"What else?" Franks asked.

Edward took a breath. "Just the look the victim saw in the big one's eyes. He said he looked like the devil. He said if he lives to be a hundred, he'll never forget that look."

Franks cursed beneath his breath. "Silver! I'd bet on it. You could have him arrested and held without a charge."

"And let the Americans turn him into a cause? That would do us more damage than we would have stopped. And, if it is Silver, it would serve his purposes."

"What's the alternative?"

"We watch him," Edward said. "Unless I'm very mistaken, whoever did this tonight meant it as the first act in an as yet unwritten play."

"Starring himself," muttered Franks.

"Who else?" Edward agreed. "I'd be surprised if he wasn't in some tavern celebrating right now and basking in the reaction this is sure to stir up among his compatriots."

"I'm on my way," murmured Franks, glancing again at the walls. "Why don't we meet tomorrow night and I'll tell you what I've learned."

"Eight o'clock?" said Edward.

"Eight o'clock is fine," Franks answered as he turned to leave the church.

Edward turned with him. As he did, he kicked something on the ground. Stooping, he groped until he found it with his hand. It was too dark to see it, but he could feel what it was: a cockade, such as the patriots wore on the rims of their hats. He carried it out of the church and to the nearest Broad Way lamp, where he and Franks inspected it in turn.

It was like a thousand others of its kind: a bit of pleated ribbon, gathered into a rosette and held by a metal clip. The only thing that made it special was that the clip was silver and on it were stamped the tiny initials A.B.

"A.B.," murmured Franks. It meant nothing to him. He glanced at Edward, but Edward didn't seem to have heard. He was staring down at the cockade but seemed to be thinking of something else. "Do you want to keep it or should I?" asked Franks.

This time Edward heard him. "I'll keep it," he said. He closed his hand on the ribbon.

Franks glanced at the shadows that banked either side of the street. "I'd best be on my way, then," he murmured. "I'll see you tomorrow night."

"Tomorrow," Edward answered, and stood listening to Franks's footsteps fade. When he was alone, he opened his hand again and stared at the bit of ribbon with it's en-

graved clip. To be sure, there must be dozens of other
A.B.'s in New York. It didn't have to be Alex Beckwith. But
then again, it could be. He remembered the argument between Susannah and Alex that he'd overheard that last day
at William Street. And then, too, he remembered how Alex
had turned down his chance at parole. No doubt about it:
Alex Beckwith hated the British as much as any man could.
He hated them enough to have done this. But had Alex
done it? That was the question—and the question whose
answer Edward was bound by duty to learn.

No. That wasn't strictly true. It wasn't as though he had
no choice about pursuing this. Franks had offered to take
the ribbon. He could have told Franks his suspicions about
Alex and sent him to find out. That way, if Alex was im-
plicated, Susannah would never know that he, Edward, had
even been involved. The possibility had hovered before
him, but then he had swept it aside. He couldn't send
Franks like a bloodhound into Susannah's life. Whatever
problems or pain that all led to, he had to go himself.

A dog barked hollowly from somewhere in the night.
Edward began walking in the direction of his rooms. As he
went, he recalled the last time he and Susannah had met.
He remembered the look of worry he'd seen on her face
when he'd mentioned Alex's name. Could Susannah have
known what Alex was doing? Could that be what her look
had meant? Then a new thought struck him. What if Susannah was involved?

He stopped dead in his tracks. But even as his heart began to sink, his mind reasoned that this was not her style.
Susannah wouldn't condone secret violence. Her style was
direct. She wouldn't be a part of creeping around and
scaring people in the night. If she was angry, she'd say so
right out loud. Or was he rationalizing? Was Susannah
guilty, too? And then there was the hardest question. What
was he planning to do?

Hearing the watch approaching, he began to walk again.
As he walked, the image of Susannah rose up in his mind.

Do you mean to trail my brother like an animal? she asked. Is it because you hate me for what I said to you?

No. No, it wasn't. He wasn't a vindictive man. He took no pleasure in the prospect of bringing Susannah more grief than she'd been dealt already in these last seven years. He didn't want to hurt her, but on the other hand, he had a duty to his country. He also had a belief. He believed that acts of violence such as this one tonight hurt not only Britain's rule. He believed that they also hurt America's chances for success. Lawlessness was demoralizing for both sides. It created fear and dissension at an already difficult time. Every ounce of energy that went into vengeful attacks would deplete the effort it would take to rebuild New York. Good people would become disgusted and bad ones would run wild.

You'd do the same in my position, he told Susannah in his mind. You said as much that day when I left William Street. You said that one should not let personal feelings interfere with one's principles. But what if those feelings were for your twin brother? Would you say the same?

He started with surprise as he heard a voice call out "Halt! Who goes?"

It was the watchman, holding his lantern aloft.

"I'm Captain Steel from General Carleton's staff."

"Have you something to prove it?"

Edward pulled out Carleton's pass and handed it across. The watchman scanned it by his lantern then handed it back. "I'd stay away from the American taverns if I were you. From what I hear the Americans are drinking hard tonight."

"I'll keep it in mind," said Edward, folding the pass away. He had no need to visit the taverns. Franks would take care of that—and, he hoped, have news to report when they met tomorrow night.

His problem was the Beckwiths. Slowly he walked toward his rooms, grappling with the prospect of discovering whether Alex was the A.B. of the cockade. If Alex had been there tonight, he'd been the little man, and the big one had been Silver—if Franks was right. If Franks was right about Silver, then he was the one to catch. Edward suspected that Alex was more of a follower, though just how dedicated a follower remained to be seen. Recalling the victim's description about being set afire by the torch, Edward wondered if Alex was having second thoughts about his new leader's sanity. Perhaps the knowledge that he was under suspicion would be enough to sever his involvement with Silver and the Sons. And what if, in addition, Susannah was also to urge him to give it up?

Silver, however, was a different case. He'd meant what he said to Franks. Unless they were careful, they might turn Silver into a martyr to extremists and moderates alike. But if they caught him in the middle of an act like tonight's, good citizens would be disgusted and cut him off.

Edward walked slowly all the way to his rooms, and by the time he approached them, he had the framework of his plan both for dealing with Alex and with Silver and the Sons. If it was Alex, he reminded himself. He had no doubts that he'd be able to learn the truth. The only question was what that knowledge was bound to cost.

Chapter Twelve

"Hanging from the beam he was, naked as when he was born and with a note pinned to him giving the Tories two days to be gone from New York!" Milly reached the end of both her story and her breath. She stood in the door of the drawing room, panting expectantly. She reminded Susannah of a dog they'd had before the war, who was always dragging the neighbor's possessions into the yard and presenting them to the family for reward and praise. "Two days!" repeated Milly, waggling her head.

"But if he was naked," pointed out Susannah, "then where could the note have been pinned?"

"To the skin of his chest!" declared Milly as Alex's door opened up above and his feet sounded on the stairs. He appeared, running lightly, straightening his stock with his right hand while he gripped his hat in his left.

"I might not be home for dinner," he called.

"Dinner! But what about breakfast!" Susannah planted her hands on her hips. "You're not as strong as you should be yet, you know. If you don't eat well, you'll end up back in bed!"

Alex only smiled. "I'll have something in town." His stock straightened, he pinched her cheek as he passed. "Don't worry, I won't starve, Susie!" He laughed as he went out.

"I declare!" clucked Milly. "He's in a rare good mood. And for having come in so late last night—I'd say he's got back his health! Do you suppose—"

But Susannah was already out the door. "Alex! Where are you going?" She caught him at the gate.

"Out and about." He grinned broadly and winked. "I guess you've heard about last night's fire. I want to hear what they're saying this morning."

"What were they saying last night? That's why you were out so late, wasn't it?" She held him by the sleeve, feeling more jealous than worried—the same jealousy she'd felt all those years ago when he'd marched off with the army and she'd been left at home.

Alex nodded. Susannah realized that Milly was right. He was looking better than he had since he'd been sick. "Last night they were saying it's about time that someone paid the Tories back for what they've done to New York."

"Did the note really give them two days to leave?"

"It gave them two weeks. And it served notice of what they can expect if they decide to stay." His grin broadened. "I don't think you'll see so many Tories strutting through the markets this morning as there were yesterday!"

"Good riddance." She released his sleeve, smoothing the material as she said, "The water boy told Milly that the note was signed 'Sons of Justice.' Have you ever heard of them?"

Alex's eyes narrowed and he paused before he replied. "Last night was the first time people heard of them. But I have the feeling that you'll be hearing again, and soon. Very soon, if I'm not mistaken." He drew a deep breath and looked up. "My, what a fine morning! The finest I've ever seen! Have a good time in your garden," he teased, pinching her cheek again.

She swatted his hand absently. "I want to come along."

"What? To the taverns? Don't be a goose!" He laughed. "All the men will be in the taprooms and you'll cause a scandal if you come in there!"

She tossed her head and retorted, "I don't care if I do!"

"But you will care," he assured her, "when I have to fight a duel to protect your honor! No, you sit tight here. I'll try to come home for dinner and I'll tell you everything." This time he gave her cheek a pat as he swung out the gate.

Susannah watched him stride away, a mutinous frown on her face—a frown that only darkened when Alex turned to wave. A moment later he turned the corner and disappeared. She stood there another minute, then marched back to the house, where she found Milly—as expected—watching from the door.

"You don't have to go to the taverns," Milly offered as she came in. "They'll be full of it in the markets."

Susannah turned and looked back at the street. Did Alex think she'd spend her morning weeding while he enjoyed himself? Did he think that things had changed so much from the good old days when they'd run down to the Fields or the Bowling Green together to listen to patriotic speeches and mingle with the crowds? She was glad that his dark mood had lifted, but just because it had didn't mean she'd turn into some docile woman to be left behind at home when excitement was stirring in the streets.

"Please fetch my basket," she said to Milly.

"Yes, mistress," Milly said. "Shall I go and carry it for you? I've already dusted downstairs and I've straightened the rooms except for Master Alex's, because he was still—"

"Yes, yes. Whatever you want," Susannah agreed, knowing that Milly would get nothing done if she left her behind. She also felt obliged to Milly and her mother, the cook, for staying at William Street after Edward had left on nothing more than the promise of future wages. Monsieur Binchot's draft had finally arrived a week ago, to Susannah's great relief, though it had been for less money than Susannah had hoped.

"It won't take me a minute!" Milly promised, and this time she flew, straightening her apron and cap as she disappeared.

"Men!" muttered Susannah, yanking her bonnet down from its hook. "Thinking they've got all the right to enjoy themselves!" She remembered what Amy had said about the war giving her the chance to do things she couldn't have done otherwise. If Alex's attitude was any indication, those chances wouldn't last for long. She hoped she'd run into him in the street. She wanted to see his face.

"Could we walk up to the Broad Way?" Milly asked, returning with the basket on her arm. "That's where they hung him. On a cross in Trinity Church!"

Tying her bonnet ribbons, Susannah nodded. "I don't see why not. Then we can walk down Wall Street."

"Oh, my, yes!" Milly gasped, almost undone by the promise of such an unexpected treat.

The sight of Milly's excitement made Susannah laugh, and she was still laughing when Milly threw open the door—and almost crashed into Edward, who was coming up the steps.

With a strong little gurgle, her laughter died away.

"Why, Captain Steel!" Milly exclaimed with undisguised delight. "Mistress Susannah and I were just going out! I guess you've already heard the news about last night! That is—" Flushing, she caught herself as she realized that Edward wouldn't have been overjoyed by the news. She started to apologize, but Susannah cut her off.

"Captain Steel hardly came here to gossip or pay a social call. What is your business?" she demanded in her brusquest tone, trying to ignore her heart, which had—as always at his appearance—begun to run away. He looked as tired as he had when they'd last met. But it wasn't his fatigue that stopped her. It was the expression in his eyes. He looked almost regretful. Regretful about what? For one baffled moment she wondered if he'd come today to reclaim the house.

"There's something I'd like to ask you," he said in a neutral tone. Pausing, he added, "Is your brother at home?"

"No. He's left already. What is it you wanted to ask?"

His eyes shifted briefly to Milly. "I'd prefer to ask it alone."

Something about his expression sent a little chill down Susannah's spine. Whatever was on Edward's mind was bigger than the house. What could be bigger? "Yes. All right," she agreed, and telling Milly to see to Alex's room, she led the way to the drawing room. Edward stood in silence as she shut the door.

"Well, what is it?" she demanded as soon as the doors were closed, hiding her misgivings behind an impatient tone. It was strange to be here with him again in this room. It brought back memories—and feelings—she'd prefer to forget.

For a moment he didn't answer. Then he held out his hand. "I wonder if you've ever seen this?" he asked as he opened it.

Susannah leaned forward. There, lying on his palm, was the liberty symbol: a red, white and blue cockade. "Yes. Of course I've seen it!" Looking up, she raised one brow. "What are you doing with that? Don't tell me you've decided to change sides?"

"It isn't mine," he said bluntly. "I'm wondering whose it is. I wonder if you know."

"How would I know?" she asked, as her eyes returned of their own volition to the ribbon in his hand. She looked at the ribbon, but she saw the hand—steady, long-fingered—a hand she knew all too well. Her legs began to tremble as if they, too, recalled the heat of those long fingers sliding across her skin.

"You might, if you looked at it," he persisted, holding the cockade out to her.

She jumped back as his hand came near, then she caught herself. Her heart was beating quickly, too quickly by far, and despite her best intentions, her cheeks had begun to burn. Embarrassed, she looked up and saw him read her mind. As he read it, his eyes changed completely. The look of regret fell away, and in less than a second they went from cool to hot. The trembling was spreading up through her abdomen. She was powerless to stop it.

Then Edward stopped it for her. With an effort that fairly crackled in the warm morning air, he quenched the fire in his eyes. Understanding her fear of them touching as though she'd spoken it aloud, he picked up the cockade with two fingers and held it out to her. "Take it, Susannah." This time it was a command.

Susannah obeyed in silence, holding out her palm. He dropped the ribbon into it, and although it was almost weightless, she gave a little jump.

She studied it closely, glad for an excuse to ignore both Edward and the hammering of her heart. The cockade was unremarkable: a ribbon gathered up into a rosette and held in the middle with a metal clip.

"Turn if over," ordered Edward.

She turned it in her hand, and saw the initials printed on the back. A.B. Alex Beckwith? She looked up, confused. "Where did you get this?"

His eyes bored into hers. She'd seen them like that before, but she couldn't begin to guess the reason for his present intensity until he spoke. "On the ground after the fire at Trinity Church last night."

"At Trinity Church?" she repeated. Then she understood. She saw how it might have happened. Fear and anger flashed through her. "Why did you bring it to me?"

"Was Alex at home last night?"

"What business is that of yours?"

"Why not ask yourself the same? You gave your parole for him, Susannah. You're responsible for what he does."

Another thrill of fear shot through her. Again, she pushed it off. "I trust my brother!" she retorted. "I'm gladly responsible."

His eyes shifted to the ribbon lying on her palm. She fisted her hand to hide it before she caught herself. "What makes you think that Alex is the only A.B. in New York? And even if it was his, what would that mean? It could have gotten into the church in a hundred different ways. He might have gone there last week—people do all the time. They find the ruins peaceful!'' She spat the word out with scorn.

"He might have gone to fight the fire, for all you know," she went on. "Or somebody else might have dropped it, hoping it would be found. You might have dropped it!'' she added, then cringed as she saw the astonishment ice over Edward's eyes. "I don't care what you think of me!'' She tossed her head defiantly. "And since you ask, let me ask you—what were you doing there last night?''

"I treated the victim," he said quietly.

For the first time she faltered. "Was he—was he hurt? I thought he was only frightened.''

"For the most part," he agreed.

"Well then," she concluded, "I don't see why you're so concerned.''

"He was only frightened, but he might have been killed. Two men took part in last night's attack. As they were leaving, one of them deliberately touched a torch to the coat of the victim until it caught fire. He would have been badly injured, had the other not put it out.''

"And you're implying that Alex would do such a thing?'' Fear bubbled up as anger, shouldering all other feelings aside. She was angry at his accusations and at the way he made her feel—all too conscious of her body, even at a moment like this.

Edward shook his head once. "I'm implying no such thing. I don't believe that Alex was the man with the torch. But if he's associated with such a man, I believe that someone should stop him before he stumbles into something very bad.''

"How do you know that man would have been injured?'' she challenged, struggling against what she felt. "For all you know, lighting his coat was part of their plan.

Maybe they did that just to frighten him, and they'd always intended to put the fire out."

"I don't think so," said Edward. "Not from what the victim said. Either way, Susannah, such violence leads to no good."

"It leads to no good for Tories."

"It leads to no good for either side." He was silent for a moment, his eyes studying her in a way that touched her pulse like a spark to a waiting fuse. He'd come to accuse her brother, and still she responded to him—and despite the cool logic in his eyes, she knew he felt the same. What was this force that bound them against reason and will? Had her pride not prevented her, she would have stepped away. It took a real effort just to stand her ground.

"Can't you see, Susannah?" Edward said at last. "What happened last night abases the cause your country fought for. It demeans your suffering. I saw the victim, Susannah. He wasn't the King. He wasn't a Lord Bridgeham. He wasn't even a Marguerite. He was just a man who was minding his own business when he was grabbed at random and frightened half to death."

"He was a Tory," Susannah maintained stubbornly.

Edward exhaled with impatience. "He was a loyalist. So, therefore, now the loyalists will have to avenge his fright by frightening a patriot—then the patriots will strike back, until there's a full-fledged battle raging in New York. And who will have been served by it? Who will have won?"

"If the British gave up New York, it wouldn't be your concern."

They were standing so close together she could feel him recoil at her words. "But it would be yours, Susannah. Goddamn it, can't you see!" In his frustration, without thinking, he seized her by the arms. "Can't you see?" he demanded, giving her a shake that caught her off balance and tumbled her into him.

She jerked at the contact as though she'd been burned. By the force of pure resolve, though his body ached for her touch, Edward held her from him, breathing heavily as though the force he was resisting were more than invisible desire. Was it invisible? His eyes locked into hers, which seemed to have ignited in the space of a single breath.

"You're hurting me!" she whispered.

"I can't help it," he whispered back, and gave up the struggle, pulling her hard against him.

She came without resistance, burning through to his very skin, burning beneath it, into his muscle and blood. Their mouths locked together, both devouring at once. Their hands grasped and grappled, straining for a tighter grip. They pressed against each other, trying to blot out the world, striving to drown out reason with their thundering hearts.

Edward held her shoulders; when he curved them back, her breasts thrust against him, their tips so hard that he could feel them drilling through all the layers of interfering cloth. She was wearing her bonnet, whose rim clipped his cheek. He tried to pull it off, and when that didn't work, he reached up underneath it, driving his fingers into her hair and pulling her head back until her mouth was pointing up. Then he bent forward, engulfing it with his.

Susannah groaned in pleasure as Edward's mouth covered hers, his tongue swooping and plunging so that she felt it everywhere. When his mouth released hers, she turned her head back and forth, offering him her cheeks, her forehead and her neck. It was as though nothing had happened since that moment in the root cellar—as though they'd stepped apart for an instant and now had stepped back again at the same pinnacle of yearning and desire.

His hands cupped her buttocks as his lips came down her throat and she arched against him, offering her breasts. He let his lips take her, then his lips were not enough. One hand remained behind her, but the other came up, cupping her breast and caressing, lifting it to his lips. She felt the heat of his breath through her bodice and she felt his teasing teeth. She thought she would swoon from the pleasure, but for his encircling arm. She felt him hard against her as she'd felt him once before, and everything ran together in a breathless, blinding swirl.

She gasped as he pleasured her other breast. One hand clung to the broadcloth of his coat, the other curled into a fist on his chest. As the sensation mounted, she brought her fist against his cheek, running her knuckle along the line of his jaw. At her touch, he turned his head and pulled her knuckle against his teeth, first biting, then stroking with his darting tongue.

His tongue found the sensitive places where her fingers joined her palm. It teased and invaded; she found it astonishing that such a small contact could make her feel so much, as if she were all bound together. As if she were bound to him. His tongue probed and darted, teasing open her fist—as though he were teasing open something else. Perhaps that was why she tried to resist him, and perhaps that was why it gave her so much pleasure to give in at last.

Her eyelids flickered open to watch the surrender. She saw that Edward's eyes were closed in the same ecstasy she felt, though where hers was of surrender, his was of possession. The sight of him made her tremble. It made her want to weep. His manliness alone sucked her breath away. Something hot and sweet washed through her as she uncurled her fist, exposing to Edward her open, virgin palm. His eyelids flickered open. In the same instant they both froze, for there, resting in her palm, was the forgotten cockade, which might or might not place Alex at the scene of last night's crime.

Susannah grunted as her breath left her lungs. Their bodies loosened and slowly disentwined, while all the time they both kept their eyes on the cockade.

At last they were fully separate, Susannah's palm out flat. She stared at it, feeling as though she were coming back from a long, long trip.

"I don't know," she whispered.

"Don't know what?" Edward rasped.

"I don't know if it's Alex's." She drew a long, shaken breath and raised her eyes to his. She saw herself reflected there, framed by the thin black circle around his irises. She saw that her lips were swollen and her eyes looked wild. She looked stunned and regretful, and Edward looked the same. She drew another breath and said, "But even if I did, I wouldn't tell you. Alex is my brother."

She felt him exhale, an exhalation that went on forever, like a bladder emptying of air. She almost expected him to collapse like an empty sack. But he kept on standing, looking down at her.

Edward stood that way for a long time, thinking of something to say. But there was nothing. There was no point in speech. In the end, there was only his tricorn, lying where he'd dropped it on the rug. He stooped to retrieve it and straightened his wig and clothes without looking at Susannah or she looking at him. He left without saying goodbye, and it wasn't until he was in the street that he remembered that the cockade was still in her hand. Then again, maybe he'd intended to leave it with her all along.

"Mistress Susannah?" Milly tapped timidly on the door. When she opened it, Susannah saw the basket on her arm. "Do you still want to go to the market?"

"What?" Susannah stared.

"To the markets. And down Wall Street. And to Trinity Church. You know, to see where the fire was."

"Oh. No, I don't think so. Why don't you go alone, Milly," Susannah said, feeling incapable of moving from the room. She would stay here forever. She would grow old and die. She would die thinking of Edward and with a heart full of guilty regret.

"But what shall I buy?" asked Milly. "I haven't got a list." She looked disappointed at having to go alone. But she'd rather have to go alone than stay at home.

"Buy whatever you like," said Susannah, fumbling in her purse for enough silver to cover the cost of a meal. It didn't really matter to her what Milly bought, since she doubted that she'd be hungry for at least another year, and she also doubted that Alex would be home to eat.

She was right about Alex. He didn't come home until late afternoon. He found her in the garden—Milly must have told him she was there. She heard him whistling as he came out the back door. She was on her knees weeding among the beans. She stayed as she was, waiting, until she heard his voice.

"Susie!" He was grinning. "I see that you took my advice."

"Advice?"

"About spending the day in the garden!" He was grinning to himself, thinking, as he'd thought all day, how very right Barney had been. Both last night and this morning, men were coming out of the walls, wanting to join up by the dozen with the Sons of Justice, "or whoever it was that strung that Tory up at Trinity!" Naturally, he and Barney had not announced their role, but it had tickled Alex to be sharing the secret. It had also tickled him to think of what lay ahead. He'd more than forgiven Barney for setting the torch to the Tory last night. If the redcoats had raped his wife, he'd probably feel the same. Besides, Barney must have realized that Alex would put out the fire.

"What's that you're doing, Susie?" he asked, bending forward and squinting for a better view. He'd drunk a lot of rum both last night and today, and his body still wasn't used to its effects.

Susannah didn't answer. Leaning back on her heels, she brushed off her hands and, reaching into her pocket, held something out to him.

He peered at her hand closely. It was dirty, and in the middle of the palm rested a little red, white and blue cockade.

"Is this yours?' she asked him.

He was carrying his hat beneath his arm. Straightening, he held it out and turned it all around. It was missing its cockade. Then he took the one she was holding. His initials were on the back. "Yes. It's mine." He nodded. "Did I lose it in the house?"

Susannah shook her head slowly. "No. You lost it at Trinity Church. Captain Steel found it last night. He brought it here today."

"He—what?" Alex lost his good-humored glow. "That redcoat scum! You let him into this house! I thought I told you—"

Susannah cut him off. "Were you there, Alex? Did you light that fire last night?"

Alex's mouth hung open. He closed it and studied her. "What if I did, Susannah? Are you going to turn me in? Do you mean to report me to your Captain Steel?"

"Of course not!" she snapped. "What do you think I am!" Standing up angrily, she brushed off her skirts.

"I think you're my sister," Alex said heavily, wishing that he was sober or at least seeing straight. "But you're not pleased with it, are you?"

"I don't know what I am," she answered, which was the perfect truth—a truth she'd discovered over the course of an afternoon's thought. "Did you do it, Alex?"

He nodded once. "Yes, I did, and what's more, I plan to do it again—and damn your Captain Steel!"

"Stop saying that!" snapped Susannah "He's not mine at all!"

"He won't stop me," Alex went on. "And neither will you. Do you want to stop me, Susannah?"

"I don't know," Susannah said. She turned to squint up at the sun, which blazed far too cheerfully for her present mood. "You know I hate the Tories as much as anyone. But I can't help but wonder where all this will lead. Scaring a thousand Tories won't bring Mother back. It won't give you Marguerite."

"I wouldn't take her if it did!" Alex's mouth turned hard with disgust. "But it will make our enemies taste the bitterness they've forced us to eat."

"Then what?" she wondered. "And aren't they bitter enough? The Tories are leaving, and so are the British. It's only a matter of time."

Alex was staring at her, his face drawn with surprise. "Listen to you," he said softly. "I can't believe that you're saying these things. You don't sound like the sister that I used to know."

"Maybe I'm not that sister. Maybe she's grown up."

"I've grown up, too, Susannah. I've gone to war—and to jail." The bitterness that had been gone that morning had all come creeping back.

The sight of it pained Susannah and made her feel more confused. "I'm sorry," she murmured. "It's just that I'm worried about you, doing things like that. People who play with fire can get burned, and I don't want you burned, Alex. I don't want you hurt at all. I want you safe, here with me."

"I'll be safe," Alex promised, his face relaxing at last. "I won't be hurt. I swear it. This is nothing compared to the war."

"But you don't know what kind of people you're working with. They could be—well, even crazy, for all you know."

For just a moment a shadow flickered across Alex's face as he thought of Barney raising the torch last night. Then he shook the doubt off and he smiled. "You worry too much, Susie. Nothing will happen to me." Moving to stand beside her, he slipped his arm around her waist. "I'm sorry about leaving you at home today. I know how you must have been feeling, and I won't do it again. It's been quite a day, Susie—just like after Lexington. In the taverns and the markets, people are talking of nothing else. Come back to the house and clean up, and I'll tell you everything!"

So he began to tell her, and she listened as best she could, but mostly as she listened, she was thinking of Edward Steel. However much Alex protested, she wasn't pleased with his new plan—except for the fact that it might help hurry the British home. Amid so much confusion, she was sure of only one thing: she wouldn't be safe from Edward Steel until he was gone from New York.

Chapter Thirteen

Edward pulled his watch out of his pocket and held it up to the candle that the tobacconist had left him to light the back room. Franks had said two o'clock and it was half past three. Anything could have happened. There was no way to know and nothing for him to do but to sit and wait. He slipped the watch back into his pocket and, for want of anything else to do, reopened the letter from his brother that had come on a packet from London that had docked yesterday.

St. John wrote that London's political atmosphere was every bit as unsettled as it had been when Edward had left. Portland's coalition was still doing its best to guide the government, while Pitt and Fox were fighting over it like dogs over a meaty bone.

> The King's devotion to Pitt is as strong as ever—almost as strong as the King's displeasure at the treaty terms. Still, it is generally hoped that he will not refuse to sign the final treaty, at such time as the terms are reached. And as far as we hear from Paris, that time may be soon. But no doubt you will have more news on that than I.

Leaving politics aside, St. John reached his bigger news. He was gong to be married! Or, as he said, "England's staunchest bachelor has finally succumbed!" Edward didn't know the lucky woman, whom St. John described as "Not so very beautiful, but very, very good."

> Which is to say that she is generally pronounced not to be "a great beauty." I suppose you'd think me besotted if I confessed that I find her more lovely than any woman on earth.
>
> Her parents are holding a betrothal party in a month, but we shan't have the wedding until you can be home—to hold me up at the altar in case my legs give way! But seriously, Edward, I'm the happiest of men. I know that when you meet her, you'll see the reason why. She sends you her warm regards and looks forward to your return.

After that, St. John turned abruptly to questions about New York—no doubt to curb his natural urge to go on about his fiancée. Edward smiled at his brother's happiness. Since he could recall, St. John had made friends of women rather than fall in love with them. There had been a time when he'd envied him the skill. Now he felt no envy. St. John deserved all his happiness. His smile lingered, until his eyes touched the letter's last lines.

> By the by, there's been a scandal here. Darbyshire's oldest son has run off and left his wife. Darbyshire ordered him back, but he flatly refused. Worst of all, at least to the gossips, is that his mistress is a chambermaid and unforgivably plain. Since his defection, his wife has not been seen.

So Catherine had been humiliated before all of society. The prize for which she'd betrayed him had eluded her. Edward stared at the letter, wondering that the story didn't make him feel glad—wondering that he felt so very little at all.

He'd been so quick to accept what he'd felt for Catherine as love. He wasn't so quick to say the same of his feel-

ings for Susannah, but all the same, he knew that whatever
he called it, it dwarfed anything he'd experienced before in
depth and intensity. If he hadn't admitted it before, their
last meeting had shown him just how uncontrollably strong
was the fire that burned between them—and how easily it
could flare. And how dangerous it was, he added. How
very dangerous, especially given what he knew about her
brother and what she didn't know about him. If she didn't
already, she might come to hate him one day.

He heard footsteps. He tensed, listening, and a moment
later, Franks opened the door.

He was out of breath from hurrying and apologized. "I
would have come sooner, but Silver was watching me. I had
to hang around the tavern until I was sure he was gone."

"You're certain he didn't follow you?"

"Yes, sir. Positive." Sweat glistened on Franks's forehead; he wiped it with his sleeve, bracing his hands against
his thighs as he caught his breath. The two weeks' grace
given the Tories by the Sons of Justice was up today, and
Franks had spent the interim working his way into Barney
Silver's trust—which was no small matter, given Silver's
suspicious mind. By this point Franks was virtually certain
that Silver was their man. Though Silver hadn't said so
plainly, he'd implied as much. There had been no further
actions by the Sons of Justice since the fire, but according
to Silver there would be one tonight.

Edward had told Franks his suspicions about Alex
Beckwith, as duty had required. He'd nursed a thin hope
that even if Alex was involved, somehow Susannah might
be able to change his mind. But his hope had been short-
lived in the extreme, for no sooner had he described Alex
than Franks had identified him as the man with whom Silver had been drinking the night of the fire. And since then,
Silver and Alex had continued to keep company, though
when Franks met with Silver, they always met alone.

Clearly Silver had been recruiting ever since the fire, but
except for Alex, Franks couldn't be certain as to who his
recruits were. Silver met with his men one by one, and

Franks didn't want to rouse his suspicions by watching him.
Now, however, all that was about to change. Barney had
invited Franks to a meeting that afternoon, at which Franks
had expected to meet the group's full membership and learn
the plans for tonight's action. Edward had already chosen
a dozen of the sharpest men in the city's barracks to go with
him tonight. All he needed was for Franks to furnish the
specifics of the rendezvous.

"How was the meeting?" he prompted, his eyes on
Franks.

"There wasn't one, if you can believe it." Franks shook
his head between breaths. "Not as we thought, anyways. It
was just me and Silver. He's still keeping us all apart—so
if anyone is a spy, we won't know the others until tonight.
And then—presumably—it will be too late." He wiped
away the sweat again and leaned back against the wall.

"But he told you the target?"

"Not even that." Franks blew out his breath in frustration, inhaled again, then said, "Silver wouldn't give me
anything but the point of rendezvous. We're to gather in a
warehouse down past Peck's Slip. Then we'll learn the
plan."

"Not even a hint?" asked Edward, keeping his own
frustration at bay. The cagier Silver became the more he
wanted him.

"Only that I'd approve." Franks grinned crookedly.
"Which narrows the target down to twenty thousand pos-
sibilities."

Edward didn't bother to return the smile. "What time are
you meeting?"

"Half past nine. I thought you could hide near the
warehouse and follow us from there. I went down there just
now to check it. That's why I'm so late."

"And?"

Franks straightened from the wall and shook his head.
"Silver's done his planning. There's nowhere near to hide.
The warehouse is isolated, and if there's a guard, you'll

have to keep your distance—too much distance, I'm afraid."

"Damn!" Edward cursed Silver beneath his breath. As much as he wanted the man on his own terms, he couldn't risk letting him get away and hurting whatever innocent victim he'd chosen for tonight. "We'll have to arrest him, if there's no other way—both him and Beckwith," he added, though Alex's name caught in his throat.

"I'm not convinced," Franks said slowly. "I think there's another way. When I was looking at the warehouse I had another idea. I found a place where you can hide not very far away. There's an alley off Water Street, just past the chandler's shop. I figure that we'll have to split up to get from the warehouse to wherever tonight's action is. If we trooped through the streets together, the sentries would be after us in a flash. So when I leave the warehouse, I'll manage to slip away."

"You think that you can do it?"

"I know I can." Franks met Edward's eye. "I know Silver. I know that he's got to be caught. He's been careful up till now. But he's also got a crazy streak, and crazy men aren't cautious. They forget and make mistakes. I believe that by the time we leave that warehouse tonight, Silver will have one thing and only one thing in mind. I don't believe I'll have any problem getting away."

After six months of working together, Edward trusted Franks. "All right." He nodded. "I'll be there at half past nine."

"We'll get him, sir," Franks promised.

"We'd better," Edward said.

Alone again after Franks left him, Edward stared at the flickering candle flame. Through it, he saw Susannah laughing and crying at dawn after Alex's fever had broken and she knew that he'd survive. He couldn't warn her of the trap. He wanted to, but he couldn't. They were standing on two different sides. The war still wasn't over, no matter what anyone said, and at this moment Edward wondered if it would ever be. He remembered how pleased he'd been when Carleton had given him this job. He'd seen it as a challenge. He must have been blind.

"Have some more of the trifle," Susannah offered Mr. Van Rijn. "It's made from those lovely eggs you sent us yesterday."

"Not even a spoonful. I couldn't!" Mr. Van Rijn touched his stomach and pretended to groan.

"Not even a spoonful, Father?" Amy clucked her tongue. "Why, I seem to remember a time not too long ago when you swore that when the war was over and there was enough to eat again, you'd eat a whole pudding by yourself each and every day!"

"I know, I know." Mr. Van Rijn patted his stomach again. "The mind is willing but the body must regain its capacity. It is something to look forward to!" he concluded happily.

"One thing among many others," Mrs. Van Rijn agreed.

"Many, many!" declared Amy, meeting Susannah's eye and exchanging a smile. It had taken well over a month to bring this dinner off. Most of the delay had been due to a bad summer cold that had made its stubborn, pernicious way through the whole Van Rijn family. But Amy had not forgotten, and as soon as the family was well, she'd sent word to Susannah that she'd spoken with her father and he was ready and willing to play his appointed part. Given Alex's involvement in the Sons of Justice, Susannah couldn't wait. Maybe she and the Van Rijns between them could talk some sense into him.

"Father will talk to Alex after dinner," Amy had confided when they'd arrived, her murmur covered by the rest of the family's chattering. "That way no one else can ruin the plan. I've only told Mother, and she thinks it's a splendid idea!"

Now, detecting the light blush of Amy's cheek, Susannah realized for the first time the plan's hidden benefits. Perhaps being around Amy would help Alex get over Marguerite. Susannah's smile broadened as she considered the idea.

"What about you, Alex?" she said, turning to him. "Can you fit in a bit more trifle? Alex?"

He jumped at his name. He'd been daydreaming, staring at his plate. "What? I'm sorry. What was it you asked?"

"If you wanted any more trifle," Susannah repeated patiently. For a prospective suitor, Alex was being very vague.

"Trifle? Oh, no thank you." He glanced around. "What about you, sir? More trifle?" he asked Mr. Van Rijn. He looked bewildered when everybody laughed.

"Woolgathering," fifteen-year-old Maria observed. "When a girl does that, it means that she's in love. I wonder what it means in a man?" She gave him a pert smile.

"Maria!" scolded her mother, but everyone laughed again—this time including Alex.

"Are you flirting with me?" he inquired, and Maria looked greatly pleased.

After the fruit was passed and eaten, the women left the men to their wine and went into the drawing room, where the balmy evening breeze tickled the draperies. Though September was waning, the weather had stayed warm—a boon to all the refugees who were living in tents.

"I hope Father doesn't forget," Amy murmured, watching as Susannah poured the tea.

"Doesn't forget what?" asked Maria, who had overheard.

"Doesn't forget none of your business," Amy replied. "And what you said to Mr. Beckwith was very rude."

"He liked it," Maria asserted, putting out her tongue. "I believe you're jealous of Mr. Beckwith's attention to me!"

"Why, of course I'm not!" declared Amy, turning almost as red as her hair.

That delighted Maria. "Amy's in love!" she crowed.

"Girls, please!" their mother clucked. She'd brought her workbasket and was knitting a sock. "My goodness, you'll make Susannah regret the hour that she asked us here!"

"Never," averred Susannah, passing her the first cup of tea. "I'm so happy to have you. It feels just like old times." She looked around and smiled. "Do you remember how it was before the British came? The house was always full of people, laughing and arguing."

"Mostly arguing, as I recall," observed Mrs. Van Rijn. She held up her sock and added, "Before the war this would have been a bit of fancywork."

"It will be again," Amy assured her. "There'll be plenty of time for tatting after the British are gone!" She smiled again at Susannah.

Susannah smiled back, but this time her smile was forced. Even the glow of old times couldn't soothe the distress that came with the thought of Edward—and, despite her best efforts, that thought came with everything. "I hope they leave soon," she murmured.

"They will," promised Mrs. Van Rijn. "Why, for all we know the treaty's already been signed and at this very moment the news is on the way to us! Then, Tories or no Tories, they'll just have to leave."

"The Tories will leave much sooner!" Maria looked up from stirring her tea. "The Sons of Justice gave them two weeks, and two weeks is almost up! Everybody's saying that something will happen soon."

"Who's saying that?" Susannah's stomach tightened with fear.

"Oh, people." Maria gave a vague wave with her spoon before laying it in her saucer in order to raise her cup. "I wonder what they'll do next!" she murmured over the rim.

"Do stop!" Amy hushed her. "What a thing to hope for! Anyway, I'm sure that note was an idle threat. The Sons of Justice were probably a couple of pranksters who had too much to drink one night. Don't you think so, Susannah?"

"Of course," Susannah said, already busy planning how she'd keep Alex in tonight.

The Van Rijns left at eight. When they were gone, Su-sannah slipped her arm through Alex's and led him back to the drawing room. First she'd try talking and then maybe a game of checkers. And then—well, she'd see then. Maybe Amy had been right. Maybe the two-week ultimatum had been an idle threat.

"Wasn't that nice?" she began when they were back in the drawing room. "It reminded me of the old days."

"With exceptions," he pointed out.

"Yes, of course with exceptions. But it was nice all the same. What did you and Mr. Van Rijn talk about after we'd gone?" She'd opened her own workbasket and was mend-ing one of his shirts.

"Nothing much." He shrugged. He was standing at the mantel, which was still bare, save for the clock. She'd kept the statuettes in their box; they reminded her too much of that night. "Mostly he was talking about his store. About how they're rebuilding."

"I think they're so brave." She sighed. "To do it all themselves. Other people might just let their debts sweep them away. But Mr. Van Rijn's determined to start again— and at his age!" She tied off the thread and snipped it, then examined the mended rent. "And without Gilbert to help him. Amy's helping him, you know." She smoothed the shirt and folded it with deliberate care.

"No wonder." Alex chuckled.

"No wonder what?"

"No wonder he asked me to help him, if he's reduced to relying on girls!"

"I'm sure that Amy's a fine—" Susannah began, then stopped. "He asked you to help him?"

Alex nodded once. "It was a generous offer. My help now in exchange for a percentage of the trade."

"I'll say it was generous! I hope you told him yes. Heaven knows we can use the money—at least till Father gets home!"

"I told him I'd consider it. After all, I ought to see to our affairs before I see to someone else's."

Susannah opened her mouth to point out that there was ample time for both, just as the clock on the mantel struck half past eight.

At the sound, Alex straightened. "I've got to be going out."

"No!" she cried, so sharply that his brows came down. "That is, I was hoping you'd stay in for once. Feeling so much like the old days makes me remember so much. Supper made me think about Mother and Father and how we all used to be. I'll be all right with the memories so long as you are here. But if you go out, Alex, I know I'll feel bad." The sentiment was maudlin, but the assertion was true. For a moment she thought that her plea had succeeded. His face flooded with regret.

Then he shook his head. "I'm sorry. But I've got to go. I'll stay in tomorrow."

"Why not tonight?"

"Because I've got an appointment."

"An appointment? With who?"

"With no one you know, Susie," he answered. Then he smiled. "Don't look so worried. It's nothing bad, I swear. I give you my word on tomorrow," he added, coming to where she sat and laying his hands on her shoulders as he bent to kiss the top of her head.

"Wait!" she called again as he left the room. But this time he didn't hear her—or pretended not to hear. Thrusting aside her mending, she went after him.

She followed him upstairs to his room, where she found him undressing. His coat and his waistcoat were lying on the bed and he had his back to her, rummaging in the chest. She stood at the door and watched him, unsure of what to say—until he straightened and she saw what he had in his hands.

"What's that for?" she demanded as he shrugged his arms into the shapeless homespun coat he'd worn when he'd first come home. "Alex, where are you going?"

"You sound like you already know."

"Is it the Sons of Justice?"

"It is, and don't look like that. It's not a funeral, Susie. Not mine, in any case." He left the coat unbuttoned and reached for his hat.

"What do you mean, funeral? Are you planning to kill someone?" Her voice inched up toward hysteria.

"Of course not!" Alex said. "Nobody's going to get killed. Only a bit shook up—or more than a bit," he added, his eyes hardening as they moved beyond her face. "But no one who doesn't deserve it. You can depend on that. When you hear the news tomorrow, you'll be glad of it. I guarantee."

Her heart froze with a sudden panic. "It isn't Captain Steel?"

"What do you take me for?" Then Alex's eyes sharpened as they scanned her face. "Would you care if it was, Susannah?"

"Of course not!" She tossed her head, if only because it let her turn her face so that he couldn't see the troubled relief in her eyes. But she was still worried. "Please don't, Alex," she begged.

"I have to go," he answered. "I've given my word. And even if I hadn't, I'd go anyway. I wouldn't miss tonight's action for all the gold in the world! I wouldn't trade it for a clear shot at King George!"

The lines of his face softening, he reached out to tousle her hair. "Don't worry so much, Susie. I promise I'll be fine. The only ones who'll suffer tonight deserve everything they'll get. Wait up, if you want to. I'll tell you about it afterward."

"Why can't you tell me now?" she protested.

"I'm sworn to secrecy." He bent to kiss her on the cheek, then left whistling "Yankee Doodle," a tune she'd once adored.

She listened as his footsteps faded down the stairs. When the front door didn't open, she got up and went into the hall. He hadn't gone out by the back door, for she'd have heard that one, as well. Then she heard him coming up the kitchen stairs. Why had he gone to the kitchen? She frowned as she moved down the hall. She ran down the first flight of the staircase, across the landing, then halfway down to where she could lean over and catch a glimpse of the rear hall.

She leaned over just as Alex came into the back hall. He had a sack in his left hand and something she couldn't see in his right. Then, as he reached the door, he pushed back his jacket and stuck the object in his belt. It was a pistol. He dropped his coat back into place, shouldered the sack and disappeared out the door. Susannah watched him, too startled to call out.

Not that her calling would have made a difference, she realized as her senses returned. She doubted she could have stopped Alex with anything short of physical restraint, and she couldn't have restrained him—not by herself, anyway. The urge toward hysterical laughter rose up in her again as she saw the fleeting image of her binding Alex to his bed-posts with Milly's bewildered help.

Hysteria wouldn't help her. She swallowed hard. Alex had had a gun. Why—since he'd promised that no one would be hurt? And what had been in that sack, which he'd hoisted so effortlessly? And why had he gone to the kitchen? she wondered last of all. But this last puzzle was the easiest to solve. He must have hidden the things in the root cellar—his old trusted spot. Was there something else still hidden? she wondered as she came down the stairs. Perhaps there was still something that might give her a clue as to where he was going. Suddenly she had to know.

She picked up the candle he'd left burning in the hall and used it to light her way down the kitchen stairs. She hesitated for a moment outside the cellar door as all the old fears and demons reached out to tickle the back of her neck. Then she pushed the door open, turning as she did so that the first draft of coolness wouldn't extinguish her light.

Slowly she turned back, trying to ignore the shadows that danced along the walls, and also trying to ignore the echo of Edward's voice whispering, "I want you!"

She shivered despite herself, sweeping the candle over the floor in a search for where Alex had hidden his things. She hadn't been down here since that night Edward had dug up the statuettes, and now she saw that he had filled in the hole and scattered it with sand so that she could hardly tell where the spot had been. As if it had never happened. Except for the fact that it had.

She dragged her eyes away from the spot and found Alex's hiding place in one corner, behind the barrel on which she'd sat as she'd watched Edward dig. The sand there had been scooped out to fit the sack, in which he must have hidden the gun. Alex wouldn't have gone to the trouble of burying his things, believing that the cellar was unlikely to be disturbed. The last of the previous winter's stored vegetables would have long since been used up, and it was still too early to think of storing this year's—all of which made the cellar a perfect hiding place. Alex would have known that his things would be safe just tucked out of plain sight.

She held the candle close to the ground in her search for clues. But the ground yielded nothing but a scattering of chicken feathers drifted about on the sand.

Feathers. She straightened up. That's why Alex had hoisted the sack with such ease. It had been full of feathers! And someone else must have the tar. In a flash, Susannah knew the substance of the plan—and unless she was mistaken, she knew its object, too.

"When you hear the news tomorrow, you'll be glad of it, I guarantee," Alex had answered when she'd asked him for the victim's name. And then there was the grim look that had hardened his face. She was almost certain he'd been thinking of Marguerite.

Did he mean to tar and feather Marguerite? She'd seen Tories tarred and feathered in the years just before the war. It was a painful procedure and often left dreadful scars, especially when combined with being ridden on a rail. But women weren't tarred and feathered; it simply wasn't done.

Which meant that tonight's victim was probably Bridgeham himself—and if he didn't deserve what was coming, she didn't know who did.

Holding the candle aloft, she looked around the room. Again she heard Edward, but this time with different words. This time he was asking her about the purpose of violence, and describing its dangers as well as its pointlessness. Alex had promised that he'd be all right, but Alex had taken a gun. And Alex had promised the same thing when he'd left eight years before. He'd promised he'd be back soon and they'd all celebrate. But she wasn't celebrating, she was afraid. This time the cause wasn't freedom. This time the cause was revenge.

For the first time, with chilling clarity, she saw the difference between the two. Freedom was a thing of the light, but revenge was dark. It gave men secrets and sent them creeping like criminals in the night. Suddenly she recalled what Edward had said about the second man at Trinity Church, the man who had deliberately touched the torch to the Tory's coat. A deep fear loomed up before her and embraced her with icy arms.

She shivered violently. The cellar was freezing cold. She pulled the door open and practically ran up the stairs. But even the balmy drawing room felt chilly now, and she couldn't get away from the image of the terrified Tory and the specter of what could go wrong. What if someone shot Bridgeham or Marguerite? What if someone betrayed the Sons of Justice and Alex was hurt, even killed?

The night lay inky black against the tall windows. She set the candle on a table and wrapped herself in a knitted shawl. But the coldness was inside her and she couldn't drive it out. She saw a man raising a torch and touching it to Marguerite. Marguerite was screaming, her mouth a gash of red, and there was fire, awful fire everywhere.

Her head jerked up. Was she dreaming? The scream had sounded so real. Her heart was racing wildly and her cheeks were clammy with fear. Had the scream in her mind been a warning? She didn't believe in such things, but she had an awful premonition that she ought to believe this time. Alex was in danger. There was danger everywhere. She had to stop it. She sprang to her feet.

She was out the door and into the street before she paused to ponder what she intended to do. Did she mean to burst into the middle of the attack on Bridgeham and try to stop the Sons? If she did, Alex would never forgive her and the rest would think her insane. Nor would that do any good. If she couldn't stop her own brother she had no hope with the larger group, and her interfering would only make things worse.

But had that really been her intention when she'd rushed out the door? Hadn't her first thought been, as always, to run for Edward's help?

At the thought of Edward, her heart leapt, then fell. How could she go to him this time? He was the enemy. He was a redcoat captain. He'd turn Alex in. But better to have Alex reported than outright killed. Besides, Edward hadn't reported Alex when he'd found that cockade. Instead, he'd used that bit of ribbon to try to reason with her. And before that, he'd gotten Alex out of jail and moved them back to William Street and saved Alex's life. Edward had solved every problem she'd laid at his door.

Suddenly, in the midst of her panic, she knew that, redcoat or not, she trusted Edward more than she did anyone else in New York. She trusted him more than she trusted Alex—perhaps more than she trusted herself. Suddenly, all she wanted was Edward at her side, with his comfort, his reassurance, his strength and his wit. She wanted the part of him that saved her and the part that stirred her both.

The scope of her wanting might have slowed her, but the urgency drove her on. She knew where he was living because he'd had his things sent and Milly had seen the address and repeated it to her. She ran there as quickly as her legs and her lungs would allow, and with every step she was praying that she'd find him in. He wouldn't turn her away if she asked him. And he'd know what to do.

William, the sloe-eyed valet, opened the door when she knocked. In response to her urgent question, he said that his master was out.

"Out where?" she demanded, dangerously close to tears.

"Can't tell you that, mistress," William replied with a genial shrug. "He went out after supper and said that I shouldn't wait up." His brows rose suggestively at the thought of where Edward might have gone.

Tonight she was beyond the pettiness of William's look. She didn't care what Edward was doing, so long as she knew where he was. "If he does come back," she told William, "please tell him that I called. Please ask him if he would come to my house right away. Right away," she repeated.

"Yes'm," William said. "I'll be sure to tell him," he assured her, and shut the door.

Alone and empty-handed, Susannah turned back to the night. She could still hear the fire roaring in her ears and Marguerite was still screaming. What was she going to do? Without Edward, who could she turn to for help?

Chapter Fourteen

Light from the full moon filtered through cracks in the warehouse and lay in milky splotches on the walls. It reflected with pale silver on the faces of the men who were gathered in a circle, listening while Barney spoke. The men numbered two dozen, give or take a few. They were all watching Barney, though most of them glanced away once or twice to scan the faces of their comrades, whom they'd never met before. Alex lounged against a wall, the sack lying at his feet. Beside it was a pile of sheets. The tar was waiting for them, hidden away near the Bridgehams' house.

"I'll go in through the window and open the back door," Barney said. "Beckwith and three others of you will be waiting there for me. While we tie up the servants and grab the lord and his lady, the rest of you will wait outside. You'll have to keep an eye out in case any neighbor overcomes his fear of cutthroats and robbers enough to spread the alarm to the guard."

"What about sentries?" someone asked.

"There won't be any," said Barney. "We'll take care of them first." He held up a coil of rope and a strip of cloth. "Knock them out, bind them and gag them."

"What if they put up a fuss?"

"Hit harder," Barney said. "Redcoats have hard heads and Tories are even worse. Don't worry about being gentle."

A couple of the men guffawed. The mood was restless and eager, but it was wary, too. From where he was standing, Franks surveyed the group. Some of the men had been drinking and seemed to be spoiling for a fight, but none of them had Barney Silver's calm intensity—not even the man called Beckwith, who was standing at his side. The sight of Silver's calmness reminded Franks of his assurance to Captain Steel that crazy men make mistakes. Just now Silver didn't look too crazy. He'd better hope that he'd been right.

At Silver's direction, Beckwith began to hand out sheets. "These are our disguises," Silver explained. "Take a minute to add your eyeholes wherever they're comfortable, then refold the sheets and tuck them beneath your coats. We'll put them on at the Bridgehams'. You can fasten them with your belts."

"Are we going there together?"

"To be sure!" Silver's smile was cold. "Carrying the feathers and beating on a drum! What do you think?" he demanded to the questioner's embarrassment. "We'll split up by twos when we leave here and all take different routes. Stick with your partners and be quick. If anyone does stop you, remember that one of you's drunk and the other is taking him home. Think up a name and address, preferably not your own. Any questions?"

There were none. Silver scanned the group. "We'll meet in the backyard along the house. Not a word, not a sneeze, not a sound. Understood?"

It was. A few muttered. The rest of them bobbed their heads. Silver and Beckwith stood at the warehouse doorway, counting them out by twos and holding the next two back until the last had vanished into the night.

Franks lined himself up beside a man whose shaggy beard didn't hide the timidity in his eyes. The man would be easy to shake off, he thought as they moved to the door. But just as they reached it, Silver's eyes swept over Franks, then he pulled him out of line.

"You'll go with Beckwith," he said. Franks nodded acquiescence, as he had no choice. He stepped aside and waited while the rest of the men passed by, appraising his new partner out of the corner of his eye. Beckwith held himself with the particular quiet of the high-strung. He was small but Franks guessed he'd be agile in a fight. Moreover, he had a pistol stuck into his belt. His expression left no doubt that he was looking forward to what lay ahead, and that he wouldn't take kindly to anyone who interfered.

Silver paired himself with the last of the men. Before he left, he drew Beckwith aside for a brief whispered conference. Then they all left at once: Silver and his partner up Ferry, Franks and Beckwith along Queen.

Beckwith set a brisk pace that Franks easily matched, though as he jogged along he was wondering what Silver had been whispering about. But there was no time for second-guessing. He knew what he had to do. He jogged a few yards farther, then stopped suddenly.

"Wait up!" he whispered, but Beckwith had already stopped. "Nature calls," he apologized, clutching his stomach with both arms. "It was always like this before battle." He glanced at the house closest to them. "There must be a necessary in the yard. Go on without me if you don't want to wait."

"I'll wait," Beckwith muttered, though he looked far less than pleased.

For a moment Franks thought that Beckwith would follow him into the yard, but to his relief, Beckwith stayed on the street. As closely as he could gauge it, the yard he'd picked ought to back onto the alley in which he was supposed to meet Steel. He ran silently through the shadows and vaulted the wall.

Crouching, he scanned the alley, but it was too narrow and deep to profit from the silvery light of the moon. He squinted through the shadows and thought he heard something move. Cupping his hands to his mouth, he half whispered, half called, "Steel?"

"No such luck, Franks," said a cool voice in his ear.

Damn! It was Beckwith. Franks knew it was even before he turned. Even in the dimness, he could see that Beckwith's face looked as unforgiving as did the pistol he held. He nudged Franks with the barrel to push him against the wall. "The Steel you were calling isn't a captain by any chance?"

Franks didn't bother wasting his breath in reply. He wondered if Beckwith meant to kill him. He assumed that he did and was running through possible defenses when another voice cut the night.

"I told you. The man's a Tory. I can smell them a mile away!" declared Barney Silver, emerging from the night.

Alex turned, startled. He hadn't heard Barney's approach. Moreover, he didn't like Barney's being here, when they'd agreed that Alex would handle Franks if Barney's sense about him turned out to be correct.

"Where's your partner?" Alex asked Barney.

"I sent him on ahead." Barney jerked his head in the direction. "What are you waiting for? Kill him. Even if someone hears the noise, they'll only bolt their windows so that the robbers don't come in."

"I want the name," said Alex. "Of the man he's supposed to meet."

"Forget it," grunted Barney. "We've got more important affairs. The man's a traitor. That's all you need to know." He glanced at Franks, then spat sideways on the ground. "Goddamn stinking Tory," he muttered beneath his breath.

Alex cocked the trigger and swallowed hard. He could feel both Barney's and Franks's eyes watching him: Barney's insistent and Franks's resigned. He'd fought five years as a soldier and killed his share of men. But those men had been coming at him and they'd all been armed. This man was defenseless. This was murder in cold blood. "Why don't we take him with us. We can question him later on."

"I've got no questions for him," said Barney. Before Alex could blink, he pulled his knife from his belt and drove it into Franks's chest. Franks grunted thickly and collapsed when the knife came out. Barney leaned down briefly to wipe it on Franks's coat. Then he touched Alex. "Come on. Let's go."

He set off and Alex followed, turning once to look back at the huddled shadow that had been Franks. Of course the man had been a traitor and had probably deserved to die. But his sudden death had sapped the excitement out of the night, so that when they emerged from the alley, the moon seemed so dim that Alex glanced up without thinking to see if it had gone behind clouds.

Edward jogged down the street, trailed by a dozen fully armed men who were doing their best to keep their footsteps light. He'd been at the barracks collecting his troops when someone had rushed in to summons him to the barracks master's house. The barracks master's daughter had fallen on her hearth and terribly burned her left arm and the side of her face. He couldn't leave her as she'd been, so he'd done what he could do—keeping a wary eye on the barracks master's clock. It wasn't until he'd finished and checked his own watch that he realized the clock had been half an hour slow. Even running, he was cutting the time very close. He prayed that the meeting at the warehouse would have delayed Franks.

He signaled the men to slow down a block away, then proceeded more slowly toward the alley's mouth. The alley lay in shadow.

"Franks!" he called. He listened and heard silence. Then, as his eyes adjusted, he saw the heap on the ground. A knot gripped his stomach. With luck it might not be Franks. It might be a pile of garbage. But his luck was not in tonight. He dropped to his knees in the darkness and felt Franks's neck for a pulse.

He located a weak one. He also found the blood, and the warmth of it told him by how little he'd missed. With terse, murmured directions, he sent three men out for a lantern and for the means to carry Franks. Then, in what light the moon afforded, he bent down to do what he could.

In loosening Franks's clothing, he discovered a sheet tucked beneath his coat, which he ripped into pieces and used to stanch the flow of blood. When this was accomplished, he made a quick survey of his pockets in the glimmering hope that Franks might have been the victim of a robbery. But the hope ended with his discovery of an untouched purse—which meant that Franks had been left for dead by the members of his group.

"Damn!" cursed Edward in anger and in guilt. If he'd been here sooner, Franks might not have been hurt, or at least there would have been two of them to confront the attackers. Worst of all, he had no way of knowing where the rest had gone or who else might be left to die before the night was through.

Footsteps sounded in the alley as the men returned with the lantern and a stretcher they'd gotten from a house.

"Take him back to the barracks hospital," he ordered two of them. "If he regains consciousness, ask him to tell you the plan. Report it to the nearest officer before you come looking for me."

"Where will you be, sir?"

"Looking for trouble," Edward said.

The rest of the men followed him from the alley back into the street. He had no way of guessing where the Sons might be bound, but he could think of someone who might know. Whether or not she'd tell him was a different case, but he had no choice but to ask her. She was his only chance.

They were running up Beekman Street when he heard someone call his name. Turning, he saw Susannah. She was running, too, waving one hand while the other clutched at a shawl, which was trailing behind her as she rushed up the street.

"Edward! Oh, Edward!" She was badly out of breath. "William said you'd gone out! I've been looking everywhere!" With her free hand, she grasped his coat sleeve as if to hold herself up.

He covered her hand with his. It was icy cold, though she was dripping with perspiration. "What is it, Susannah? Why are you looking for me?" He chafed her hand without thinking, trying to bring her some warmth.

"Alex!" she gasped, her eyes wild. Then she saw the men, who had stopped and were watching this latest development.

"Never mind them," he commanded. "Tell me where Alex has gone."

"To the—" she began. Then her eyes widened. "How did you know?" she asked.

"I haven't time to tell you. Susannah, a man's been stabbed. There might be others if we don't get there in time. You've got to tell me!"

"To Lord Bridgeham's!" she burst out. "At least that's what I think. They've got tar and feathers and a gun—Oh, Edward, take care of Alex. Please don't let him be hurt!" Her hand turned to grasp his hard.

"I'll do what I can," he said grimly, disengaging his fingers from hers. He squeezed her hand, then released it. "Go home and wait there."

"Please let me go with you!" Her eyes, dark and frightened, pleaded with his.

He shook his head slowly. "No, Susannah. It's no place for you. If you go home I promise I'll do my very best. If you do, I'll come to you as soon as I possibly can. I promise," he repeated, his voice softening. He took her by the shoulders and held her a moment before he turned her back toward William Street and gave her a little push. She glanced back over her shoulder, that same haunted look in her eyes, but to his relief she began moving away. He waited until he was sure. Then he turned back to his men.

"To the Broad Way, and quickly! There's no time to lose!"

Susannah turned back in time to see him go. Her body was still freezing except for the places he'd touched, and she could feel her whole soul trying to curl into those bits of warmth. She ached to go with him, not only to have him near, but also to spare herself the awful ordeal of waiting alone and imagining what was happening out there in the night with tar and feathers and Alex and Edward—and a gun. She knew that there was nothing she'd be able to do except add to the confusion of the darkness and the men. Whatever could be done for Alex, she knew that Edward would do.

"But, oh, Edward," she whispered, "take care of yourself, too!" She pressed her hand to her icy lips and stared at the spot where he'd been. But the emptiness scared her, so at last she turned away and began walking back home to William Street, praying that when she got there that Marguerite's screaming, which still echoed in her ears, would have stopped.

Marguerite was dreaming about being presented at court when she was awakened abruptly by something clamped over her mouth. It was a man's rough-palmed hand. She tried to scream and gagged. Then she saw two empty-eyed ghosts bending over her bed. She gagged again, this time in terror. The man took his hand away, and in the next instant a cloth was stuffed into her mouth and another one tied tightly around her head.

"Tie her hands behind her," ordered a voice.

Despite her terror and confusion, Marguerite realized that the ghosts were human: men dressed up in sheets. The fact brought small comfort, for she could only guess what they were doing in her chamber. Mutely, she pleaded with them. Take my jewels, my clothing. Don't hurt me, please! The words came out as a whimper. One of the ghosts glanced at her, and from deep within the eyeholes she sensed his contempt.

She was afraid that they meant to rape her after they'd robbed her room, but as soon as they'd bound her, they dragged her up off the bed and half dragged, half prodded her across the rug to the door. At that point she became aware of other people in the house. In the hallway she came

face-to-face with her husband, who was being propelled
along by two more ghosts.

Both groups came to a standstill when they met, and the
ghosts that were holding Lord Bridgeham looked her up
and down with an attention to detail that made her skin
crawl. "She's a looker, all right," one ghost said. "Though
I can't say much for him."

"He's got money," replied the one of her captors who'd
shown her his contempt. His voice was familiar, though she
was far too shaken to put a name to it. Then the pause was
over and they were moving again, she first, then Bridgeham following, down the hall toward the servants' stairs.

There was no sign of the servants. She wondered if they'd
been killed or merely bound and gagged as she was, somewhere in the house. A new fear seized her as she wondered
what lay in store. If these people weren't robbers, then what
did they want?

She lost her footing on the stairway and would have
tumbled headfirst had the ghost whose voice was familiar
not caught her before she fell. For a moment his arms
gripped like iron, then he let her go as though her very
presence were repulsive to him.

They shoved her out the back door into the arms of a
dozen more ghosts. A bad smell assailed her nostrils: the
smell of heated tar. Then she saw the barrel. She gagged
and began to fight.

"Be still!" Her captor gave her a shake. "It's meant for
his lordship!"

That was bad enough, but not quite as awful as the
prospect of being stripped of her nightgown and subjected
to the pain and humiliation that Bridgeham was about to
face. She turned her head to where they had just led him
out. He was also struggling and must have seen the tar.
Despite his gag, he was bellowing. The sound was terrible.
Had Marguerite's hands been free she would have pressed
them to her ears. Had she not been so terrified, she would
have shut her eyes. She had never felt so helpless, not even
during the war.

One of the ghosts struck Bridgeham a blow across the back. He staggered, but they caught him before he could fall.

"That ought to keep him quiet," a muffled voice observed. "Let's get him ready."

Now they were stripping him. His body looked pale and bloated in the harsh light of the moon. Marguerite turned her head away, then felt it turned back again.

"Look at him," her captor commanded. "You chose him, now look at him!"

That voice... They had the tar now. They were starting to smear it on. At the first touch Bridgeham's eyes dilated and tears of pain poured from them. The sounds that he was making were almost animal. Marguerite realized she was crying, choking on her own tears. Bridgeham's bellowing grew louder: awful, muffled shrieks.

Then, all of a sudden the ghosts threw down the tar and everyone was running, like a blizzard in the yard. Through the blizzard she heard shouting.

"Bloody hell!" someone cursed behind her, and she felt herself released. She staggered, thrown off balance, but managed to keep on her feet as the hooded captors vanished over the back wall and soldiers poured out from the house and scattered, some going where the ghosts had gone and others staying behind.

Bridgeham had toppled and was writhing on the ground, horribly naked and streaked and reeking with tar. Marguerite stared at him, too horrified to turn. A moment later a man knelt at his side, and she was astonished to recognize Captain Steel.

The arrival of two soldiers to aid her blocked him from her view. One unbound her while the other untied her gag. Between them they helped her up the back stairs and into the house. They'd just found her some brandy when Captain Steel reappeared.

"Captain Steel, thank goodness! You saved our lives!" She clutched his hand with both hers. "Is Lord Bridgeham all right? Did you catch them?"

Gently but firmly, he freed his hand and replaced it with her brandy glass. "Your husband is sore but will recover. We've caught a few of your attackers, but most of them got away. You didn't recognize any of them?"

"How could I? They were wrapped in sheets. I woke up and saw them. I believed that they were ghosts!" She shuddered at the memory. He guided her glass to her lips. After a long swallow, she felt her calm return. Memory returned with it. She raised puzzled eyes to him. "One of them did sound familiar," she said slowly. "The one who told me to look at Bridgeham when they—" Her eyes opened very wide. "It was Alex—Alex Beckwith! I'm positive it was!" She stared at Captain Steel in shock and surprise.

He seemed almost unsurprised. "Anyone else?" he asked calmly.

No, and she didn't care. "I want him arrested!" she demanded. "I want him locked up! How can my husband or I feel safe with him loose on the streets? He's a dangerous criminal! His whole family is dangerous! This is the second time they've attacked us! You will arrest him?"

"Yes, we'll arrest him." Captain Steel bowed his head. He seemed almost reluctant.

She narrowed her eyes. "Don't you believe me?"

He sighed and raised his eyes. "Yes, I believe you, Lady Bridgeham."

"Well, that's better." She sniffed—and it wasn't until sometime later, when the brandy had done its work, that she recalled his connection with the Beckwiths and the rumors that she'd heard. When she did, she smiled smugly. It would serve Susannah right. And as for Captain Steel, she didn't feel sorry for him. She'd warned him about the Beckwiths from the very first.

Susannah threw open the back door as soon as Alex knocked. "Then he found you—thank God!"

He didn't pause to reply, brushing past her welcome with the briefest of caveats. "No one! Tell no one! I was here with you all night."

"But—"

But he was gone, through the hallway and running down the kitchen stairs, hiding who knew what in the root cellar this time.

She collapsed against the closed door, grateful for the support, since her entire body was trembling with relief. She couldn't have said how long she'd been waiting since Edward had sent her home. She had been so frightened it had seemed like a lifetime since. And Edward had kept his promise—Alex was safe and whole.

"Thank God!" she murmured, brushing away a tear.

Alex climbed the stairs more slowly than he had gone down. Almost with deliberation, she thought as she waited for him. When he reappeared, he was frowning.

"Then *who* found me?" he asked. "What did you say when I came in just now? Thank God that *who* found me, then? Tell me, Susannah." He crossed the hall to her with a look on his face that made her feel almost afraid.

"Alex—" She took a step backward.

"Who did you tell?" he demanded. "Was it that redcoat captain? Was that how he knew where we were?"

She wanted to deny it, his anger was so cold. Then she remembered what Edward had told her about someone being stabbed.

"Who was stabbed, Alex?"

"Nobody," he said. "A Tory informer." He shrugged the words away, not wanting to be deflected from the issue at hand. "Did you tell that redcoat Steel?"

"Yes, I did." She straightened from the door's support and faced him defiantly. "I was scared, Alex. I was afraid for you. I kept thinking about that man setting the Tory on fire, and then, with Marguerite, I thought you might lose your head."

"So you betrayed me to a redcoat?" His voice rose incredulously. Then he flinched physically before an even more dreadful thought. "How did you know where we were going? Were you in league with them?"

"Alex! You know I wasn't. I guessed it from what you said. Tell me what happened?"

"Tell you!" He spun away and threw up his hands. "You betrayed us to the redcoats. They've got some of the men. The rest of us were lucky. We managed to get away. How could you do it, Susannah? How could you turn on me?"

I didn't turn! she wanted to cry. I was trying to save you from yourself!

"Who stabbed the man, Alex?"

"What man?" He glanced around. His eyes were like ice in winter when the river freezes hard. "I don't know about any man. I was at home all evening. I was right here with you."

She faced him, pale and heartsick. Then someone pounded on the door.

Alex stiffened. Fear and anger shot through his eyes. "With you!" he rasped, reminding her. Then he bounded away up the stairs.

Susannah listened to his footsteps, sickened clear through to her soul. Then, as the pounding was repeated, she went to open the door.

To her relief, it was Edward. "Oh, Ed—"

He cut her off. "Is Alex here, Susannah?"

At his expression, the sickness came rushing back. Silently she nodded.

"Where?"

"What do you want with him?"

"I'm going to arrest him."

"No!"

"I have no choice." He didn't have to say he was sorry. She saw it in his eyes. But that didn't help Alex. That didn't change anything. "Where is he, Susannah?"

"Please, Edward."

"I'm sorry." He turned to his men. "You three go downstairs to search the root cellar. You three try upstairs. His bedroom is the first one on the left."

"No!" cried Susannah, lunging toward the stairs, but Edward caught her before she could get away. "No!" She struggled against him, though she knew it was no use, for his hands held her with a steely grip. Even in her distress, she saw how careful he was to hold her away from him. He'd betrayed her and he knew it. He would not make it worse by reminding her of their past intimacy. But nothing, nothing helped.

The men had vanished in both directions by the time that she gave up and stood with her chest heaving and her hair disheveled from the violence of her fight. Edward's breathing was less than even and he kept his hold on her.

Tossing her hair back, she looked up at him. "I trusted you, Edward," she whispered, the words aching in her heart. "You said you'd take care of Alex. How could you come here now?"

"Because it's my duty. Susannah, there was a man almost murdered tonight," he answered with a bitterness that chilled the night. But that didn't stop the struggle she heard up above as all three of Edward's soldiers manhandled Alex down the stairs.

"Let me go, goddamn you!" Alex cursed, flailing from side to side. "You don't know what you're doing! I was home all night. Tell them, Susannah!" He came to a halt at the foot of the stairs. He was wigless and his hair was a tousled mess. He'd shed his old coat—back into the chest, she guessed—and his resistance had almost cost him the left sleeve of his shirt.

"Tell them," he urged again, his eyes on her. Dark gray eyes, just like hers, but filled with so much hate. Even now, with Edward's betrayal, she couldn't share that hate, though she would have been glad to, if it had dulled the hurt.

She felt Edward watching, which made her lift her chin. "He's right," she said, turning. "He was at home all night. He was right here with me."

She saw Edward's eyes darken with the knowledge of her lie. "Susannah," he entreated, "you told me yourself." His voice was gentle, but it might as well have been harsh.

She shook her head slowly. "I don't know what I meant. Alex was here the whole time. I'd take an oath on it."

They were interrupted by the men coming up the stairs with the dirty sheet cut with eyeholes and with the gun. They held them up to Edward. "Right where you said they'd be."

Alex's eyes swung back to Susannah, filled with utter disbelief. She knew what he was thinking and she would have given her life to explain. But the explanation would only have made things worse.

Edward was talking in a strange, cold voice. "Alexander Beckwith, in the name of His Majesty, King George, I hereby place you under arrest for the attempted murder of Lieutenant Aaron Franks, for breaking and entering into a private residence, for assault and battery, and for false imprisonment of Lord Bridgeham and his wife. Take him to Bridewell," he directed his men.

"Alex!" cried Susannah, but Edward's hand stopped her again. She watched in helpless horror as Alex's eyes fixed on that hand with a look of contemptuous comprehension that hurt more than words could have done.

Alex's eyes rose slowly until they reached her face. "I'll kill him yet," he promised. "Thanks for all your help."

"Alex!" she whispered as the men led him away.

Stunned and sickened as she was, it was several minutes before she realized that Edward had stayed behind. She felt his presence beside her but she could not bring herself to look up. If hell was here on earth, surely she'd found it tonight.

Edward wasn't thinking of hell. He was thinking of love as he stood in the hallway, gazing at Susannah's bowed head. Love for his home and his country flowed in his very blood, but for the first time he wished with all his heart that he'd never seen England or heard her name. He'd squabbled with Susannah and he'd held her in his arms, but until this moment he hadn't known for certain that what he felt was love. Somehow, in these six months, she'd become part of his heart. But what did any of that matter when the knowledge came too late?

"Susannah... If this world were different..."

He saw her start at his words. Then slowly she lifted her anguished eyes to his. "If it were. But it's not, Edward. It's the only one. And now I've lost Alex because—" She shook her head.

He knew what she was thinking. Because she'd trusted him. "Lady Bridgeham knew," he said softly, for her sake more than his. Susannah would never blame him half as much as she blamed herself. "She recognized Alex."

Susannah raised her head and fixed him with a level gaze. "And if she hadn't, Edward? Would you have still come?"

Both of them knew the answer. Slowly he nodded once. "It's my duty," he repeated, and saw her shoulders flinch.

He wanted to pull her to him. He wanted to call her "my heart." She was his heart, which was breaking as he stood watching her. In the six months since he'd scooped her up unconscious from the stoop he'd learned to read her body as well as he could read his own. At this moment he could hear it crying out for the love and comfort that was no longer his to give. Not now and not ever. He'd forfeited that tonight.

"Susannah, I'm sorry."

"Take *me*," she said, looking up.

"Take you?" he repeated, wondering if she'd lost her mind. He searched her face for her reason.

She held up her wrists. "Take me to prison, Edward. I've given my parole for Alex's good behavior. So take me to Bridewell, too."

"No, Susannah" He pushed her wrists away. "It won't help Alex for you to go to jail."

"Never mind helping!" she cried, thrusting her wrists up again. "Take me! It's your duty!"

"Stop!" Self-control cracking, he seized her arms and shook her back and forth. "Stop it, Susannah! This won't help anything!"

"Take me! Take me!" she cried, pounding her fists on his chest, until the only way to stop her was to hold her as he'd sworn he wouldn't do.

"Hush, hush!" he murmured above her stormy sobs, torn between the pain and the wonder of her in his arms. Pressing her against him, he prayed for a miracle. But there was no miracle, only Susannah's wild sobs, and he let her go because he had no choice.

"I wish I had never met you!" she said. "I should have let Alex die instead of coming after you! I trusted you, Edward!"

"Yes, I know," he said. "But I'm British, Susannah. And you're American."

His words affected Susannah as nothing else had done. All at once she stopped shaking and her shoulders slumped. "Yes," she said slowly, her eyes on the floor. "Yes. You're right. I should have known better. It was all my fault."

He opened his mouth to tell her that she was wrong, but he knew she couldn't listen, not with Alex in jail. So instead he told her, "I'll do what I can to see that he's treated fairly. And I'll cancel your parole."

"Thank you," she said with a flatness that was harder to hear than her rage.

By instinct his hand came up and moved toward her, but he caught himself at the last moment and forced it down again. To stay any longer would be to burden her, though leaving seemed no better than drowning in the sea.

"God bless you," he murmured, and when he turned away she was still standing with her head bowed, staring down at the floor.

Chapter Fifteen

"A nice crisp juicy apple, all crunchy and sweet! Wouldn't it taste just perfect right now?" Maria Van Rijn looked from the orchard to her sister, Amy, who had paused at her side by the fence. "It won't take a second, Amy, just in and out again. No one will see us, and if they do, we'll just run away. A nice Tory apple—mmm!" Maria teased.

Amy was sorely tempted. They'd walked a long way, a good ways beyond Greenwich village to the woods where the hazelnuts grew, and the baskets they'd filled were heavy. A crisp apple would taste very good. "But if they do see us, we can't run or the nuts will spill. And what would we tell Mother?"

"We won't have to tell her anything, because they won't see us, we'll be so quick," Maria assured her. Then, with a sigh of impatience, she hitched up her skirts. "All right, if you're such a scaredy-cat, I'll do it myself!"

Before Amy could stop her, Maria was up and over the fence to the nearest tree in the orchard. A minute later she was back, her apron bulging with apples, which she thrust into Amy's hands, then she flung herself back over the fence, breathless and giggling.

Amy was also giggling, though she couldn't have said why. "I thought you said only two!"

"They fell into my hand. Come on, put them in your basket, and hurry up!" Lugging their burdens, they hur-

ried down the road as though the Tory farmer were in hot
pursuit. He wasn't—a fact that for some reason made them
giggle even more, until they were laughing so hard they
could barely walk. Staggering like two drunks, they wobbled to the side of the lane and collapsed against each other
on the grassy bank.

Amy pressed her hand to her side where she had a stitch.
"We'll have to make up a story when Mother asks where
the apples came from."

"Or we could eat them all up." Maria polished the biggest, reddest apple on her skirt, then she opened her mouth
to its widest and took an enormous bite. "Mmm!" Her eyes
fluttered shut with pleasure.

"You've got juice on your chin." Amy grinned and chose
an apple for herself.

They crunched in companionable silence, warmed by the
afternoon sun and serenaded by the birds in the trees. Maria helped herself to a second apple as soon as she'd finished her first, but when Amy had finished, she pulled out
the paper she'd folded in her pocket and settled back to
read.

"Anything interesting?" Maria's blue eyes flitted with
the mildest of interest over the printed page. Far from dis-
tinguishing herself as the family scholar, Maria had welcomed the disruption the war had brought to her education.
Not that, in her family, she ever needed to read. Among the
Van Rijns there was always someone to report the news to
her.

Right now the reporter was Amy. "The final treaty terms
have been reached in Paris."

"As if Father and you haven't been discussing those
boring old terms for the past two weeks!" Maria stuck her
tongue out to catch a drop of juice as it rolled over her apple.

"Two days," corrected Amy. "That's when we first
heard the news. And we didn't know the exact terms, which
are printed here."

"Any surprises?" asked Maria.

"Not really. No. Mostly they're just the same as the pre-liminary ones."

"There, you see—boring, boring!" Maria leaned closer. "I meant, is there anything really interesting? I'll bet there's not."

"Move back," protested Amy. "You're chewing in my ear!"

"I'm not." Maria chuckled, but she did move back, leaving the paper to Amy, who scanned the middle page.

"Here's something! The Dawes house is offered for sale. I guess that means the Bridgehams are leaving."

"And good riddance!" Maria declared. Tossing the re-mains of her apple over her shoulder, she clasped her hands to her breasts and recited, "'He dragged me from my very bed and hurled me down the stairs! I was frozen with ter-ror! I knew I was going to die! If Captain Steel hadn't ap-peared when he did, I have no doubt that Alex Beckwith would have killed me and my husband both!' It's too bad they didn't kill her!" Maria concluded, unclasping her hands and wiping them off on her skirt.

"She's awful," agreed Amy, laughing at her sister's im-itation of Marguerite. Sobering, she added, "You'd think it would have been enough for her to have jilted Alex for that gross husband of hers. And then the way Lord Bridgeham stood up at the end of everything and asked the judge to have Alex sent to an English jail so he won't be pardoned by the Americans after the British leave! Poor Susannah—as if she hasn't been through enough!"

Maria nodded in concurrence. "Susannah looked terri-ble in court. As white as a sheet! She looked so white, a couple of times I was sure she was going to faint. And Mr. Beckwith never looked at her once. He never looked at anyone—except that Captain Steel. Imagine Captain Steel being the one to save his life, then the one to arrest him and send him to jail. And him giving testimony that Mr. Beck-with himself refused to speak in his own defense! It's like a story from a novel!"

"What do you know of novels?" Amy scoffed.

"You've told me stories." Maria turned dreamy eyes to her. "Who do you think is handsomer, Alex Beckwith or Captain Steel?"

"Maria! What a question!" Amy clucked. But she was thinking of a different kind of look. Maria was wrong about Alex. He had looked at Susannah once. He'd looked at her just after they'd called Captain Steel to the stand. Amy had been sitting just behind Susannah, so she'd caught the full force of that look, which had been so bitter she'd shivered and turned away.

Sitting where she had been, she'd noticed something else. She'd noticed that Captain Steel had also looked at Susannah, once. It had been only for an instant, when he was leaving the stand—after he'd sworn that in his opinion Alex had never intended to harm Lady Bridgeham or do more than frighten her husband. He'd looked at Susannah after that, but later on Amy had wondered if she might have imagined that look, for it had held more sorrow than she had ever seen.

Maria's eyes sharpened as she studied her sister's face. "You're sweet on him, aren't you?"

"Who, on Captain Steel?"

Maria snorted with exasperation. "You know who I mean! Alex Beckwith. Are you sweet on him?"

"No, I'm not." Amy took her sister's question seriously. "Not in the way you mean it. But when I look at him I wish I could do something to change the way he feels."

"Maybe you'll have a chance," said Maria. "If they don't send him to England, I bet he'll be free by Christmastime."

"I hope he is," sighed Amy, folding the paper away. As she did, the thrum of hoofbeats reached them from down the lane.

"Quick! Hide the apples," Maria hissed. "Your shawl, Amy!"

They threw the shawl over the baskets just as two riders appeared. Both were riding at an easy canter, but when they saw the two women, they slowed their horses to a trot so as not to kick up dust. Both men touched their hats to the women as they rode by. The younger of the two recognized Amy and his eyes swung back and lingered for a minute after he'd passed.

"Speak of the devil!" hissed Maria. "Captain Steel himself! And who was that with him? It looked like General Washington!" She stared at Amy, almost beside herself. They'd seen a lot of Washington in the early days of the war, when he'd come to supervise the defense of New York.

"It wasn't. It was Carleton. They look very alike."

"I'll say," breathed Maria. Coming out of her shock, she blinked. "My goodness, Amy! What about the way Captain Steel looked at you! He's even more handsome up close. For a redcoat," she added quickly, brushing invisible dust off her skirt. "I wonder why he was looking. Maybe he recognized you from court."

Amy looked after the two men and slowly shook her head. "No. I met him with Susannah several months ago." She sighed deeply for the second time. "We'd better get going. We've still got a long walk home." She reclaimed her shawl from the baskets and retied it around her neck. Her share of the nuts felt heavier than it had when she'd set it down. "We've got so many nuts," she mused aloud. "Maybe when we get back I'll take a package to Susannah. I haven't seen her since the trial."

They'd hardly set off toward home when they heard hoofbeats again. "I wonder who this time," Maria said as they moved to the side of the lane, for the horse was rapidly approaching.

It passed them at a fast canter. The rider didn't think about the dust his hooves would kick up—or if he thought, he didn't care.

"Lord Bridgeham!" exclaimed Maria. "And he didn't look too pleased! Maybe someone made a low offer on the house!" She chuckled at her own wit until the dust reached her nose and she began to cough. Covering her mouth with her free hand, she set off after Amy toward home.

* * *

Edward and Carleton continued to trot after they'd slowed, for their purpose was pleasure rather than haste. They rode in silence, each lost in private thought. Carleton was thinking about transports and Edward was recalling where he'd met Susannah's red-haired friend. He'd met her at the market, then seen her again in court at Alex Beckwith's trial. She had a nice face. Open. That comforted him. It pleased him to think of Susannah having a friend like that.

Susannah. With a stab of pain, he recalled how she'd looked at the trial. If he lived to be a hundred he'd never forget the awful whiteness, the terrible blankness in her face. She'd looked like a different woman from the one who'd fainted on his doorstep six months ago. Of all the things that pained him, the one that hurt the most was the thought that he'd played a part in quenching the fire he'd seen that day when her eyes had fluttered open as she lay on the couch. Maybe when all this was over, that fire would burn again. With good friends and kind treatment, maybe her wounds would heal. Then he thought of her brother and heaved an unconscious sigh.

His horse's ears pricked forward.

"What's this?" Carleton turned. Then Edward heard the hoofbeats hammering up from behind. He pulled his horse over just as the rider appeared.

"Bridgeham!" muttered Carleton.

Bridgeham reined his horse so abruptly that the startled animal reared. "Get down, damn you!" cursed the furious lord. But the mare's compliance didn't improve his mood. Plunging one hand into his pocket, he dragged a paper out and shook it at Carleton.

"Is this the thanks I get from my King? After all my loyal service—I'm sorry, sir, but I must demand better than this!" He thrust the paper at Carleton.

Carleton read, then shook his head. "I wish I could help you, Lord Bridgeham. But this is out of my hands."

"Nothing is out of the hands of a man who's made up his mind! The man was convicted in the King's court. He's the King's prisoner. Then send him to the King's prison! That's all I'm asking you."

"He is in the King's prison," Carleton said patiently. "As the judge has declared right here." He tapped his reins on the paper, which Bridgeham had thrust into his hands. "I know how you feel about Beckwith," he said with more patience than he felt. "But if he were sent to England, think of the trouble that would stir up. America would make him a cause célèbre."

"Let them and damn them!" Bridgeham stormed. "If you leave him here, they'll make him a hero!"

"I don't think so," Carleton said. "I don't think the Americans who take power will favor terror any more than we do. If I were a fledgling government taking over in New York, I'd be sorely tempted to leave Alex Beckwith in jail."

"But you're not," said Bridgeham bluntly. "And I promise you, they won't. Americans act, they don't think. They're scarcely better than animals—as Beckwith's case well proves!"

Carleton raised one eyebrow. "Quite a strong indictment from a man who is married to an American."

Bridgeham's face turned livid. "An entirely different affair! This man's committed mayhem! I demand that he pay!"

At Bridgeham's strident insistence, Carleton's manner changed in a way that Edward had seen often enough before. Carleton's expression turned quietly steely as he faced the outraged Bridgeham. "I'm sorry," he said coolly, "but I cannot comply. Good day, your lordship." He handed the paper back. Without waiting for Edward, he turned his horse up the lane.

Edward turned and followed before Bridgeham could start in with him. In the past, Alex Beckwith had angered and frustrated him. But at this moment he was feeling a strange empathy. Had he been in Alex's position on the night of the raid, he'd have been sorely tempted to shoot both his lordship and his vindictive wife.

They cantered a brisk half mile before Carleton slowed to a trot. "At times like this," he mused, "I'm surprised that there is any peace at all. You know what was in that paper?"

"Bridgeham's?" Edward shrugged. "I assume an order transferring Alex Beckwith to an English jail."

"An unsigned one," answered Carleton with an impatient sound. "Can you imagine a more perfect affront to the Americans? If I were Washington, I'd be hard-pressed not to take such a move personally. And yet his lordship presses on, thinking only of himself!"

Carleton shook his head with disgust. Then he shot a look at Edward. "I wonder what his lordship would say if he knew that he had Beckwith's sister to thank for saving his skin!"

"I'm grateful that you didn't tell him, sir."

"Did you really think that I might?" Carleton's eyes scanned Edward's with a look that made Edward wonder how much the general had guessed. He'd told Carleton about Susannah's role in the night's events. Then he'd asked for the general's help in keeping that role out of the testimony. He'd also gotten the general's aid in releasing her from her parole. Perhaps most importantly, Carleton had agreed that Alex Beckwith should not be tried for the stabbing of Franks.

Thankfully, Franks had survived to swear an affidavit that Barney Silver had stabbed him, and that when Silver had ordered Alex to kill him, Alex had refused. Not that Alex had lifted a finger in his own defense. Instead he'd maintained a stony silence throughout the questioning. And in order to try Silver, they'd have to catch him first.

"I don't suppose Silver will turn up until we're long gone," Carleton said, increasing Edward's suspicion that the general had read his mind.

"He won't, if we're lucky, sir."

"Don't blame yourself," Carleton said. "The man's a chameleon. Even Franks couldn't do better than average build and height."

"Except for the eyes," said Edward. "Franks was exact about those. Piercing and demented." He shivered despite himself. "In this case I bet even Washington would agree to a long term in jail."

They rode on a ways in silence, each following his own thoughts. Carleton broke the silence. "Whether or not Silver reappears, your part in this business is done. After the trial, all of New York knows who you are."

"I suppose you're right," agreed Edward with a sense of relief. He'd had enough of espionage to last him all his life. Beyond that, there were still thousands of loyalists to ship off to wherever they were going, and as soon as possible. Now that the treaty was final, there was nothing keeping them in New York. All that was left for them was to finish their business as fast as they could and go.

"You don't sound disappointed." Carleton shot him another look. Then, before he could answer, Carleton went on. "In any case, I've got another assignment for you. This one's slightly different."

"Slightly?" Edward repeated with dread.

"Very," amended Carleton. "I've calculated as best I can, and I've reached the conclusion that we can be out of New York in four weeks."

"Four?" repeated Edward, trying to keep his tone calm at the thought of all the remaining loyalists and the property still to be sold.

Carleton, however, nodded. "I'm not sure that the Americans will put up with us any longer than that. I've set the fifteenth of November as our official departure date. I believe that we can do it, if we give it our best." His lips curled briefly. "As Lord Bridgeham says, a man can do anything if he puts his mind to it."

"Without doubt," Edward agreed dryly. As much work as it would be, he couldn't help but feel relief to know that the end was near. It would be easier to forswear Susannah

with an ocean dividing them instead of his willpower and
the force of her brother's hate.

Carleton must have felt the same relief, for at that moment he sighed. "We came to America almost two hundred years ago. It will be a dubious honor to be the last to
leave. On the other hand, if you look at the matter more
broadly, you could say that we're not leaving at all. In the
broader sense 'we' are also the Americans.

"A philosophical point at best," he concluded with another sigh. "And you're waiting to hear your assignment
and not philosophy. Well, it's a simple one. You'll be my
liaison in working with the Americans to coordinate the final day. Their entrance and our departure will have to be
aligned."

Simple, thought Edward. He could envision its simplic-
ity—and the dozens and dozens of details that would go
into making it so. "I'm flattered that you trust me with
such a delicate task."

"I do trust you," said Carleton. "You did a fine job of
stopping the Sons. Beyond that, you seem to have a feel for
the Americans. Since we first had the news of the treaty,
we've been doing our best to leave America in an atmosphere of goodwill. I'd like that to continue, right up
through the final day. I believe it will be invaluable in the
future relationship not only of the United States and England, but also with Canada."

As always, Edward was impressed with the wisdom of
Carleton's words. "The Americans are lucky to have you,
sir."

Carleton laughed. "If only they knew! Well, well, they'll
be done with me soon enough. They'll be done with all of
us. Are you homesick for England, Edward?"

"A bit." Edward smiled. "St. John's gotten himself engaged. He'll be married when I get back."

"Has he! It's about time!" Carleton slapped Edward on
the back. "Send him my congratulations. Tell him I'll give
them to him myself! It's your turn next, Edward."

"Yes, sir," Edward said, and was surprised at the wave of longing that swept over him. The longing was for Susannah, and though he knew it was unreasonable, he couldn't stop it from rolling on and on, down the years and the empty seasons that lay ahead. It was powerful enough to make him forget even Carleton until the general spoke again.

"Speaking of the Beckwith girl, I imagine she'll be glad to hear that Bridgeham's order was refused."

Edward turned his head. "We weren't speaking of her, General."

"Weren't we?" Carleton smiled. "Too much work, Edward. It does strange things to one's mind." Without waiting for an answer, he spurred his horse ahead, leaving a thoughtful Edward to follow as he would.

"Captain Steel!" Milly's eyes bulged at the sight of Edward standing on the stoop. For a full minute she was too astonished to ask him in. Then she made up for the lapse by half dragging him into the hall. "Come in! It's fine to see you! So, you're still in New York!"

"To the bitter end, Milly," he said with a smile. But his smile quickly faded as he glanced around. "I wonder if Mistress Beckwith is in. I thought if she was, that perhaps..."

"Oh, she's in all right, Captain. She hardly goes out anymore except to carry a basket of food down to Bridewell and back. A full basket both ways, if you get what I mean. Not a crust will he accept from her, not a word will he speak! He might as well have died instead of been sent to jail!" Then Milly realized to whom she was speaking and flushed to the lace of her cap. "Begging your pardon, Captain!"

"It's all right," Edward said, though he couldn't help but flinch physically at the thought of Susannah's pain. Duty. It was such a cold word to cause so much hurt. "I've got something to tell her," he added. "Something that might help a bit. That is, if she'll see me."

At that, Milly flushed again. "She don't see many people," she said falteringly. "Just sits up in her bedroom at her spinning wheel. You could probably clothe the whole city from the wool she's spun! I could go up and ask her," she offered.

"I'd like that," Edward said.

Milly took two steps toward the stairs then stopped and turned around. "Come to think of it, Captain, maybe it would be better if you was to go up yourself. I know some folks wouldn't think it proper, but seeing how you've lived here yourself..."

"You're right," Edward said quickly before Milly could change her mind.

He knew what Milly was thinking. If she was given the choice, Susannah would refuse to see him out of loyalty to Alex alone. And he wanted to see her. He wanted to see her so much that he doubted he'd have had the strength to leave if Milly had sent him away.

He came up the stairs softly as he had once before—that day when he'd first met her and returned from headquarters to find her valise still in the hall. She'd been holding the book of sonnets, and he'd grabbed it from her in anger about Catherine. Now he couldn't believe he had done that. It seemed so long ago.

The door to her room was open and he saw her from the hall. She was sitting at the window, at her wheel with her back to him. The sight of her froze him. After a month without her, it was almost enough. Almost, but not quite. His heart was already aching as he raised his hand to knock. Before he could, she sensed him and turned her head.

The spindle fell with a rattle, and from the way she stared, he knew that she wasn't sure if he was really in her doorway or she was seeing a ghost.

"Edward?" she faltered.

"Yes. It's really me. I'm sorry to surprise you." He stepped into the room. "Milly let me in. She said I should come up." He rattled on without paying attention. Dear

Lord, she looked so thin! Her eyes seemed enormous in her pale, strained face.

She rose to face him. "What—what do you want?"

"To see you," he said without thinking. Then he added, "I've got news. Good news, Susannah. Why don't you sit down?" She looked so pale and unsteady he was afraid she might faint. He knew he ought to hate himself for doing this to her, but instead he found himself hating Alex for withholding out of stubbornness the comfort she needed so desperately.

"I'm all right," she murmured, touching the wheel for support. "What is your news? Please tell me."

He took a step toward her then forced himself to stop. "It's about Alex. I've just heard that Lord Bridgeham's request has been turned down, so Alex won't be sent to England. They'll keep him here."

"Oh, thank God!" she gasped.

Edward moved quickly to catch her before she fell. Her arm felt as thin as a child's. "Susannah, you're wasting away!" He could feel the bones along her back through the wool of her dress, and it took all his effort not to press his lips to her hair.

"No, no! I'm all right," she assured him as he lowered her into the chair. "Milly and her mother take good care of me."

"I believe they try," he said slowly, looking down at her. "Milly told me about Alex not taking the food that you bring. Do you think you can change his mind if you starve yourself?"

"That's not it!" she protested. Without thinking, she reached out with her hands for the wheel and the spindle and her feet began to tread.

She worked in silence for a minute, then suddenly she stopped as her head bent forward and her hands fell into her lap. "He hates me, Edward," she whispered. "He's cut me out of his heart!"

Edward dropped to one knee beside her and took her hands in his. They were freezing cold despite the fire burning in the hearth. "No, Susannah," he murmured, chafing her icy hands. "He's only angry and even that will pass. He wouldn't act this way if he didn't love you still." Silently he added, Believe me, I ought to know how much that love can hurt. He tried not to hate Alex for doing this to her. More hate was surely the last thing Susannah could use.

She shook her head slowly, staring down at their joined hands, his so strong and busy, hers so thin and still. She hadn't known just how much she missed him until she'd seen him at the door. Or perhaps she'd only been trying to ignore the truth—that she loved Edward, even with Alex in jail. And that she didn't blame him, although Alex would say she should. Alex had vowed to kill him. She sighed and her shoulders slumped.

"How did this happen? I can't understand. When I first heard about the treaty, I was so glad. I imagined just how it would be. Alex and I would work together to make everything right. I wasn't afraid of the hard work. I even welcomed it. I thought that the worst was over and the best was about to begin. But now everything's ruined. I've ruined everything."

Her hands remained passive as his tightened over them. "Don't say that, Susannah!" he pleaded. "You're not the one to blame. If you must blame someone, blame me, but not yourself!" He spoke without thinking, but he spoke from love. Closing his eyes, he brought one of her hands to his lips. She didn't resist him, and when he opened his eyes he found her looking at him.

"You blame Alex, don't you, Edward?"

He moved her hand from his lips to touch it to his cheek. He did it without thinking, unable to let her go. "I'm angry at Alex for hurting you," he said. "But I don't really blame him. Blame doesn't help anything. It only breeds revenge and revenge brings hurt. You've been hurt enough, Susannah. You need kindness and love."

At his words, she tried to pull her hand back, but he didn't let it go. "I love you, Susannah. You know that, don't you?'' he asked, trying to drink the essence of her through the palm of her hand.

Silently she nodded, turning her head away.

He took a breath and said, ''I think you love me, too.''

Susannah squeezed her eyes shut and gave her head a halfhearted shake.

He ignored it. He remembered the terrible emptiness he'd foreseen that afternoon when he'd imagined a lifetime without her. He had nothing to lose and everything to gain. He pressed her hand to his cheek and held it there.

''Marry me, Susannah,'' he said.

She jerked her hand free. ''What are you saying!''

''I'm saying marry me!'' Tilting her face to him, he smoothed the hair back from her brow. Her freckles stood out sharply against the paleness of her skin, bringing back that first day when he'd watched her sleep. ''Let me love you, Susannah. Let me take care of you,'' he pleaded, and felt a spark of hope at the yearning he saw in her eyes.

''I know you're thinking about Alex,'' he said before she could reply. ''But Alex is a grown man and he's got his own life. The Americans will free him as soon as they take New York, and after that what he does will be up to him. I don't want you to spend the rest of your life begging his forgiveness. I want more than that for you. I want you to have my love. And I want yours, Susannah!''

Turning her hand, he pressed a trail of kisses along the inside of her wrist and up her arm. He felt her pulse quicken and her head fell back. ''Please, Susannah!'' he murmured.

''Edward, no!'' she moaned, but she didn't try to stop him and he didn't stop until his lips had reached her elbow. By that time her fingers were twined within his hair and she'd begun to tremble in the way he knew.

He raised his head to find her flushed, and he knew from the look in her eyes that she wouldn't stop him, no matter what he did. And at the same moment he knew that no amount of kisses would convince her to marry him. She would give herself to him in need and passion, but marriage, the thing he most wanted, she would have to decide for herself.

Slowly he pulled the cuff of her sleeve back into place, which slowed his heart slightly. Then he asked again, "Will you marry me, Susannah?"

"And live in England?" she asked. "Flee my own country to escape my own brother's hate?"

For a long, silent minute the question hung in the air, and Edward could feel Susannah struggling with herself. Choose me, he begged silently, again and again and again. But when the minute ended, Susannah shook her head.

"I can't," she said softly. "I don't know how to explain it to make you understand. I've ruined things with Alex, but I have one more chance. My country is another chance. This dream of America. It's my dream, Edward. It's kept me going all these years. In those months after Mother died, sometimes I'd get so low. But then I'd think, when this is over, when we've won, we can make things right. I'd think there was a reason for all our suffering and the reason was good. I can go to England, but I can't bring my heart."

As she spoke she was crying, the tears pouring down her cheeks. He held her very gently, murmuring, "Hush, my dear."

"Do you hate me?" she whispered.

"You know I don't."

"Will you hate me later?"

"Never! I give you my word."

"And you understand why?"

"I understand," he murmured, and in truth he did. But understanding didn't help the ache in his heart.

He waited until she'd stopped crying before he smoothed back her hair and found yet another handkerchief for her to blow her nose. "I want you to promise me something."

"What is it?"

"That you'll eat. And that you'll go out walking and see your friends. That one with the red hair."

Susannah nodded. "Amy Van Rijn." Her eyes searched his face and she wondered how it was possible that she could love Edward and not spend her life with him. "Maybe someday," she murmured.

"Maybe," Edward replied, but she saw the real answer in the sadness of his eyes. "Will you promise, Susannah?"

"I promise," she said, and she lifted her lips to kiss him when he bent to her.

His kiss was as gentle as his hands had been, and he stopped it before it could catch hold, for between them there was no limit short of eternity. She curled her hands into fists to keep them in her lap as he stood, but she couldn't resist calling out as he moved toward the door.

"When will you be leaving?"

"Not till the very end. I've just gotten a new job. Organizing the final day."

"You'll do a good job." She smiled and meant it. Then a shadow crossed her face. "Don't leave without saying goodbye. Unless you think it's better—"

He shook his head. "I don't think it's better. Goodbye, my love."

"Goodbye," Susannah whispered, and watched him walk out the door.

Chapter Sixteen

NOTICE is hereby given to all Loyalists within the Lines, desirous to emigrate from this place before the final Evacuation, that they must give their names at the Adjutant General's office on or before the 7th instant, and be ready to embark by the end of the following week.

NOTICE! The Board on Debt hereby notices all concerned that they will be meeting for the last time on Monday next, after which time no further claims may be filed.

The Commissary General hereby advises that his accounts are closed and no further claims will be accepted. GOD SAVE THE KING.

The final day was approaching. You could feel it in the air. You could see it in the harbor, thick with the masts of ships, which were now increasingly bearing American flags. You could see it most of all in the city streets, where the final wave of Tories were liquidating their estates. Now there were auctions six days a week on Broad Street and on the bridge by the Merchants' Exchange, and most of the goods went cheap. Few people had money, but there was a profit to be made by anyone who did.

"Some Americans is as bad as Tories," grumbled one toothless man who'd gathered with the crowd that was observing the sale of the Dawes estate. Catching the eye of the man beside him, he nodded toward the front, where a man in a well-cut frock coat was bidding on a four-poster bed. "Don't look too much to me like he's lacking a bed!"

"'Course he ain't!" a thin woman agreed. "More likely plans to resell it—and for a good price, too. Better than the likes of us could afford—not beds, but lodging, too! My husband was a soldier. It's a downright disgrace!"

A third voice spoke from behind her. "It is. But grumbling won't help."

"What's there to do but grumble?" asked the man, while the woman swiveled her scrawny neck to see who the speaker might be. "There ain't jobs for us to work, and if we work we ain't hardly paid."

"Grumbling is useless," replied the speaker in the same low tone. "Action is what counts." He was a man of middling height, wearing a tradesman's coat, itself in middling condition and slightly the worse for wear.

The woman's eyes narrowed. "I've gone to the authorities. I've gone to everyone. But they don't want to see me." She spat from the side of her mouth.

"Not by yourself," he replied. "Numbers make a difference, especially now, when the redcoats are in such a rush to get out. Don't wait for the Tories to sell to the man with cash. Take it before they can sell it."

"What—houses?" The woman gaped.

The man looked at her with pity. "No. Goods that can turn into coin. Such as those there." He nodded past her toward the auctioneer's block, where a pair of fine andirons were being offered for seven pounds.

"Seven pounds!" muttered the woman. "That's more than I've seen in a year!" But when she looked back at the speaker, she found he'd disappeared.

The toothless man caught her looking and shrugged. "He went into thin air. Ordinary-looking fellow. But not such a bad idea. Take from the Tories before the Tories sell."

"In numbers, he said," added the woman. The two exchanged a look.

"It don't sound quite honest," murmured the man.

"Honest?" The woman stiffened. "Is it honest that a dead soldier's family is starving on the street?"

"Well, now that you put it that way..." the man said thoughtfully. He turned around and searched the crowd but he caught no glimpse of the stranger with the intriguing idea. Too bad he'd vanished. He'd seemed like a good sort to know—the sort who knew how to make the best of even the worst of times.

Barney Silver let the crowd carry him along Great Dock Street through the tent slum called Canvas Town. He walked with his hands in his pockets and without fear of recognition. Why should he fear? He'd been in the city these last weeks, coming and going as he pleased, planting the seeds of dissatisfaction wherever he found fertile minds. Not everyone had as few wits as that woman back there. Most caught on more quickly to Barney's well-placed hints.

Did the redcoats think he'd give up that easily? Barney was an American. Adversity fed his resolve. He'd had some nervous moments when Beckwith had come to trial, but they'd gone predictably easy on him. He'd be out before he knew it, Barney thought with a little smile. The British were gutless. No wonder they'd lost the war. And as for the Tories, their biggest surprise was yet to come. In these last weeks of roving the city, Barney had formed a plan so brilliant he'd even impressed himself—a plan to ensure driving every last Tory out of New York. And the best thing about it was how few people it would take. Just Barney and Beckwith. Just as they'd started out. Barney strolled through Canvas Town, a smile on his face.

"Sir, here's the copy of General Carleton's letter to General Washington." The corporal laid the letter on top of all the other papers piled on Edward's desk—papers he meant to get to and some that he would not. He'd felt a brief breath of respite when Carleton had pushed back their departure date. But that respite had quickly dissipated before the flood of tasks left to complete.

Edward scanned the letter briefly. It was dated two days before and addressed to West Point, from which Washington had already departed on the first leg of his journey south—a journey that would finish with his triumphant entry into New York City in the same hour that the last British soldier marched out.

"My goal," Carleton had written, "is to relinquish New York on November 21 . . ."

The corporal stood at attention. "Sir, is there anything else?"

Anything else? Six days to quit Manhattan and the corporal asked was there anything else? Edward's mouth twitched into the grimmest of smiles. "There's everything else, Corporal. There's whether we've got enough transports to take out all that want to go—and where they'll all be sent to once we've got them on their ships. And then there's the question of whether the winds will ever pick up, so that once the ships are loaded they can sail anywhere!"

Pausing, he raised a sheaf of papers, which he held up one by one. "I've got an order from General Carleton requesting that the worst of the damage done to churches in the city be repaired as an act of British goodwill. To the same effect, here's an order that you must have read—the one about every soldier discharging each outstanding personal obligation before he embarks.

"Then there are the big issues, such as can we really be gone on that date or will we have to hold off General Washington—who is already convinced beyond reason that we're intentionally lingering on. And then there's the formal withdrawal—there's that to consider, too. Have I mentioned the growing numbers of thieves and prostitutes who may destroy the city before we can hand it to the Americans? If not, you can add them to the list. In other words, Corporal, the answer to your question is yes!"

"Sir." The corporal swallowed, his eyes jerking nervously from the floor up to Edward, then back to the floor again. The captain wasn't joking. The question was, was he mad?

"No, I haven't lost my mind, Corporal. Not yet, anyway." Edward sighed. "I'm just another soldier suffering from a bad case of overwork. You're dismissed, Corporal. Or rather, no, you're not. I've got a message to be delivered to the adjutant general, if I can only find it . . ."

But he hadn't found the message when a regular burst in to announce that there was a riot down at the Fly Market because the inspector of markets had absconded with the market bell and could Edward come and stop it before someone was killed.

Edward went to stop it, not because it was his job but because if he didn't, nobody else was likely to. It turned out that the inspector had stolen it purely out of spite. It took Edward half an hour to make him give it back—and recant his threat to burn the market down. By that time it was almost noon, which meant he'd wasted half of one valuable day.

He had lists to check at Whitehall, so he walked south on Queen Street, past Hanover Square and into the morass of Canvas Town. When he'd first come to the city five years ago, the area had housed refugees. But in the years since Yorktown, its first tenants had been forced out by the criminal element that had flooded the town, outgrowing its old neighborhood behind St. Paul's and spilling over down here.

Canvas Town was a disheartening spectacle at any time of day, home to the desperate and the dispossessed. Unemployed soldiers and unemployed camp followers watched Edward passing from beneath lowered lids, while pigs fought with humans for the right of way, rutting through gutters overflowing with filth. A few of the more energetic watchers spat as Edward passed. He was in full uniform. He was all the time these days. It wasn't any more comfortable than it had ever been, but it helped him to remember just who and where he was.

A thin girl with dark hair blocked his way, swiveling her hips mockingly. For an instant he thought of Susannah, mostly because of the hair. The thought ran through him like a spear with a red-hot tip. It wouldn't be much longer, then he'd have the rest of his life to forget. He stepped wide to avoid the girl and continued on his way. He was picking his way past a pair of pigs when he felt a light tug on his coat. A hand was in his pocket. Without thinking, he clamped down on the wrist.

"Ow! Leave off! You're hurting me!" cried the dark-haired girl.

"Its what you deserve for stealing." He pulled her in front of him.

"I wasn't stealing!" she protested.

"Your hand was in my pocket."

"It wasn't, either! You're just saying that because I'm American."

"I'm saying it because it's true." Still holding her tightly, he began walking again.

"What are you doing? Where are you taking me?"

"To jail," said Edward. "Thieving's against the law. Or didn't you know it?"

"Damn redcoat!" spat the girl, her hair flopping in her face as she fought his grip. But he was too strong for her, so she gave up her struggle and switched to another tack. "I know something. I'll tell you if you let me go."

"What will you tell me?" he asked, steering her around a cart full of bricks—probably filched from someone's half-ruined house, despite the standing order against exactly that manner of theft.

"Something important. A plot to disturb the peace."

"I'll bet you know," he said wryly.

"I do—it's the truth!" she declared.

"What kind of a plot?" he asked, steering her around a mongrel fighting a pig over waste.

"Will you let me go if I tell you?"

"Tell me, and then I'll decide."

This time when she pulled back, he let her stop. She eyed him with the same sullen expression he'd just seen on the inspector's face. But she only took to the count of six to change her mind. "All right. I'll tell you. Then you'd better let me go. There's a plot to plunder the city when Washington comes in."

"Whose plot?" he demanded, feeling half a fool to be having this conversation with a common thief.

"Who do you think—the Tories! Who else would think of that? Not a good American!" she added indignantly.

"How did you hear this?"

"From a couple of men I was with."

"I can imagine," Edward muttered, his lip curling with disgust at the scene she was describing. They'd been standing in one place too long: people were starting to notice. He began walking, pulling her along by her arm.

"Where are we going? You said you'd let me go!"

"I didn't. I said I'd decide. When did you hear this?"

"I don't know. A few days ago."

"But you never told anyone?"

"Who would I tell?" she sneered. "You bloody redcoats? You'd probably be glad—or you'd call me a liar, and drag me around by the arm!"

"What did the men who told you look like?"

"Like Tories!" She tossed her head. "Silk coats and waistcoats, and powdered wigs. One was bigger than the other. He had blue eyes. The other—the small one—had a wart on his nose."

Edward felt a twinge of disappointment. Neither man could be Barney Silver—if either existed at all. Not that there was any reason why Silver should be involved in what she insisted was a Tory plot—except that Edward wanted Silver caught. Until this moment he hadn't realized how much he did.

On impulse he asked her, "Have you seen a man of average height with a strange look in his eyes?"

She tossed her hair back and looked at him with disgust. "Now that's a fine description! How'm I supposed to know?"

"You aren't," growled Edward, losing patience all at once. He dragged her along, despite her objections, all the way to jail, where he had her locked up for the night.

The next morning she was still insisting that her story was true. "Except about the Tories. It isn't a Tory plot. It's the men from Canvas Town, and they mean to rob from the Tories that decided not to leave. They say there'll be no one to stop them since Congress let the Army go and Washington won't come in with but a handful of troops."

Her dark hair hung forward, practically over her eyes. "There's something else," she added. "That man you were asking about. I've seen him."

Edward hid his reaction. "Why should I believe you today?"

"Then don't believe me! I've seen him, and that's the truth." She folded her arms over her thin chest and glared at him through her hair.

The trouble was that he did believe her, or at least he didn't disbelieve her enough to ignore what she was saying.

"Where are we going now?" she asked a minute later as he led her from the jail. "Are you setting me free, then?"

"Not quite yet," he said. "First there's someone else who'll want to hear what you have to say."

She only grumbled a little on the ride to headquarters and was visibly impressed by the Beekman house—so much so that Edward specifically instructed the guard to keep an eye on her nimble fingers while he spoke to Carleton alone.

Carleton listened, frowning. "Silver?"

"It could be. Chances are she's still lying. But if she's not..."

Still frowning, Carleton nodded. "You'd better bring her in." He questioned the girl closely, and although she seemed abashed by Carleton's stature, she repeated her story much as she'd told it before. When she'd finished, they sent her out again.

Carleton paced while Edward waited. Once or twice Carleton stopped, as though he'd made up his mind. But then he must have had second thoughts, for he began to pace again. Finally he halted. "You're right. It's a plausible tale. In view of which," he concluded, "Washington ought to be told. I'll write him a letter. You'll take it right away."

"I?" Edward had already lost valuable time with the girl. With a mental groan he thought of the piles of work on his desk. "With all due respect, sir, I can't really spare the time. Not if I'm to be finished by the twenty-second, as you've said. And then there are the prevailing winds—"

"The twenty-fifth," said Carleton. "That gives you three more days. It's the most I can give you." As he spoke, he was reaching for quill and paper to write to Washington. "He's somewhere upriver," he said as he wrote. "You'll have to ask the Americans. I'll give you a pass. I want you to speak to him personally—if he'll see you, that is. Wait for his reply, if there is one. Bring it straight to me. As for the girl, I think we'd better keep her under guard."

When the pass and the letter were blotted and sealed, Edward tucked them into his coat.

"Do you have a good horse?"

"Yes, sir. Good enough."

"Then I'll wish you Godspeed. I know you'll hurry back."

The girl screeched like a banshee when she learned her fate. "But you promised!"

"I never did. It's for your own safety."

"Damned bloody lying Brit!"

She was still screeching when Edward rode off, as fast as his horse would carry him, along the river north.

He encountered the first American pickets just across the Kingsbridge. They accepted the pass from Carleton but couldn't tell him where Washington was. They suggested he try the Van Cortlandt mansion in Yonkers.

He tried it, but Washington wasn't there, though they said they'd had a message from him from Tarrytown. Edward paused only long enough to water his horse, then set out again. He lost time in Dobbs Ferry when his horse lost a shoe, but an hour later he was finally in Tarrytown, where he was directed to Edward Cowenhaven's house.

They were sitting late at the table at the Cowenhaven house. The candlelight from the window shone on the frozen ground as Edward rode into the yard. Cowenhaven's stable boy took his horse, then a pair of Continental regulars ushered him into the house.

They showed him to a study at the back of the main hall, though not far enough to block out the tantalizing smells of food. He'd missed dinner hours before, when he'd taken the girl to Carleton, and now he'd missed supper, too. He wondered if the Cowenhaven kitchen would be kindly disposed toward a hungry redcoat captain with a long ride home ahead. Maybe if he was lucky—"Captain Steel?"

Edward jumped. He'd been thinking so hard about supper that he hadn't heard the footsteps approaching or the door swing ajar. He turned quickly and stiffened with surprise, thinking for a fleeting moment that he was seeing Carleton.

But the man in the doorway wasn't Carleton. He had the same size and build; even the face was superficially similar. But the eyes, thought Edward, the eyes were unique.

The eyes regarded him with interest. "You have a letter for me from your commander?"

Damn! He'd been gaping at Washington like a fool. "Yes, sir," he muttered, and groped within his coat until he had the letter, which he passed across.

There was a light burning at the table to the right of the door. The aide who'd returned with the general held it aloft while Washington read, and though he tried not to, Edward continued to stare.

What was there about the man? he wondered as Washington read. He was dressed well but plainly in a brown coat and breeches to match, his own hair hidden beneath a powdered wig. Carleton's news displeased him, for Edward saw his frown, and he felt himself shrinking before he caught himself in surprise. He wasn't one to quail before displeasure, even from powerful men.

When he'd finished the letter, Washington folded it and looked up. "I'm sorry to hear that there will be another delay in the evacuation. We have waited a long time and we are impatient to reclaim our homes. In our position no doubt you would feel the same way."

He made it a statement, not a question. In any case, he was right. Edward nodded in concurrence. Washington went on. "General Carleton has also informed me of a rumor he has learned—about a disturbance that might take place at that time. He offers to send his informant if I care for an interview. That will not be necessary," he said. "Please tell General Carleton that I have received his message but I am not concerned."

"If I may, General." Edward cleared his throat. "I believe that General Carleton was less concerned by the general rumor than by the identity of one of the participants. There's a man named—"

"Yes, Silver. So your commander says. And adds that he may be demented and is definitely dangerous." Washington's gaze rested on Edward, and Edward had the sense of being transformed from an abstract presence into a specific one in the general's eyes. He was no longer Carleton's envoy but Edward Steel.

"Life is dangerous," Washington said. "It is also demented at times. We know this and yet we continue to face it as best we can. And often the very act of facing danger diminishes it. For more years than I might have wished to, I've commanded all sorts of men. The ones like Silver try to cause trouble but they don't succeed, because the others don't let them, when all is said and done. I have faith in Americans, Captain. I've got faith in them today."

"There is always a first time, General," Edward pointed out.

"There is," Washington acknowledged, his eyes on Edward still. "But I don't believe that time will meet us as we ride into New York. Not if there is justice, and I believe that there is. I'll be riding into the city amid men who've ridden with me for years. They've seen me through darker threats than the one you've described. We'll be riding from war into peacetime on that day. Think about that, Captain Steel. I believe that you'll understand."

Edward hadn't realized how open the general's face had become, until it resumed its stiff formality. "Please thank General Carleton for his warning and tell him that I will be looking forward to saluting his rear guard on the twenty-fifth."

"I will tell him, General," Edward replied—though by the time he said it, Washington was already out of the room. His aide lingered behind him only long enough to add that there would be a message to Carleton, if Edward would care to wait. He left, and a moment later a regular appeared to lead Edward down to the kitchen for a belated meal.

The regular sat with Edward as he ate his bread and meat. He was a young man with an open face who looked as though he'd grown up on a farm. He looked brawny enough to have been able to plow fields without a team. "So you come from Carleton," he said after a spell. "They say he resembles George Washington."

"So he does," Edward agreed. "But the two are different."

"How's that?"

He tried to think. But it was hard to think of Carleton with Washington in his mind. And Washington was in his mind, filling it so thoroughly that even the farm-boy regular had no trouble reading his thoughts.

"I know how it is," he told Edward with an understanding grin. "I've been with him ever since Morristown. I was with him that terrible winter in Valley Forge. Scant food, scanter fires, hardly a blanket to cover us. There was times when we'd get to thinking that perhaps we'd best give up. And just when things was their darkest, here General Washington would come. He's not much of a one for telling stories and I've never seen him laugh. He'd speak a few words. He'd listen. Then he'd move on. But just them few words was enough to give us faith. There was times when he held us together with just his two hands." He held out his own two massive hands to demonstrate. "I wouldn't have wanted to fight the war without General Washington."

The soldier fell silent, at home with his memories, while Edward chewed slowly, considering his words. He didn't have to tax his imagination to know what the soldier meant. He'd had the same feeling in the upstairs room—as though Washington's belief in justice were an invisible shield that would protect him against Barney Silver and every other threat. His faith was in his soldiers and their faith was in him.

Think about that, Captain Steel, Washington had said. I believe that you'll understand. All at once Edward did understand, and not just about the day to come. He understood about the war. He saw things about America he'd never seen before. All because of two minutes he'd spent with Washington.

In a rush he felt Susannah's presence at his side, as sometimes happened when he let down his guard. He could bar her from his mind, but never from his heart. Now he found himself thinking of her with a sense of hope. He knew that Washington would take care of her. Not in the same way that he would have himself, but nonetheless in an important way. He believed that Washington could give her the peace in which to heal her wounds, and that thought was as reassuring as any he'd had in months. Perhaps that reassurance would make his loss of her bearable.

He slept a few hours at Cowenhaven's and started out at dawn. Washington would be leaving sometime later; he would sup with the Van Cortlandts tonight. As Edward galloped south along the empty road, he carried last night's reassurance and his new insights along. Perhaps that was the reason he couldn't help but wish that Barnett Silver was safely locked in jail. Now that he saw Susannah's well-being so tied to Washington and peace, he had a new reason for wanting to ensure that both would succeed. There was still a week left. Perhaps if he was sharp... Perhaps if he was lucky, he thought as he rode.

He delivered Washington's letter to Carleton, who read it and shrugged. "We've warned him. It's the best we can do. It won't be much longer."

"No, sir," agreed Edward. Not much, then eternity.

The next days passed in a dizzying blur, each with its crises, changes and endless details. Committees of patriotic New Yorkers met daily to plan for the big day, while Washington and his forces continued to move south. As promised, the British had pulled back below McGowan's Pass on the twenty-first. That same day the Continentals crossed over the Kingsbridge. Washington was staying in Harlem until the twenty-fifth.

On Monday, the twenty-fourth, the American committee published a broadside announcing the order of procession for the following day. The broadside ended with the warning Citizens Take Care! Under this was printed an urgent call for every able-bodied man to form himself into a guard to patrol the city during the night, starting at an early hour. "It is requested that such Inhabitants who are not on the patrols, and sickness does not prevent, will keep themselves awake."

Edward's desk was empty. His papers had all been destroyed or else carried out to the ship, which would leave for England with the first favorable winds. He'd done everything he could do except put Barney Silver in jail. But after a week of searching thousands of pairs of eyes, he was beginning to believe that Silver must be gone. And he hadn't heard any new rumors about the plundering. He locked the office behind him then added his key to the board, which would be carried to City Hall and left for the Americans.

In his room his things were packed, except for his uniform, which he would wear tomorrow for the final ceremony. Again, he'd missed supper, but he wasn't thinking of food. Ten hours remained until morning, and he had only one thing left to do.

Chapter Seventeen

The last night. Susannah sat in the drawing room close to the warming fire, counting the minutes by the pass of the patrols. All citizens, whom "sickness does not prevent," should keep themselves awake. Not that she worried about sleeping. Not on a night such as this.

How long had she waited for this night? How long had she dreaded it? She'd been waiting forever, only now it seemed that she must have always looked toward it with dread. She couldn't imagine not knowing Edward, he seemed such a part of her life. But of course he wasn't a part of it at all. And tomorrow he would be leaving. It was what she had been awaiting and yet it seemed impossible. She thought her mind must be mocking her when she heard the knock on the door. It came again and she answered, her heart aching in her throat.

It was Edward! She couldn't believe it at first. His face was ruddy from the cold, but beneath that he looked tired. She had to squeeze her hand in a fist to keep from touching his face.

"Susannah. I hope you don't mind. I had to come." He stood looking down at her, drinking in her presence as she was drinking his.

"I'm glad you came," she murmured. Why not? It was the truth. The cold night air clung to him when he followed her into the hall. "The others are sleeping," she told him softly. "They wanted to get an early start tomorrow."

"What about maintaining vigilance?" he asked with a ghost of a smile.

"I promised I'd maintain it for them. I didn't think I'd sleep." She echoed his smile. "Would—would you like to come into the drawing room? I haven't got any wine, but—"

"No," he said softly. "I don't want any wine. That's not why I came, Susannah."

She caught her breath. "Why did you come?"

"I came to say goodbye."

"Oh, Edward!" she whispered. She looked up at his eyes, as blue as she'd remembered, and at the same time as gray. They drew her within their dearness until the ring of black encircled her like a fortress and protected her from all the world. For the moment nothing mattered except that she and Edward were together again. She would cling to this moment, until it was torn away.

His eyes never released hers as he shook his head. "No," he murmured deeply. "I can't just say goodbye. We have one night, Susannah. Will you share it with me?"

Silently, she nodded, not trusting her voice. But already that sweet fire had begun to untangle the tightness in her throat. She didn't have to move to reach him, she only had to lift her arms. She laid her hands on his lapels and raised herself onto her toes. She watched as his eyes came closer, then her eyelids fluttered down at the very instant that his lips touched hers.

Their touch was light, but she shivered down to her toes, and her own lips opened in an endless sigh of relief, as though she'd been holding her breath forever, waiting for this kiss. She felt his lips stir and leave hers as they opened to drink in her sigh.

His hands rose to frame her face, his fingers twining gently into the thickness of her hair. He tilted her face upward and her eyes opened into his. They were dark and so full of loving that to look at them was like a kiss.

She had no idea how long they stood thus, gazing into each other's eyes, before their lips came back together as lightly as before. Lightly, so lightly: just the cushion of skin against skin. But at the same time, deep within her, she could feel the fire begin and slowly travel upward, growing as it rose. As it grew, the kiss deepened. In the same moment their lips opened and she felt the heat of his tongue, shooting sharp bursts of sensation with every searching thrust. Her fingers closed tightly on the thick stuff of his coat. His slid more deeply into her tumbling curls, holding her a willing prisoner to the plunder of his mouth.

In waves and in rounded ripples, her body began to respond, drawn into the rhythm of this endless kiss. Her breasts stirred against him and her hips began to move as they had on that other night. He groaned when her body touched his; his tongue disappeared and in the next instant she felt hers sucked into his mouth with a pressure that both satisfied and started fresh longings. Her hands left his shoulders and slid around his back to pull him closer to her restless hips.

Her cheeks were burning. His hands released her head and slid around and down her as hers had done to him. One spanned the small of her back. The other pressed her to him—she could feel the reason why. She eased forward in encouragement and heard him groan again. His lips left hers then, moving hotly to her ear. His tongue flicked and tasted. When it plunged inside she felt her whole body shudder involuntarily. A feeling inside was growing, trembling and tickling, warm, hot, expanding, filling up her chest. Pleasure and joy flooded through her, untwisting every tightness and tossing off every weight. His hot tongue stroked her and his big hands held her near. Then suddenly her body was shaking everywhere.

"Susannah? What's the matter? Are you crying?" Edward's face rose over hers, flooded with tender concern. As

she watched, that concern changed to astonishment. "Susannah—you're laughing! But why—in heaven's name?"

"I don't know. Because I'm happy!" Shaking, she clung
to him as wave after wave of laughter convulsed her body
with mirth. Every part of her was laughing, right down to
her toes.

She caught his hand and brought it up against her cheek.
"Oh, Edward, I'm so happy! Happier than I've been in
years! I know you'll be gone tomorrow. But you're here
right now and that's a lifetime more than I expected a day—
just an hour ago! Let's forget about tomorrow. Let's not be
sad tonight! Let's not hurry or look backward, or think
about what's gone wrong. Then later we can remember—
well, you know what I mean."

He knew exactly. More than that, he knew she was right.
Later there would be plenty of time to fill with regrets. Tonight was the time for magic and ecstasy and joy. He found
he could easily smile. "Tomorrow? Never heard of the
word." With his thumb he traced her smile until she bit it
teasingly.

"Ouch!" He jerked back, pretending to be hurt. "You're
quite the brazen hussy!"

"Am I?" She grinned with delight.

Her hair had fallen forward with his first embrace. Long
curls lay across her shoulder and drifted down her chest. He
hooked his finger behind one and followed it down to its
end, rubbing lightly over the fullness of her breast.

"Oh!" breathed Susannah as her grin disappeared.

His fingertip touched the skin just above her bodice, then
traced the bodice edge up to her right shoulder, gathering
up the hair and letting it fall behind her back. He did the
same on the other side, and by the time he was done her
breasts were straining against her bodice so hard they'd
begun to hurt. She concentrated on his fingers, willing him
to touch her there.

His hands ignored her message, resting briefly on her
shoulders before sliding down her arms to her elbows, then

back up again. His eyes lingered on her bodice, then slid up to her face, and the little dimple teased her as he gave her a lazy smile. "Do you like me to touch you?" he murmured.

Her nod was hesitant, not because she was uncertain but because she was still concentrating on other things. Maybe if she stayed very still, he'd touch her there again. She gave a little restless movement beneath his hands.

He felt it. His eyes darkened and the dimple disappeared. "Oh, God!" he half whispered, half groaned. She felt his fingers bite into her flesh as he dragged her against him for another kiss that left her vibrating and breathless and so weak in the knees that she knew if he released her, she'd crumple to the floor. Not that she cared if she crumpled, so long as he came with her.

"Susannah, Susannah!" he whispered in her ear, his tongue moving hotly, wetly, seductively.

She arched and rubbed against him, trying to soothe the fire but stoking it instead. His hands dropped back behind her, and she felt him rucking up her skirts. Her breathing grew shallow as she felt cool air on her thighs, then the searing heat of his fingertips brushing against her skin.

"Yes, please!" she whispered. She was wanton. She didn't care. Only let him touch her until he'd stilled the aching that threatened to tear her apart. As they had that night in the root cellar, the tips of his fingers grazed her inner thighs as his hands rose to cup her buttocks. When he squeezed them, she groaned aloud. Sensation spurted through her and her body began to shake.

She clung to him. "Edward!" Then, inexplicably, he stopped. "No! No!" she whispered, and heard him chuckle deep in his chest.

"What—in the hallway?" he murmured in her ear. "You are a brazen hussy!" Then, as if she weighed no more than a sack of feathers, he scooped her up into his arms.

"Wait—I'll take the candle," she said with a giggle as he started toward the stairs. "No point in taking a tumble."

''No, not on the stairs!'' he agreed, and bent at the table for her to grab the light.

She held it aloft with her right hand while she circled his neck with her left. She left navigation to him, devoting herself instead to as much of his neck as her tongue could reach and then to his left ear.

''I'll drop you,'' he threatened huskily, and shifted his hold just enough to make her gasp. The light jerked like a drunken thing, throwing wild shadows up through the hall as he turned on the landing and practically ran up the second flight. She was seized by a fit of giggles at his hurry to open her door.

''Laugh at me, will you?'' he demanded, and tossed her onto the bed so energetically that she almost let the candle drop. She held it, lying back on the pillows while he stood over her, winded, his eyes blazing with a fierce, wild joy. ''I love to see you laughing,'' he said in a different tone, shaking his head slowly as though he thought it must all be a dream.

''Where are you going?'' she asked when he turned away.

''Only to light the fire.'' He knelt on the hearth at the fire Milly had laid.

She watched his broad back and shoulders as he worked with flint and steel. ''Do you think we really need one? The room feels nice and warm.''

''Nice and warm, does it?'' He chuckled deep in his chest, but she noticed that he didn't linger after the flame had caught.

The shadows loomed behind him as he crossed back to the bed. He looked so tall and powerful as he stood staring down at her that she couldn't help but feel a little bit afraid. The fear must have shown in her eyes, for his whole expression changed. ''I won't hurt you, Susannah,'' he murmured tenderly.

''Yes, I know,'' she answered, and held out her arms to him.

The mattress shifted as he rested his weight on one knee and braced himself above her with his palms resting flat on each side of her head. She watched as his eyes moved slowly over her face and her tousled hair. Her heartbeat had steadied itself once more, but she knew it was only waiting for his touch to explode again.

Suddenly he smiled. "That first day, when you fainted and I was waiting for you to wake up, I had the impression that you meant to throw yourself on my mercy—or some such thing."

Her eyes sparkled with amusement. "You must have been surprised."

"Not as surprised as you were, I'll wager!" he allowed.

His uniform. She remembered. "It seems so long ago."

"It does," he agreed softly, his eyes sobering. This time she wasn't smiling when his thumb traced the line of her lips. His own lips followed, gentle at first, then with an increasing insistence until her limbs had begun to quake and her heartbeat was racing again.

She kissed him back when he kissed her and moaned as his lips left her mouth to trace a languid, burning trail down her throat and below, to the top of her bodice, where her breasts were thrusting again. Her fingers pushed aside his wig, seeking his own fair hair. This time she didn't mean to let him stop.

She needn't have worried. His lips lingered and stayed, moving along her bodice hem as his tongue teased and darted below. Then he moved lower and she felt the heat of his breath searing through the layers of her bodice and stays. The feeling was exquisite and awful. One of her hands clutched his hair while the other was flung back to circle the bolster. Her hips were moving again.

He heated her with his closed lips, then with his open mouth, until she was whimpering like a kitten and tossing from side to side. Then at last, his fingers came to her aid, unfastening her bodice and unlacing her stays. Her breasts sprang to freedom, shocked by the room's cool air. For a moment they trembled, untaken. Then his mouth came down.

"Oh!" she cried out, opening her eyes as images flooded her mind. She thought of the height of summer, of honey being poured off just after it has boiled, thick and hot and golden and lushly sweet—and the sound of his ragged breathing only increased the heat.

He loved her from height to height, with lips and tongue and even cheeks—the scratchiness of his nighttime beard exciting her tender skin. Then his lips moved lower and the mattress shifted again as he nudged her over to bring his other knee up onto the bed.

Her breath caught in alertness as she felt her petticoat stir, and she shuddered as the heat of his lips touched her ankle and began to move slowly up. He pushed her skirts before him, over her calf to her knee, seeking the top of her stocking and the first band of sensitive skin. She shuddered again when he found it, then froze when she felt him stop.

"Are you afraid, Susannah?"

"No, oh no!" she gasped. "It's just that I've never..." But she couldn't say. It didn't matter. His lips touched her other leg. Slowly they moved upward over her trembling thighs, which wanted to clamp together until he coaxed them apart.

Suddenly she was lonely and wanted to feel his arms. "Edward, please," she whispered, reaching down to touch his sleeve.

He raised his head and looked down. His eyes were very dark, as dark as hers or darker. "What's wrong?"

"I need you to hold me, please."

"Oh, my darling!" he whispered, and the mattress moved violently as his arms came around her, suffusing her with his warmth. "My heart!" he whispered, nuzzling her cheek and her ear. He stroked her and held her. "I went too fast. I'm sorry."

"No, no." She shook her head. "I only missed you. I wanted to feel you here." She moved her hand between them, flat against his chest, and began to unbutton his waistcoat and then his shirt. Still holding her, he let her, pausing between breaths. As she reached the last of the buttons, the length of his pauses increased. At last his shirt fell open. She ran her palm over his chest and felt the gusty heat of his exhaled breath. His muscles jumped and rippled beneath her hand. His skin was hot and silky, except for the mat of hair that tapered as it descended toward his abdomen. She followed its trail and he sucked in his stomach in a convulsive gasp, then in the next moment his hand closed over hers and pushed her fingers lower, to the swelling that was almost bursting the buttons of his breeches' fall.

"Ah...!" he murmured, molding her hand to the shape. She felt movement beneath the fabric; her heart lurched crazily. He pressed harder, then released her, reaching out with both arms and drawing her in toward him until her naked breasts touched his chest.

Her skirts were bunched between them. He fumbled for the fastenings. She did her best to help him but hindered him instead. Incredibly, laughter found them in the midst of her desire.

"Always pushy," he muttered.

"Arrogant Brit!" she whispered back. But she let him finish and raised her hips when he pulled her skirts down. He shucked off her stockings and shoes when he got that far. She thought he'd take off his breeches, but he didn't, yet. Instead he held her to him, released her, then held again, as if searching for the absolute perfection of their fit. Every fit was perfect: his chest, his hands on her back, then molding her buttocks, moving around and around until she understood what he'd intended by leaving his breeches on.

His hands fell quiet when hers began to unbutton his fall. "You're sure you're ready?"

"I'm sure," she whispered back. She paused, then she added, "What if I said I wanted to stop?"

"Do you want to?"

"What do you think?" she asked as her fingers worked busily.

He groaned and pressed toward her. "How can you tease at a moment like this?"

"Because I'm happy!" she whispered as the last of the buttons gave. She touched him and held him to show him that she wasn't afraid. She wasn't, only surprised at his burning heat. He lay still for a moment, savoring the touch of her hand. Then he peeled off the remains of his clothing and turned back to her.

She came to him, arms open, the perfect fit, first time. "I'll try to be gentle," he whispered. Their bodies had already begun to move.

"You won't hurt me," she promised. "Not when I want you so much."

She was silk beneath his body, a river of velvety fire. She was like no other woman he had ever known. He knew the reason. Still moving, he lifted his head and gazed down at her flushed and lovely face. "How I love you," he whispered. "You are dearest of all to me."

Her eyes blazed. "Oh, Edward, I love you, too! Don't ask for more—just let me love you now!"

"Now is enough, my darling," he said tenderly. And so it felt to him.

He watched her as long as he could. He wanted to see her, but he wanted to feel her, too. Then he forgot about seeing and feeling as he passed into some other land where everything was Susannah in passion and ecstasy, and they'd found themselves together in a perfect paradise.

Piece by stunned and languid piece, he drifted back to earth, blissfully entwined with Susannah in the feather bed. One of her legs lay between his, and her breasts cushioned his chest. Her hair was his pillow, fragrant and warm with her scent. Turning his face, he touched her naked shoulder with his lips.

She purred at the touch of his kiss, but her skin was cool. During their time in paradise, the fire had burned low. He tucked the quilt up around them, and she purred again.

"Are you cold?"

"No. I'm happy."

"I ought to tend the fire."

"You've done that well enough already," she murmured.

He smiled and carefully, tenderly smoothed the hair back from her cheek. He had never imagined that love could be like this—not only the passion, but this state of quiet grace. He loved her ear, her shoulder, the way she rolled her eyes so that she could see him without turning her head.

"You stay. I'll tend the fire," she offered.

He laughed. "You! You look as though you can barely lift your head."

"Humph," she muttered. She stirred, then lifted her head a bare inch from the pillows. She gave him a lazy smile. "There."

He laughed again. "Stay where you are. I believe you," he said, disentangling himself and padding across the room, naked, to add wood from the pile.

Susannah watched him, admiring his tight buttocks and long muscular legs, and the way the shadows played on his back as he bent. He stayed until he was sure that the fire would not smoke, then padded back. She kept watching, admiring him from the front as much as she had from the rear: broad chest with its tapering of golden hair, flat narrow abdomen.

"You are shameless," he told her, climbing back into bed.

She shivered when he touched her. "You're freezing!"

"Warm me, then." He held out his arms to her and she nestled into them, first frontward, then backward, his arms cradling her breasts. "Mmm...lovely!" He cupped them.

"You're insatiable." She wriggled as he gently squeezed.

"You bet I am, with just one night!" he replied, then stopped. He sighed. "I'm sorry."

"Hush. Never mind. Quickly change the subject and we'll pretend we didn't hear."

He racked his brain to oblige her and found something to his surprise. "I saw your General Washington."

"You did!"

"Mmm." He nodded against her, brushing her neck with his lips. "I had to take him a message. He was in Tarrytown."

"What did you think of him?"

"He is a man among men."

"Don't tease!"

"I wasn't teasing. I meant it. He is unique. Meeting him was like finding the missing clue to the United States. Suddenly I could understand how you'd won the war. And why you believe that you can make a go of self-government. He's a born leader. He'd be a boon to any land." He paused, then added, "He'd make a better king than our George."

"That's treason," said Susannah but she was moved.

"I trust you," he murmured, raising his chin to rest it on her head. "Take care of him," he told her.

"Who? Of Washington?"

He nodded against her. "Your future rests with him. If you take care of him, he'll take care of you."

They lay listening to the fire, which was crackling merrily. They were both thinking of Edward's leaving, and both trying not to think.

Susannah shifted. "I have something for you." She unwrapped his arms from her and reached out to open the drawer of the table beside the bed. Hiking the covers up to cover her breasts, she turned around and handed him two folded squares of white.

"Your handkerchiefs," she told him. "The ones you loaned to me."

He remembered all too clearly the times when he'd lent them to her. "Where do you think I should put them?" he asked, glancing down the contours of his body under Susannah's quilt.

"Hmm..." Frowning, she picked up the quilt to peek. When she dropped it, she was grinning. "Not there, anyway. How about your waistcoat pocket?" she added, wriggling away again, this time to reach for his clothing on the floor. She couldn't quite reach it, but she tried anyway. Edward grabbed, but too late, as she pitched headfirst off the bed.

"Ow!" Her voice sounded muffled. He slid forward to look and found her nursing a bruised elbow and naked as the day she'd been born, except for her wild mane of hair.

Without thinking, he smiled. She looked adorable. "Come up here and let me see it. I'm a doctor, after all."

At that, she forgot her elbow. "It's nothing. Just a bruise." Retrieving the handkerchiefs, she tucked them into the pocket of his coat, which she hung on the bedpost before climbing back into bed.

He moved back to give her room, then moved up again.

"What are you doing?" she asked when he took her arm.

"Looking at your elbow."

"I told you it was fine."

"I know," he said mildly, holding it up to the light. It was red and looked sore. He touched it with his lips. "If I can't take care of you forever, at least I can tonight."

"I wish you could forever."

"I know. So do I." He released her elbow, and she settled into his arms. He held her and gently stroked her hair. At first she lay quietly, but presently she began to stroke him, too, first his forearm, then his chest, then his abdomen. He felt himself stir and come back to life. Her fingers moved lower to touch then encircle him. He lay back, concentrating. It felt so very good. So good. Too good. He shifted his hips and groaned.

She stopped. "Does that hurt you?"

"Not exactly. No."

"What, then?" Her brow puckered as she turned.

"It feels too good," he whispered, covering her hand with his. He raised it and kissed it, then laid it beside her leg. "I'll show you," he murmured, running his hand up her thigh, then languidly back again, first on the outside, then gradually moving in. Her thighs closed. He left them to stroke her stomach and breasts until he felt her relaxing. Then his hand moved down again. This time when his fingers reached them, her thighs drifted apart.

As he stroked, he kissed her. He nuzzled her ear and her neck, murmuring endearments until she began to move. Then he stopped stroking to slide down the bed. "Stop. Where are you going?" she asked, raising her head.

"To show you." He smiled. "Lie back and close your eyes."

For once she obeyed him, and then she urged him on. "Please, please!" she murmured, her hands restless in his hair. She knew that she should stop him. She thought that she might die. She thought he meant to kill her, but she knew that he did not.

He did not—only nudged her up and up, to the brink, then over the far edge to pitch and tumble head over heels back to earth. At the last moment she saw a hole gaping beneath, but just before she reached it, he snatched her in midair, enfolded her in his strong arms and took her back up again.

"What are you thinking?" he asked, long after that. The fire had burned low again, but this time they'd let it go.

She sighed and turned to the window. "That it's still dark." She stared into that darkness, feeling warm and content. "Where do you live in England?"

"Why do you want to know?"

She nestled closer to him. "So I can imagine you there."

Her words brought a pang of sadness, which her warmth eased away. How could he not feel happy with Susannah here in his arms, so soft and supple, all of his dreams come true? Surely a night such as this one came only once in a lifetime. He should be grateful for it.

He covered her more closely. "In Kent," he said. "It's something like Pennsylvania, but more green and lush. My father has a big house, bigger than the houses here."

"A castle?"

"Yes. Sort of," he said, and felt her smile. "Why is that funny?"

"I don't know." She sighed. "I'm picturing you in armor, like an old-fashioned knight."

"There's armor," he admitted. "But it's only for display. It's not a real castle, just a country house. My grandfather bought it when he became a lord."

"Your grandfather is a lord?"

He nodded. "He was. My brother's the lord now."

"But never you?"

"Never," he answered, thinking of Catherine. His arms tightened around her.

"What's wrong?" she asked.

"Nothing. I was thinking of something that happened a long time ago."

"Of the same thing you were thinking of that night in the root cellar—when you said you hated titles?"

"Yes. Of the same thing," he said.

She rubbed her cheek against his chest. "Tell me," she said.

"There was a woman. I thought we were in love. But it turned out she only wanted to be the wife of a lord."

"It was she who hurt you? She was the lily who festered?"

He frowned, his eyes blank.

"The sonnet from Shakespeare I quoted that first day. You grabbed the book and shut it."

His brow cleared. "I recall. Yes. She was the lily who festered. But that doesn't matter now. I'm better. You've made me better," he whispered against her hair.

"I'm glad for that," she said. It wasn't a lie. She was glad. How could she be anything else with Edward's heartbeat strong and steady against her cheek?

He cradled her against him. "Alex will be out of jail soon."

"I hope so." She closed her eyes. She didn't want to think of Alex, not just now, anyway. But she knew why he was asking—for the same reason that she had. He wanted to know that she'd be all right after he had gone.

"In time he'll forgive you. After the wounds have healed. He's stubborn, but not heartless."

"Yes, I'm sure you're right."

His arms tightened around her. "I wish there was something I could do."

"Hush." She laid her finger across his lips. "You've done so much already. Everything you could."

"I wish I could take you with me."

"I wish that I could go. But I can't. It's not only Alex. It's leaving America. I'd feel like a deserter."

"I know. I understand." He drew her even closer, speaking to her without words—speaking to her with his heart, which she understood.

They made love once more, very gently and as slowly as they could, then fell asleep, sated and wrapped in each other's arms.

The late watch calling six o'clock dragged open Edward's eyes. The last day. The last morning—and he had plenty enough to do.

Susannah was still sleeping, her hair fanned across his chest. He looked down at its darkness on his own light skin and wished he could freeze the image in his mind so that he could have it back, whole and perfect, in the years to come. He looked around the darkened room, wanting to remember it all, and most of all Susannah, all cozy and flushed with sleep.

Right now, everything was so vivid he could not believe it would fade. But just as time eased the bad memories, it faded good ones. Right now, Susannah was with him, warm and vital in his arms. But tomorrow, and all the tomorrows, he knew he'd wake from dreams of her to find himself embracing air.

What if he hadn't stopped Alex? Could they have found a way to be together then? Useless, useless question, for all of them were as they were. To have betrayed his country would have tainted their love, not only in his own eyes but in Susannah's, too. And even in her brother's—they were alike that way. America was about to embark upon a great adventure, but the greatest of adventures took their toll on private lives.

Susannah stirred beside him. He wanted to go while she slept. He believed it would be easier, and in any case, there was no way to tell her goodbye. Gently, he disentwined himself from her grasp, then left the bed slowly so as not to jolt her awake. He dressed in the darkness, groping for his clothes and remembering all too clearly just how they'd come off. Never again, he was thinking. He wondered how many people had known such a perfect love? Perhaps it was better that they were parting now. Wouldn't their love only diminish from this pinnacle? But even as the thought came, he knew he was fooling himself. A thousand nights with Susannah wouldn't dim his desire for her.

He carried his shoes with him. He'd put them on down below—and hopefully manage to miss Milly and her mother. He stood over Susannah, gazing down at her face in repose. Then he bent down and kissed her softly and finally.

"God bless you," he whispered. Then he turned and left the room.

Outside the air was razor sharp, the sky spangled with the last flush of stars, which glittered like bits of diamonds caught in winter ice. Edward turned up his collar and hurried along to his rooms, where he stripped off the clothes he'd just put on and changed them for his uniform. He checked his reflection in the looking glass, which brought back the day that he'd first met Susannah—which in turn reminded him of the handkerchiefs she'd returned.

He found them in his coat pocket and held them to his face, inhaling her sweet scent and seeing once again the fleeting glimpse of her bottom as it tumbled off the bed. It's nothing, she'd said of her elbow. She was used to caring for herself. She'd be all right from now on. Sad, but she'd be all right. He placed the handkerchiefs on top of the coat in the trunk that William, if he remembered, would be taking down to the ship. On second thought, he took the handkerchiefs out again and tucked them inside his shirt so he'd have them with him even if William did forget. Then he closed the trunk and locked it and went out to begin his last round of duties in New York.

Chapter Eighteen

Alex Beckwith cursed silently at the sound of keys jangling in the hall. He knew who that sound would bring: his jailers, for one last round of insults before they surrendered their command. He wondered if this round would include any physical blows. They hadn't so far, which he suspected was because of Susannah's precious Captain Steel—as was the higher quality of the meals that he'd been fed. Under those conditions, he'd have preferred beatings and starvation. Now that the redcoats were leaving, Captain Steel would never know if his keepers knocked off his head. And this shift had been drinking ever since they'd come on. He'd been enduring their drunken abuse through the bars of his door all night.

The key grated against the fittings of the lock. Let them come, thought Alex, clenching his fists and moving to the wall beside the door. Even if it made things worse, he'd put up a fight. The crunch of British muscle and bone would feel good against his fists. In that instant he remembered the crunch of the Tory's nose when Barney had knocked him down outside the City Arms. That night he'd been disgusted by Barney's violence. If he'd known then what he knew now, he'd have felt differently. How could she have done it? His own sister—his own twin? How could she have held out for eight years, then suddenly given in? It was Steel's doing, he knew it, and he'd make him pay one day.

If he had to follow him to England, by God, he'd make him pay!

Alex tensed in readiness as the door swung back. He was stiff from lack of exercise and he was still weak. But if they were as drunk as he thought they'd be, he ought to have a chance to hurt them a little before they took him down. He planted his feet in readiness and prepared to swing as the familiar detested scarlet jacket filled the open door.

He swung his right arm, low and hard toward the fifth button from the top.

"Bloody—what!" grunted a familiar voice as a hand clamped on his wrist. He felt it jerked sharply upward, and before he could draw breath, he found himself glaring into Barney Silver's face.

"Barney!" He almost collapsed, he went so limp with surprise. "What are you doing here?" Blinking, he tired to make sense of the color of Barney's coat.

"Springing you," muttered Barney. "At least that was my plan before you tried to kill me!" He pushed Alex back into the cell, speaking in an undertone.

Alex dropped his voice, too. "But how did you get in here?"

"In case you haven't noticed, most of the guards are drunk. And those who aren't are too busy getting ready to leave. I came in through a cellar window and slipped past all of the guards—except for the closest to your cell. I got the jacket from him."

"Where'd you leave him?"

"Out in the hall. I figured you could give me a hand dragging him in here." Barney cast a quick glance over Alex, judging his state of health.

"I'm hale," Alex assured him. "Come on. Let's go."

Following Barney into the hall, Alex saw the soldier slumped a few yards away. They each grabbed a shoulder and dragged him easily. "What if they find him?" Alex asked while they were binding and gagging him in the cell.

"What if?" Barney shrugged. "It's too late to look for you. Besides, they know the Americans would have most likely let you go. We need to get you a uniform to get you out. There's a guard on the stairway. I'll get him up here and we can knock him out."

They crept down the hallway and Alex stood pressed to the wall while Barney walked forward and called down to the guard. He clumped up the stairs heavily. When he reached the top, Barney pulled him forward, then struck him hard with the butt of his gun. Alex caught him as he slumped forward, and they manhandled him down the hall.

"He's big for you," Barney noted as they stripped off his coat.

Alex paused to grin. "Do you want to keep knocking them unconscious until we find one small enough?"

"If we had time, I wouldn't mind it." Barney returned Alex's grin with the smile that Alex remembered: one that chilled you when you saw his eyes.

"Where are we rushing off to?" Alex asked as he buttoned the coat—over his own, as Barney had directed—then tucked under the sleeves.

"You'll see," Barney told him, binding the second guard fast. The first one was still out cold. Barney kicked him hard in the ribs, but he didn't stir. "You ready?" His eyes ran over Alex appraisingly. "You'll do," he concluded, and passed the second guard's musket to him.

When they were back out in the hallway, Barney locked the cell. Then they crept down the hall to the stairway, pausing to listen after every few steps. It took them no more than several minutes to reach the ground floor. There they found a handful of guards clustered at the front door.

They ducked back up the stairway, flat against the wall.

"Where to now?" whispered Alex.

"The opposite end of the hall. Follow me and walk slowly. You're a redcoat now."

Alex nodded. Meeting Barney's eyes, he realized that Barney had the same air of total calm he'd had the night of the fire and the night that they'd gone to the Bridgehams'. That told more than words could that Barney had a plan. He wondered what, this time. He was game for anything.

As it turned out, at the moment that Barney stepped into the hall, something happened outside the front door. Relaxing their vigilance, all the soldiers went out to see.

"Quick!" Barney seized Alex's arm and sent him marching toward the unguarded front door.

Alex's heart was pounding as he came into the light. All one of the redcoats had to do was to recognize his face. But all the redcoats were too busy with the spectacle, which was—what else?—a pig that must have gotten into some ale and was lurching drunkenly around the prison yard. The soldiers were roaring with laughter, though in fact few of them were any steadier than the pig.

"Good morning, New Yorker!" One of them tipped his hat and almost tumbled over his neighbor, who caught him with a roar.

"They're all pigs," muttered Barney, leading Alex past. "Ramrod spine, Beckwith. You're a redcoat now!"

Once beyond the prison, they walked briskly west. Downhill they could see the harbor, bristling with masts. The sight pleased Alex. "I hope they've brought enough ships to take them all away."

"They have," Barney said. "And I've got a plan for making sure that they'll all aboard. By tomorrow morning there won't be anyone except for true Americans in New York."

"What plan?" panted Alex. He was running out of breath, for he had not walked farther than across his cell in two months.

"You'll see." Glancing at Alex, Barney slowed his pace. "How did they treat you?"

"Like a prisoner." Alex brushed his forehead to wipe away the sweat. He wasn't about to tell Barney about his suspicions about Captain Steel. Susannah's betrayal hurt too much to share, not even with Barney. Or maybe especially with him—particularly when he had that look in his eye. "Where've you been these last months? I figured you'd left New York."

"I did for a few days," Barney admitted. "But then I came back."

"And they never caught you?"

"No, and they never will." Barney opened his mouth to say more, then he shut it and stopped.

"What's wrong?" Alex stopped at his side.

"Nothing. Keep going." Barney began to walk again. "We're being followed. No—don't look around." He seized Alex's arm to pull him forward as Alex turned his head.

"How can you tell for certain?"

"I have an extra sense—the same one that told me Franks was a spy. Just keep walking like you don't know, while I think of what to do."

Alex kept walking. Now the sweat on his neck felt cold. Had they discovered his absence at the prison and the guards locked in his cell? No, that couldn't be it, because if they had, they'd be after him in numbers, not sneaking like a spy. He thought of the Tory, Franks. Then he thought of Steel. "Did you recognize him?"

Barney shook his head. "All right," he murmured. "I've got a plan. Pay attention, Beckwith, and listen to what I say." And, while they were still walking, Barney described what they'd do.

The sun was streaming through the edges of the draperies when Susannah opened her eyes. She must have dozed off again after Edward left. She'd been awake when he'd gotten up, but she'd pretended to be asleep, because she knew there was nothing more that they could say, and they'd said goodbye in the best way before they'd gone to sleep. She'd waited until she'd heard him close the front door, then she'd gotten up to gather her scattered clothing and put on a nightgown so that Milly wouldn't die of shock when she came in with the tea.

She stretched to her full length, then curled back up again. Turning her head into the pillow, she inhaled Edward's smell. The scent of him made her smile. Yes, he was gone, but how could she feel sorry after the most perfect night in her life? She couldn't feel embarrassed or regretful or ashamed. Whatever they'd done together had been sanctified by their love. If she lived for a hundred years without seeing Edward again, she knew that she would never feel the same for another man. The memories he'd left her were like a wonderful box of jewels. She lifted them into the sunlight and watched them glitter through her hands. They were too many, too perfect and too varied to view one by one—not yet. Later she would do that. Just now she was happy merely possessing them.

The door opened abruptly and Milly hurried in, the dishes rattling on the morning tray. She pursed her lips at Susannah as she set down the tray. "I guess it's a good thing that nothing went amiss last night, with all of us sleeping like children in our beds!"

"Oh, I was awake," Susannah assured her. "Right through to the dawn. Then I put on my nightgown and had a little nap." It was the truth—in its broadest sense—she thought with a secret smile. "I can report that there was no trouble. Not a single whit!" Her smile deepened as she ran her hand over the sheet, where she could still determine the depression where Edward had lain.

Milly brought her her saucer of tea. "In any event, this is no morning to lie abed! You'll miss the procession. General Knox and his gentlemen will be leaving Cape's Tavern at nine o'clock and it's already eight!"

"Eight o'clock," murmured Susannah, wondering where Edward was. Imagine if they were married and he was coming back tonight. Closing her eyes, she pretended that she had that to look forward to.

Sunlight scoured the polished floor as Milly swept back the drapes. "Mother and I are going directly." Her voice came in puffs as she worked. "That is, unless you need us."

"Not at all." Susannah stretched again, then sat up so that Milly wouldn't think her a total sloth. "I'm meeting the Van Rijns at nine or so out at the Teawater pump."

"You'll never be ready."

"Probably not. But it doesn't really matter, since the first rank isn't supposed to pass until noon, and they'll probably be late. You know how these things are."

"That's true," admitted Milly, moving to the last set of drapes. "But if you wait, such a crowd will gather you'll never see over their heads!"

"Then maybe I'll bring a ladder." Susannah laughed, then laughed again at Milly's expression. "I feel wonderful today!"

"No wonder!" Milly turned as she finished with the drapes. "It's a great day for all of us. Just think, by nightfall there'll be no British left in New York!" Then her conscience smote her. "'Course they weren't all so bad. Captain Steel, for instance." Then she frowned again. "Excepting what he did to Master Beckwith, but—"

"It's all right," Susannah said. "You go off with your mother and have a fine time for yourselves. Stay out as late as you want to. I'll take care of myself."

"You enjoy yourself, too, mistress!" Milly beamed and bustled from the room.

Alone, Susannah lay back, thinking of Edward again. She blushed, then she smiled, thinking of what they'd done. The sky through the windows was a blinding blue. Right now General Washington would be waiting with his men to enter the city he'd fled seven years ago. She remembered what Edward had said about Washington. Stretching again with reluctance, she got up and began to dress.

The sun was brilliant, but the day remained crisply cold. Edward walked briskly in an effort to keep himself warm.

Carleton had given up the Beekman mansion and had spent last night in town. Edward had just been to see him—for the last time in New York—to report on the final arrangements and the fact that all was calm. In a few hours Carleton would be rowed across to Staten Island, where he'd stay until the end. He'd invited Edward to come with him, but Edward had declined. Instead he'd requested to be on the first ship that sailed. He might as well be in England if he couldn't be in New York.

He pulled out his watch and checked it. The time was a quarter to nine. New Yorkers had already gathered at Cape's Tavern with General Knox. Presently they would march up the Broad Way to meet Washington and the troops. Simultaneously, more or less, the British would march down. A messenger would be waiting on the wharfs. When the final British soldier was shipboard, the formal entrance would begin. Such a simple procedure, thought Edward, to have taken so long to arrange. He paused, shading his eyes to sweep the harbor beyond the Battery, thick as a forest with the masts of waiting ships.

He turned back, blinking from the reflection of the sun. Two redcoat soldiers were approaching him. One of them looked familiar, dark, with his hair in a queue. For a moment Edward watched him. Then, with a shock, he knew. The soldier was Alex Beckwith—Alex who should be in jail, not marching up the High Road in a British uniform. His first impulse was to call out. His second was to hide. He spun into a doorway and pressed against the side just as the two strode past him. Neither of them looked his way.

He gave them to the count of ten, then stepped back into the street. There were enough other people in the street to screen him from their vision in case they looked back. He kept a safe distance behind them, being sure to keep out of sight. The man with whom Alex was walking was a stranger to him. He looked tall beside Alex but in reality he was of no more than average height. Average, thought Edward, and he had brown hair. He quickened his pace to stay with them as his skin began to crawl.

Beckwith and his partner were heading in the direction of Chatham Square, beyond which lay the Bowery—and the routes for both processions. They weren't the only ones headed out that way. The street here was swarming with expectant crowds. After all, this was the day they'd all been waiting for.

Using the crowd as his screen, Edward tailed the two. Once, he saw Beckwith's partner stop and Beckwith glance around. But they only stopped for a moment before they began to walk again. Edward knew that they couldn't have seen him but, just to be safe, he dropped back even farther—as far as he dared. If Beckwith's partner was Silver, he'd have eyes in the back of his head. And by this point Edward was fairly sure that he was.

Shortly before they reached Chatham Square the two split up. Alex headed east—toward the river and also toward William Street. Edward thought of Susannah and wondered what Alex had in mind. But he couldn't lose Silver. There was no question of that.

Silver continued straight for a short ways, then turned into an alley between an abandoned ropewalk and a livery. Edward paused at the mouth of the alley, then turned in after him. It was still morning and the shadows were thick. Edward stayed among them as he crept forward on silent feet. He heard a door open, then Silver disappeared up into the ropewalk. Edward crept toward the door.

He tried it. It was open and squeaked faintly as he pulled, so he pulled slowly. Then he slipped inside, taking care to control his breathing so the dust wouldn't make him sneeze. Pressing himself against the wall, he quickly scanned the vast litter-strewn emptiness of the ropewalk's main floor. Slowly, very slowly, he reached down to ease his pistol from his belt as he forced his eyes to move carefully over everything. From what he knew about Silver, he could be hiding in thin air. He hadn't finished searching when he heard footsteps coming from the loft overhead. Silver wasn't in thin air. He was in the loft. With the same careful movement, Edward started for the stairs.

He crept up inch by inch, testing for creaking treads, the image of Franks, stabbed, all too clear in his mind. To be taken by Silver would mean being killed, and Alex—if he reappeared—would provide little help. Alex had balked at the idea of Franks's murder, but Edward doubted he'd balk today. Which meant he'd have to deal with Silver quickly in case Alex was coming back.

He caught sight of Silver as he neared the top of the steps. Silver was at the window at the far end of the loft, kneeling with his back to Edward, too busy with whatever he was doing to turn around. There were a number of barrels a few yards straight ahead. If Edward could reach them, they'd offer him cover to watch. He flexed his muscles, relaxed, inhaled and began to move, keeping low to the ground with his eyes on Silver's back.

He'd almost reached the barrels and Silver hadn't turned, when suddenly he felt a cold breeze on his back. Someone was moving behind him. He froze, but before he could turn, his head exploded with a sudden and terrific pain. Darkness rushed toward him. He tried to fight it off, but it was no use. He thought he heard someone chuckle as he pitched into the black.

"I think I see them coming!" Maria Van Rijn cried, and immediately, all around them, the crowd began to stir and press forward into the roadway, peering toward the north for the first sight of the redcoats marching out of town.

Susannah moved up with the others, craning her neck to see. But it was only a boy on horseback, crying to be let through.

"Have you seen them? Are they coming?" people cried out as he passed.

"They're forming ranks up at the Bull's Head. It won't be much longer now!"

"Still at the Bull's Head." Maria rolled her eyes and groaned. "And just because they're forming up doesn't mean they're about to move. Why, it must be hours since General Knox marched past."

"You're cranky because you're hungry," Amy said peaceably. "Have another muffin." She offered her sister the sack. Maria took one gladly.

Susannah declined. "Thanks. I'm not hungry. I guess it's the excitement."

"I know. Isn't it wonderful!" Amy squeezed her arm. "And to think how long we've waited!"

"Seven years," Susannah said.

"Seven years?" A man behind them who'd overheard shook his head. "Why, I've been waiting for this morning since before you girls were born! The first news of the Stamp Act was nigh unto twenty years ago. We fought 'em on that one, and we've been fighting ever since!"

"A great day!" others agreed.

Susannah and Amy exchanged a smile. "You're looking so much better than you were at the trial," Amy murmured in her ear.

"I'm feeling so much better!" Susannah giggled in spite of herself. Part of her wanted to tell Amy about her magical night, but most of her wanted to savor its intimate secrecy. She knew that her present mood would give way in time, but she meant to keep it alive for as long as she could. She'd have the rest of her life to miss Edward's love. Now, while it was still vital, she meant to relish it.

She wondered if Edward was feeling the same way. She pictured how he'd look smiling, the dimple scooped next to his mouth, and just a hint of sadness in his wonderful eyes. A bittersweet pang cut through her. She shivered and squeezed Amy's arm. "Thank goodness for the sun this morning!" she declared, lifting her face to its warmth.

"Morning!" grumbled Maria, brushing the last muffin crumbs from her sleeve. "It's long past morning. It's already afternoon. What's holding up the British? I hope they haven't changed their minds!''

"They won't dare!" vowed the man behind her, and he spat for emphasis. Even before Susannah had time to pull in her skirts, a swelling cry reached them from the crowd up ahead.

"Here come the redcoats! They're coming down the Bowery!"

Then they heard the distant pulsing of the drums and the faint piping of the fifes. As the music grew nearer, the hautbois and bassoons joined in, filling the crisp November air with their jaunty tune. Boys strove to break from their mothers' grasp and rush to join the march.

"Not yet!" their mothers scolded. "Wait till our own men come."

"They're leaving! They're really leaving!" Amy chanted in Susannah's ear as the two of them stood on tiptoe to watch the passing parade. Against the day's clear brilliance, the red of their coats fairly gleamed, set off by their crossed white belts, white breeches and polished boots. They paraded in companies with a captain heading each, looking neither left nor right as they marched to the beat of the drums.

Although she doubted he'd be with these soldiers, Susannah searched each captain's face for Edward's chiseled features and his gray-blue eyes. Then the last of the troops had passed them and the crowd turned to watch them leave.

"Down Queen Street," murmured Amy, repeating the parade's published route. "Then left, to the river. Then to the ships and off."

Susannah said nothing, but she shivered as the first pang of desolation crept into her heart. Last night had been magic, but now Edward was gone and no amount of imagining would bring him back again! But the pang was quickly shattered by the next round of rousing shouts.

"Here come our troops! Look—here comes Washington!"

Washington! Even Susannah's heart leapt at the name, and she pressed forward with the others for the first thrilling glimpse.

Chapter Nineteen

The first thing Edward was conscious of was the pounding in his head. Then he heard voices speaking a short ways off.

"I can't guess," one was saying. "Can't you even give me a hint? After all, I'm in it with you, whatever you've got in mind."

"In due time," replied the other. "Curb your impatience. I should think you'd be happy just to be free."

"Happy!" scoffed the first one.

Edward recognized that voice. It belonged to Alex Beckwith. He remembered now how he'd spotted Alex and followed Silver when the two had split up. He'd followed him to the ropewalk and up to the loft. He'd been creeping toward some barrels when someone had knocked him out. Alex, he realized—who hadn't gone home or to the river but instead had come up here. They must have spotted him, and Silver must have guessed that if the two separated, Edward would follow him. So he'd sent Alex on ahead to surprise him and knock him out. So much for his best shot at Silver, he thought through the drumming pain.

The light from the windows stabbed his eyes when he opened them. He'd been moved from where he'd gone down. The barrels were now to his right, and the window where he'd seen Silver was a few yards away, to his left. Silver sat to one side of the window while Beckwith sat opposite. From below came the faint hubbub of voices—the crowds gathered at Chatham Square to watch the processions. Edward wondered how long he'd been out and what Silver had in mind.

"I should have guessed Steel would be following," Alex was saying now. "The only thing I can't figure is how he knew you'd get me out."

"Dumb luck," answered Silver. "No redcoat could be that smart. And our luck," he added. "There's a part for him in my plan. His appearance was made to order," Silver said, looking around and catching Edward watching him. "Look who's rejoined the living!" he sneered, seeing Edward awake.

Edward met Silver's sneer coolly, despite his aching head. "Barnett Silver. So we meet at last."

If anything, Silver seemed delighted that Edward knew his name. "At last is right!" He chuckled—a sound to make one's blood run cold. "Last for you, redcoat!"

Edward shifted his weight and discovered he'd been bound.

"Bonds too tight?" mocked Silver. "Don't worry. It won't be for long. You'll be feeling no pain pretty soon." He chuckled again.

"You don't scare me, Silver," Edward said, which was the truth. He was too disgusted by the man to feel fear. There was no question that the man was insane. The only question, therefore, was what he had in mind.

His eyes shifted to the rifle lying at Barney's side. A rifle and a window: that wasn't hard to read. He meant to shoot someone. Someone British, presumably. A flash of fear shot through him as Carleton came to mind. But to the best of his knowledge, the general was already gone.

Who then? Edward wondered. Even Alex didn't know. From what he'd heard when he'd awakened, Silver was also keeping Alex in the dark. His eyes shifted to Alex, and his heart gave a crazy leap as visions of Susannah swept into his mind. But Alex's expression was completely his own. All the old hate and anger were fixed as if in stone as he glared at Edward, just as he'd done at the trial.

Edward felt a rush of hot anger of his own. He was furious at Alex for causing Susannah pain when he ought to be helping her through her difficult time. The temptation to blame Alex was suddenly so strong that it almost swept away his consciousness of Silver and the gun.

Almost, but not quite. He had to stop Silver, impossible as it seemed. And he had no weapons but his words and his mind. Glancing from Alex to Silver, he saw that his only chance was to play the two against each other—if they could be played.

He decided to start with Alex. "Welcome back to life," he said. "I guess you've got Silver to thank for getting you out."

"What if I do?" Alex's dark eyes swung to him—so disturbingly like Susannah's, except for their bitterness.

"Nothing." Edward's bonds bit hard when he shrugged. "Except that I'll wager when this is over you'll wish he'd left you in your cell."

"What do you know about it?" Alex sneered.

"I know Silver," Edward said calmly. "I know that if you follow him you're bound for bigger trouble than you've had yet." He gestured toward the rifle with a nod of his head. "Last time you were lucky. Silver's victim lived. This time maybe they'll hang you for the murder Silver's got in mind."

"They won't hang him," scoffed Silver. "It'll never cross their minds. Not when they've already got their criminal—you!"

"Murder!" Alex's dark brows flew up the same way that Susannah's did when she was surprised. Then his eyes fixed on Edward. "What's Steel got to do with it?"

"Everything." Silver grinned. "Embittered by his country's humiliating defeat, Captain Steel, the gallant redcoat, decides to exact revenge. He hides in the ropewalk, waiting for the parade. He takes aim, fires and shoots—"

"George Washington!" His voice raw with revolted comprehension, Edward concluded Silver's speech.

"Washington!" gasped Alex, his face going white. "That's not it, is it, Silver?"

Silver ignored Edward as his eyes fixed on Alex's face, hard and glassy with the look that Franks had described. "Don't you see, Beckwith? It's the perfect plan! At first I'd planned to find a Tory to take the blame. But then your redcoat captain obligingly presented himself. First we'll shoot Washington, then we'll shoot Captain Steel and leave him by the window, his pistol in his hand. The scene will be self-evident. Redcoat acts in revenge, then takes his own life, knowing what will happen to him if he's caught.

"The Americans will go wild!" Silver went on, his eyes alight. "They'll drive every last Tory into the sea! They'll fire the shiploads of redcoats stuck waiting for the wind!"

Alex was still gaping. "Washington?" he breathed. "You can't mean to shoot Washington?"

"Yes. But not mortally. Even a slight injury ought to do the trick."

"But he could die," said Edward, his eyes glued to Alex's face. "You're risking the life of your country's finest man. You're mad, Silver. You're out of you head."

"Shut up, bloody redcoat!" Silver snarled at him, seizing the rifle and pointing it at Edward just as the first strains of music drifted up from the square down below.

Forgetting Edward, Silver pivoted to the window.

At the same moment, Alex cried, "Don't!" and lunged at Silver, grabbing the rifle with both hands. He refused to release it when Silver yanked it back.

"Let it go!" Silver demanded. "I'm not going to shoot him yet."

"Not yet—not ever!" panted Alex, grimly hanging on. "I'll kill you with my bare hands before I stand by for that! You've gone too far, Barney!"

"Too far—I'll show you too far!" Silver threatened, giving Alex a mighty shove that sent him crashing back toward the wall near where Edward lay.

Alex hit the wall and staggered, but managed to keep to his feet. As he lunged again toward the window, Silver lifted the rifle and fired.

The shot caught Alex in the shoulder, threw him back and spun him around. He collapsed on the floor next to Edward, who froze, not daring to move for fear that Silver would reload and fire at him. The man was completely demented. There was no reading him.

Silver stood, his shoulders heaving on each ragged breath as he glared at Alex's bloody, unmoving shape. "Damned coward!" he muttered at last. The music was very loud now. Silver moved to the window to watch. Then he glanced back at Edward. "Here come your fine friends," he sneered. "Too bad I'm waiting for bigger game, or I'd shoot a couple of them just for good measure!"

"You're not God, Silver. They'll catch you in the end." But even as he said so, Edward knew that Silver didn't care. He was too in love with the violence to care who it struck. He watched as Silver reloaded and knelt at the window to wait. In his mind he saw Washington's lined and patient face and he heard the general saying, "I'm not afraid."

Washington, who'd so often been almost clairvoyant, this time had been wrong. Terribly wrong, thought Edward. Perhaps even fatally.

The music was very loud now. The troops must be just down below. With little hope of freeing himself, he began to work his hands in a desperate effort to loosen his bonds. But instead he made them tighter. The rope cut into his wrists and he felt the tips of his fingers begin to tingle as the blood ceased to flow. Hopelessness rose within him. He was going to die. He thought of Susannah and regretted what this would do to her—Alex's death and his own alleged suicide and crime. Would Susannah believe that of him? He prayed that she would not. He prayed—his thoughts were cut off by something cold and wet pushed into his hand.

He turned his head and saw that while he'd been struggling, Alex had managed to move inches closer to him—close enough to reach out and pass him a knife. Alex's face was paper white and his eyes were closed. But his lips formed the word "Hurry!" as Edward looked down at him.

The wetness with which the knife was covered was Alex's blood. Edward grasped the handle and positioned the blade as best he could, but the angle was awkward and his fingers were half-numb. The music was growing fainter. The British were marching south. The Americans would be coming now. He didn't have much time, and at any moment Silver would turn and fire at him. But Silver wasn't turning. He was transfixed at his post. Edward sawed frantically. Too fast, he dropped the knife!

He groped with his fingers and touched the blade. Reaching out, he accidentally pushed it away. His eyes on Silver, he moved sideways until he had it again. He could hardly hear the British music by the time the ropes were cut. He heard a new burst of cheering as he started on his legs. Barney Silver's finger tensed on the trigger as Washington appeared. Edward gave a mighty thrust and his legs were free.

He had no time for caution and his legs wobbled as he stood, but he ignored them as he lunged forward, grabbing for the gun. His fingers felt hard wood and grasped, but they were still weak and sticky with Alex's blood. With a roar of anger, Silver shoved him aside. Edward tried to hang on, slipped and tumbled, scrambling to his knees just in time to see Silver plunge the butt straight toward his face.

"It's him! It's him!" cried Amy as the first rank of horses appeared, carrying George Clinton, the first governor of free New York, and General George Washington, the new country's greatest man. Amy clung to Susannah and jumped up and down without knowing what she was doing, she was so carried away. Other people were jumping or pounding one another on the back. Some, like Susannah, were staring, overwhelmed by the sight.

He was beautiful, thought Susannah, the tears streaming down her cheeks. He'd stood by them through their troubles and he'd led them to peace. She watched as his steady eyes scanned the crowd and she felt her breath catch as they came to her. They only lingered for an instant and then they passed on, but even that brief contact left something behind. The happiness she'd felt that morning all came rushing back, carrying with it a new sense of calm. A belief in the future, that was what she felt. A new pride and self-assurance straightened her back. She remembered what Edward had said to her last night, about how Washington would take care of her.

As if they'd shared her reaction, all around her people were standing up straight. They were no longer shoving but giving one another room, turning their heads for a final look at the general before turning back to welcome the lieutenant governor and the city's council, who were riding behind. After them came Knox and his entourage, then those citizens lucky enough to own or have rented horses for the day. Those citizens not lucky enough brought up the rear, walking eight abreast. Susannah applauded them all till her hands were raw. Then she pulled on her woolen gloves and clapped again.

She waited with the Van Rijns until the parade had passed. The main unit would follow the course of the British troops down Queen Street to Wall, then turn up toward the Broad Way, where they'd stop at Cape's Tavern to fire a salute. The force under Knox would head west from here toward the Fields, where the British guard was waiting to surrender the jails. The Van Rijns were for taking Nassau in order to avoid the crowds, but Susannah told them she wanted to follow Knox.

"Maybe I can convince them to release Alex so he can watch them raise the flag," she explained.

"I'll go with you," offered Amy. "We'll meet you at the Battery," she told her family before Susannah could object.

They reached the prison at the changing of the guard and stood with a group of civilians watching from the side. Although the ceremony had obviously been planned, there was some confusion after the British had gone. Nobody was quite certain who was in charge of what, so in the end Susannah approached General Knox himself.

"I know you're very busy, but my brother is inside. He joined the army when he was sixteen and fought until he was captured. He spent eighteen months on a brig. I know it would mean a great deal to him to see them raising the flag."

"Beckwith," Knox murmured when she told him the name. "Yes, I do recall the incident. It would be highly irregular for us to let him out."

"Yes, I know," Susannah admitted. "That's why I'm asking you. He's very bitter, General. This might help to heal his wounds." She knew how young and earnest she looked, and for once she didn't mind.

At last the general nodded. "Yes, all right," he said, and calling to a regular, he issued instructions for him to find Alex and release him into Susannah's custody.

"How wonderful!" Amy whispered as the man went off. But he was back a few minutes later to report that apparently the British had already let Alex go.

"Let him go?" wondered Susannah as she and Amy exchanged a look.

"Perhaps as an act of goodwill," Amy suggested. "Likely he's already at Cape's Tavern listening to the salute. Come on, let's hurry! Maybe we'll see him there."

But there were too many people to see Alex in the crowd, and as they flocked down to the Battery, the throng only seemed to swell. All they could see was the top of the flag-pole and they waited for the flag to appear.

"What's taking so long?" Amy wondered, but it was another ten minutes before the news filtered back to them.

"Bloody Brits tore down the halyards, took the cleats and greased the pole! There's a boy trying to climb it. Look now—there he goes!"

They looked and saw the lithe form battling his way up the pole.

"I believe he's going to make it!"

The boy clawed his way to within inches of the top before he hit a patch of grease and slid back down again.

"Oh, no!" Susannah and Amy groaned with the crowd. The same thing happened twice more before someone had the bright idea of sending to the nearest ironmonger's for a hammer and new cleats. A soldier filled his pockets with the cleats, wrapped new halyards around his neck and climbed up inch by inch, tapping in a cleat, then using it to advance. When he'd strung the halyards, he climbed down, and with a collective sigh of relief the flag was raised. It caught the afternoon breeze and fluttered, proud and free.

"Hurrah for the United States! Hurrah! Hurrah! Hurrah!"

The crowd went wild with seven years' worth of pent-up joy. Susannah hugged total strangers and they pounded her on the back. They were cheering so hard they hardly heard the thirteen-gun salute: one round fired for each brand-new state.

She looked around for Alex as the crowd was breaking up.

"Come home with us," urged Amy. "We'll all celebrate."

"I want to go to William Street to see if Alex is there."

"Bring him along if you want to."

Susannah smiled. "I'll do my best. Don't worry if I don't make it." The two women hugged, then Amy went off with her family, and Susannah headed for home.

She passed Cape's Tavern, the flag fluttering out front and the sounds of a celebration issuing from within. Everyone was celebrating, Susannah thought, glancing back toward the harbor and wondering which of the masts belonged to Edward's ship.

She opened the door with her key and stepped into the silent hall. Milly and her mother would most likely be out all night. Let them be. She sighed and looked around the hall. So then, it was over. The suffering was through. Alex was out of prison and America was free. She remembered the day she'd left here, and also the day she'd returned. The day that she had met Edward: the most fateful day in her life. Edward was gone now, but she still had the house. Her eyes drifted over walls and doors, so full of memories.

"Susannah?"

She started as she heard her name called softly from above. Her first thought was of Alex. But it sounded like Edward's voice.

"Susannah?"

Then she looked up and saw him on the stairs. "Edward! What are you doing here? What's happened?" she cried when she caught sight of his appearance. His jacket was off, his shirtsleeves and breeches were filthy and his waistcoat streaked with blood. She rushed forward. "Are you hurt?"

"No, I'm all right." He caught her as she reached him and wrapped her briefly in his arms. "It's Alex, Susannah."

"Alex!" She sprang away, but he had her hand already and was leading her up the stairs.

Déja vu was the French expression for what she felt, standing in the doorway and looking at Alex stretched out on his bed. Alex's face was just as white, but this time there was blood staining the bandages that covered his chest.

"My God! What is it? What's happened?" She pressed her hands to her mouth.

"He was shot." Edward's hands on her shoulders moved her into the room. "I'll explain later. You've got to help me now. Susannah, can you help me?"

She nodded, still struck mute. Edward's hands gripped more tightly. "Susannah?"

"Yes. I'm all right." She forced her eyes from her brother and turned them to him instead. "Yes. Really. Just tell me what to do."

"Fetch clean linen, a basin of water and extra water besides. And tallow to stanch the bleeding—" He began to fire orders in a voice that she recalled, and she left the room, her ears ringing with his commands.

They toiled together as they had toiled once before, while the sky outside exploded in fireworks and flares. Susannah was conscious of nothing but Edward's familiar hands and the persistent red stain on the bandages she held.

"How can he bleed so much?" she murmured.

"He was shot at close range," Edward said grimly. "It makes for a messy wound."

The world still lay in the deepest darkness when at last the bleeding stopped. Susannah's arms were aching as though she'd fought fires through the night. She stood, quaking with weariness, when she heard a sound. Turning toward the window, she watched in bewilderment as the sky beyond it filled with colored light.

"Fireworks," explained Edward, coming to stand by her side. "They're celebrating the British leaving."

She had forgotten that. She raised her eyes to Edward. "But you're still here," she said.

His mouth curved in a wry, weary smile. "I was delayed en route."

Susannah ignored his smile. "Delayed? By what? And what are you doing with Alex? Tell me how he was hurt." Her hands grasped his without thinking and she brought them to her breast, pressing them close for comfort as she gazed up at him.

Edward looked down into her worried, puzzled eyes. At some point during the ordeal of getting Alex home, he'd made up his mind not to tell her, at least not everything. Now, with his hands cradled against the soft warmth of her breasts, he wondered that he could have considered holding anything back from her.

"I'll tell you," he said softly, bringing her hands to his lips. He kissed each one gently, then he guided her to a chair—to the same chair in which she'd slept those other nights. He settled her and then settled himself at her feet, chafing her hands gently between his as he began to speak.

"I was on my way to the harbor when I saw Alex in the street, wearing a British uniform and walking with a man I thought must be Barnett Silver."

"Silver!" Susannah gasped. Her eyes flew to Alex, then back to Edward again.

He nodded in confirmation. "He'd sprung Alex from jail. I followed them to a ropewalk above Chatham Square. I didn't think they'd seen me, but it turned out that they had. They knocked me unconscious and tied me up. When I came to again, Silver was at the window with a gun."

"He meant to shoot Alex?" She shivered with violence.

He brought her hands to his lips again as he shook his head. "Hush. No," he told her. Then he took a deep breath. "He didn't mean to shoot Alex. He meant to shoot Washington."

"Washington!" She gaped at him in utter disbelief. "But Silver's American! Why would he do such a thing?"

"To stir up hate against the loyalists and drive the last of them out of New York. He wanted to make it look as though I'd shot him. That was his plan. He'd shoot Washington then he'd shoot me with my pistol and leave my body there."

"You!" Disbelief faded and horror flooded her eyes. "Oh, Edward!" she sobbed, and covered her face with her hands.

"Hush, it's all right," he murmured, taking her in his arms. "Hush, now, my darling," he murmured against her hair. "I'm fine and so is Washington. And Alex—"

"Alex!" She gasped, pulling away as her eyes flew again to the bed.

He shook his head to reassure her. "Alex didn't know. He had no idea what Silver had in mind. When he found out, he tried to stop him. That's why he was shot. Afterward he managed to slip me a knife so that I could cut free and stop Silver in time."

"And you did stop him." Her face was as white as Alex's as her eyes locked with his.

Edward nodded slowly. "The only way I could."

She gulped. "You killed Barney Silver?"

"I choked him to death."

"I'm glad!" she whispered fiercely. "He was an evil man. I'm glad you killed him, Edward. He deserves to be dead!"

He looked from her flashing eyes down to his hands. "I've never killed a man before."

"You had no choice." Susannah covered his hands with hers. "You had no choice, Edward. And think of the life you saved! The lives," she amended, glancing again toward the bed.

Edward followed her gaze. She didn't try to hold him when he withdrew his hands. She watched as he walked to the window, where the sky was exploding again.

"Susannah," he said without turning. "There's something you ought to know. Tonight, when I was bringing Alex to the house, the thought crossed my mind that if he did die you'd have lost the biggest part of what was keeping you here."

"But he didn't," she murmured. "Because you saved him all the same."

He spread his hands. "I'm a doctor."

"No, Edward. You are who you are." She moved to stand behind him and rested her cheek on his back, closing her eyes to savor the warm, solid feel of him. When she began speaking, she could hear her words in his chest, as though she were speaking directly to his heart.

"Before, when I came in—before you called my name—I was standing in the hallway thinking to myself that this was the moment I'd been waiting for all these years. For seven years I've looked forward to the day when the redcoats would sail back to England and New York would be ours again. But you know what I felt, Edward?"

"Tell me," he said quietly.

She could hear his heartbeat, which was steady against the erratic boom of ships' cannon and of the fireworks. Moving closer until they were touching from shoulder to thigh, she slid her hands up around him, her palms open flat on his chest. "What I felt in my heart was a wish that you were here. As much as I love Alex and America, I'm only half a person living apart from you."

She felt his breath catch. "Susannah—"

"No, wait. There's more. When Alex is well, if you want me, I'll come to England with you."

The air left his lungs in a rush. "Want you!" He turned, cupping her face with his two hands and tilting it up to his. "Want you! Oh, my darling! How can you ask such a thing?" He kissed her lips, her eyelids, murmuring, "My heart! I'll make you happy!"

"Yes, I know you will." She opened to his kisses, which were strong and deep and swept away the last thread of lingering doubt. She had been born to love him and her surrender was sweet. When his hands moved up her bodice, she arched to meet their touch. She whimpered with disappointment when he raised his head.

"What about Alex, Susannah?" he asked soberly. "Today may have changed our future, but it didn't change the past. Alex may wake up hating me as much as he did before."

His arms still held her. She rested back in them, still caught in the physical wonder of the magic of his touch.

"All the time, growing up, Alex was a part of me. I always thought of him as my other half. I thought no one but Alex could really understand. But then I met you, Edward, and I knew that I was wrong.

"Alex is my brother. But you're my other half. I love him dearly and I always will. But as you once told me, he's got to make his own way. I can't really help him, even if he wanted my help. And I can't let his bitterness defeat our love. Who knows, maybe one day our love will bring him around."

He pulled her against him because he couldn't resist, and held her so close that she could feel both his heart and his desire. Still holding her, he murmured, "What about America? What about your chance to make things come out right?"

"I will miss her," she said honestly. "But I don't think I need her the way I did before. Today, standing with the others, seeing General Washington and watching the troops marching in . . . I felt more faith in the future than I have before. America has plenty of eager hearts and hands to help her out. She doesn't need me, Edward, as much as I need you."

"And I need you, Susannah. Before God, I do!" Overcome by emotion, he took her lips again. This time his kiss was searing, lighting a fire that left her trembling.

She clung to him and whispered, "Edward, take me, please!"

"What about Alex?" His question was more than half-lost in his kiss.

She whimpered as he found one of her sensitive spots. "We could be very quiet."

Despite himself he laughed, and was as surprised as Susannah when his laughter ended in a sob.

"Edward!"

"Never leave me!"

"No, never!" she swore, clinging to him as tightly but no longer trembling. After that he took her as she'd begged him to, after he'd scooped her up and carried her to her room across the hall. They weren't very quiet, but they were very quick, driven by the fierceness of their passion and lulled by the security of the days and nights ahead. Then Edward left Susannah to redress her hair and returned to Alex, who was still sound asleep.

Sometime toward morning Alex opened his eyes. The first thing he saw was Susannah. She was smiling.

"Can you manage a swallow of broth?"

"Broth sounds like heaven," he tried to reply. It came out as a garbled croak, which she took as a "yes."

He noticed Steel when she'd left the room. He was sitting near the window, and from the look of his clothes they were the same ones he'd been wearing when Alex had seen him last. Closing his eyes, Alex let the memories filter back—Barney's insane declaration, his own ineffective attempt to wrestle free the gun and the desperate struggle between Steel and Barney, which had ended in Barney's death. The last thing he remembered was Steel lifting him. After that he must have blacked out from loss of blood and the pain. But he could fill in the spaces. Steel had carried him home and saved him with Susannah's help. Just as he had the last time, Alex thought to himself.

He opened his eyes and found Steel watching him. "Water," he managed, and watched Steel fill a glass.

Steel propped his head up and held the glass as he drank. After that, his voice worked better when he tried it again.

"Silver's dead?"

Steel nodded.

"It's no more than he deserves." Alex paused, then added, "I don't deserve much better myself."

"Your sister wouldn't agree with that."

"Susannah." He closed his eyes. "You did your best to warn her and she tried to pass it on. I wouldn't listen. I must have been a fool."

"Mostly you were angry. War does that to a man."

Alex opened his eyes and studied Steel. "If it hadn't been for you, at this very moment Washington might be dead."

Steel shook his head slowly. "I could say the same to you. If you hadn't passed me that knife, I wouldn't be here now."

"Then I guess we've both got something to thank each other for," said Alex as Susannah reappeared.

She was carrying three steaming bowls on a tray. "I brought up one for each of us," she announced with a smile. But her smile faltered as she glanced from face to face. Had they been fighting again, so soon?

Alex supplied the answer. "I was just trying to apologize to Captain Steel."

"Were you?" Susannah's eyes shifted between them, then back to the bowls. As she carried the first to Alex, she fought back the urge to grin. She set it on the table.

"Just a minute," he said. "I want to apologize to you, too, Susannah. And to thank you for standing by me— when it was more than I deserved. You were right about Silver. I should have listened to you."

"When have you ever done that?" she asked dryly, still struggling to hide her delight. "Now hush and drink your broth. You'll have plenty of time for saying you're sorry when you've gotten back your strength!"

Alex's brief speech had exhausted him. He fell asleep as soon as he'd drunk his broth.

Susannah took hers to the window to drink. Outside, the fireworks had ended and the sky was lightening with dawn. From here she could see empty space where the city had burned, and the masts of the British ships readying to depart. Soon she and Edward would be sailing on one of those ships. Maybe he'd sail first and she'd follow when Alex was well.

England wouldn't be so bad, she told herself, recalling Edward's description of fine houses and lush green fields. It would be an adventure, and the thing to keep in mind was that if she'd come to love one Briton, maybe the rest of them weren't so bad. So she shouldn't mind about leaving.

But she did mind, that was the truth. Right now, looking over the city, she was longing to stay and be part of this great adventure that was about to begin. She'd done her part to earn it and it seemed such a pity to leave, especially now that Alex and Edward seemed to be making their peace.

Absorbed in her thoughts as she was, she didn't hear him get up until he was standing beside her, also looking out at the dawn.

"Another clear day," he noted.

"Clear but cold," she agreed. Her bowl was empty. She set it on the windowsill, chiding herself briskly for having selfish thoughts when she already had so much.

"I've heard they're already arguing in your Congress about how much power the states ought to give up to the new government."

"That's easy," she answered, her eyes scanning the view. "They should give it as much power as it needs."

"Easy to say," he observed. "But just how much is that? That's the question, you see, Susannah—capable of endless debate. It makes a man wonder which way they'll go in the end. It makes a man want to stick around to see what happens next."

That caught her attention. She looked up, suddenly very still. "A man?" she said slowly. "What sort of a man?"

"An Englishman," said Alex, meeting Susannah's gaze. When her eyes widened, he nodded. "I know it's hard to believe after all the things I've said in the past. And I'm not saying that those things aren't still true. Americans are too bumptious and headstrong for their own good. And New York is a rough-and-tumble town."

"But . . . ?" prompted Susannah, her eyes still hard on him.

"But America is on the verge of beginning something big—perhaps the biggest adventure any country has known to date. Maybe it will prove too big for her to handle in the end. Or maybe she'll handle it as she did the war. Either way, it's tempting to stick around to see. Besides," he added, a slow smile spreading on his face, "with all these hotheads bumping one another, they'll need a good doctor to patch up the wounds."

Susannah began to smile, then forced herself to stop. "You don't have to do this, Edward, if you're doing it for me. I said I'd go to England. I'll still go if you want."

Reaching out, Edward caught Susannah's hand. "I know you will, my darling, and knowing makes me love you more—if that is possible. But you don't have to. I meant what I said." He pressed her hand to his lips, then added, "Welcome home, my dear."

"Welcome home!" she whispered, moving into his arms. Her hand sneaked beneath his waistcoat, up the soft cotton of his shirt, her fingers running over the hard muscles of his back. "You're sure you won't miss England?"

"Oh, I'll miss it," he said with a laugh as his fingers began a journey of their own. "But I trust that you'll do your best to take my thoughts from homesickness."

"My very best!" she promised, tilting back her head to offer the distraction he'd been thinking of.

* * * * *

HARLEQUIN
American Romance

From the Alaskan wilderness to sultry New Orleans . . . from New England seashores to the rugged Rockies . . . American Romance brings you the best of America. And with each trip, you'll find the best in romance.

Each month, American Romance brings you the magic of falling in love with that special American man. Whether an untamed cowboy or a polished executive, he has that sensuality, that special spark sure to capture your heart.

For stories of today, with women just like you and the men they dream about, read American Romance. Four new titles each month.

HARLEQUIN AMERICAN ROMANCE—the love stories you can believe in.

AMERICAN

HARLEQUIN
Romance

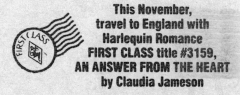

**This November,
travel to England with
Harlequin Romance
FIRST CLASS title #3159,
AN ANSWER FROM THE HEART
by Claudia Jameson**

It was unsettling enough that the company she worked for was being taken over, but Maxine was appalled at the prospect of having Kurt Raynor as her new boss. She was quite content with things the way they were, even if the arrogant, dynamic Mr. Raynor had other ideas and was expecting her to be there whenever he whistled. However Maxine wasn't about to hand in her notice yet; Kurt had offered her a challenge and she was going to rise to it—after all, he wasn't asking her to change her whole life . . . was he?